13.

2

10

Wives & Mothers

Wives & Mothers

Jeanne Whitmee

PIATKUS

For — Leslie, Ann, Julie and Phyllis.

All of the characters and some of the locations in this
book exist only in the imagination of the author. Any
resemblance to known people or places is entirely
coincidental.

Copyright © 1991 by Jeanne Whitmee

First published in Great Britain in 1991 by
Judy Piatkus (Publishers) Ltd of
5 Windmill Street, London W1

*The moral right of the author
has been asserted*

*A catalogue record for this book is available
from the British Library*

ISBN 0 7499 01047 7

Phototypeset in Compugraphic Times 11/12 pt by
Action Typesetting Limited, Gloucester
Printed and bound in Great Britain by
Bookcraft (Bath) Ltd

Chapter One

The war had been over a year and a half when Grace first met Harry Wendover. He had joined the pit orchestra at the local variety theatre and was lodging with Mrs Grainger who lived next door to the Manse.

Mary Pringle, Grace's mother, had died a month before VE Day, giving birth to her sixth child, a boy, which had died with her. Rodney Pringle had borne his loss with stoic forbearance, true to his Methodist beliefs.

'It is God's will that your mother has been taken from us,' he told Grace in his booming, lugubrious voice. 'Now it is up to you to take her place.'

And so she had, to the best of her sixteen-year-old ability, caring for her four sisters as well as she knew how. The three youngest girls were still at elementary school but thirteen-year-old Rachel had won a scholarship to the local grammar school and Rodney was determined that she should stay there. When Grace had tentatively suggested that Rachel might share the work, he had been adamant.

'Your sister has her studies to attend to. She has a good brain.' he said, intimating that Grace had not. 'And I want her to have the opportunity to use it.'

So Grace had meekly accepted her role of substitute mother, falling into the gruelling routine and managing as best she could. Getting up early every morning, she did the housework and got the younger girls ready for school before going to her job behind the drapery counter at the Co-op. Each evening when she came home she would cook the evening meal and do the washing and ironing, sometimes not falling into bed until well past midnight. On Sundays she dressed the children in their best and took them to chapel to hear their father preach.

1

By the time a year had passed Grace had slipped into the gap her mother had left. She accepted her lot in life because she could find no reason to rebel. But she often longed to go out with the other girls at work. She listened enviously to their chatter, hearing them talk about dances or the films they had seen; the boys they'd been out with. But she knew better than to ask if she could join them. Her father strongly disapproved of what he considered the 'Temptations of the Devil'. The cinema was iniquitous, and as for boys — she knew better than even to mention them.

It was a Sunday morning when she first saw Harry. He was leaving the house next door just as she was marshalling the younger ones on the pavement outside the Manse, ready for the walk to chapel.

'Good morning. What a lot of children. Are they all yours?'

Grace looked up. 'They're my sisters,' she told him rather crossly, re-buttoning little Christine's coat and pushing a stray curl under the brim of Victoria's straw hat.

'Where are you going? I'll walk along with you if you like — give you a hand.'

'I can manage perfectly well, thank you.' Grace took the hand of each of the two youngest ones while Rachel walked behind with ten-year-old Sarah. Undeterred, Harry fell in companionably beside her.

'Well, I'll walk along with you anyway. I'm going this way too.'

'Suit yourself. I suppose I can't stop you.' Grace took a sidelong glance at the tall young man striding along beside her. He had crisply curling brown hair and the bluest eyes she had ever seen. He was very attractive and she couldn't help feeling flattered that he wanted to walk with her. He wore a smart tweed sports jacket and grey flannels and she wished her own coat had been newer and more up to date. All the other girls at work had gone in for the New Look and she would have given anything for one of those coats with a nipped-in waist, flared skirt and alluring velvet stand-up collar. Red, she would have chosen, to complement her dark hair. And with it she'd wear one of those little feathered caps. But there was no money for fancy coats and hats. All the spare money went on keeping Rachel smart in her school uniform and the little ones in socks and shoes.

'You've got pretty hair.'

The remark startled her out of her dreams of fashion and her hand rose involuntarily to the glossy dark hair which she wore tied back in a pony tail. That was another thing, she longed to have it cut in one of the smart fringed bobs that were so popular, but her father wouldn't allow it.

2

'I'd like to have it all cut off,' she said wistfully.

'Oh, no.' He sounded horrified. 'Girls with hair like yours should never have it cut. It's beautiful.' He smiled at her and she noticed his mouth for the first time. It turned up at the corners as though he was always smiling and a fascinating dimple twinkled elusively in his left cheek. His lips were firm and well shaped and when they parted they revealed even white teeth. 'I'd like to see what it looks like when you untie it and let it down,' he said daringly.

Grace blushed, suddenly acutely aware of his eyes on her face as they walked side by side along the narrow pavement. They were nearing the chapel now and she slowed her pace. 'Are you going to chapel too?' she asked.

He threw back his head and laughed. 'No fear. We've got a band call — rehearsal,' he added, seeing her puzzled expression. 'I'm a musician. I play the piano — at the Theatre Royal in Bridge Street.'

Grace stared at him speechlessly. The Theatre Royal was out of bounds to her, just like the cinemas. And she had never met a musician before, unless you counted Miss Aitkin who played the asthmatic harmonium in chapel on Sundays.

Seeing her expression, Harry laughed. 'Does that make me completely unspeakable? I'm not always going to play in a theatre pit, you know. One day I'll be a concert pianist, or on the wireless at least.'

Grace stared at him. She fully believed he would. It was a world utterly outside her comprehension where anything might be possible and she longed to know more about it.

By now they were standing outside the chapel door. 'Well, I expect I'll be seeing you around.' Harry was already beginning to walk away, but he stopped. 'I'm Harry, by the way. Harry Wendover.' He paused. 'What's your name?'

'Oh — Grace Pringle.' She blushed. She hated the name. It sounded so stuffy and old fashioned. But Harry was smiling.

'I might have known,' he said. 'Grace. The name was made for you.' He reached out one finger and touched her cheek. 'Bye then, Grace. Be seeing you.'

She watched him swing away down the road, utterly captivated by this debonair, carefree young man. She wondered wistfully if he had a girlfriend, imagining a fashionably dressed laughing girl with short blond hair and endless legs, like Lana Turner in her photograph outside the Roxy last week. Or maybe he took out one of the dancers from the theatre. She'd seen photographs of them displayed outside too, all dressed in wonderful spangled costumes with elaborate feathered head-dresses. She looked down at her shabby brown coat. It had been her mother's and was a size too large for her. The style was out of date too, but the cloth was good – or so her father said. Harry Wendover had only spoken to her out of kindness, she told herself. Why should she interest him, surrounded as he was by so much glamour?

'Come on, Gracie.' Rachel nudged her, her pale blue eyes reproachful behind the steel-rimmed spectacles. 'You know how cross Father gets if we're late.'

Reluctantly she ushered them all into chapel. They filed down the aisle in front of her and settled into their pew. Each of them knelt. Five dark heads bent over folded hands, eyes tightly shut. Four pairs of lips moved in a mechanical 'Our Father'. But the fifth pair remained still. Inside her head Grace was praying for a red coat with a velvet collar.

She saw Harry often after that Sunday, going in and out of the house next door. Once or twice they exchanged a few words, but Grace was always acutely aware of her father's eyes watching from his study window. It inhibited her and she always hurried away as fast as she could, her eyes lowered. Harry couldn't know how he occupied all her dreams and fantasies. In them she was always beautifully dressed and wearing powder and lipstick. He would take her in his arms and they would dance together, under a crystal chandelier, their steps matching perfectly. The dreams warmed her on the coldest nights. They cheered her when her hands were red and raw from the washtub or scrubbing the kitchen floor; when her back ached and she knew that all her friends were out enjoying themselves. She hugged the dreams to her and made herself believe that they would some day come true. Later they helped her to bear the shame and humiliation of the other, nameless thing her father called 'her duty.'

Mary Pringle had been dead a year and a half when her father first told her about that 'duty'. In a voice that trembled with emotion he described to her how much he missed her mother and how hard it was for a man alone to fight temptation. It was late at night and he had surprised Grace by coming to her room when she was getting ready for bed.

'I could never take another wife,' he told her, his head in his hands. 'No other woman could take the place of your mother, and anyway, the parishioners would not approve.'

She had felt so sorry for him that she had sat down beside him on the edge of the bed and put her arm around his shoulders. 'You have us, Father,' she said gently.

4

He lifted his head and looked at her and suddenly she was afraid of what she saw in his eyes. He clutched suddenly at her shoulders. 'You're a good daughter, Grace. A good daughter and a lovely young woman. You've taken your mother's place well. But there are other duties a daughter can — and sometimes must — perform.'

Even in her innocence, apprehension stirred some instinct deep within her and she shrank from him, shaking her head and backing away. 'Father . . .?'

'Don't you see, child, we're both tormented by temptation. We can save one another, you and I. I've seen the young men ogling you with their lustful eyes. I won't let them have you, do you understand?'

'No, Father. They don't ogle me. I don't want them even if they do.' She was uneasy — afraid, of the wild glint in his eyes and the flecks of spittle at the corners of his mouth.

What he did, then and at other times, late at night when the house was silent and her sisters were asleep, left her with profound feelings of guilt and shame. Although he always insisted afterwards that she was a good girl, performing her Christian duty in keeping her father from temptation, she still felt guilty. And somehow she knew that it was the kind of guilt that would never be erased if she lived to be a hundred. Her father bought her the coat she had wanted for so long. He bought her other things too — small treats that she suspected he could ill afford. His generosity led her to wonder if he felt guilty too, but she pushed the thought from her. She'd been brought up to believe that her father could never do anything wrong. After all, he was a man of God, wasn't he? It must be all right if he said so.

When Harry saw her for the first time in the red coat he gave a long low whistle.

'You look lovely, Grace.'

She was walking home from work one evening in late March. The first daffodils were beginning to open and there was a feeling of spring in the air. He fell into step beside her.

'Why don't you ever come to the theatre?' he asked.

She shook her head. 'My father doesn't approve of theatres.'

He stared at her. 'You're kidding. Do everything your dad tells you, do you?' When she didn't reply he asked: 'How old are you, Grace?'

'Almost eighteen.'

'Don't you think you're old enough to make up your own mind?'

'Old enough to know that it's none of your business.'

He grinned good naturedly. 'Fair enough. Look, I've got a couple of comps. Want one? Have them both and bring one of your sisters if you want.'

'Comps?'

'Complimentary tickets — free seats. Oh come on, Grace. I could meet you for a drink afterwards and walk you home.'

She was just about to refuse when something suddenly occurred to her. Maybe her father wouldn't mind? He'd bought her the coat, hadn't he? And he'd been much less strict with her lately. Her spirits rose. 'All right,' she said suddenly. 'I'll come.'

Sitting in her seat in the front stalls, wearing her red coat, Grace felt like royalty. Harry looked so handsome in his black dinner jacket and bow tie. When the lights went down and the band struck up she glowed with pride at the sight of him, sitting there at the piano. She wanted to turn and tell those sitting around her that he was her friend.

To Grace, who had never been to the theatre in her life, it was a magic world of colour and music. She loved it all, from the blue plush seats and the usherettes in their smart uniforms, to the acts on the bill — comedians, acrobats, jugglers and singers, not to mention the chorus, scantily clad girls who could kick higher than she would ever have thought possible. When the lights went up she treated herself to an ice-cream and looked around her, wishing she could see someone she knew and that they could see her.

She met Harry afterwards, waiting for him at the stage door round at the back of the theatre as he'd told her. He came out with several of the other musicians who eyed her speculatively, nudging Harry and winking knowingly. She felt slightly embarrassed but the feeling soon left her when Harry took her arm and smiled down at her. He wore a dark overcoat over his evening suit, with a dashing white silk scarf.

'Enjoy the show?'

'Oh, yes. It was wonderful.'

He laughed. 'Easy to see you're not a regular theatre goer,' he said. 'It's a load of old tat compared to the West End shows.' As they walked he regaled her with descriptions of some of the shows he'd seen — describing how some of the theatres had stages that could revolve and equipment that could produce special magical effects. He took her to the Crown and Anchor, a pub in the next street to the theatre. Grace had never seen the inside of a public house before and she gazed around her, wide-eyed with curiosity, while Harry went to the bar to buy drinks. It seemed to be full of smoke and pungent yeasty smells; of people laughing and talking, every one of them with a glass in their hand. There was so much to see: the fascinating mirror behind the bar that reflected the lights and the bottles, the golden-haired barmaid in her black, low-cut blouse and glittering earrings; and the customers. She recognised some of Harry's fellow musicians and returned their smiles shyly from her seat in the corner, but she gazed in awe when some of the performers from the show came in. Even in their outdoor clothes they still looked special to Grace. They had panache — a kind of gloss — that made them stand out from ordinary people in some indefinable way that made her want to stare and stare at them.

Harry had asked her when they first came in: 'What will you have?' and she'd shaken her head. How silly and naive he must think her.

'Oh, whatever you're having,' she'd replied. Now he reappeared, shouldering his way to her through the crush, carrying two glasses of golden liquid which he put down on the table in front of her.

She looked at it apprehensively. 'What is it?'

'Whisky — with a dash of ginger.' He laughed. 'It'll bring the roses to your cheeks. All right?'

'Oh — yes, thank you.' When she took a sip and swallowed it she thought her throat would burst into flames, but she smiled at Harry, blinking back the moisture that sprang to her eyes. 'It's lovely.'

He reached for her hand, his eyes suddenly serious. 'Grace, I've got something to tell you.'

'What's that?'

'I've got another job. I'm leaving here.'

She felt her heart turn to ice. 'Oh — when?'

'Tomorrow. I leave in the morning.' His fingers tightened round hers. 'I really wish we could have got to know each other better, Grace. I've tried, but I thought you didn't like me.'

'Oh, no ...' She looked at him, speechless with disappointment. 'I — it was Father. He ...'

'I know. I realised that later.' He nodded. 'He's pretty strict with you, isn't he? But when I saw you in that red coat, I though perhaps he was easing up a bit.'

Grace was silent. What would she do when he was gone? All her dreams, all her hopes of happiness, seemed to turn to dust and she saw her future stretching endlessly ahead of her, grey and dull and forbidding. She tried hard to swallow the tears that thickened her throat and made herself ask: 'What sort of job is it?'

He launched enthusiastically into a description of his new job, but she hardly heard any of it except to register that it was in London

7

somewhere and that he was excited about it. It was as though the bottom had dropped out of her world. Presently she said: 'I think I should be going home now.'

'Of course.' Harry got to his feet.

'You'll be wanting to be with your friends as it's your last night. It's all right, I can find my own way.'

He looked hurt. 'Of course I'll come. You don't think I'd let you walk home on your own, do you?'

They walked in silence. She wanted to tell him how much their brief acquaintance had meant to her; how much she would miss him; but the words refused to come. Besides, she asked herself, what was the point? A week from now he would have forgotten her. Somehow she found she had voiced this last thought. Harry stopped walking and took her arm, swinging her round to face him.

'That isn't true, Grace, honestly.' His blue eyes were grave as they looked into hers. 'You're special — different from all the others. If I'd been staying — if things had been different ...' He drew her towards him and kissed her gently on the lips. 'Look, tell you what, will you write to me?'

She looked up at him, her eyes luminous with tears.

'Oh yes, Harry. Of course I will.'

'And maybe you could come up to Town and meet me sometimes?'

For the moment she couldn't quite see that as a possibility but she nodded her head just the same. Somehow she would manage it — for him.

'Yes, Harry.'

He kissed her again and she felt a glow of happiness enfolding her like a warm blanket. He loved her. He must love her to say such things and to kiss her.

'I'll write as soon as I can and let you have the address of my digs,' he said. 'Take care of yourself, Grace. I've got to go now. I've got all my packing to do. Bye for now, love.'

Her father was waiting for her in his darkened study. As she let herself in through the front door her thoughts were all of Harry. She could still feel his lips on hers and the warmth of his strong young arms around her. She didn't notice that the study door was ajar. When Rodney's voice sawed through the silence it made her start violently.

'*Where have you been*?'

She had reached the foot of the stairs but she stopped in her tracks. 'To the theatre, Father.'

'And who gave you the money for such fripperies, may I ask?'

8

'I was given a free ticket. I didn't think you'd mind.'

'How *dare* you go out without asking my permission?' His brow was dark with anger as he glowered at her and her heart began to thump with apprehension. He flung out an arm, pushing the study door open behind him. 'Take off that coat and come in here.' When she hesitated he strode towards her, grasping her arm and pulling her across the hall. 'Do as you're told, girl. How dare you defy me?'

In the study he turned to face her and she shrank from the raw fury in his eyes. 'So you think you can do as you please, do you?'

She stared at him. 'You − you've been so much − kinder lately, I thought . . .'

'You thought you could take advantage,' he thundered. 'You thought you could betray me − your own father. I saw you out there,' he said in a voice that trembled. 'I saw you − making yourself cheap with that common young man, behaving like a street woman.' When she didn't reply he went on: 'Don't you care? Are you so completely abandoned that you don't *care* who sees you making free with yourself?'

'I wasn't. I told you, Father, I was given a free ticket . . .'

'Don't you know, girl, that nothing is free in this world? If that man gave you a ticket for the theatre it was because he expected something from you in return.' He stepped towards her. 'Or perhaps you knew that. Perhaps you expected and welcomed it.' He stopped suddenly to sniff at her. 'You've been drinking.' He glared at her accusingly. 'Well, *have* you? Tell me. I'll have the truth from you if I have to beat it out of you.'

His anger was like a wall of flame. Grace cowered from it. 'Harry isn't like you say, Father. He bought me a drink after the theatre − just one − and then brought me straight home.'

'Don't lie to me, girl. I saw you out there with my own eyes − *kissing* − kissing and letting that − that *creature* paw you about. How could you, a child of mine?' She didn't answer and he thundered: 'Well − can you deny it?'

'It wasn't the way you make it sound, Father. It was because he's going away.' A sudden flash of defiance made her burst out: 'All the girls I know go out and enjoy themselves. They have boyfriends too. It doesn't make them bad. I've done nothing wrong. There's no harm in it.'

'Really? I happen to think I'm the best judge of that.' He drew in his breath sharply and turned from her, walking round his desk and opening the drawer. 'I thought I'd brought up my daughters to know right from wrong. Obviously in your case I failed. Painful as it will be for me, I will have to chastise you, Grace. You realise that?'

Now she saw what it was that he had taken out of the desk drawer and shrank back in disbelief. 'No, Father, you can't. I'm not a child any more. You can't. *You can't.*'

'Do not tell me what I can and cannot do.' He advanced towards her, flexing the cane between his hands. But what she saw in his eyes terrified her even more than the prospect of a thrashing. She made a dash for the door and twisted the handle frantically, but it was locked. With her back pressed against it she made one last desperate appeal.

'Please, Father − *please don't.*' But even as she was saying the words she knew they were falling on deaf ears. The violent emotion that had taken possession of Rodney Pringle could hear and feel nothing but the urge that drove him; the irresistible urge to inflict pain − pain that would satisfy the perverted lust eating at his repressed being.

It was five am when Harry was awakened by something tapping on his bedroom window. He lay for a moment, wondering if it was part of the dream he'd been having, but when it came again he got out of bed to look down into the back garden. What he saw below shocked and puzzled him. Grace, her hair wild and her clothes torn, stared up at his window as though transfixed. Pulling on trousers and a sweater he crept downstairs and quietly let himself out through the back door. She was still there, huddled on the garden seat beneath his window, a handful of gravel still clutched in her hand.

'Grace. My God, what's happened to you?'

She got shakily to her feet and fell into his outstretched arms. 'It was Father. He − he saw us last night. He was watching from the study. He − he − beat me.'

Speechless with shock, he stared down at her. Her hair hung in damp strands around her bruised and swollen face, and her blouse was ripped almost to shreds. 'He did *this* to you − your own father? Just for going out with me?' He looked disbelievingly at her cut lip and the livid wheels and lacerations made by the cane on her shoulders and arms. 'But surely . . .'

'Please, Harry − don't ask me to tell you about it. Take me with you,' she begged. 'I can't stay here any longer. You don't know what he's like.'

He held her trembling body close and felt the chill of her flesh through his sweater. 'Where have you been all night?' he asked.

She nodded towards the garden shed. 'In there. I was afraid he might kill me if I stayed in the house.'

Harry sank on to the garden seat with her and pulled her head

10

against his shoulder. After a moment he said: 'You'll have to go back to fetch your things. Can you get back into the house? I'll come with you if you're afraid.'

She looked up at him with frightened eyes. 'I can't. I can't go back in there.'

'If you're going away you'll have to.' He touched the torn sleeve of her ruined blouse, trying to cover her shoulder with the tattered shreds. 'You can't go like this. You'll need a change of clothes — your ration book — clothing coupons and things. No good going anywhere without them.'

She swallowed hard. 'Yes, of course. I'll go by myself — now, before he wakes up.' She looked up at him hopefully, trying to read his expression. 'Does that mean I *can* come with you then, Harry? I promise I won't be a nuisance. I won't get in your way and spoil things for you. I'll get a job as soon as we get there.'

'Shhh. Don't worry about things like that.' He held her close, rocking her soothingly back and forth and stroking her tangled hair, his mind working on the problem. At last he made his decision.

'We can't be together like this,' he said slowly. 'But if we were ...' He grinned down at her. 'It's a funny old time to be asking you, but will you marry me, Grace?'

She gazed up at him, her eyes round with astonishment. 'Oh, Harry, *yes*. Yes, please.'

Chapter Two

Grace stood at one of the long windows of the tiny flat, looking down on to the Hackney Road. It was early evening and Harry had just left for work. As she watched the traffic below, she wondered vaguely about the people rushing past in the street. There were so many of them, each with their own life. Were they happy? What were they thinking about as they made their way home or out for the evening? Surely none of them could possibly be as confused and unhappy, feel as inadequate as she did.

She turned despondently back to look at the room behind her, seeing it as though for the first time; the shabbiness of the furniture, the mockery of the double bed with its frayed and faded pink eiderdown. The evening sunshine showed up the threadbare patches in the worn carpet. It made the curtains look dusty, and glaringly lit the places Grace had so carefully darned. The whole room epitomised the way she felt – impoverished and bewildered.

The flat was part of a converted Georgian terrace. The once elegant, beautifully proportioned family house had been divided crudely and unimaginatively into four flats by a greedy landlord. Each one consisted of a tiny hall, a large bed-sitting room and a small kitchen; each of the kitchens had a bath and water heater in one corner, but the toilet facilities on the ground floor were shared by the tenants of all four flats. It was their first home and when Grace had first seen it she'd felt like singing with happiness. To her it had looked like a palace and she had longed to move in with Harry and begin their new life together there and then.

When they'd first arrived in London, Harry's landlady had reluctantly found Grace a tiny box room which she referred to as her 'top floor back', but she had insisted that it was only a temporary measure. Her mouth pulled down at the corners, she had warned them both that she didn't hold with what she called 'hanky-panky', and that she didn't let her rooms to married couples. It seemed they would have to postpone their wedding until they could find a flat. In the meantime Harry had been busy rehearsing with the dance band he had joined and Grace had occupied her time looking for work. She found a job on the haberdashery counter in one of the big department stores in the West End and soon settled into it.

When Harry had heard of the flat through one of the other boys in the band they had taken the bus out to Hackney at the very first opportunity. When they were told it was still vacant they had been as excited as two children.

'It'll mean a bit of travelling for us both each day,' he had said. 'But it's quite cheap. It'll do nicely for a start, eh?'

'Oh, Harry, it's beautiful.' Grace had stood at one of the two long elegant windows in the living room, her eyes shining as she pictured the velvet curtains she would make to replace the dingy brown brocade ones, and the smart new furniture they would save up for. She and Harry had hardly spent any time together since they came to London. He played with the band in the evenings at various venues all over London, often not getting home until after midnight. Grace worked in the daytime from nine till six. Often they only passed each other on the stairs, he on his way out, she on her way in. Sunday was the only day when they had time together and they made the most of it. Anxious to save as much money as they could they would go to all the places that were free: parks and museums, The Serpentine or Hampstead Heath, sometimes a bus ride to Hampton Court. Hand in hand with Harry on those days, Grace thought that no one could ever possibly have been as happy as they were.

The wedding took place at Hackney Register Office on a blustery day in early May. Grace wore a blue two-piece, bought at special staff discount from the store where she worked. Harry looked handsome in the navy pin-stripe suit he wore when the band played for tea dances. Instead of a honeymoon they had gone straight back to the flat. And that was when the trouble had begun.

When Harry had pulled her into his arms that night in bed and tried to make love to her, Grace had gone rigid, seized with a violent panic. Somehow it was not what she had visualised. Without really thinking about it she had foreseen their marriage as innocent of all intimate contact; pure and beautiful. Every time Harry touched her a vision of her father's face rose to haunt her. She saw again the indescribable look in his eyes. In Harry's gentle touch she felt again the obscene softness of her father's hands, heard again the excuses he had made for what he was doing, which she now saw through

13

as weak and wanton. Were all men the same? Did they all want to use a woman's body for their own gratification? Her father had made her feel soiled and guilty. She would not allow Harry to do the same. She would not let him spoil their marriage.

To begin with he had been patient, soothing and caressing her until her tears had subsided and she slept. He had begged her to talk about her problem but she couldn't. How could she tell him what she had allowed to happen? How could she make him understand that the only way she could forget was never to let another man near her? But she was married now. Once more the despised and hated word 'duty' arose. One night in exasperation Harry himself had used it.

'It's the least a man can expect from his wife,' he had said, getting up to pace the room in frustration. 'You took a vow to love and cherish. If nothing else you might think of it as a duty, but if you loved me you'd want to.'

She did love him and she told him so − over and over. But he could not believe that a woman who loved her husband could shrink with revulsion every time he so much as reached out for her.

The weeks passed into months. Grace worked by day and Harry in the evenings. She was always in bed when he arrived home and when she heard him coming up the stairs she would turn her back and feign sleep. Last night he'd been particularly late and instead of climbing quietly into bed beside her, he shook her shoulder roughly.

'Grace, come on, love. I know you're not asleep.'

She turned to look at him and saw at once that he'd been drinking. His eyes were slightly bloodshot and his breath was sickly sweet with the smell of whisky.

'Don't look at me like that. You make me feel like a sex-mad swine,' he said, slurring his words slightly. 'Damn it all, I only want what every married man has a right to expect.'

She pushed him from her. 'Go away. You've been drinking.'

'You bet I've been drinking,' he said raggedly. 'What other pleasures have I got?' He pulled at her nightdress. 'What's so repulsive about me that you can't bear me to touch you, Grace? Tell me that − just *tell* me.'

'Leave me alone.' She pushed him away and pulled the neck of her nightdress together. But before she knew what was happening he had snatched her hand away, ripping the thin material until it revealed one breast. He bent, fastening his mouth on it, ignoring her cries. Holding her threshing arms above her head he moved over her and forced her thighs apart, thrusting into her. It was over quickly and Harry rolled from her with a groan and lay on his side for a moment, listening to her sobbing. Then he turned,

14

but this time, instead of taking her in his arms and gently soothing her as he had done in the past, he rounded on her angrily, suddenly stone cold sober.

'Why do you have to make me feel like some dirty animal every time?' he demanded. 'You don't know the meaning of the word love.'

She sat up, drawing her torn nightdress around her and staring at him reproachfully. '*Love*? You call that love?'

He shook his head. 'No, I don't, but it's all I'm ever likely to get from you, isn't it? What's the matter with you, Grace. Why are you so bloody frigid?'

She should have told him them. She knew instinctively that this was the moment and that if she let it pass there would never be another. She opened her mouth to begin, but her courage failed her. She imagined the look of incredulous horror on his face. He would blame her. How could he *not* blame her? If she told him what there had been between her and her father their marriage would be over. He would stop loving her − if he hadn't already. There would be no chance for them once he knew. She turned away.

'It's all you ever think about,' she muttered, getting out of bed and pulling on her dressing gown. 'There are other things in life besides sex.'

They stayed together, establishing a kind of uneasy truce. As long as it wasn't too often Grace would submit to Harry's lovemaking. But he knew she hated it; sensed she was gritting her teeth, just waiting and praying for it to be over. It undermined his confidence and made him bad-tempered. It even affected his work. God only knew there was no pleasure in it for him, and gradually − to Grace's relief − their love life almost ceased to exist.

As time went by and winter came, she began to think more and more about her sisters, left behind in the Manse at Easthampton. Sitting in the flat alone during the long evenings she worried about them. With her gone would one of them be forced to take her place − or would her father have learnt his lesson? She thought more and more about them until at last she could bear the uncertainty no longer and told Harry one morning at breakfast that she wanted to make the trip home.

'Just for one day − to see that they're all right,' she assured him. 'I've got some time off due to me. I'll go next week. I could stay one night at the Great Eastern Hotel, then I could take the little ones out for a treat after they got home from school.'

He didn't argue, but shrugged in acquiescence. Grace was a law unto herself. He had long since given up trying to understand her.

The town looked just the same. When she came out of the station forecourt and stood waiting for one of the familiar red buses she was faintly surprised to see the same shops and buildings. Somehow she had felt that it would all have changed, just as her own life had changed.

She waited until she knew her father would be out, then went to the Manse and rang the front door bell. Rachel answered. She was wiping her hands on the front of a grubby print pinafore. Grace was shocked at her appearance. Gone the neat hair and smart school uniform. Her hair hung around her face in greasy strands and she looked like a middle-aged woman instead of a sixteen-year-old girl. She stared at Grace with undisguised hostility.

'Oh, it's you.'

'I came to see if you were all right. Can I come in?' Grace made to step over the threshold but Rachel barred the way.

'You're not welcome here,' she said. 'Going off like that. I had to leave school because of you. You're a selfish cat, Grace Pringle. And Father says you're a bad girl.'

Grace held out her left hand. 'I'm Grace Wendover now. Harry and I got married soon after I left here. Father's wrong about me.'

'Well, you're not coming in.' Rachel stood her ground. 'If I were you I'd clear off before Father gets back and sees you. He said if you ever came back I wasn't to let you in or even speak to you.'

Grace felt the hot colour creeping up her neck. 'I suppose he didn't happen to tell you *why* I left?' she asked. 'Did he ever tell you what he did to me? Did he ever try . . .?' She stopped in mid-sentence. She could tell by Rachel's face that he hadn't. That was a relief, but at least she could defend herself. 'He thrashed me,' she went on. 'That night, just because I went out with Harry. He thrashed me with a stick — within an inch of my life. That's why I left.'

Rachel began to close the door. 'Liar,' she said, thrusting an accusing chin at Grace. 'He said you'd come back with a lot of wicked lies and that I wasn't to believe them. And I don't.'

'It's true.' Grace put her hand against the door. 'Let me see Sarah and the little ones — please, Rachel.'

'No. Father said we weren't to have anything more to do with you.'

'He isn't telling you the truth. He's the one telling lies,' Grace insisted.

'I know who *I'd* rather believe.' Rachel pushed the door and it clicked shut abruptly in Grace's face, leaving her standing on the step. She walked slowly down the path but as she turned to fasten the gate she saw the net curtains next door twitch and caught a glimpse of Mrs Grainger's grey head whisking out of sight. Apparently even their kindly neighbour's mind had been fed with lies about the Minister's errant eldest daughter. There was nothing more for her here, she told herself. Easthampton wasn't home to her any more. She wondered dejectedly if anywhere was.

There was no point in staying the night. She caught the first train back to London and sat miserably in her corner seat throughout the two-hour journey, feeling rejected and alone. In her mind she relived that terrible night when her father had beaten her, remembering the pain and the terror as she fled from the house; the chill of the night air on her bruised flesh and the eerie skeletal rattling of the tree branches in Mrs Grainger's garden as she crouched in the draughty garden shed all night. What had she done that her sisters should turn against her? It had all been for Harry and now it seemed that even he didn't want her. What had gone wrong between them? More important, how could she put it right? If she lost Harry she'd have no one.

At Liverpool Street she caught a bus, getting off at the stop before hers to buy bread and milk at the little corner grocer's shop she often used. Harry wouldn't bother for himself, but she was dying for a cup of tea and something to eat.

She climbed the stairs wearily and let herself into the flat. She took her purchases into the kitchen and put the kettle on, then she turned towards the living room. It was then she heard the quiet buzz of voices. Frowning she turned the door handle quietly, pushing the door open a few inches. It was then that she saw them, reflected in the mirror on the opposite wall. The girl had blonde hair. She and Harry lay side by side on the bed — both of them naked. It was all too clear that they had just made love.

The shock seemed to bring all the injustices of the day to a head. Afterwards she realised that she must have gone a little mad. Bursting into the room, she screamed shrilly at the girl.

'Get out. Do you hear me? *Get out.*' She picked up one of the female garments that lay strewn about the floor and began to tear it into shreds. Harry leapt up and tried to restrain her, but she pulled away from him, letting loose a torrent of words she'd hardly been aware that she knew. Going to the window she threw it open and began to hurl the girl's clothes down into the street. Later she vaguely remembered the pale upturned faces, blank with surprise, as the flimsy garments fluttered down, but at the time she neither saw

17

nor cared. When the clothes had all gone she turned her attention on to the girl, now cowering by the door, wrapped in Harry's dressing gown, her eyes wide with shock and her mouth a round O of fear. Grace leapt at her, tearing wildly at the blond hair, clawing at her face, oblivious to the girl's screams, or to Harry shouting at her, until he grasped her flailing arms and held them behind her back, urging the girl to leave; bundling her out of the flat.

Suddenly it was quiet; uncannily quiet. The flat was empty. Harry had pushed her into a chair and hustled the girl outside on to the landing, taking her — as it later transpired — to safety in the flat below. Grace slammed the door and locked it, leaning against it breathlessly. He would not come back — *ever*. He wasn't her husband any more. Now she was all alone. She began to weep, silent, furious tears that seared her cheeks like acid and tore agonisingly at her chest and throat. Now she was really alone. Perhaps she had always been alone. Perhaps she always would be.

Grace was slightly breathless when she reached the top floor of the building in Charing Cross Road. She'd been here once before with Harry but she'd had to rack her memory really hard this morning to remember the name of his agent. Tapping on the half-glazed door and receiving no reply, she pushed it open and went in. A bored looking girl sitting at a desk, looked up without interest.

'Yes?'

'Can I see Mr Sylvester, please?'

'What's it about?'

'It's — a personal matter.'

A small spark of interest glimmered in the girl's eyes for a second, then faded again. She stood up. 'I'll see if he's free.'

She went through to the next office and Grace heard a murmured conversation. When she reappeared the girl said grudgingly: 'He can give you five minutes.'

Gerry Sylvester looked up. The young woman standing in front of him didn't look like a musician, but he had been in the business long enough to know never to judge by appearances. Some of the most unlikely people could produce music that sounded as though it came straight from heaven. He smiled. 'Good morning. How can I help you?'

Clutching nervously at the strap of her handbag, Grace came straight to the point: 'Can you tell me where Alfredo's Rumba Band is playing this week, please?'

It wasn't the usual approach and his bushy eyebrows rose in surprise. 'Now why would you want to know that?' he asked.

'I'm trying to find Harry Wendover,' she told him, her heart thumping uncomfortably. 'It – it's important that I find him – quickly.'

Gerry leaned back in his chair, regarding her with curiosity. Harry was one of his better clients. He worked hard and he was ambitious. The job with Alfredo was working out well. He'd just booked them a summer season at Bournemouth. Gerry had even got Harry a couple of BBC engagements recently too. Only accompanist work, but still . . . The boy wasn't brilliant but there was no doubt that he had a good steady career in front of him. He wouldn't like anything to happen to spoil it. On closer inspection he saw that the woman in front of him was hardly more than a girl. His shrewd eyes took in the down at heel shoes and shabby handbag; the red coat whose buttons strained a little at the front – his spirits sank. Oh God, no. What sort of mess had Harry got himself into here?

'Well now,' he said slowly, lighting a cigarette to give himself time to think, 'it's my rule not to give out information about my clients. I'm sure you can understand that?'

'Yes – but you see, I'm his wife.' She held out her left hand.

The cigarette almost dropped out of Gerry's mouth in surprise. He had no idea that Harry was married. Odd he'd said nothing. 'Forgive me, but if you're his wife, my dear, how come you have to ask me where he's working?'

Grace coloured. 'We – had a row. And parted. Several weeks ago.'

After a moment's hesitation, Gerry pulled a notepad towards him and scribbled something on it, then he tore off the page and passed it to her. 'This is where the band is working this week,' he said. 'It's a Palais de Danse in South London – think you can find it?'

Grace nodded gratefully, pushing the paper into her bag.

'You won't make a scene, love, will you?' he asked. 'I mean, he *will* be pleased to see you, I take it?'

Grace turned at the door. Was it possible he had heard about the humiliating evening she'd found Harry at the flat with the girl? Summoning every last shred of her dignity she said: 'Don't worry, Mr Sylvester. There won't be any trouble – not this time. Thank you for helping me.'

Grace was acutely aware from the moment she entered the building that she looked incongruously out of place at The Palais. She wore the blue two-piece that she had been married in, but, like the red coat, she'd had trouble fastening it. It was ten weeks since the terrible night when she had returned from Easthampton to find

19

Harry in bed with the girl. He'd tried to come back several times, knocking on the door and begging to be allowed in to talk, but she'd sat silently, her hands over her ears and her lips pressed tightly together, determined not to see or speak to him again. He'd even sent her money for the first few weeks, but she'd sent the cheque back, care of the bank, enclosing a note addressed to Harry saying that she wanted nothing more from him. Unable to afford the rent of the flat on her own meagre wage, she'd moved out, taking a dingy bed-sitting room in Bow, telling herself that she'd manage all right somehow. But the long winter nights were cold and the hissing little gas fire ate her shillings voraciously so that she had to exist mainly on baked beans on toast and bread and jam.

Discovering she was pregnant came as a shattering blow. Somehow she didn't associate pregnancy with the barely endured couplings she and Harry had shared. At first she ignored the tell-tale symptoms, hoping that perhaps it might be a mistake after all − the result of her poor diet. But as the weeks passed she was forced to acknowledge the fact that her condition would not be ignored. Each morning she retched miserably in the dingy bathroom two floors below, whilst the other tenants of the house rattled the door handle impatiently. Every time she fastened her skirt it was a little harder to make the waistband meet. Soon it would show and she'd have to give up work. What would become of her then? Eventually she had to face the fact that she must pocket her pride and find Harry again. After all, he was responsible.

She'd never been in a dance hall before and the opulent Victorian splendour awed and intimidated her; as did the brash young people in their flounced dresses or draped suits. She bought herself a glass of lemonade and found a quiet corner in which to sit and drink it, wondering how she could manage to speak to Harry alone in this crowded place.

When the band came on and began to play, the floor soon filled up with dancers. Grace's heart sank. She could see Harry, smiling and looking as handsome as ever there at the piano, but he would never see her among all these people. She didn't see the remotest possibility of being able to speak to him. She might just as well go home now. But she sat on, hoping against hope that some way of attracting his attention would present itself to her.

In the end it was by sheer accident that they met. During the interval, when the band left the stand, Grace decided that she had had enough. She wasn't going to see Harry this way. She would have to write to him. Somehow find the words to make her humiliating capitulation and send it here, hoping that it would reach him. Before

20

facing the bus queue she went to find the Ladies. It was packed with giggling girls renewing their lipstick and straightening their stocking seams. Most of them were about Grace's own age, but she felt much older, an interloper among their frivolous camaraderie. She shrank from the way they looked at her – curious; pitying. Some of them glanced critically at her clothes without bothering to hide their patronising smiles. As soon as she came out of the lavatory cubicle she left, going through the swing door and into the corridor again with relief.

It was as she was walking towards the front entrance that she heard him call her name: 'Grace!'

She turned, stopping in her tracks as she found herself face to face with Harry.

He walked towards her.'What are you doing here?'

'I – came to see you.'

'But why? I don't understand. You never came to see me play before ...' He touched her arm, his eyes suddenly concerned. 'Are you all right?' He didn't tell her that Gerry Sylvester had already warned him that Grace was looking for him and that she seemed unwell.

'Yes – well, no.' She'd dropped her gaze but now she looked up into his eyes. It was important suddenly for her to see his expression when she told him. 'I'm going to have a baby, Harry.'

For a second his eyes registered the same disbelief that she herself had felt. Perhaps he too hadn't thought it possible to make a baby out of revulsion and coldness. Then, slowly, a look of wonder and excitement came into his eyes. 'A *baby*? How – how long?'

'Almost five months,' she told him.

'Five? Then you must have been ...'

'Yes. But I didn't know.'

Reaching out he pulled her into his arms and held her. 'Oh, Grace, love. I'm sorry. If only I could turn the clock back. That day – it didn't mean anything, you know. I'd give anything for it not to have happened.' He looked down at her. 'Look, I'll make it up to you, I promise.'

His words brought the tears she'd so far denied herself. 'I will too. It was my fault, I know that. I always knew it really.' She hid her head against his shoulder. 'Oh, Harry, I *do* love you. It will be all right, won't it?'

'Of course it will.' He kissed the tears from her cheeks.

A crowd of girls came out of the Ladies and gazed at them in amazement. That dowdy girl in the awful blue dress, what could the handsome pianist possibly see in *her*, they wondered? But Grace was

21

oblivious to their envious glances. Harry and she were back together. She wouldn't have to be alone any more. Everything was going to be all right.

Harry's summer season at the Pavilion, Bournemouth, began in the second week of May. Grace went with him and they managed to find a nice flat on the edge of town. It was in a tree-lined road of rather grand Victorian houses, quite close to the railway station. For Grace it was an idyllic time. Once her initial morning sickness was over, pregnancy suited her. She lost her pinched, undernourished look and grew rounded and serene, her complexion smooth and golden from fresh air and sun. When Harry was at rehearsals she would walk down into the town and look at the shops. Sometimes she would walk to the East Cliff, past the smart, newly refurbished hotels and down on to the beach by way of the zig zag path, to spend an afternoon sunbathing on the beach; riding back up later in the cliff lift. On some days she would make sandwiches and meet Harry in the pleasure gardens for a picnic lunch. She loved sitting under the pine trees and watching the children paddling in the Bourne stream, while the tame squirrels scampered for scraps of food.

It was on a humid night in late July when she wakened Harry at two in the morning with the first pains.

'Harry, I think the baby's coming.'

He was awake instantly, helping her to dress and gather her belongings together, going downstairs to telephone for a taxi. He'd stayed at the hospital for the rest of the night and all next morning, but when it was time for him to gɔ to the theatre for the afternoon performance, the baby still hadn't been born. Grace was exhausted. They allowed him to see her for a few minutes before he had to leave, but she hardly seemed to know he was there. Her rambling words and glazed eyes, her flushed face and damp hair, alarmed him.

'She seems in such terrible pain. Will she be all right?' he'd asked the sister anxiously. But the staff hadn't seemed unduly concerned about her.

He returned at teatime to spend a couple of hours at her bedside, then went reluctantly to the theatre for the evening show.

Left on her own Grace felt abandoned. Exhausted and racked with pain she called out for Harry time and again, until the sister came into the small side ward where she was and told her quite crossly that she was disturbing the other patients and must be quiet. It was nine o'clock when they wheeled her down the corridor to the labour ward, and half-past ten when her baby daughter was delivered. Miraculously, the moment the baby was laid in her

22

arms, Grace felt well again; refreshed and charged with a new and powerful energy. She gazed down into the baby's dark blue eyes, touching the fine black down on her head with her fingertips, afraid to look away in case it was all a dream. 'My baby.' She said the words experimentally to herself, over and over. 'My daughter. A real person of my very own — made out of my own flesh and blood.' It seemed like a miracle. Now it didn't matter that her family had rejected her. She need never be alone again, whatever happened.

Harry came as soon as the show was over and stood by the bed holding the baby tenderly in his arms and looking down at her with an expression of love and wonder in his eyes.

'What shall we call her?' Grace asked, watching them happily, intoxicated with the new potent power that coursed through her veins.

'Elaine,' he said without hesitation. 'I've always liked that name. It was my mother's. We'll call her Elaine Grace.'

Elaine grew fast in those warm, golden weeks of late summer. As soon as Grace brought her home from the hospital, Harry had taken them out to buy a pram and during the weeks that followed Grace took her for long walks. Even though she knew Elaine was too young to understand she showed her all the sight and sounds and smells she had discovered for herself in the weeks before the baby was born. The beach with its tangy salt air; the ordered profusion of colour and the clean scent of pine and bruised grass in the gardens. She loved to push the pram down to the clifftop in the evenings, to hear the plaintive crying of the gulls and watch the sky turn to mother-of-pearl as the sun dipped beneath a sea of molten gold.

Elaine's little arms and legs grew honey brown and rounded, her hair grew into soft dark curls and her cheeks became rosy. The holidaymakers on the beach often looked into the pram to coo at the pretty, happy baby kicking and laughing under the canopy, while Grace stood proudly looking on. She loved everything about Bournemouth. It was a beautiful town, but to Grace it was far more. She had been happier here than in any other place and she never wanted to leave. As the summer days began to shorten, Harry occasionally reminded her, with a word or a reference to people they both knew, that it would soon be time to leave, but she refused to allow herself to think of their return to London; the noise and fumes of the traffic, the grimy city streets, and the dreariness of the coming winter.

'Can't we stay here?' she asked once. 'You could get a job with the resident band at The Pavilion, couldn't you?'

But Harry had shaken his head. He was excited. That morning he'd had a letter from Gerry Sylvester with the news that he'd fixed him an audition with the Geraldo orchestra. He showed it to her.

'It'll mean twice the money I've been getting, love. We'll even be able to put down the deposit on a house of our own, somewhere in the suburbs maybe, with a garden for Elaine to play in. You'd like that, wouldn't you?'

All too soon September was upon them. Time to pack and leave. But as they prepared to move back to London, Grace's heart was heavy. Something told her that she would never be as happy as she'd been that summer.

Chapter Three

To begin with Harry said that the house in Stanmore was too expensive, but Grace had set her heart on it from the moment she walked in through the front door. She insisted that they could manage the mortgage if she found a job too.

'With you at home in the daytime we don't have to worry about Elaine,' she reminded him. And at last Harry had allowed himself to be persuaded, secretly looking forward to having his little daughter to himself for a few hours each day.

It was a semi-detached villa in a road lined with flowering cherry trees. Each pair of houses had a timbered gable and a rounded front porch. They had been built in the mid-thirties, just before the war. Inside there were three bedrooms, a pretty green bathroom, a lounge, dining room and a kitchen with what the estate agent had called 'every mod con'. The previous owners had moved in a couple of years after the war ended, and modernised, putting in a stainless steel sink, something which Grace had never seen before, as well as brightly painted cupboards and units. At the back was a garden neatly laid out with a lawn and flowerbeds that reminded her nostalgically of Bournemouth. There was even a gnarled old apple tree with a swing hanging from one of the lower branches. It was perfect – and far too good to miss.

Grace had quite easily found a job as manageress of a small draper's shop in the Honeypot Lane shopping centre. The house was within walking distance of it, and of Elaine's new school. Even the station was handy enough for Harry to get up to Town in under an hour. And so the three of them had moved into number forty-seven St Olaf's Avenue and settled happily into a new routine.

Elaine was seven when they moved to Stanmore. A bright, happy child, she had adjusted easily at school and was the apple of her parents' eyes.

Since the family had moved back to London the autumn after her birth, they had lived in a flat in Edgware over an ironmonger's shop. Harry was happy and busy with his regular dance band job and Gerry Sylvester found him plenty of additional engagements with the BBC to augment his income. More recently he had managed to get Harry work with some of the major film studios too, providing background music for the sound tracks. For himself, Harry would have been content to remain in Edgware, but Grace had never forgotten his promise of a little house in the suburbs. Bournemouth had given her a taste for fresh air and the good things of life and she was determined that they would have something better. When she found the house in St Olaf's Avenue, she knew at once that it was the home she had always dreamed of.

On the surface Grace and Harry's marriage was ideal. Everyone who knew them thought them the perfect couple. And Grace herself was happy enough. They agreed about most things and they were both devoted to Elaine. But under the bland surface their relationship was still far from idyllic. It was for this reason that Harry sat in the waiting room of the local GP one spring afternoon, nervously waiting for his name to be called.

The family had registered with Doctor Bradshaw when they first came to live in Stanmore six months ago, but so far none of them had had any reason to visit him. Harry had no idea whether he was old or young, and as he sat there, staring unseeingly at the magazine on his lap, he wondered how on earth he would approach the problem he had come to discuss.

When he was ushered into the surgery he was relieved to see that the doctor was middle-aged. A younger man would have inhibited him, whilst a man of an older generation would have made him feel even more embarrassed than he was.

After the usual preliminaries, the doctor looked up at him expectantly.

'So, Mr. Wendover, what can I do for you today?'

Harry took a deep breath. 'It's my wife really, Doctor.'

'I see. Couldn't she come herself?'

'She doesn't know I'm here. It's rather embarrassing. You see she's − she won't − doesn't like ...'

'How long have you been married?' the doctor asked helpfully.

'Almost eight years.'

'Any children?'

'One − a daughter of seven.'

'So this problem is recent?'

'No. It's always been — difficult.'

The doctor turned his chair round to face Harry. 'Why is this, do you think? Is there pain? Did she have a difficult confinement?'

Harry frowned. 'Well, yes. But even before that she was — unwilling.'

'Have you talked about it?'

Harry shook his head. 'I've tried. She just gets upset.'

'Could there have been some traumatic incident perhaps, when she was younger?'

'Oh, I doubt it. She had a very strict upbringing,' Harry said. 'Her father was a Methodist minister. As a young girl she was hardly allowed out of the house.'

'Mmm.' The doctor looked thoughtful. 'If the birth of your daughter was difficult and painful, perhaps fear of another pregnancy is inhibiting her. What do you do about contraception?'

Harry frowned. 'Well, I'm always *careful*.'

The doctor smiled. 'You mean you don't use anything.'

'Well, no.'

The doctor sighed. 'I wonder if you realise how vulnerable that makes a woman feel.'

'I hadn't thought of that.'

'She must feel tense and anxious every time, and that isn't conducive to a relaxed and enjoyable intercourse for either of you, is it? Look, why don't you bring your wife along to see me? I'm sure the three of us could sort something out.'

'Oh, I'm pretty sure she wouldn't come,' Harry said quickly. Grace had no idea that he was here this afternoon. If she knew that he was sitting here now, discussing their unmentionable problem with a total stranger, she'd be horrified. 'She's very sensitive about these things. Her upbringing, you see ...'

'Then why not try buying some condoms and using them? Show your wife that you care — that you're willing to take the responsibility.'

'Yes, all right.' Harry knew deep inside that this wasn't the answer.

'I see I haven't convinced you.' The doctor was peering at him. 'Is there anything else you want to tell me? In what way does she object to lovemaking?'

Harry swallowed and ran a finger round his collar. 'She just seems to find the whole business disgusting.'

Doctor Bradshaw regarded him for a long moment, then he said: 'Tell me a little about yourself,'

Harry looked at his watch. 'I don't want to hold you up ...'

27

'It's perfectly all right. You can let me worry about that. Anyway you're my last patient this afternoon. Tell me, are your parents still living? Were you an only child?'

Slightly irritated, Harry outlined his background as briefly as he could, seeing no relevance whatever to his marriage problem. 'I'm thirty-two, and yes, I was an only child. Both my parents are dead. They were killed by a V2 in 1944. I was in the RAF at the time. I'm a musician, by the way.'

'So you were in the airforce? Did you have many girlfriends during that time?'

Harry shrugged. He was getting tired of this interrogation. 'No more than most.'

'Sexual experience?'

'Some.'

'Compare notes with your friends?'

'Yes, I suppose so.' Harry felt beads of perspiration break out on his forehead. He felt like an insect under a microscope.

Doctor Bradshaw turned his chair back to the desk and pulled his pad towards him. All the signs were there. Clearly the problem was with the young man, not his wife. He was just embarrassed and ashamed to admit he was inexperienced. The solution was quite simple. 'I suggest that you buy a book that I shall recommend,' he said, writing down the title. 'Take it home and when you have studied it yourself, show it to your wife. Pick your moment, of course. A quiet evening after dinner when you're both relaxed. Learn about lovemaking together. I'm sure you'll find it most rewarding.'

'Oh – thanks.' Harry took the slip of paper the doctor handed him.

'Don't forget what I said about contraception. And, Mr Wendover . . .'

'Yes?'

'Don't be too hesitant. Most women like a positive approach.'

'I'll try to remember.' With some relief Harry got to his feet and backed towards the door. 'Good afternoon then, doctor.'

'Good afternoon, Mr Wendover.' Doctor Bradshaw shook his head as the door closed. Eight years. It had taken eight years to pluck up the courage to ask about something as basic as sex. The sooner they taught it as part of the general curriculum in schools, the better, in his view.

'Grace . . .'

'Yes?' She looked up from the dining-room table. It was late.

Elaine was in bed and she had been working, bringing the books from the shop up to date. 'What is it?'

He cleared his throat.'You're not afraid of having another baby, are you?'

She frowned. 'You know we couldn't afford another child. I'd have to give up my job and we'd never meet the mortage ...'

'No, I'm not *suggesting* we have another child – just asking if you're afraid of getting pregnant.'

Grace began to feel the familiar prickly uneasiness creeping over her. 'No, not particularly.' She lowered her head over the books again, hoping he would let the subject drop. But he didn't. Getting up from his chair he came across to her and closed the ledger she was working on.

'Harry, don't do that. I have to get these books ...'

'They can wait,' he said firmly. 'This is more important.'

'What is?'

'Look, Grace ...' He sat down next to her, covering her hand with his. 'We can't go on as we are.'

'I don't know what you mean.'

'Yes, you do. You hardly ever let me near you. It isn't natural.'

She felt tears fill her eyes and the hated panic beginning to stifle her. 'I can't help it, Harry.'

He squeezed her hand. 'I know, love. But why? You say you love me.'

'I do. Of course I do!'

'Then if you love me ...' He broke off. They'd been down that road countless times and found it a dead end. 'Look, love, maybe it *is* the fear of another baby, even though you don't realise it. You said yourself we couldn't afford it. I've been thinking about it and I've got something to prevent it.'

'Have you?'

'Yes, because I *want* you, Grace. I don't think you realise what it's like for me. I want us to have a proper marriage – to be happy. I want you to know what love is *really* like.'

She sighed. She was unfair to him, she realised that. He loved her. He'd tried hard to do what he thought was best. He deserved better. If only there was some way she could overcome her aversion.

Harry was watching her face. She seemed to be softening. Maybe the doctor had been right. He wondered whether this was the right moment to get the book out. Then he pushed the idea aside. Some of those diagrams ... She wasn't ready for that yet. Maybe later. He took her hand.

29

'Let's go up, love. Now that you know it's safe, you'll be all right. I know you will.'

She hung back. 'Something to prevent it,' he'd said. What did he mean? Perhaps he was right. Maybe she would be all right this time.

In their room they undressed in silence, each of them tense and nervous. Sliding into his eager arms under the covers Grace tried hard to relax and found it difficult. Harry took his time, caressing her, employing everything he knew and more that he had learned from the manual the doctor had recommended. At last he felt her body begin to lose its rigidity. Her response to his kisses grew warmer and she began to caress him in return. He heard her breath catch as he ran one hand down the length of her body, cupping one breast, stroking over the curve of her waist and the roundness of one buttock to her thigh. Now was the time. He slid his hand under the pillow for what he had put there earlier. Taking her hand he pressed something into it.

'Put it on for me.'

Her eyes flew open. 'What is it?'

'I told you, it's to prevent ... *Grace*. What is it? Where are you going?' She was out of bed in an instant. He jumped out and made a move towards her, but she held both hands up defensively in front of her, backing towards the door.

'*Don't*! Stay away. Don't come near me.' Pulling the door open she fled into the bathroom and he heard her turn the key. Sighing, he flopped back on the bed again and closed his eyes tightly against the pain that tore through his lower body. What the hell was the matter with her? Couldn't she see what she was doing to him — to their marriage? What on earth was he to do with her?

In the bathroom Grace huddled in the corner, sitting on the cork-topped stool by the bath. She wrapped both her arms around herself and rocked backwards and forwards, trying to shut out the images that haunted her. She could still feel the sensation of thin, slippery rubber between her fingers — still hear her father's voice as he explained to her what must be done with it. That voice, low and rumbling, gloating with letchery. So different to the sanctimonious boom he used in the pulpit on Sundays. The horror and revulsion she had felt then intensified a hundred times. It was as though her father and Harry had become one and the same person.

Much later, stiff with tension and chilled with cold, she got up and splashed her face with cold water at the washbasin. Taking a clean nightdress from the airing cupboard she slipped it over her head, then crept into Elaine's room and slid into bed beside the sleeping child.

In the next room Harry was still awake, lying on his back, staring up at the ceiling. He heard her stealthy movements and turned on his side. Was she afraid — actually *afraid* — to come back to him? Did she think he was going to rape her? One thing he knew: he'd never ask for outside advice any more. And tomorrow he'd burn that book. If Grace found that, God only knew what she'd think. As for his needs — he'd satisfy them elsewhere. There was never any shortage of girls hanging around the stand when they played for dances. After all, what was there to be faithful to? he asked himself bitterly.

Ever since Elaine's birth Harry had taught music as an addition to the family income. He had a dozen or so piano pupils, most of whom came to the Wendovers' home for lessons. Elaine had been fascinated from babyhood, learning as she watched her father's patient skill; hearing him coax the first stumbling efforts into real music. Soon after they moved to Stanmore she begged him to give her lessons too and to his delight he found her a bright pupil with a good ear. She picked it up with a speed that amazed him.

That first year at Stanmore, Harry taught his daughter to swim at the local pool. On her eighth birthday he bought her a shiny red bicycle and taught her to ride it. It was always Harry who was waiting when she came home from school, with tea ready so they could sit and eat together companionably before it was time for Grace to come home. They would relate to each other all that had happened during the day, laughing together at their own private little jokes and shared likes and dislikes. When the summer holidays came, the long warm days spent in each other's company were a delight to both of them and as the months went by father and daughter grew closer.

Harry couldn't always be home during the day. Sometimes he had to go up to Town to rehearse and on these occasions he would take Elaine with him. This she enjoyed more than anything else. Sitting quietly in her seat at the back of the rehearsal hall she would listen to the band going through new numbers, her quick ear picking up every badly turned phrase, every wrong note and discord, until she felt convinced that she could have conducted it herself.

Harry was inordinately proud of his small daughter with her intelligent little face and her bouncing dark durls. Maybe she was becoming a little precocious — even spoilt. The lads in the band made a great fuss of her and she responded by showing off a little; airing her musical knowledge; making them laugh with her quaint grown-up remarks.

31

Coming home tired after long days at the shop, Grace became increasingly aware of the way her small daughter's character was developing and didn't care for it.

'You're making her grow up too soon,' she accused Harry. 'She's too much indoors in the company of older people. She should have some friends of her own age.'

They disagreed over it time and again, Harry arguing that he had his job to go to and if Grace wasn't at home to care for Elaine, the child would have to go with him. The arguments developed into rows and, although she would not admit it to herself, Grace resented the closeness developing between her husband and daughter. They had a way of closing ranks against her, which made her feel in the wrong and shut out. There she was, working her fingers to the bone to help provide a nice home for them all, and that was all the thanks she got. The resentment grew into animosity without either she or Harry realising that they were making their daughter the scapegoat for deeper, much more serious issues for which they had both stopped seeking a solution.

It was in the spring of 1960 that Harry was engaged to accompany Stella Rainbow on a series of broadcasts.

Grace could not understand her husband's obvious excitement. 'I've never heard of her. What a silly name. Who is she?' she asked scathingly after he'd read the letter to her over breakfast.

'She's a singer. Her father was black American, a trumpeter with the Nat Gonella band. He married a white girl over here and stayed on. I know her slightly from when she sang with the band with two other girls a while back,' Harry told her. 'Did you see what Gerry says? It seems she asked for me specially.'

'Why should she do that?'

'I accompanied the girls a few times when they were rehearsing. Stella told me then that she was planning to go solo and we tried one or two numbers out together. It was me who recommended her to Gerry.'

'Mmm. Is she any good?' Without waiting for his reply, Grace got up and opened the kitchen door to shout up the stairs after Elaine. 'That child will be late for school if she doesn't get a move on.' She looked at him. 'Well, will you take the job with this Stella thingummy person?'

'Yes, I think so.' Harry smiled reminiscently and Grace asked: 'What's she like?'

'She has rythym in her very bones, and a voice like smooth rich

32

cream. You should hear her. I'm sure she's going to make a big name for herself.'

'Well, just as long as you get paid what you deserve.' With one eye on the clock, Grace began to gather her things together. 'And I shall have to get going or *I'll* be late.'

The programmes were twenty minutes long. There were six of them. It entailed a week of rehearsals in a little theatre in Camden Town, after which the programmes went out live on Tuesday afternoons at four o'clock. It meant that Elaine had to go to her mother at the shop when she came out of school which she resented deeply. The draper's shop with its bolts of material on one side and baby linen on the other, was a poor substitute for the excitement of a rehearsal theatre or a broadcasting studio.

Stella was twenty-three. She was tall, almost as tall as Harry, and her figure was willowy and perfectly proportioned. Huge dark eyes were set in a heart-shaped face whose complexion was honey-coloured rather than brown, and her hair, although raven black, was long, straight and as shiny as satin. Oddly enough it reminded Harry of Grace's hair as it had been when he had first seen her in Easthampton, before she'd had it cut.

Stella's voice was perfect for the songs she sang, bringing a special soft richness to Gershwin, Cole Porter and the newer songs of Bart and Newly that made up her programme. To Harry it was sheer pleasure accompanying her, listening to her − looking at her. She seemed to *live* the songs she sang, acting out the wistfulness of the lyrics − the love and the aching nostalgia − in a way that twisted his heart. He'd seen few other singers achieve the special and original effects she got from her material. He considered her wasted on radio and told her so one day as they finished rehearsing.

'I can't understand why Gerry hasn't tried to get you some television. You'd get a wider audience that way. If they could see you as well as hear you, they'd go wild.'

Stella smiled. 'Harry, what a lovely thing to say.'

'No, I mean it. You've got a great career ahead of you. You just need handling the right way.'

'So how about you doing that?' Stella laid a hand on his shoulder. He could feel its warmth through the material of his jacket. Laughing uneasily, he said: 'Me? I'm only an accompanist. You've got Gerry for that.'

'You know, you underestimate yourself, Harry. You understand the business. You could do a lot for me. We could do a lot for each other, perhaps.' She slid on to the piano stool beside him, slipping

33

her hand easily through his arm. 'I've got an agent, yes. What I really need is an arranger. And you're the best accompanist I've ever had. I sing better with you than with anyone else. I knew that from the first time, with the band, remember? That's why I asked for you again.' She leaned forward to smile into his face. 'So why don't we give it a try?'

There was nothing flirtatious about her manner. She spoke to him as one musician to another. She was as guileless as Elaine; coaxing and cajoling, just as his daughter did when she wanted something badly. But in spite, or perhaps because of it, he felt the force of her sexuality more strongly than he had with any other woman. The fact that she was unaware of her seductiveness made it even more powerful and, with a sudden stab of guilt, Harry moved away from her to stand up.

'It's a lovely idea, Stella, but I don't think so. There must be a hundred other people you could get, ten times better than me.'

The smile left her face. 'It's a pity you feel that way. I think we could make a great team.'

On the day of the last broadcast Stella gave him her address and telephone number. They'd gone out for a drink to celebrate the completion of the series and were sitting in a little pub when she pressed a slip of paper in his hand.

'I've really enjoyed working with you, Harry,' she said almost shyly. 'And if you ever change your mind about becoming my arranger, just give me a ring.'

He looked at her. He had no idea what constituted a fashionable woman, but he did know that Stella always dressed in a style that was perfect for her. Today she wore a well-cut grey suit that fitted her slim figure to perfection. The jacket was open to reveal a vermillion blouse that complemented the honey skin and brought out the amber light in her eyes. Almost without knowing that he did it, he reached for her hand. Immediately the long, coral-tipped fingers curled round his and her eyes met his.

'You're good for me, Harry.' she said softly. 'You bring out the best in me. When you play, I feel I can sing anything.'

He laughed, pleased and flattered. 'Nonsense! You've got star quality, Stella. You're going right to the top. You'd sound good against someone banging tin cans.'

'No.' She shook her head. 'It's more than just your playing. You give me confidence. It's a kind of magic.' She laughed her soft, husky laugh. 'Don't ask me to explain it. Look ...' Thoughtfully she laced her fingers through his, totally unaware of the effect it had on him. 'I promised myself I wouldn't tell you about this, but

34

Gerry rang me this morning. There's an offer of a trip on the P&O ship, *The Himalaya*. It's a world cruise. I don't know about these things but he tells me *The Himalaya* is the flagship and it'll be an important engagement − a good chance for me to be seen by some influential people.' The amber-gold eyes looked into his. 'I told him I'd only accept it if you came too, Harry.'

Stunned, he looked at her. 'Stella, you know I couldn't do that, don't you? You'll be fine who ever accompanies you. Don't pass up the chance just because I can't go.'

She looked like a disappointed child. 'I've told you, Harry, no one brings out the best in me like you do. I've already told Gerry it's all down to you.'

'But I couldn't. It'd mean − what − six months away from home?' He shook his head but he was wavering and she saw it. A smile twinkled the golden eyes.

'Four, actually. Sailing date is July 22nd. You'd be home for Christmas.'

'That's less than a month away.' Harry shook his head, the temptation wrenching at him. 'Much as I'd like to, I don't see how ...'

'Do you mean that? Would you *really* like to, Harry?' She looked intently into his eyes. 'I won't accept it without you, but it's nice to know that you'd have liked to go.'

Just as Harry could never refuse Elaine when she was being sweet and reasonable, he found Stella's wistful resignation irresistible. He squeezed her hand. 'Look, how long before you have to let them know?'

Her eyes lit up with excitement. 'I've still got a couple of days.'

'Leave it with me,' he said. 'I can't promise, but I'll see what I can do.'

Grace was excited. That afternoon at the shop she'd had an unexpected visit from Mrs Chapman, the elderly owner, who had run the shop herself until her arthritis had forced her to give up. Mrs Chapman was not alone. Her companion was a woman in her early forties, smartly dressed in a black suit and white blouse. Grace noticed that instead of a handbag she carried a briefcase, and wondered if she might be some kind of rep' who wanted to show them a new line. Mrs Chapman surprised her by asking if the three of them could talk in the back room, and if it would be possible for Grace to make some tea.

Somewhat puzzled she had left her young girl assistant in charge and gone through to the back with her visitors. Seated at the table that also served as a desk on which Grace did the accounts, Mrs Chapman came straight to the point.

'Perhaps you won't be surprised to know that I've decided to give up, Mrs Wendover. I've sold the shop to Mrs Bennett here and she'll be taking over in a month's time.'

'Oh − I see.' Grace's heart sank. Was she to be out of a job?

For the first time Mrs Bennett spoke. 'I'm sure you'll be glad to know that Mrs Chapman would sell to me only on the assurance that I would offer you a job at the salary you're getting now.' Grace blushed with pleasure. 'That's very kind,' she muttered.

'That is, of course, if you want to stay on,' Mrs Bennett continued. 'You see, I have plans for this shop.' She looked around the cluttered stock room with a hint of disapproval in her grey eyes. 'With all due respect to Mrs Chapman, I feel that this kind of establishment has had its day. I plan to turn it into a boutique − subject to my getting the necessary planning permission, of course.'

Grace felt her interest aroused. 'A boutique?'

'Yes, exclusive dresses, costume jewellery and accessories − that kind of thing. The shop will have to be modernised and refitted, of course ...' Another look around at the dingy brown-painted cupboards and shelves. While she had been speaking, Margaret Bennett had been taking in Grace's clothes and appearance. She'd pictured a little grey mouse of a woman whom she'd hoped would be put off by all the new innovations, but she was pleasantly surprised by Grace's looks and efficient manner. With a little tactful advice she could probably be turned into quite a presentable asset. She decided it wasn't going to be as difficult as she'd imagined.

When she left the shop that afternoon, Grace's head was buzzing. Elaine had gone to a friend's house straight from school. It was only three doors down the road and Grace picked her up on her way back. She was a little disappointed that Harry wasn't home, but, unable to contain her news any longer, she threw off her coat and launched into her news.

'Guess what?'

Elaine looked up from her homework. 'Don't know.'

'Chapman's is being taken over. It's going to be a boutique − really modern and smart. And guess who's got the job of manageress?'

'You?'

Elaine's casual guess somewhat took the wind out of Grace's sails, but she continued: 'Mrs Bennett, the new owner, will be there too, but she'll be away a lot of the time, buying, so I'm to be in charge.'

Elaine looked up, chewing the end of her pen. 'Does that mean you'll be getting lots of money and we'll be rich?'

Grace frowned. 'Of course not. But Margaret – Mrs Bennett – is taking me up to Town after we've closed the shop for refitting, to buy something to wear in the shop. She suggests a smart black dress.'

The front door slammed and Elaine jumped up from her work with a squeak of delight. 'Daddy's home. Put the kettle on, Mummy. You know how he always wants a cup of tea.'

Grace looked ruefully after her daughter as she whisked out of the room, Those two. Still, *she* was the one with exciting news today. Wait till she told Harry about the boutique.

But Elaine had spiked her guns, telling Harry about the new owner of Chapman's shop while he took off his coat. Not that he was listening very intently. He was too busy wondering how to break the news to Grace that he was thinking of going on the P&O world cruise as Stella's manager and pianist. Over tea Grace told him about her new job in detail.

'First I'm to organise a closing down sale. Then there's to be advertising in the press. Margaret is taking me up to Town on one of her buying trips and we'll be getting me a new business outfit at the same time.'

Harry nodded abstractedly, stirring his tea. 'Grace – listen, love. There's something I have to tell you.'

Harry's solemn look stopped her in mid-sentence. 'What? What is it? Is something wrong?'

'No – well, not exactly. I've had an offer too today. It's a good one, but I don't know how you'll feel about it.'

Grace's heart turned to stone. She might have known it. They were going to have to move – just when she'd been offered this exciting new job. 'Go on,' she said dully. 'Tell me the worst.'

'It's on a cruise ship. Pianist arranger to Stella Rainbow. It's a really good chance. She's going places, Grace. The only thing is, it's a world cruise. I'd leave in July and I wouldn't be back until just before Christmas.'

'Oh, *Daddy*.' The cry came from Elaine. 'All that time? You wouldn't be away for my birthday?' She'd come to stand beside him and he slipped his arm around her and hugged her to him.

'No, puss. I don't sail till the 22nd. We'll have a grand celebration. Tell you what, I'll take you both out to dinner, somewhere posh, up West.' He glanced at Grace. 'That's if Mummy agrees.'

'Of course. I can't stand in your way if it's a really good job. I mean, it's for all of us, isn't it?' She was trying hard not to show

how relieved she was. It couldn't be better. Harry obviously wanted this job, and with him away she would be able to give all of her concentration to the new job. Elaine's friend Jenny lived close and her mother had said that Elaine was welcome there at any time. It couldn't be better. She looked at Elaine's crestfallen face and felt a sudden stab of guilt. 'We'll miss you, of course,' she said.

Harry's face broke into a relieved smile. 'Well, if you're really sure, I'll get on to Gerry about it first thing in the morning.'

On the day that Harry sailed, Chapman's closed for business and the shop fitters moved in. To Grace it was almost the most exciting day of her life. Elaine had clung to Harry tearfully when he left that morning, making him promise to send postcards from every port and write to her every day. For herself, Grace had felt a little impatient with the child's emotional display, glancing at her watch as the minutes ticked by, itching to lock the house and get down to the shop. She and Harry had said their goodbyes last night. He had held her close, saying how much he was going to miss her. She told him − truthfully − that she would miss him too, and assured him that she loved him as much as ever; all the time uncomfortably aware that she was arousing him, inviting the intimacy she dreaded so much. She'd tried her hardest to pretend to want him, especially as it was his last night, but after their brief lovemaking was over and Harry had fallen asleep she lay for a long time staring into the darkness; trying to quell the waves of disgust and revulsion that swept sickeningly through her.

Harry was a good man. He was a kind and considerate husband. Why couldn't she respond to him as she should? Why, after all these years, did the horrific images still rise inside her tightly closed eyelids the moment he began to make love to her? It was all so long ago. Would she never be free of it? She needed Harry's love so much − but Grace could only equate sex with hate, bitterness and betrayal, not love. The love she felt for Harry was pure and beautiful. It had nothing to do with those dirty, repellent acts. If only there were some way she could make him understand.

All that day she felt oddly bereft. And guilty too. She'd actually been glad when Harry had told her about the cruise. Her first thought, that for sixteen weeks she would not have to dread the thought of bedtime. But now she felt sad and uneasy about it. As the men worked and the dust of years rose from the dismembered shop fittings to cloud the air, Grace applied herself with vigour. At the back of one of the stockroom cupboards she found a box of corsets, circa 1920, and she and Margaret Bennett laughed at

38

the bright pink calico monstrosities, with their uncompromising whalebone and torturous laces.

'More like armour plating,' Margaret laughed. 'Did they wear them for their figures or to keep the men out? I think we'll present them to the local museum.'

Thoughtfully, Grace watched the old shelves and counters being ripped out. She couldn't help feeling that a part of her own life was being ripped apart too. For some time now she had felt the changes that were taking place all around her and she knew instinctively that it was a case of go with them or be left behind.

'Everything's changing, isn't it?' she said, speaking the thought aloud.

'It certainly is,' Margaret said cheerfully. 'It's a new era, a new decade. The *sixties*. Everything's new. Anything goes. Exciting, isn't it?'

Grace wasn't quite so sure.

Stella had bought a whole new wardrobe of glamorous evening dresses for the cruise. She confided in Harry that she'd borrowed the money to pay for them. 'It's an investment,' she said huskily, holding up crossed fingers. 'I just hope it pays off.'

Harry looked at the jewel-coloured mountain of satin, lace and sparkling sequins laid out on her bed, ready for hanging in the spacious wardrobes of her stateroom. 'I'm sure it will,' he said. He'd come to give her a card and the posy of flowers he'd bought as a good luck gesture before they sailed. 'But I can tell you here and now that you'd still be a hit if you walked out there in sackcloth.'

She laughed. 'I hope it won't ever come to that.' Opening a cupboard she produced a bottle of champagne. 'I was keeping this till after our first show, but let's drink it now,' she said impulsively. 'It may be warm and we'll have to use tooth mugs, but what the hell?'

Harry went through the open door to the bathroom and returned with the tooth mugs. He held them out to her, grinning. 'You're right,' he said. 'What the hell?'

Chapter Four

In her bedroom, Grace took off her smart black 'shop' dress and arranged it carefully on a hanger. As she pulled on a skirt and blouse she heard Elaine downstairs begin her piano practice. Ever since Harry had left six weeks ago she had practised for an hour after school each day, even before starting on her homework. Grace was vaguely irritated. She'd quite thought that with her father away Elaine would have let her music lapse. It seemed that Harry's influence affected her even from the other side of the world. Though at least she didn't have to sit silently by while they discussed the technical difficulties of Chopin and Beethoven before switching with equal enjoyment and bewildering speed to the instrumental dexterity of Louis Armstrong and Duke Ellington.

He'd written regularly − separate letters to her and Elaine, from every port. Places with romantic-sounding names: Madeira, Capetown, Bombay, Columbo, Rangoon, Bankok. The letters were short. They said that he was enjoying the trip − seeing all the exciting foreign places; that Stella's singing was going down well; and that he missed them both. Grace had no idea what was in Elaine's letters. As soon as the child had read them, she folded the flimsy blue air letters and hid them away in a drawer with her most prized possessions.

She walked out on to the landing and stood for a moment in the doorway of her daughter's room. As usual it was untidy. Her bed was still unmade and an open geography book lay face down on the eiderdown. From the arrival of the first letter, Elaine had looked up all Harry's ports of call in her school atlas and read avidly about them in her geography book.

Grace looked around at the schoolgirl clutter: the pictures of Cliff Richard and the Shadows pinned to the walls; the record player Harry had bought her, records lying on the stool beside it. Rachmaninov's Second Piano Concerto incongruously cheek by jowl with 'What Do Ya Want If Ya Don't Want Money?' The floppy-haired likeness of Adam Faith smiled brashly up at her from the record sleeve as she tidied the pile.

Absently she picked up the discarded green and white school frock, flung carelessly over the back of a chair in favour of jeans and tee-shirt. For a girl nearing her teens, Elaine wasn't at all interested in clothes or her appearance. Grace found that she slightly resented the fact that her daughter was far more interested in music than in the exciting new stock that was arriving daily at the shop. She hadn't even wanted to come to the Grand Opening, even though it was during the holidays and Margaret had very generously invited her. On the day that 'Margot's' had opened she'd gone with her friend Jenny to the swimming pool − just as though it were an ordinary day and not important at all.

Grace was missing Harry even more than she'd expected to. Apart from his company he did a lot around the home while she was at work all day. More than she'd realised. She stood at the landing window, looking down into the garden. The lawn needed mowing again. And there were weeds everywhere. She would have to get down to it this Sunday. And Elaine would have to help, whether she liked it or not. Recently she had asked if she could join the local church youth club. Her friend, Jenny sang in the church choir and she wanted to be involved too. Grace had been vehement in her refusal, her voice rising shrilly as she told Elaine that the church was a sham. For days the thought had upset and haunted her. It was all a confidence trick, she told herself. It swallowed people whole, drained them of everything they had that was worthwhile, and then tossed them mercilessly aside. No daughter of hers would ever become sucked into it. Bitterly she recalled the Sunday when she'd spoken to Harry for the first time, and how she'd asked God to send her a red coat. He'd answered her prayer, but He'd made her pay a cruel and terrible price. She'd no time for Him any more.

She was enjoying her new job. A whole new world had opened for her with the arrival of Margaret Bennett. On their first buying trip together Margaret had taken her to lunch in an Italian restaurant in The Strand. For the first time she had eaten spaghetti that was called 'pasta' and hadn't come out of a tin, and been outrageously flattered by the handsome dark-eyed young waiter who had insisted that 'The signora's figure is far too slim for her to deny herself a second helping.'

In the train on the way back to Stanmore she learned a little more about Margaret's background. Grace had often wondered about her husband. Now she learned that Margaret had divorced.

'Jim and I married far too young,' she said. 'It was during the war. We hardly knew each other really. Once the war was over and he came home for good, it just didn't work. The romance had gone. In civvy street he was a grocer's assistant.' She smiled ruefully at Grace. 'Can you imagine anything more boring that being married to a man who turns the handle of a bacon slicer all day?'

Grace surprised herself by saying: 'Not if you loved him, surely?'

Margaret shrugged. 'What you think is love at eighteen often turns out to be mere sexual drive.'

Grace digested this piece of psychology in silence. Was what she felt for Harry really love? she wondered. It certainly wasn't 'sexual drive', whatever that was. Most people seemed to take it for granted that the sexual side of marriage was a pleasure. Was she alone in finding it so repellant? Was the thing that Margaret called 'sexual drive' something women were supposed to have as well as men?

'Yours is a happy marriage, isn't it?' Margaret was looking at her. 'You're lucky. Handsome, talented husband, nice little home and a pretty daughter.'

'Yes, I'm very lucky.'

'Is this the first time Harry has worked away from home?'

'Yes. Except for summer seasons. When Elaine was little, we used to go with him.'

'That must have been nice.'

'It was.' Grace looked dreamily out of the window, thinking longingly of Bournemouth and the idyllic summer when Elaine had been born.

'This singer — how old did you say she was?'

Grace turned in surprise. 'I'm not sure. Young, though.'

'Oh. You haven't met her then?'

'No.'

Margaret's eyebrows rose. 'Trusting, aren't you?'

Grace looked at her, frowning a little, then she laughed. 'Oh no, there's no danger of anything like that. They're both musicians. Professionals, working together.'

'Really?' Margaret was tempted to say something, then changed her mind. Was Grace really as naive as she seemed, or was the marriage that secure? 'Are you managing all right with Elaine at home for the holidays?' she asked, changing the subject.

'Everything's fine, thanks. Anyway, they've gone back now.' Grace stifled a sigh. Elaine had been difficult since Harry had left. She was missing him. She resented having to go to Jenny's

42

each day after school and begged to be allowed to have a key so that she could let herself into the house. Grace was adamant.

'It's only for an hour and a half. I've made arrangements with Mrs Smith. She'd be offended if I changed it all now.'

'But I could be getting on with my piano practice.'

'No.'

'My homework then.' In her disarmingly perceptive way, Elaine sensed that her mother resented her having music in common with her father.

Having her daughter see through her annoyed Grace intensely. 'I've told you, Elaine, the answer's no. We'll have no more arguments. It's only for a few weeks after all.'

'Why can't you be at home like other mothers?' Elaine had demanded accusingly. 'I'm fed up with going to Jenny's. We have Marmite for tea *every single day*. I hate Marmite.'

But Grace had won. It gave her quite a lot of satisfaction to see Elaine not getting her own way for a change. Harry always gave in to her, especially when she wheedled and flattered him. If Grace had her way there would be a lot more no's said. She had to put up with Elaine's sulks for an hour or two but it was worth it. Besides, Grace had so much to think about. She was learning so much — more with every day that passed; — about fashion and make-up, about clothes and what to wear with what.

On her visits to fashion warehouses with Margaret on half-closing days she saw that subtle changes were taking place. Skirts were becoming shorter and straighter, trouser bottoms wider. Colours were brighter, brasher, more adventurous.

She and Margaret were becoming good friends. And though Grace was never left in any doubt that Margaret was the boss she was allowed more and more say in the running of 'Margot's'. She discovered a new skill for window dressing, gleaned from window shopping expeditions in Bond Street. Taking one good garment, a small gilt chair and a scarf, she could create an ambiance of good taste and luxury which the customers found irresistible. On her half days she had started attending a flower arranging class too, so that she could create tasteful flower arrangements for the shop. Yes, life was opening out for Grace in the most exciting way.

Stella was a big hit. Every evening she appeared with Harry for fifteen minutes' cabaret during the after dinner dancing. Her performance always brought thunderous applause and compliments from admirers during the day, who would seek her out when she was relaxing on the boat deck. The young ship's officers were particularly attentive, asking her repeatedly to have a drink with them. But none of them interested Stella in the least. She fobbed them off, saying that she needed to rehearse or rest.

The rehearsal part was true. Though her repertoire was wide, frequent shows before the same audience soon exhausted it. They did a nightly request spot and the same numbers were asked for time and time again, but new material was constantly needed. She and Harry usually rehearsed the new numbers they had brought with them in the mornings when the dining saloon was empty.

In comparison to the luxury of Stella's stateroom, Harry's cabin was cramped and small. On 'E' deck, it grew hotter and stuffier as they neared the Equator, the throb of the engines making sleep impossible for him. Stella was indignant.

'Why should you have to pig it down there while I have all this luxury?' she complained one evening when he saw her back to her room.

'Because you're the star,' he told her with a good-natured grin. 'I'm only the hired help.'

'Don't say that.' She looked wounded. 'Never say that, Harry.'

He laughed. 'I'm only joking. I'm happy with my job anyway. I'm going to enjoy watching you going places.'

'I hate to hear you put yourself down. You have talent too.' She sighed. 'Maybe I didn't do you any favours, asking you to be my pianist.'

He took both her hands. 'It was the best thing that ever happened to me. Look, Stella, I'm not a bad pianist, but I don't kid myself I'm ever going to make a name for myself. This is the highest I'm likely to get. I'm happy to bask in your reflected glory.'

'I wish you wouldn't say things like that. It's not true anyway.' She shook her head. 'You're a *real* musician, not just good at playing the piano. You're sensitive, perceptive, quick to pick up my slightest mood or thought.' She smiled. 'Even before I've thought it. I know my performance wouldn't be half as good without you.'

He smiled. 'That's nice to know.'

'It's true. Sometimes I feel you can read my mind.'

He laughed. 'Maybe I can.'

She removed the diamante clip that held her hair, so that the silky black mass fell heavily down her back. She turned to him, moving closer. 'Can you read it now?'

She wore a shimmering black and silver dress, moulded closely to her body to flounce out into a fishtail of sequinned net around her calves. She stood so close that he could feel the length of her body against him and smell the exotic perfume that he was becoming so familiar with as they worked together. She looked into his eyes.

'What is it, Harry? Do you miss your family — your little girl and your — wife?'

He didn't miss the slight hesitation before she spoke that last word. It seemed to hold much more than the question she asked.

'Yes, of course I miss them,' he said, his tongue feeling thick in his mouth. 'Elaine's a wonderful girl. I've a feeling she's going to be a better musician than her old dad ...' He caught the look in her eye and knew she was waiting. Moving away from her he went and sat down, taking out a cigarette he didn't want and lighting it with trembling fingers. She'd guessed, with typical feminine intuition — about what was missing from his life, about Grace's coldness. Was it really that obvious? God, what a stupid, inept fool he felt. Panic made him want to get up and leave — now, before he made an even bigger fool of himself. Their working relationship was fine. He didn't want anything to happen that would spoil it. He didn't want anything to spoil his marriage, such as it was, or his family life either. But he couldn't deny that he found Stella irresistibly attractive. He wanted her more strongly with every breath he took. He stood up suddenly, stubbing out his unwanted cigarette.

'Look, I'd better go. You need your sleep.'

'Not yet, Harry.' She stepped between him and the door, putting her hands on his shoulders. 'Why don't you stay here tonight? You'll sleep better.'

Very firmly he took the hands from his shoulders and held them, looking into her eyes. 'You know I can't do that.'

'You could if you wanted to. It's as simple as that.'

He tried to avoid her hypnotic golden eyes as they looked levelly into his.

'Look, when I said I'd take this job ...'

'When you said you'd take the job, I was so happy,' she interrupted. 'I wanted a good pianist and manager. But more than that, Harry — oh *much* more than that — I wanted *you*.'

He could hear his own heart beating as her fingers curled around his neck and she laid her cheek gently against his. 'Stella, you know there can't be anything permanent — you know I'm married.'

'I know you're unhappy,' she whispered, her breath soft in his ear. 'I saw it from the very first day. We're so good together in every way, Harry. It was inevitable — perfectly natural — that we should want each other like this too, eventually.' She drew back her head to look at him. 'You do want me, don't you?'

With a great shuddering breath he put his arms around her

45

and crushed her to him. 'You know damned well I do,' he said raggedly.

When he kissed her her lips parted beneath his and her tongue explored his mouth. Her sweetness was as heady and intoxicating as wine and he heard himself groan with desire as he unzipped the black and silver creation, his fingers fumbling awkwardly in their eagerness. As it slipped to the floor he drew in his breath sharply at the beauty of her. She wore nothing under the dress and her skin was like coffee-coloured silk, warm and slightly moist, the scent of her perfume mingling with her own rich musky fragrance. Gazing in wonder, he took in the high, firm breasts with their rosy brown nipples, the slender waist and softly rounded stomach. She was far more beautiful than he could ever have imagined. Slowly, almost as though he were afraid she might disintegrate beneath his hands, he traced her cheek and the line of her throat with trembling fingers, following the smooth rounded shoulder to the curve of her breasts. Tenderly cupping them, he touched his lips to the brown nipples and felt them spring into hard little peaks at his touch. Sinking to his knees he buried his face in the gentle curve of her waist, his tongue finding her navel and dipping into it while his hands encircled her hips to draw her closer.

Stella sank to her knees to face him. Without taking her eyes from his, she began to loosen his tie, unfasten the studs of his evening dress shirt, pull at the waistband of his trousers. Gently she removed each garment, the touch of her hands arousing him to fever pitch. Then finally she took his face between her hands and kissed him long and deeply as he had never been kissed by any woman before.

Making love with Stella was a revelation. She was as eager and uninhibited as he, as hungry and full of longing, and yet restrained — not wanting to hurry and spoil the exquisite pleasure of anticipation. She welcomed his seeking hands and lips as they covered every inch of her, lingering over the melting dewy flesh inside her thighs and between her breasts. She explored his body in return, her lips following her long sensuous fingers as she sought out the smooth and the rough of him, the hardening muscles and the sensitive, vulnerable places. She was imaginative, employing all she had ever learned to excite and delight, until at last, unable to hold himself in check any longer, he took her shoulders and pressed them back against the pillows, moving urgently over her. She opened for him like an exotic flower, receiving him with a warmth and passion that thrilled him as nothing else ever had. She moved her hips against him, heightening his pleasure, sending the blood singing through his veins until at last they came together in a climax so intense it was almost unbearable.

Reluctant to let her go, Harry rolled on to his side, still inside her, his arms wrapped tightly round her, and they lay for a moment, waiting for their breathing to steady. He felt her moist skin sticking succulently to his; her warm breath caressing his cheek and the beat of her heart drumming insistently against his ribs. In that moment they were one being, and Harry knew that he had never felt so alive — never known such a depth of happiness in his life.

She moved her head back a little to look at him, smoothing a strand of his damply curling hair from his forehead. 'I love you, Harry,' she said simply. 'I've loved you since the day we met.'

He kissed her and drew her head down into the hollow of his shoulder. 'I love you too. You're so lovely, Stella. What did I do to deserve this?'

'It's not just sex,' she told him gravely. 'I could have had that with anyone. There have been plenty of other men, I admit that. But no one — I swear, no one like you.'

A vague uneasiness stirred for the first time at the back of Harry's mind as reality slowly seeped back. As always Stella sensed it.

'I know you're married. And I know you don't want anything to spoil it,' she said. 'So if you want to stop, just say so now, darling, and this need never happen again.'

For a fleeting second Harry wondered if she knew quite well that it was already too late. How could he not want her again after what they had just shared? Three more months of being together — working with each other every day. Having her unavoidably and tantalisingly close to him. It was too much — far too much to ask. He knew he wasn't strong enough to resist that kind of temptation. He was pretty sure she knew it too.

She touched his cheek. 'Tell me about it, Harry. Tell me why you're so unhappy.'

He was silent, staring up at the ceiling. How could he betray Grace by telling another woman about her shortcomings, her lack of response? To a woman like Stella, warm and uninhibited, it would be impossible to understand. Besides, it wasn't only Grace's revulsion for sex that made the marriage dead. There were other things too: the way she refused to share his interests with him, almost as though she were punishing him for something. Sometimes he thought she despised his work too. She hadn't said so, but he knew instinctively that she resented his closeness with Elaine and the fact that the child took after him, sharing his interest in music.

Elaine. An instant picture of his daughter sprang into his mind,

47

making him feel ashamed of what he had just done. He adored Elaine; loved her a little more with each year. She was growing into a lovely girl, a daughter for any father to be proud of. She would have her mother's classic looks, and more talent for music than he had ever had. Already he could feel that in her. She worked hard at it too – never shirking her practice – always eager to improve. In her childishly penned letters she had told him that she practised every day and he believed her, touched by her diligence and her desire to please him.

'Harry?' Stella leaned across him to brush his cheek with her lips. 'What is it, darling? Why do you look so sad? Please – you can tell me.'

'Grace doesn't love me,' he said. 'I don't think she ever did. She married me to get away from an unhappy home. We parted soon afterwards, but then she found that Elaine was on the way so we patched things up. But it never really worked.'

She raised herself on one elbow and looked down at him. 'And you – what about you, Harry? Do you love her?'

For a long moment he looked into the golden eyes, reaching up he stroked the thick black skein of hair that fell across her shoulder on to his chest. 'If I did I wouldn't be here,' he said. 'I'm a one woman man, Stella.' And in that moment he knew that what he said was true.

On the day that the *Himalaya* docked it was wet and misty, a typical English December morning. Southampton was a grey, rain-washed blur on the skyline as they stood together on the crowded deck, waiting for the pilot to come on board. Stella huddled into the collar of the fur coat she had bought in New York and moved a little closer to Harry. Without looking at him she said: 'You'll be going straight home?'

He sighed. 'I have to, love. It's nearly Christmas – there's Elaine to think of.'

'I know.'

Her lovely face looked so unhappy that his heart contracted. During the trip they had made a lot of contacts. There had been offers galore, which Stella would have snapped up, but Harry was more cautious. He had deflected them all, advising that Stella's agent should be contacted and giving out Gerry Sylvester's card. All that remained now was for her to sit tight and wait to see if the offers were genuine.

'What will you do at Christmas?' he asked, slipping an arm round her.

'Nothing.' She shrugged. 'I haven't thought about it.'

'I daresay the offers will have been rolling in,' he said, trying to cheer her. 'All we have to do is pick the best. I shall be looking in on Gerry tomorrow morning. Shall I meet you there?'

She looked up at him hopefully. 'Could we have lunch afterwards?'

'Of course.' He frowned. 'But after that ...'

'I know. Play it down for a while.' She looked at him again, her eyes uncertain. 'When will you tell her, Harry?'

'Not yet – not until after Christmas. For Elaine's sake.'

She was silent. If anything was going to keep Harry from her it would be Elaine. She was the pull – the person he dreaded hurting most. Elaine was her greatest rival. Not Grace.

Seeing the look on her face he drew her into a sheltered corner and kissed her. 'We knew all along that this day would come,' he told her, cupping her face. 'We must face it bravely. It won't be for long. We'll soon be working together again whatever happens.'

Whatever happens. She searched his eyes. What did he mean by that? Now that the time had come to part she was so afraid that something would happen to take him from her again. It wasn't easy to walk away from a family, however much in love you were. She knew that. On board ship, right away from home ties, it was easy enough to pretend they didn't exist. But once he was at home with Grace and Elaine again ... She shivered.

'Yes. We'll be working together,' she said almost inaudibly. 'At least I can look forward to that.'

At 'Margot's' it was all pre-Christmas bustle. The shop was tastefully decorated. In the window, discreetly dressed with Christmas roses and frosted evergreens, a white fur jacket and a scarlet silk dress tempted passers-by. Margaret Bennett was delighted with the first months' success. On Christmas Eve when they closed the shop, she gave Grace a handsome bonus along with her pay envelope, and presented her with a gift-wrapped blouse from stock that she knew Grace had had her eye on.

'I think we're going to make a great team, Grace,' she said. 'Before long we'll be able to open another branch at this rate.' She opened a bottle of wine and poured two glasses. 'Have a drink with me before you go.'

Grace sipped at the sweet sparkling wine with satisfaction. She felt like a real businesswoman. Before, she'd simply had a job. Now, thanks to Margaret, she had a career.

'Tell me about your Christmas,' Margaret invited. 'You must be

49

looking forward to it — planning a celebration. It must be nice to have Harry home again.'

Grace nodded, forcing a smile. It had been good to see him home again. She'd found herself quite excited on the day he'd been due. Elaine could hardly contain herself, running to the window every ten minutes to see if he was coming down the road. It had been late afternoon when he'd arrived. And Grace had known the moment she saw him that there was something wrong. He looked well enough; tanned from all the sunny weather, fitter and more handsome than she'd ever seen him, in fact. He'd kissed them both warmly enough, but was it her imagination that he couldn't quite meet her eyes?

Elaine wouldn't leave him alone, sitting on his knee and chattering incessantly; asking him a dozen questions all at once. He'd unpacked all the presents he'd brought, souvenirs for both of them from almost every place he'd visited. They'd sat down to the special evening meal that Grace had prepared and Harry had invited them to tell him their news too. But before she could tell him how well the shop was doing and how excited she was about her new career, Elaine had jumped up and gone to the piano to show him how hard she had practised. Late, after Elaine had finally been persuaded to go to bed, Grace had told him about 'Margot's', but even then she couldn't be sure that he was really listening. He was tired. She told herself that it was understandable. Finally they'd gone to bed and she had steeled herself for the inevitable, but to her surprise it hadn't happened. Instead, Harry had patted her absently, briefly kissing her cheek.

'It's been a long day, love. I expect you're as tired as I am,' he'd said, rolling away from her to lie on his side. But she'd known he wasn't asleep. For a long time she lay there looking into the darkness, wondering why her relief should be tempered with such uneasiness.

Harry had lain awake too, thinking about Stella alone in her flat; longing for her, wondering how he was going to break the news to Grace that their marriage was over. While Stella and he had been together everything had been so simple and straightforward, but now that he was home it all seemed hideously complicated — almost unreal. Lying there, he recalled unhappily the day he'd brought the girl from Alfredo's band back to the flat for a drink that had led to other things. And Grace's reaction when she had come home unexpectedly and caught them. It was a long time ago but the memory of her hysterical violence still sent shivers down his spine. Grace hadn't wanted him herself. She'd made him feel worthless and rejected. The girl had obviously found him attractive. She'd been a temptation he'd foolishly and disastrously succumbed to. If — *when* — Grace knew about Stella would her reaction be the same? And Elaine, what about Elaine? How did he explain the situation to an eleven-year-old girl? His heart ached at the prospect of losing his daughter. So much so that he pushed the thought from his mind. She was his, after all. Grace couldn't alter that — couldn't prevent him from seeing his own daughter. Finally he fell asleep from sheer exhaustion to dream muddled confused dreams that made him wake with a thick head and stinging eyes.

He arrived at Gerry's office half an hour before Stella next morning. The girl in the outer office wore her usual disgruntled expression. She looked vaguely put out when he walked in, looking pointedly at her watch. But she went grudgingly through to Gerry's office and came back to say that he was free.

By contrast, Gerry greeted him jovially, rising to shake his hand. 'Well, how are you, Harry, old fellow? I must say you look well.'

'I am, thank you. The trip was marvellous, the experience of a lifetime.'

Gerry sat down and looked at his appointment book. 'Stella is coming in too this morning. I expected to see the two of you together. She's had no shortage of offers — some of them quite promising too.'

'I know. That's partly why I'm here early. I need to talk to you.'

Gerry looked at his client with narrowed eyes. He and Harry went back a long way and he knew him well enough to sense his uneasiness. 'What is it? Not happy about continuing as her arranger, that it?' He pushed his cigarette box across the desk. Harry took one and lit it thoughtfully.

'Too happy, if the truth were known,' he said at last.

Gerry frowned and leaned back in his chair. 'Ah. If you mean what I think you mean . . .'

'I do.' Harry leaned forward to stub out the barely smoked cigarette. 'I know what you'll probably say, Gerry — a shipboard romance; unnatural conditions and all that. But it isn't like that. It's real. We love each other.'

Gerry was reminded sharply of the day when Grace had come to him, begging for information about her husband — waiflike and deserted — her pride in her hands as she'd appealed to him. He'd never known the reason for their parting that time but he'd felt sorry for them both and been glad he was able to help get them back together again.

'I see. So what are you going to do about it?'

51

'Christ, Gerry, I wish I knew.' Harry reached for another cigarette.

'Well, as I see it, you only have two options. Either you make a clean break at home and stay with Stella, or you let me fix her up with one of the overseas offers she'd had and you make a fresh start.'

'I can't let her go, Gerry.' Harry's voice was heavy with misery. 'I *can't*.'

There was a moment's silence as Gerry thoughtfully watched his friend. He'd had his doubts about the success of his marriage for some time, but he did know how much Harry's daughter meant to him. He had brought her up to the office with him many times and the two were obviously close. He must be seriously besotted with Stella to contemplate leaving Elaine. Why was it that some people made such a mess of their lives? Still, it wasn't for him to judge. If his clients weren't happy in their private lives, they didn't work well. Their success at work was his priority. He opened a file that lay on the desk before him. 'I received a new offer for Stella just yesterday,' he said. 'It's to appear in a new American musical. Off Broadway to begin with, but the backers are confident it'll move up.' He looked up at Harry. 'They'll take her alone, or if you're willing they'll have you both. You'd arrange her numbers, play for rehearsals, and generally see fair play. How to you feel about it?'

'I'll have to have time to talk to Stella — see what she thinks.'

Gerry leaned across the desk. 'But what do *you* want, Harry? If you take my advice you'll think very carefully before you do take a step like this.' He closed the file and pushed it away. 'Look, I'll be frank with you. Under normal circumstances I wouldn't even offer you a job like this. It's hack work. You deserve better. It's not going to advance your career one bit, and you have to think of yourself too, you know.' He chewed his lip. 'Why don't you let her go alone, lad? Give yourself some time to get her out of your system? Okay, so she's a dish and you've got the hots for her right at this moment, but it'll pass.'

Harry looked up angrily. 'You make it sound so cheap and sordid. It's not like that.' He ran a hand through his hair. 'Look, Gerry, leaving work out of it for a minute — Grace and I haven't really been hitting it off for years. She's a fine woman, a good wife and mother in many ways except ...'

Gerry nodded perceptively. 'Except in the area that matters most, is that it?'

Once again Gerry had made it sound sordid; made Harry feel shallow and faithless. No one would ever understand what he had been through if they hadn't experienced it themselves. He wouldn't know how to begin to describe the aridity of the last eleven years.

Gerry was lighting another cigar, meticulously cutting the end and holding it in the flame of his lighter. 'Come on, lad,' he said calmly. 'There are always ways of easing that kind of problem. Surely there's no need to break up your home and family? You'll only regret it, you know.'

'I'll take the job — if Stella wants it too,' Harry said decisively.

Gerry looked up with raised eyebrows. 'Just as you say, Harry.' he said with a shrug. 'It's your life.'

Stella did want it. When she came in and heard about it her face lit up with delight. An hour later they walked out of the office arm in arm and made for their own special little pub in Villiers Street. As he sat opposite her, their drinks on the table in front of them, Harry thought she had never looked so beautiful. She was almost incandescent with happiness.

'I can hardly believe it, Harry,' she said. 'You and me in New York. A brand new musical. I shan't mind being alone for a little while now.' She reached for his hand and held it tightly. 'You are happy, aren't you, darling?'

Harry swallowed hard. 'I will be when we're on the plane — on our way,' he told her with a smile. 'Until then, I can't quite believe it's happening.' What he didn't tell her was how much he dreaded all that must inevitably come before.

Christmas Day was for Elaine. Both Grace and Harry made sure that she enjoyed it, but by then both were aware of the gathering storm. Harry knew that it could no longer be postponed. Grace had already steeled herself for whatever was to come. Ever since he had come home, especially since he had been to see Gerry Sylvester on the morning after, there had been an abstracted, brooding air about him. Some feminine instinct deep inside told her that her marriage was about to fall apart. But that instinct was overlaid by the practicalities of everyday life. The Christmas preparations, the daily routine of work and home that forced everything to appear normal — made it possible to believe for just a little longer that whatever it was, wasn't happening.'

It was after Elaine had gone to bed and he had been up to make sure that she was asleep that Harry decided that he could put off the moment no longer. Sitting opposite Grace in the living room, the coloured lights of the Christmas tree twinkling in the firelight, he said awkwardly: 'Grace, there's something I have to tell you.'

She looked up, meeting his eyes defensively, and he saw in that moment that she already knew. 'There's someone else, isn't there?'

'Yes.'

'That girl – that singer? Ruby Rainbow or whatever her silly name is?' Her voice was tight and tears of hurt stood in her eyes. He saw them glistening in the flickering light of the flames.

'Grace – I never meant – never *wanted* to hurt you. But you never wanted me, did you? Not really.' He trailed off. What he was saying suddenly sounded so superficial, so shallow. And yet . . .

'How could you?' she said reproachfully. Then her tone sharpened. 'The dirty little slut invited you into her bed and now you think you're in love with her. Can't you see that it's only – only sexual drive. Are you really so stupid that you think it'll last? A woman like that isn't satisfied with one man.'

He stared at her. What did Grace know about sexual drive, for Christ's sake? Roused to sudden anger he lashed out at her: 'Yes, it will last, and I'll tell you why, shall I? Stella is warm and generous. She isn't afraid to show her love in the way a real woman should. All these years, Grace, you've made me feel ashamed just because I wanted to make love to you – *my wife*. You made me feel that I was making unreasonable demands – that I was doing something nasty and grubby that I should be ashamed of. If you really want to know Stella makes me feel like a man again. She wants *me* – not just for material things or even for my music, but because I'm the man she loves and wants.'

'Stop it!' Grace had her hands over her ears. 'I don't want to hear any more about her and her disgusting needs. Go to her if that's what you want. If all you really want from life is someone to – to *copulate* with.' She choked on the last word, blinking back the tears.

Flinching, Harry stood up and looked down at her. 'You're the one who's digusting if you really want to know, Grace.' he said quietly. 'Not me – not Stella. It's *you*. You're warped. To you a relationship between a man and a woman is something dirty. You don't understand the meaning of the word love. I feel sorry for you.'

'I don't want your pity,' she snapped. 'Just get your things and go.'

At the door he turned. 'I want to talk to Elaine. I think you owe me that. I'll come back tomorrow afternoon.'

'No!' She was on her feet instantly. 'I won't have you telling her a lot of lies to make yourself look good. If you go, you'll never come

54

back here again. You walk out on me and you walk out on her too. I'll make sure she knows the truth about her precious father.'

'Grace, don't be vindictive. None of this is Elaine's fault. Don't take it out on her.'

She shook her head. 'She'll have to learn as I have that life has a nasty habit of kicking you in the face. She might as well start learning now.'

He withdrew quietly. He would come back tomorrow anyway. Grace would have to let him in. There were things they must discuss. She would see that when she calmed down. This wasn't the time to argue about access.

When he had gone Grace stared at the closed door. Her face crumpled as the tightness in her chest sharpened painfully. Dry, silent sobs racked her as she sank into a chair and buried her face in her hands. The old hated images of her father rose to mock her. She felt his soft hands again and heard his voice coaxing and wheedling. Hate filled her throat and chest like poisonous gas, choking and suffocating her. If her father had been in the room with her at that moment she would have killed him with her bare hands.

Elaine sat huddled on the top stair, her nightdress pulled over her knees. As Harry came up the stairs, she held out her arms to him. 'Don't go, Daddy. Please.'

He drew her into his arms and carried her into her room. Setting her down on the bed he sat beside her. 'I have to go, Elaine,' he said softly. 'But you'll always be my girl. We won't lose touch.'

She threw her arms tightly round his waist and buried her face against his chest. 'You can't go. I missed you so much while you were away. When will you come back again?'

Looking down at the tearstained little face, he wondered guiltily just how much she had heard. Stroking the springy curls he said: 'I may not be back, my love. Not to stay, anyway. Sometimes people find they can't live together. Your mummy and I don't make each other happy any more and − I've found someone else I want to be with.'

'But what about *me*?' She was sobbing now. 'Don't *I* make you happy? Don't you want to be with me any more? Did I do something wrong? Is it my fault?'

Harry swallowed the choking lump in his throat and held her tightly to him. 'Sweetheart, if I could take you with me, I would. But your place is here, at home with Mummy.' For a moment he let her cry against him, anger at his own inadequacy wrenching his heart. How did one explain to a child of this age? One day perhaps she would understand. But she was hurting now. *He* was hurting her and it tore him apart. Putting her gently from him, he took a card from his wallet. 'Here, put this away safely somewhere. It's Mr Sylvester's address. If ever you want me, he'll know where to find me.'

He held both her hands and kissed her damp face. 'Be a good girl for me, sweetheart. Mummy will need you. She loves you very much, you know.'

'But I love *you*, Daddy.'

'I know, pet, and I love you too. I'll see you again, I promise.' He lifted her legs and slid them under the bedclothes, tucking her in warmly, bending to kiss her one last time.

Elaine lay with Gerry Sylvester's card clutched tightly in her hand, listening helplessly as her father moved about in the next room. She heard him opening drawers and cupboards; imagined him throwing his clothes back into the suitcase he had only recently unpacked. She wanted to jump out of bed and run to him again, beg him to stay. But some newly adult instinct in her told her it was already too late. Tears streamed down her cheeks as she heard his footsteps going down the stairs. She heard the front door open and close quietly behind him, and she knew that he had gone. Gone out into the night — the Christmas night. And she knew then that Christmas would never come again without her remembering the night her father went away and left her.

Chapter Five

'How old are you, Grace?'

Margaret faced her employee across the table in the back room of 'Margot's'. It was the Monday after Christmas. The shop was quiet and they were taking a coffee break before starting to price up the last of the winter stock for the coming sale.

Grace stared gloomily into her cup. 'Thirty. I was thirty last month.'

'That's no age. You're still young,' Margaret said encouragingly. 'I can give you twelve years, you know. Don't worry, dear. Harry will be back once he comes to his senses.'

'He won't.' Grace looked up, her eyes suddenly glittering with anger. 'Not this time.'

'You mean he's left you before?' Margaret couldn't quite disguise the interest in her voice and Grace immediately regretted the hasty indiscretion.

'Well, no. That time I *asked* him to leave.' She paused, sensing that Margaret was waiting for her to explain further. 'I discovered that he was − seeing someone else, you see.'

'Ah, so this isn't the first time he's kicked over the traces.' There was a pause and Margaret reached across the table to touch Grace's hand sympathetically. 'If it helps − and I know it probably won't − it's what happened to me too. In my case it was the girl from the cash desk in the grocer's where he worked. I wouldn't have minded so much but she was really plain, with glasses *and* spots.' She smiled ruefully. 'So what are you going to do?'

Grace bit her trembling lip. 'I don't know. I haven't even thought about it yet.'

'Elaine must be upset?'

Grace nodded, trying to swallow the lump in her throat. Elaine had been terrible since Harry left. For the past three days she'd been

57

impossible to cope with, spending most of the time in her room, appearing only when she was called for meals, when she sat silent and morose at the table, avoiding her mother's eyes. But last night, when Grace had finally lost her patience and tackled her, she had flared up, making it clear that she blamed her mother for Harry's leaving. When Grace told her about Stella, Elaine had accused her of lying. She had retreated to her room again in a torrent of tears, slamming the door and refusing to come out.

'She blames me,' she said dully. 'I'm at my wits' end, Margaret. I just don't know what to do with her.'

'She's at a funny age, but she'll come round. Have you sorted out the money side of things?' asked Margaret practically. 'You'll need help and you're entitled to it.'

'I don't want to take anything from him,' Grace told her. She didn't mention the fact that Harry had come to the house on Boxing Day and that she had refused to answer the door to him.

'That's just plain silly.'

'There was a letter from some solicitor's office this morning. I'm supposed to meet him there, to get something worked out.'

'Well, that's a start, at least.'

Grace shuddered, remembering the chill she had felt when the letter had arrived that morning. Her heart had almost stopped when she'd opened the typed envelope and read the formally worded request. Engaging the services of a solicitor seemed so cold and impersonal, so final somehow. 'I've made up my mind though,' she said, tight-lipped. 'I'm not going to give him a divorce whatever happens.'

Margaret sighed. 'I've heard that before. I suppose it's a natural reaction under the circumstances. You'll change your mind, of course. You're hurt now, but you'll get over it. You're still young and attractive, Grace. You'll meet someone else and then ...'

'No. Never.' Grace's tone was so vehement, so positive, that Margaret's eyebrows rose in surprise.

'They're not all the same, you know, dear,' she said gently. 'There are lots of nice men around who'd ...'

'No. I'm finished with them — all of them.' Grace got up from the table, making it clear that the conversation was at an end. Her hands shook, rattling the coffee cups as she gathered them together. 'We'd best make a start, hadn't we, if we're to open the sale on Friday?'

The appointment at the solicitor's office was arranged for the following Thursday, which was Grace's half day. As there was no school she'd arranged for Elaine to go to Jenny's for the

58

afternoon. Getting ready, she took a lot of trouble over her clothes and make-up. She wasn't going to let him think she'd gone to pieces just because of what he'd done to her.

She and Harry arrived more or less together and to Grace's surprise he looked smart, neatly dressed and well groomed. She wondered vaguely if Stella had washed and ironed the snowy shirt he wore, and pressed the pristine, knife-edged creases in his trousers, but decided that he must have used a valet service. A woman like that wouldn't know what an iron was for.

Mr Graves, the solicitor, was a tall, spare man with a balding head and a slight stoop. They sat uneasily on either side of his desk and listened to his proposals for a separation settlement. It seemed fair and Grace knew she must swallow her pride as Margaret had advised. She couldn't afford the independence she craved for, but as she sat there listening to the elderly man droning on she promised herself that she would have it one day, if she had to work her fingers to the bone for it. She tried hard to concentrate while the solicitor explained how they both stood with regard to the law, but as he came to the part about filing for divorce she raised her head and said firmly:

'There will be no divorce.'

Both men looked up at her, their expressions startled. The solicitor cleared his throat and shuffled his papers. Frowning, Harry said: 'We can talk about that later.'

'There's no point.' She looked him in the eye for the first time. 'I'm never going to release you to marry that woman, Harry. You can be sure of that.'

'No – well . . .' Harry took a deep breath. 'Grace, about Elaine? I want to see her.'

She looked down at her gloved hands. 'I'd rather you didn't.'

Again the solicitor cleared his throat. 'Er – ahem. Mrs Wendover, I must remind you that your husband does have the right to see his daughter.'

'I know.' She looked at Harry again. 'Elaine has been very upset since you left. I'm hoping to get her to come to terms with it eventually. It would unsettle her dreadfully if you were to keep seeing her. I know I can't stop you and I'm not trying to. I'm just asking you not to – for her sake.'

'I'll be going to America in a month's time,' Harry said quietly. 'For an indefinite period. If I could just see her to say goodbye?'

Grace swallowed hard. She'd expected a fight and it came as a shock to have Harry giving in so easily over Elaine; it was even more of a shock to learn that he was leaving the country again so soon, and for so long. 'Oh, well, in that case, I suppose so,' she whispered.

Mr Graves advised Grace that it would benefit all concerned if she were to sell the house, but it was agreed that Harry would continue to pay the mortgage until such time as she decided what to do. He would also pay her a maintenance allowance for herself and Elaine. Something she accepted reluctantly.

When she got home she sat down with paper and pencil and did some sums. It was clear that Mr Graves had been right. She would not be able to afford to continue living at St Olaf's Avenue. Money had been on the tight side when Harry was at home, but now, with all the overheads to pay, plus food and keeping up with Elaine's alarming rate of growth, she didn't see how she could manage it all on what she would have coming in. Tears of anger and frustration trickled down her cheeks. She remembered the lonely, dismal little room in Bow with its hissing gas fire; how ill and unhappy she had felt and the humiliation of having to find Harry and almost beg to be taken back. Well, it wouldn't happen again this time, she told herself determinedly. This time she would never let him see what he had done to her − never ask − never *allow* him to come back.

She got up and walked round the house from room to room, wondering if there was any way at all that she could stay in the beloved home she had worked so hard for, but at last she had to face the fact that it simply wasn't a practical possibility. If she was to maintain for Elaine the kind of standards she deserved, then she would have to sell the house and find a small flat somewhere. The more she thought about it, the more she knew it was best. Mr Graves had agreed to make all the necessary arrangements should she come to this decision. She would telephone him tomorrow from the shop and put things in motion. But first she must talk to Elaine. If they were to live together on their own they must each come to terms with their change in fortune. They could not go on as they were. Nothing was surer than that.

'But *why* do we have to leave here? Why doesn't Daddy want to live with us any more?'

Grace sighed. She had tried to explain to Elaine in language she would understand that grown up people weren't infallible, that they made mistakes, behaved in ways one didn't expect, but it seemed she hadn't succeeded in getting through to her.

'Elaine, I've told you; Daddy loves someone else. He doesn't want to be with me any more.' She eyed her daughter's closed face. 'And I can't make him stay with me when he doesn't love me. We couldn't be happy like that now, could we? He still loves *you* very much, though,' she added patiently. 'He's going abroad again soon and he wants to see you to say goodbye before he goes.'

'But if he still loves me, why do I have to be left behind – why can't I go with him?' Elaine's face was red and her eyes were bright with tears. Grace felt a stab of pain that she should prefer to go with her father, but, looking at the child's stricken face, she felt pity for her too. Her anger at Harry deepened.

'Daddy can't take you abroad with him. You have to stay here and go to school.'

'*She* wouldn't want me, you mean – that Stella. I'd be in the way.' Elaine poked angrily at the carpet with the toe of her shoe until Grace, her nerves raw, wanted to scream at her to stop.

'I suppose he'll marry her?' Elaine looked up. 'Will they have children of their own?'

The question startled Grace. It reminded her that Elaine was growing up fast. 'No, they won't,' she said firmly. 'Daddy and I definitely aren't getting divorced.'

The child looked relieved. 'When is he going away? When will I see him?'

'I don't know – soon. He'll let you know.' Grace reached out to touch Elaine's cheek. 'Elaine, listen darling, I'll always love you, you know that, don't you? It's just us now – you and me. We're on our own. We're going to have to make a new start. We must try to look after each other. It's been hard for me too. I ...' She swallowed hard. She didn't want Elaine to see her cry. 'I miss Daddy too, you know.'

For a moment Elaine watched her mother struggling to hold back the tears, surprise and pity softening her expression, then she stood up and went to her, putting her arms around Grace and laying her head on her shoulder. 'Why doesn't he love us any more, Mummy?' she asked miserably. '*Why* doesn't he want us? How can he love her more?'

Grace hugged her daughter's slender body close and swallowed the lump in her throat. It's me, a voice inside her head cried out. Not you – me. I'm abnormal. I'm – what was the word Harry had used? – warped. I see normal things as disgusting. I'm not fit to be anyone's wife. In a quiet, flat voice she said: 'I don't know, darling. Maybe when you see him, Daddy will be able to make you understand.'

It wasn't a successful outing. Grace put Elaine on to the train at Stanmore and Harry met her at Baker Street. It was quite a mild day for late January and for want of somewhere better to go, he took her to the zoo.

'How have you been?'

'All right, thank you.'

What would you like to see first?'

She shrugged. 'I don't know. The monkeys?'

They walked along the almost deserted pathways, side by side. Harry didn't know whether to take her hand or not. It was only four weeks since he left and yet it might have been four years. She seemed so changed, so aloof; suddenly so grown-up and controlled. Had he done that to her?

'Has term started again yet?'

'Last Monday.'

'Good to be back, eh?'

'No, not really.'

'But you still like it at the Grammar School, don't you?'

'It's all right.'

He was getting nowhere. They stood watching the monkeys for a while, he with his hands in his pockets, shoulders hunched; Elaine with a strange blank expression in her eyes that he'd never seen before. At last he said: 'Look, would you rather go to the pictures? Tiger Bay's on in Leicester Square.'

She turned to look up at him. 'We can't talk in the pictures.'

'No, 'course not.' At least she wanted to talk. 'Tea then?'

'All right.'

They found a quiet little cafe and Harry ordered tea and cakes. They sat in the steamy warmth, their knees touching under the small table, and he looked helplessly at the daughter he'd once been so close to. He wanted to reach for her hand but he stopped himself, better to keep things on an unemotional level. 'Elaine, has your mother talked to you? Has she told you that I'm going to America?'

'Yes.'

'I wanted to see you before I went. I don't know how long I'll be away, you see. I may not be back for some time.'

The candid blue eyes met his. 'You're not ever coming back, are you?'

'Well, not for a very long time.'

She met his eyes solemnly. 'Because you love her — Stella — better than us, and you want to go as far away from us as you can?'

He winced. 'No, sweetheart. Look, sometimes we have to make very hard choices. To begin with, I'm going to America because I've been offered a job there. But Mummy and I talked about it and we think that in the long run it will hurt you less if I don't see you for a while.' He tried hard to smile at her. 'You will keep on with your music, won't you?'

She shook her head. 'Mummy says that when we move to a smaller place we might not have room for the piano.' She picked abstractly at the bright pink icing on her cake. 'And, anyway, I don't like it so much now that you're not there.'

He stared at her in dismay. He'd been so proud of her musical talent. But you must keep it up. You were doing so well. He stopped himself from saying it, depression descending on him like a black cloud. He had no right to tell her what to do any more. He'd forfeited that right when he'd walked out. He shouldn't have asked to see her today. It had been a mistake. 'Have you finished your tea?' he asked. 'Do you want another cake?'

'No, thank you.'

'What would you like to do now?'

She brushed the crumbs from her hands and looked at him. 'Can I go home now, please?'

He went with her all the way to Stanmore, leaving her at the end of St Olaf's Avenue and watching as she walked the rest of the way in the gathering January dusk. His daughter, tall for her age, her brown curls bobbing on the collar of her best red coat. Suddenly he remembered another red coat, and how pretty Grace had looked in it. Soon, very soon, Elaine would be a teenager — a young woman. Next time he met her she would be a child no longer. With a stab of pain he realised it was possible he might not even recognise her. When she reached the gate, she half turned, looking to see if he was still there. He lifted his arm to wave but the next moment she had disappeared from view behind the privet hedge. It was only then that he realised that not once during the afternoon had she called him 'Daddy'. Harry pulled up the collar of his coat against the chill of the winter afternoon and turned his face towards the station.

Day by day the new spring stock was arriving at 'Margot's'. It helped to take Grace's mind off her problems. The agent's FOR SALE board outside the house had so far brought several interested parties to view, but so far none had made an offer. Grace had had no luck in finding a flat for herself and Elaine either. She worried constantly about where they would go if they found a buyer who wanted to move in quickly.

'You could always have the rooms over the shop as a temporary

63

measure,' Margaret suggested. 'But there's no bathroom or proper kitchen so it would be a last resort.'

'That's very kind of you,' Grace sighed. 'If it wasn't for the shop I'd like to move right away from here. I'm so sick of all the pitying glances I get from the neighbours, and women gossiping behind their hands when I go shopping.'

'I wouldn't worry too much about that. It'll soon blow over. Someone else'll be the butt for their gossip before long.' Margaret looked thoughtful. 'Now that you mention it though − moving away from here, I mean − I've been toying with an idea lately. I wonder what you'd think of it?'

'I'm open to any suggestions.'

'Well, you know I've been talking about opening another shop?'

'Yes.' Grace looked up with interest.

'I couldn't afford to do it on my own, of course. At least not yet. But I have a friend − a gentleman friend − who has business interests in Cambridge. He knows of a nice little property there and he's interested in buying it.' She glanced at Grace. 'As an investment of course.'

'I see.' Grace didn't see at all but she hoped her employer would eventually come to the point.

Margaret busied herself with a clothes brush, taking coats from the rail and brushing them meticulously as she spoke. 'Bryan is in property and insurance, you see, so he gets to hear of these things quickly. The shop has a flat above it. It's in Prince Regent Street − a very good position close to the town centre. I did think I'd have to turn it down. I want to stay here, you see. And I couldn't afford to put in a manageress. But if *you* were to take it on for me, I'd pay you a little more than you're getting now, and you could have the flat rent free.' She laid down the brush and turned to Grace. 'What do you think?'

Grace's heart was racing with excitement. A shop of her own to run − more money and a free flat − right away from here, where no one knew them. It was like the answer to a prayer. 'Oh, it sounds wonderful.'

'Of course you'd want to see the place. And hear more details about it,' Margaret began, but at that moment a customer came into the shop. 'We'll talk again later,' she whispered. 'After we're closed.'

When the door had been locked for the night, the two women sat in the back room over a pot of tea. Grace had been eagerly awaiting this moment all afternoon, ever since Margaret had briefly outlined her plan. Now she waited, looking forward to hearing about it in more detail.

'Bryan and I have been friends for several years,' Margaret told her. 'He's a very successful businessman, and of course I trust his judgement implicitly.' She took a sip of her tea, looking at Grace over the rim of the cup. 'He's married, which is why we have to be discreet. It's been a marriage in − er − name only for some years, if you know what I mean.' She gave Grace a knowing look as she replaced her cup on its saucer.

Hot colour rose to her cheeks. She knew only too well.

'Oh, I know what you must be thinking,' Margaret said hurriedly. 'But it's an entirely different situation to yours and Harry's. I mean, women like that have only themselves to blame, I always say. Anyway, that's besides the point. Bryan helped me buy this place, though I'm paying him back of course. It's a business arrangement, properly drawn up and all that. Our − er − personal relationship has nothing to do with the business side of things. I'd be renting the Cambridge shop from him.'

Grace was looking at Margaret with new eyes. She'd always admired her employer's fashion sense and style. She was always dressed in the height of fashion, knowing instinctively what styles and colours suited her. Recently she'd adopted the latest beehive hairstyle, her blonde hair backcombed and teased into the high bouffant coiffeur and her grey eyes dramatically emphasised with shadow, mascara and liner. Till now, Grace had taken it all at face value, assuming that it was designed to attract business. Now strange equivocal feelings about it began to stir at the back of her mind. Could it be that her employer was slightly − ever so *slightly* − common? She shook her mind free of the thought, inwardly admonishing herself as Margaret said: 'So what about all of us going up to Cambridge on Sunday to look at the place? Bryan will take us, of course. We could make a nice day out of it.'

'Next Sunday, you mean?' Grace chewed her lip. 'What about Elaine, though?'

'Oh, bring her with you,' Margaret said at once. 'I mean, her opinion counts too, doesn't it? She's going to have to live there as well.' She smiled. 'It'll be a wonderful place for a young girl growing up.' She gave an arch little giggle. 'All those dashing young undergrads. She'll be in her element a few years from now.'

Not if I have anything to do with it, Grace told herself grimly. To Margaret she merely smiled. 'Well, thank you. I'm sure we'd both love to go.'

65

The pale blue Jaguar drew up at exactly nine o'clock outside number forty-seven St Olaf's Avenue the following Sunday morning and Grace, who spotted it first from the bedroom window, called out to Elaine: 'They're here. Get a move on now. We don't want to keep them waiting, do we?'

Elaine stood at the bottom of the stairs, buttoning her coat. 'Oh, Mum, do I really *have* to go?'

'Yes, you do.' Grace tweaked at the collar of her daughter's coat and smoothed her hair. 'A lot depends on this, Elaine. I'm relying on you to behave yourself and be polite.'

'Oh, all right, but I bet I hate the place. I bet it's a rotten hole.'

Grace shook her head. 'Just don't you dare say so,' she warned. 'Even if it is.'

Margaret stood on the doorstep when Grace opened the front door. She wore a well-cut navy suit with a white ruffled blouse. Behind her stood Bryan Bostock. He was fifty-two and had been a good-looking man in his time, but too many business lunches and an over-indulgent lifestyle had turned his broad build to a podginess that strained the seams of his well-cut grey-striped suit and blurred his ample jaw-line. His dark wavy hair had begun to grey and thin and the moustache he had grown in his twenties to make him look older had now totally outgrown its purpose. His sharp eyes had not lost their twinkle, however, or their darting appreciation of an attractive woman. They lit with interest as Margaret introduced Grace.

'Delighted to meet you,' he said with a pronounced North Country accent. He took her hand and crushed it damply in his large paw. 'Heard a lot about you. Any friend of Margaret's, as they say.'

'And this is little Elaine,' Margaret said, putting her hand on the child's shoulder and drawing her forward.

'Well, well.' Bryan looked down at Elaine. 'What a bonny little lass. Takes after her mother, eh?' He winked at Grace, and Margaret frowned.

'Take no notice of him,' she said, laughing it off. 'Now, are we all set?' She nudged Bryan. 'Better get moving if we're to make Cambridge before lunch, hadn't we?'

The sleek car ate up the miles quickly, skimming along the quiet Sunday morning roads with ease. Sitting in the back and watching the countryside slip past as she leant against the soft leather upholstery, Grace began to feel excited. She had a feeling about Cambridge. Somehow she just knew everything was going to work out for them. She just wished that Elaine would try a little harder to compromise. They had fought the inevitable battle over the trip and Grace had been forced to remind her that it was her future too that they were planning.

'Don't you want to see where we're going to live? It'll be a whole new life for us both,' she'd said encouragingly. 'A new job for me, a new school for you ...'

'But I want to stay *here*,' Elaine complained. 'I only started at the Grammar School last term. I don't want to leave. I don't want to leave Jenny either.'

'You'll get a place at another grammar school,' Grace had assured her. 'All that will be taken care of. And Jenny could always come and stay with you in the holidays.'

'It wouldn't be the same. I like it here.' The argument had gone on and on until Grace's patience had snapped. Not for the first time since Harry had left she'd been sorely tempted to slap Elaine's legs as she might have done when she was a toddler. Instead she had contented herself with shouting her daughter into sullen submission.

Now she looked at the child out of the corner of her eye as she sat silently beside her in the back of the car. She deeply regretted losing her temper. She had little enough time to spend with Elaine as it was. And she'd promised herself to devote what time there was to building a good relationship between them. Since Harry had left she'd been so edgy, easily moved to tears or aroused to anger, and Elaine had often borne the brunt of it. It was hard for her too, and it was only natural that the child should want to stay in familiar surroundings with her friends under such unsettling circumstances. She reached for Elaine's hand, squeezing it warmly, and was rewarded with a tremulous smile.

'Nice car, isn't it?' Elaine whispered, returning the pressure of her mother's hand.

'Lovely,' Grace mouthed back conspiratorially.

Elaine wrinkled her nose at Bryan Bostock's bulky, grey-striped back and raised a surreptitious eyebrow at her mother. They shared a smothered giggle and immediately the rift between them was healed.

Cambridge was a surprise. As they'd approached it through the flat fenland landscape Grace had begun to wonder what kind of a place it would turn out to be. She knew it was a university town, but she hadn't been prepared for the grandeur and majesty of the ancient buildings or the friendly atmosphere of the little market town. Bryan took them on a short tour first, giving them a brief glimpse of some

67

of the colleges, then they had lunch in a small riverside restaurant on the outskirts. He was the perfect host, jovial and more than generous, encouraging them to choose the most expensive things on the menu, and ordering wine with the aplomb and flourish of the connoisseur. Sitting there with his napkin tucked under his pile of chins he beamed at them, determined that they should enjoy themselves.

'Eat, drink and be merry,' he urged them with a wave of his fork. 'After all, who knows what tomorrow'll bring?'

Grace began to reproach herself for her dubious first impression of the man and by the time they left the restaurant they were all in a mellow mood. As they climbed back into the Jaguar, Bryan rubbed his hands together.

'Right, down to business now.' he said. 'Prince Regent Street, here we come.'

It was a long, narrow street lined with shops. It led from the market place all the way to the open green stretch Bryan told them was called Parker's Piece. The shop had been a hairdresser's but now it was empty and devoid of character. Bryan unlocked the door and the four of them stood on the bare boards, looking around them.

'It's a nice size, and the window's good,' Margaret remarked.

But Grace could already see just how it would be. If she could choose she would have a charcoal-grey carpet and silver-grey walls, making a neutral background for the varying colours of her displays. She would have a gilt-framed pier glass, placed in a good position with plenty of light. And some spotlights rigged up − ones that she could direct wherever she needed light. There would be a little antique table with a tasteful flower arrangement, where customers could write cheques in comfort and privacy, and changing cubicles with silver-grey curtains ...

'Well, what do you think of it, lass?'

Bryan had asked the question, but Margaret was laughing. 'Look at her, she's well away,' she said. 'I bet she's already got the place furnished and open for business, eh, Grace?'

Grace smiled. 'It's perfect,' she said.

Upstairs, the flat consisted of a large living room with a bay window overlooking the street. There was a kitchen at the rear with a small bathroom leading off it, and Grace noticed that the water for both was heated by a convenient electric heater. A flight of stairs led to two good-sized bedrooms, one of which had a bay window to match the living room below it. A deep window seat filled the recess. Kneeling on this, Elaine looked out. The view looked over the rooftops to the green of Parker's Piece. Outside the window was a ledge, edged with a tiny wrought iron railing. A pigeon strutted and cooed, its head on one side as it tapped the window with its bill, cocking a bright enquiring eye at Elaine.

'Can this be my room, please?' she asked, looking round.

Relief almost overwhelmed Grace. At last the child was coming to terms with it all.

After the visit to Cambridge things moved fast. One of the couples who had viewed the house when it was first on the market, suddenly came up with an offer and the sale was quickly put into motion. There was so much to do: at the Stanmore end there was the packing and selling of surplus furniture. Grace was loath to part with the pieces that she and Harry had worked so hard to buy, but some of the larger things had to go. The last of these was the piano. Neither she nor Elaine had mentioned it till now, but Elaine hadn't touched the instrument since her father's departure.

'We could find room for it – *just*,' Grace told her doubtfully. 'But I'm not taking it to stand idle. Are you going to carry on with your music or not?'

Elaine shrugged. 'I don't care.'

'Think about it,' Grace urged her. 'Once the piano's gone there won't be another chance. And you were doing so well with it.'

Elaine shook her head. 'Sell it,' she said. 'Now Daddy's gone, it isn't the same. I don't want to play any more.'

At the Cambridge end there were shop fittings to buy and install, decoration of both shop and flat – all of which meant several trips up there to choose materials, paper and paint. Then there was the new stock to buy. Styles were changing fast, and on a buying trip to London Grace and Margaret discussed whether they should stick to the traditional or go in for more high fashion at the new shop.

'Better stick to what we know will sell for the time being,' Margaret said cautiously. 'We can always introduce new styles one by one when we get to know the clientele.'

There had also been some discussion between the two of them and Bryan about what the shop should be called. Margaret had wanted 'Margot's' to be exclusive to Stanmore and it had been Bryan who had come up with the answer.

'Hey, I know – we'll call it "Style 'n' Grace".'

Both women had stared at him; Grace, her cheeks flushed with surprised pleasure, while Margaret coloured for a very different reason. Bryan took the cigar he was smoking out of his mouth and laughed.

'You look right gob-smacked, the pair of you,' he said. 'Grace has come up with so many good ideas I reckon she deserves to have her name up outside.' He looked at them. 'Well, is it a good idea, or isn't it? *I* think it's brilliant.' And as Bryan was putting up the money for the venture, neither of them argued with him. 'Style 'n' Grace' it was.

Chapter Six

1966

In her room above the boutique in Prince Regent Street, Elaine unwrapped the flat square parcel and squealed with delight.

'Oooh, the latest Beatles. Thanks, Alison.' She turned to put it on the turntable of her record player, closing her eyes in delight as the opening bars of 'Yesterday' filled the room.

Alison grinned. 'I thought you'd like it. What else did you get for your birthday?'

'I'll show you.' Elaine crossed the room to her wardrobe and took out the red dress her mother had given her. Alison gasped.

'Wow! A *mini*. It's fab. Go on, put it on and let's have a look at you.'

'Mum got it last week when she went up to London buying for the shop,' Elaine said, struggling out of her jeans and tee-shirt. 'It was from Carnaby Street and I've got tights and shoes to go with it – *and* some Mary Quant make-up. Wait till you see.'

Alison threw herself down on the bed, watching as her friend twirled for her approval. 'You are lucky, being so skinny. A proper little Twiggy, aren't you? I wish my mum was a with it career woman like yours. Mum's so boring. She's never even *heard* of Billy J Kramer, and she thinks the Springfields is a place in Holland where they grow tulips.'

They collapsed into giggles, falling about like puppies. 'I don't believe you,' Elaine said. 'Anyway, your mum is a lovely cook.'

'Yeah, I s'pose I can't have everything.' Alison reached for Elaine's hairbrush and began absent-mindedly to brush her hair. It was long and fair, reaching almost to her waist, and fashionably poker straight. Elaine watched her enviously for a moment.

'I wish my hair was straight like yours. I hate the way mine curls.

71

I asked Mum if I could have it straightened so that I could grow it long, but she almost flipped her lid.'

'I don't blame her.' Alison pulled the brush through her friend's bubbly curls, watching them spring back crisply into place. 'It's so pretty. You'd spoil it.'

The two had been friends ever since Elaine had started at St Elmo's school for girls the September after she and her mother had moved to Cambridge five and a half years ago. They were the same age and although Alison was as plump as Elaine was slim, they had a lot in common.

Alison lay back against the pillow, hands clasped behind her head as she gazed up at the ceiling. 'Just think,' she said, 'only a few more days at school − then the holidays − then we'll be *students* instead of grotty little schoolgirls.'

In the coming term they were both to start a domestic science course at a local further education college. Elaine had tentatively suggested that she might try art, but her mother had talked her out of it. Elaine had given in without a fight, knowing that, in truth, she had little talent for either. She viewed the coming course with less enthusiasm than her friend.

'We're not likely to meet any decent boys at domestic science, are we?' she said pulling a face.

'Oh, I don't know. Look at all the TV chefs there are. Some of them are quite dishy. Cooking for men has a new image these days. Besides, there'll be all the other students there. They do art and designs, business studies − lots of other courses.'

'Sometimes I wish I'd kept up with my music,' Elaine said with a sigh.

Alison sat up. 'That reminds me, have you heard from your dad lately.'

'Oh, yes.' Elaine got up and went to her dressing table drawer. 'As usual I hid it from Mum. Here it is.' She handed the card, complete with its envelope bearing the American stamp to Alison. 'There was a long letter too, but that's private.' she said.

'Why do you keep all his letters and cards secret? What would your mum do if she knew?'

Elaine shrugged. 'Nothing, I suppose. I just don't want her to be hurt.'

Aliston looked at the pretty card with its bouquet of luscious roses and sighed. 'What's he doing these days? Something madly exciting, I bet. Not like my dad, beavering away in a boring old bank from nine till five every day.'

'He and Stella are rehearsing for another Broadway show,' Elaine

72

said. 'I could go over and spend the holidays with him. He's always asking me.'

'Wow – *New York*. It'd be just like on the pictures. Don't you want to go? Just think, you'd probably meet all the stars. I saw a photograph of Stella Rainbow in a magazine when she came over last year to do that telly series. There was this article all about her. It said she had an American father but was born here, in London. She's gorgeous, isn't she? And getting to be ever so famous. Fancy knowing her. If it was me, I'd want to tell everyone.'

'Not if she'd run away with your father, you wouldn't. And if you ever dare to breathe a word to anyone, Alison, I'll never speak to you again.'

'Okay, keep your hair on. You know I wouldn't anyway.'

'No, I know – sorry.' Elaine got up and walked across to stare out of the window. 'Stella's all right, I suppose, but Mum wouldn't like me going. Oh, she'd probably *let* me and pretend she didn't mind, but I know she'd feel hurt.'

'Why should she though?' Alison rolled on to her stomach. 'I mean, it all happened a long time ago, didn't it? You're seventeen now. Soon you'll have your own life to think about. I think you *should* go and visit your dad.'

'Why?' Elaine began to feel uneasy.

'Well, you haven't seen him for ages, have you? You were just a little kid when he went away. You must want to see each other.'

Elaine turned away. 'Of course – but – well – he stopped asking me a while ago. I always said no, you see, so I expect he's just given up.'

'You needn't let that stop you. You could just write and say you were coming, just turn up.'

Elaine looked round at her. 'Oh, yes? And what would I do for money?'

'I dunno – rob a bank?' They giggled again and to Elaine's relief Alison's attention was diverted as the record came to an end. She jumped up and turned it over.

'Wait till you hear the B side,' she said. 'I think it's fab.'

Alison was the only friend Elaine had confided in about her father and Stella Rainbow, but she hadn't been able to resist embroidering the situation a little to make it more romantic. Without actually saying so she had allowed Alison to think she knew Stella and, swearing the other girl to secrecy, had told about the long, affectionate letters she received almost weekly from her father – telling her how much she missed her, imploring her to cross the Atlantic by jet at his expense to stay with him and his glamorous lover.

73

In actual fact there had been no letters. On each birthday and at Christmas ever since he had left, Harry had sent Elaine a card. They always bore an American stamp but were postmarked from different states. He never enclosed any other communication or an address, so she had no way of knowing where to write back — or even if her father was still with Stella. He always signed the card in the same way: 'To Elaine with love from Daddy'. And her mother was perfectly aware that she had received them. They were all hidden carefully away in an old chocolate box at the back of her handkerchief drawer. Sometimes, when she was lonely or fed up, she would take it out and empty the contents on to the bed, looking at each fragile memento of her father with nostalgia and longing; his cards, the one blurred snapshot she had of him, and Gerry Sylvester's card, that Harry had given her on the night he left. Once she had plucked up the courage the telephone the London office, meaning to ask for her father's address, only to be told that Mr Sylvester had retired and gone to live in Worthing. Sometimes she would close her eyes and try to remember the sound of her father's voice. She wished she'd been nicer to him that last time they'd met. Could that be the reason he never wrote to her or asked to see her?

Although she still missed him, she never told her mother. She and Grace never mentioned his name. Sometimes she wondered if her mother missed him too, but somehow the tacit agreement that had grown up between them not to speak of him prevented her from asking.

Grace had changed a great deal since they had moved to Cambridge. She had had her dark hair cut in a sleek geometric style that complemented her classic features, giving her a striking look that made people turn in the street to look at her. She wore more fashionable clothes too, items that she discovered on her buying trips to fashion houses: shorter skirts; slim-fitting dresses that made her figure the envy of all her regular customers. She used more make-up too, accentuating her fine dark eyes with shadow and mascara. Yet Margaret Bennet's example had taught her not to fall into the trap of dressing younger than her thirty-six years.

'Style 'n' Grace' was doing well. Margaret now left the running of the shop entirely to her. Grace knew her own customers and catered for them. Her days were busy and her evenings were fully occupied in catching up with the housework in the flat and spending time with Elaine. There was little time for social life. Once a month Margaret would come for the day on a Sunday in the new Mini car she had acquired, and they would go through the books together. Occasionally Bryan came too and took them all out for lunch. Grace was content with the arrangement. Her days were full and satisfying. She had learned to live without Harry.

Once they had adjusted to their new life, she and Elaine had become closer. The child worked hard at school though she was not gifted academically. She was reasonably good at art and English and her domestic science teacher praised her neatness and her creative skill at needlework and cookery. On the whole Grace wasn't expecting too much in the way of exam successes and she thought that all things considered, domestic science would be the best course for her daughter to follow. It would prepare her for a career in many fields from which she could choose later. Grace also felt that it would prepare her for marriage, for deep down, although she never asked herself why, Grace half hoped that her daughter would meet a suitable young man and marry early. She wanted her to be safe and secure − and loved. All the things that she herself had missed out on.

The college Elaine and her friend Alison would attend in the autumn was within walking distance and their daily routine would be virtually unaltered. But Grace wasn't naive enough to think that nothing would change now that Elaine was leaving school. Over the past year she had watched her daughter blossom almost overnight, it seemed, from a pretty schoolgirl into a lovely young woman. Soon boys would begin to play a major part in her life and Grace was unsure of how to handle that situation. So far she'd been busy with homework and exams, and Grace had found things that they could do together in their leisure time. There was the odd visit to the theatre or cinema − jaunts around Cambridge and visits to neighbouring towns. Till now Elaine had been content but Grace knew that before long her daughter would want to try her wings and the prospect worried her a little. All the young people she saw nowadays seemed so much more sophisticated that she had been at their age; so much more adventurous − frighteningly so.

Elaine had known the facts of life since she was twelve, of course. They taught them at school nowadays, so Grace had been spared the embarrassment of having to explain them. She went cold inside at the thought of discussing sex with her daughter. It had been difficult enough explaining to her about her periods. That had been four years ago but Grace still flinched at the memory of the way Elaine had listened politely to her embarrassed stumblings, and then disarmed her totally by saying: 'Thank you, but I know all about that, Mummy. We did it in biology last term.'

Harry's name was never spoken. Sometimes Grace wished they could talk about him. She half wished that Elaine would ask her what really happened to break up the marriage, although quite how she would explain it, she didn't know. Somehow she felt that if she could find the words it would absolve her of the blame. But his name had been taboo for so long now that she wouldn't have known where to start. Although she knew that Elaine received Christmas and birthday cards it was never mentioned, and Elaine never offered to show them to her.

Last year Stella Rainbow had returned briefly to the West End stage in a musical show. During the visit she had done a short series on television, but as Grace had no set in the flat she hadn't seen it. She had read in the popular press though that Stella was enjoying a considerable success. The articles were accompanied by photographs and Grace saw, with an echo of the old hurt, that she was beautiful. Her golden skin and stunning figure made her a photographer's delight and the critics were full of praise for her voice. One had even acclaimed her as the new Ella Fitzgerald. If what one read in the gossip columns were true, it seemed that she wasn't short of admirers either.

Grace had no way of knowing whether Harry was still working with her, or if they were still together. His name never featured in any of the articles. Maybe she had used and then dropped him. Maybe it would serve him right if she had, Grace told herself bitterly. Though in moments of soul-searching honesty she admitted to herself that none of it would have happened if she had been a different kind of woman. The moments were rare and usually came in the small hours when she couldn't sleep. It was then Grace acknowledged despairingly to herself that she still loved Harry — loved him and hated him — hated herself too and everything that had happened in her life to make her the way she was.

'Oh, come on, Elaine. It'll be a fab party. You must come.'

Elaine sighed. 'You know what Mum is. She doesn't like me being out late on my own.'

Alison raised her eyes to the ceiling. 'Oh, for God's sake, Ellie. Exams are over. It's time to enjoy yourself. You're seventeen, not seven. She can't keep you in cotton wool for the rest of your life. I've asked you so many times to parties at the Carnes' I've lost count. Look, tell you what, I'll ask her shall I?'

'You can try.'

Alison took Elaine by the shoulders and looked into her eyes. 'You do want to come, don't you?'

76

'Well, the thing is, I don't suppose I'll know anyone there.'

Alison growled with exasperation. 'You'll know *me*, stupid. And Patrick and Tom are my cousins. Aunt Zoe will let us stay the night if we ask her. Then the time won't matter. Oh, come *on*. You're only chicken because you never go anywhere. You'll turn into a recluse if you're not careful.'

'Well, all right then, try. But don't blame me if she says no. I did warn you.'

But to Elaine's surprise, Grace didn't say no. Alison could be extremely persuasive when she chose. She explained that it was to be a family party at her aunt's house in Milton Road. Her uncle was giving one of his marionette shows in the loft over the old stable at the end of the garden. It all sounded quite respectable and Grace saw no reason at all why Elaine shouldn't go, especially as she'd been invited to spend the night. Margaret had telephoned to ask if she could come down on Saturday evening and stay over. If Elaine was going to be out, Margaret could have her room so it would all fit in rather well.

As it happened Grace knew Alison's uncle, Shaun Carne, or Red as everyone called him. She had bought one or two things from his antique shop at the other end of Prince Regent Street — things he had sold her cheaply because they were damaged. There was a pretty little secretaire he hadn't been able to sell because one of the back legs had been damaged; a Victorian spoon-back chair, which she and Elaine had re-upholstered in rose velvet; and a piece of Dresden-style porcelain that was chipped at the back, but which gave her window displays that extra touch of class and elegance. He had a rather abrupt manner, but humour twinkled in the bright blue eyes and he seemed to be well liked and respected by the other traders in the street.'

At forty-nine Red Carne looked scarcely older than his two sons. With his tall lean frame and his air of twitchy restlessness, he exuded a youthful energy that most men had lost by the time they turned forty. It was true that his direct, candid blue stare and forthright way of speaking were not to everyone's taste, but those who knew him well realised that although he was no soft touch, he was a good friend, and respected him for it.

Red had done many things since, as a boy of fifteen, he had left his native village in County Cork to run off and join the Merchant Navy. Since giving up the sea he had had a wide variety of jobs. He had humped coal, worked in factories, emptied dustbins; anything, in fact, that would earn him a crust and allow him time and money for painting classes. For painting was the joy of Red's life.

He met his wife, Zoe, at the Leicester art college where he attended evening classes. Small and slightly built, with her long fair har worn in a thick braid, she had a pre-Raphaelite air about her that had completely captivated Red from the moment he saw her. She was also a talented sculptress. They were married just a month after their first meeting, with scarcely a penny between them, and their first child, Patrick, was born less than a year later. When Zoe's father died, leaving her his antique shop and house in Cambridge, Red had just walked out of his job with a rather shady estate agent and Zoe was expecting their second child. It couldn't have come at a more fortuitous time.

He had loved the rambling three-storey Victorian house from the moment he saw it, and had taken to the antique business like the proverbial duck to water. Determined to make a success of the business, he had studied as much as he could about antiques from books and by talking to other dealers. What he didn't know he successfully bluffed his way through until he did. Over the years he had become quite an expert and earned the respect of his colleagues in the trade. He was a well-known personality at sales, where he had an instinctive feel for a piece that was 'right' and was frequently invited to lecture on his favourite subject, which was Victorian painting.

The loft above the old stable at the end of the garden at Mill House was full of things that Zoe's father had been unable to sell over the years. It had been while they were clearing this out that Red found the box of marionettes. They were very old, their strings broken and their costumes faded and nibbled by mice, but with Zoe's help he had restrung them and made them new costumes. Taking the marionettes apart, he had discovered how they were constructed and made more to complement the collection. He taught himself to manipulate the little dolls and he and Zoe spent winter evenings composing plays built around the various characters. Finally Red had hit on the idea of turning the loft into a puppet theatre. He furnished it with all the junk he had been about to throw away and began giving shows for his children and their friends. These had become so popular that he had found himself performing one almost every week, and soon adults as well as children were climbing the wooden stairway to what was now called the Barn Theatre to sit on every kind of seat imaginable, from tarnished gilt chairs to floor cushions, forgetting the world outside as the enchantment of the marionette plays unfolded. Over the years it had become a family team effort with Zoe and the two boys supplying the voices, Zoe helping with the manipulation, Tom standing by to hand the correct marionette to the puppeteers, and Patrick in charge of lighting and incidental music.

Alison told Elaine all this as they walked across Parker's Piece on their way to the party.

'Aunt Zoe isn't a real aunt,' she explained. 'She's a second cousin of Mum's. They're a crazy family. You'll love them. You'll like the house too. It's very big. There are six bedrooms. The family only uses three so Aunt Zoe lets the others to students. There's Toby and Mike, they're art students like Tom and Patrick, then there's James. He's at the university – he's a bit of an old sobersides, reading English and history. You'll probably meet them this evening. They usually come to all the parties.'

'They seem to give a lot,' Elaine said, a little awed at the prospect of meeting so many new people.

Alison laughed. 'There's always a party going on in someone's room. This one happens to be more formal, though. I think it's Uncle Red's birthday or something, though he'll never admit it.'

Mill House was tall and narrow with a basement and three floors above it. A flight of steps led up to a black-painted front door with a fanlight over it. There were iron railing at the front, behind which another flight of stone steps wound crookedly down to the basement. Alison led the way down these.

'Watch yourself, it's a bit steep. I said I'd give Aunt Zoe a hand with the food. You don't mind, do you?'

Zoe Carne was in the kitchen surrounded by pots and pans of every size. At forty-two she had turned from the slim nymph-like girl Red had married, into a comfortable, middle-aged dumpling of a woman. She still wore her thick fair hair in a long braid but in recent years she had taken to wearing flowing caftans to disguise her spreading waistline. She turned and smiled when Alison came in.

'Oh, there you are, darling. You can take your overnight things up in a minute. I've told Patrick to take a sleeping bag and bunk in with Tom, so you can have his room. His bed is bigger. Just give me a hand to clear up this mess first, will you? You know, however hard I try I always finish up with the kitchen looking as though it's been blitzed. That's the trouble with letting everyone do their own bloody thing in the kitchen. None of the buggers ever bothers to wash up . . .' She broke off, noticing Elaine who was standing behind Alison in the kitchen doorway. 'Oh – this must be your friend.' She wiped her hands on a tea towel and offered one to Elaine. 'Hi there. It's Elaine, isn't it?'

79

'Yes – er – how do you do, Mrs Carne?'

Zoe laughed. 'Zoe, please. And I'm not doing very well at the moment, as you can see. Grab a cloth and help Alison, there's a love.'

Elaine was slightly taken aback. When her mother entertained, which wasn't often, everything had to be just so and no one was ever allowed into the kitchen, let alone asked to wash up. Grace didn't swear either. But on Zoe's lips the words simply sounded comic, and the woman's warm informality intrigued her. She took the cloth that was handed to her and began to dry the growing pile of dishes stacked on the draining board. Zoe picked up two of the plates of sandwiches on the kitchen table.

'Better start taking some of the fodder upstairs, I suppose,' she said. 'You know, every time we give one of these bloody do's, I vow it'll be the last time.' She laughed her throaty laugh. 'But you know Red. Life without parties would be like being *embalmed* to him.'

Somewhere above them a door slammed and a moment later feet clattered down the basement stairs.

'Want any help, Ma?' The head that came round the kitchen door was covered in a mass of red-gold curls. They framed a face that looked angelic until you noticed the wickedly mischievous glint in the blue eyes. This intensified as he looked at Elaine. 'Hel*lo* – who's this?'

'It's Elaine, my friend,' Alison told him.

Well, well. And where have you been hiding this one?' He stepped forward to peer disconcertingly into Elaine's face. 'She's delicious.' He smiled. 'I'm Tom, by the way. Doesn't look as though Alison's remembered to bring her manners so I'll have to introduce myself.'

'You wouldn't know a manner if it jumped up and bit you.' Alison threw her wet dish cloth at him, but he fielded it neatly and threw it back at her.

'Take no notice of my young cousin,' he said with an apologetic expression. 'She was dropped on something vital as a baby. It's terribly sad really.' He removed the teatowel from Elaine's hand and draped it over Alison's head. 'Come upstairs with me and meet the others. You're going to be a pleasant surprise for them, I can tell you. Alison's friends usually look like her – spotty with rolls of fat.' Alison good-naturedly flicked water at him, which he ignored. He drew Elaine's hand through his arm. 'But just remember, I saw you first.'

'Oh – but – I said I'd help with the washing up,' Elaine stammered, as she looked scarlet-faced at Zoe.

80

'Guests don't wash up in this house,' Tom said. 'Not while I'm around. At least, not the pretty ones.'

Zoe's bulk all but blocked the way and she shook with laughter as they squeezed past her through the kitchen door.

'That's right. Take the poor girl upstairs out of all this squalour and give her a drink,' she said. 'Just as well for her to meet the madding crowd now, while she still has the strength to run away.'

Somewhat apprehensively, Elaine allowed Tom to lead her along the narrow basement passage.

'That's Ma's studio.' He waved an arm in the direction of a half open door. 'And the room at the front is affectionately known as the piggery. It's where we eat when we're all in together for meals, which isn't often.' Elaine glimpsed a cluttered dining room, its table covered in party food, before Tom, holding tightly to her hand, began to lead her up the narrow stairway into the hall.

Mill House was still furnished much as it had been in Zoe's parents' day. The same miscellaneous collection of antique furniture, ranging from Jacobean through Edwardian to Art Deco, filled the rooms. Even the heavily flocked wallpaper looked as though it might have been hung in Victorian days. The only real change the Carne's had made had been to the floors. Red had discarded the old threadbare carpets and sanded the wide oak floorboards, which were now varnished a rich golden and scattered with bright oriental rugs. To the front of the house a large living room looked out on to the street. Elaine had never seen any room quite like it. A grey, pink-veined marble fireplace faced the door, topped by an elaborate overmantel festooned with gilded laurel swags and fat cherubs. In the recesses on either side were shelves packed with books. Instead of the neat three-piece suite Elaine was used to at home there were three divans ranged against the walls. These were covered in striped material that looked like mattress ticking, and swathed with Indian shawls and brightly coloured cushions. A large Indian rug covered most of the floor and there were occasional tables with brass tops and intricately carved legs set with mother-of-pearl.

There were several people in the room, all of whom looked so grown-up and exotic to Elaine that she began to wish she hadn't come. To begin with she felt over dressed in her new mini dress with the matching shoes and tights. Everyone here seemed to be dressed casually, like Tom, in jeans and shirts. They all seemed to know one another too, talking and laughing together at seemingly private jokes, like old friends. She wanted to sink through the floor when Tom said in a loud voice: 'Shut up a minute, you lot, and say hello to Elaine here.'

Silence fell as all heads turned to look at her. She felt herself blushing crimson, which made her feel even worse. A tall slim young man with long fair hair stepped forward, smiling at her and holding out his hand.

'Hello, I'm Patrick. Take no notice of the baby brother. He can't help being an idiot. What can I get you to drink?' He led her across the room to a drinks table on which stood a bewildering array of bottles.

'Have you got any Coke?' Elaine wondered if he would laugh, but he didn't. Instead he nodded at his brother.

'Tom — run down to the kitchen and get Elaine a Coke, will you?'

Tom opened his mouth as though he was about to protest, then he changed his mind, turned and went out of the room. Patrick smiled and took her arm. 'Do you know any of the others?' She shook her head shyly and he said: 'Right, well, when you've got your drink I'll take you over and introduce you, though we don't stand on much ceremony here.' He pointed. 'That's Mike over there — the one with paint all over his tee-shirt, and that's Moira, his girlfriend with him. The one next to them, with the dreamy expression, is Toby. His ambition is to be a theatrical designer. The girl trying to have a conversation with him is Michelle.'

Elaine thought that Michelle was the most beautiful girl she had ever seen. She had waist length blonde hair and a wand-slim figure. Her endless legs were encased in white jeans and the shirt she wore was semi-transparent and revealed that she wore nothing underneath.

'Is she an art student too?' Elaine whispered. Patrick shook his head.

'She's the life class model at college.' He bent his head to add in a whisper: 'And between you and me, she's as thick as two planks, but don't quote me.'

'A model, I might have known,' Elaine said. 'She's very pretty.'

Patrick glanced casually across at the girl and laughed. 'So she is. Do you know, this is the first time I've seen her with her clothes on.'

At that moment Tom reappeared with the Coke and Elaine was grateful to be able to bury her burning face in the glass. Of course, she should have know. 'Life class' meant they painted a live model — usually in the nude. She cast another surreptitious, slightly awed glance in Michelle's direction. Fancy having the nerve to sit there in front of all those students with nothing on. She wondered briefly what her mother would think of it.

Tom pushed his way in between Elaine and his brother. 'Ma says when you've had your drink, better take your things upstairs. Red will be wanting us over in the Barn soon. I've brought your bag. It's in the hall. If you come with me ...'

Patrick put a hand under her elbow. 'I think not. *I'll* show Elaine the way. After all, it's my room she's having.' He gave Elaine a wry grin. 'Lesson one − don't be fooled by my brother's angelic looks.' He elbowed his way past a glaring Tom and a moment later Elaine found herself in the hall.

The staircases seemed endless but at last they reached the top floor with its sloping ceilings and odd shaped doorways.

'We call this the perch,' Patrick told her. 'Tom, Toby and I live up here. You and Alison are having my room for tonight while I move in with the angel child − for my sins.' He opened a door to reveal a room that was all odd angles. One wall was completely covered in an abstract painting of brightly coloured geometric shapes. In one corner under the sweep of sloping ceiling, a three quarter size bed was pushed against the wall. There was a record player in one corner and two shelves full of records and books. Stretched canvasses stood with their faces to the wall and under the large skylight let into the roof, an easel was set up. Beside it, a small table scattered with half-used tubes of colour, pieces of charcoal, palettes and other artists' materials. On a shelf brushes and pencils stood upright in a blue pottery jug with A PRESENT FROM HUNSTANTON painted on the side. Elaine stared around her in delight. The house was a delight; so completely different from the tidy, ordered home she had always known. The layer of dust on the furniture would have shocked her mother, but Elaine thought it was wonderful. There was such a feeling of freedom here. It was so easy-going and relaxed.'

'What a lovely room.'

Patrick's eyebrows rose and he looked around. 'Is it? We get to used to familiar surroundings that we don't really see them in the end. It *is* rather nice though, I suppose. At least up here you can always rely on privacy and we don't have the kind of mother who's always nagging us to tidy up or chasing round with a Hoover. When we can't stand the squalor any longer, we clean up ourselves.'

Elaine laughed. 'I'm surprised you can have privacy in a house as full of people as this.'

'Oh, yes. That's one of the nicest things,' he told her. 'There's always plenty of company here if you want it, but there's an unwritten law – any closed door has to be knocked on before entering. And if there's no reply, it's assumed that the occupant is either out or wants some solitude.'

To Elaine, who liked solitude but was often lonely too, it sounded like bliss. She said so and Patrick laughed.

'Well, it's Liberty Hall. Any time you feel like it, why not drop by – as long as you remember the golden rule.' He took her arm. 'We'd better go down. Everyone should have arrived by now and Red'll be wanting to start the show.'

When Alison had told Elaine that there was to be a marionette show she had been slightly put off. It sounded like the kind of entertainment she would have expected to find at a children's party, but twenty minutes later as she and Alison, along with the other guests, climbed the wooden staircase and entered the little theatre, she saw that it wasn't like that at all. The converted loft was like Aladdin's cave. Everywhere one looked there was something fascinating to see: there were stuffed birds and animals, brass dishes, jewelled swords and daggers and strangely shaped ceramics. The ceiling was draped with brightly coloured silks, the beams studded with horse brasses, Chinese lanterns and gargoyles, purloined from demolished churches. On a shelf Elaine spotted a Victorian musical toy – a glass dome inside which a galleon sat on a choppy blue sea. Carpets and faded fringed shawls decorated the walls, and there was the oddest assortment of seating that Elaine had ever seen: a chaise longue, it's ruby red upholstery faded to a soft rose; an old leather Chesterfield with some of its buttons missing; one or two small gilded chairs; a sagging divan; numerous scattered floor cushions and, right at the back on a shallow dias, a splendid 'box' affair, with looped back curtains on either side. Alison made a beeline for this, taking Elaine's hand and pulling her along.

Zoe had welcomed them all in at the door. She was the only member of the family who had changed for the party. She now wore another kaftan in fine blue Indian cotton, splendidly embroidered in bright silks and tiny flashing mirrors. Large Indian silver earrings dangled from her ears and matching bracelets jangled at her wrists.

When they were all seated Red appeared through the curtain at the side of the stage. He was splendidly attired in a burgundy cloak with a velvet lining and looked to Elaine like some sort of fairytale wizard with the lights burnishing his coppery hair. He welcomed his audience and told them a little about the play they were about to see. Then with a sweeping flourish of his cloak he disappeared again behind the curtain. The music swelled and the tiny curtains parted slowly to reveal a miniature set, perfect in every detail. The show had begun, the enchantment was about to take over, and — although she didn't know it — Elaine was about to leave her childhood behind her.

Chapter Seven

When Margaret arrived at the flat on that Friday evening Grace saw at once that she was upset. She looked tired and drawn. For the first time since Grace had known her, she looked all of her forty-five years. Her make-up looked stale and smudged, her normally well-groomed hair looked dull and lifeless, and there were bags under her eyes. Grace made no comment, but poured her an extra large gin and tonic before serving the meal she had prepared.

'Elaine won't be back tonight,' she said. 'So you can have her room.'

'That'll be nice.' Margaret sipped her drink. 'Where is she, by the way?'

'At a party.'

Margaret's eyebrows rose. 'Really? You've let her off the chain at last then, have you?'

Grace gave her employer a quick glance. 'She's never been on the chain, as you call it. She's been a good girl these past months, working for her exams. I thought she deserved a treat.'

'Well, yes, but an all-night party? A bit out of character for you, isn't it?'

Grace coloured. 'It's not an all night party. It's a birthday party at Alison's cousins' home. Mrs Carne is putting both girls up for the night, that's all.'

'Oh, yes?' Margaret laughed. 'A likely story.'

'What do you mean?' Grace demanded. 'What are you saying?'

Margaret shrugged. 'Nothing. If you're satisfied, who am I to put doubts in your mind? But we all pulled that one when we were young, didn't we?'

'Pulled ...?'

'Oh, come *on*. Didn't you ever tell fibs to get out on the loose?'

Grace was about to deny it, then she remembered the night Harry had given her the complimentary ticket for the theatre. 'I only did it once,' she said, going cold at the memory. 'It wasn't worth it.'

Margaret laughed. 'No. Many's the telling off I had too. But there — things are different nowdays, aren't they? The kids get far more freedom than we did. And all to the good, I say.'

Her comments had Grace worried, but she wasn't going to let Margaret see it. As they ate their meal she changed the subject, steering the conversation round to the shop and the success of the new lines they had been trying. But there was something about Margaret this evening — an acid sharpness about her speech and a pinched look about her eyes and mouth. Eventually Grace asked her if anything was wrong.

'You look tired. Would you rather leave the books for this week?'

'No.' Margaret straightened her back. 'Mustn't let things slide. I don't want to give Bryan anything to ...' Suddenly her face crumpled and to Grace's dismay she seemed to disintegrate before her eyes. Getting up from the table she fetched the gin and poured another generous measure into Margaret's empty glass.

'I knew something was wrong as soon as I saw you. Go on, drink that. It'll do you good, and you don't have to worry about driving back tonight.'

Margaret tossed back the neat gin gratefully. 'Thanks, Grace. I needed that.'

'Are you going to tell me what's wrong? I don't want to pry, but if you need to talk ...'

'It's Bryan — well, you must have guessed that.' Margaret found her handkerchief and blew her nose hard. 'Things finally came to a head. I've felt for some time that he was going off me.'

'Oh, surely not?' Grace said sympathetically. 'What made you think that?'

Margaret shot her a meaning look. 'What do *you* think? All the signs are there — especially the most important one.' She shook her head impatiently at Grace's blank expression. 'Oh really, Grace, sometimes I wonder how a woman of your age can be so naive. It's *bed* I'm talking about.'

'Oh, I see.'

Margaret sniffed, her eyes wistful. 'Time was when he couldn't wait. Now he doesn't seem to care one way or the other. I think — well — I'm positive, he's got someone else.'

Grace pictured Bryan's portly figure and heavy-jowelled face. Perhaps Margaret saw something in him that she didn't. 'Maybe he and his wife . . .' she ventured doubtfully. But Margaret's explosive snort stopped her in mid-sentence.

'That dried up old prune? You must be joking. He told me once, sex is just a dirty word as far as she's concerned. There's no way a woman like her is going to change.' She shook her head. 'No. He's got his eye on someone else all right – someone younger, I expect. It's happened to me before, don't forget. I know the signs.'

'Well, then, let him go.' Grace said, her voice suddenly strong. 'If that's all he's interested in, you're better off without him.'

Margaret looked irritated. 'You don't see, do you? You think it's just middle-aged vanity. Look, Grace, if I lose Bryan it could be disastrous – for you and Elaine as well as me. Apart from all the useful advice and the contacts he's helped me with, there's the financial side of the business.' She threw out her arm. 'These properties – they belong to Bryan. At one stroke of a pen, you and I could be out of a job.'

Grace's heart stood still. Out of a job – and in her case, a home too. 'I thought you said you were buying the Stanmore shop from him,' she said.

Margaret coloured. 'I was going to pay him back. It was him. He kept saying there was no need.'

'Surely he wouldn't really put us out, would he?' Grace whispered.

Somewhat mollified by Grace's crestfallen expression, Margaret shrugged. 'Who knows?'

'Yes, but surely, as you yourself once told me, business and your personal relationship are quite separate.'

'That was before we had the row,' Margaret said. 'It was the night before last. I lost my temper. I said some pretty poisonous things to him.' She lifted her head defiantly. 'Not that I've any regrets, mind. He deserved every one of them.'

'Oh dear.' Grace's heart was sinking lower by the minute. 'What happened?'

'He stormed out.' Margaret lifted her shoulders helplessly. 'I think I should warn you that I said I didn't want to see him again. I – I told him . . .' She glanced quickly at Grace. 'I told him what he could do with the shops – in *very* unladylike terms; ones he won't forgive this time. Don't be surprised if I ring to say I've heard from his solicitors before the month is out.'

Grace stared at her, appalled. 'But I thought we had a legal agreement. Surely he can't put us out on the street?'

'Not exactly, but I only rent this place on a quarterly basis. We could both be out on our ears by Christmas.'

Grace felt anger and resentment rising inside her. This was the third time that sex had risen like a spectre to spoil her life. True this time it was affecting her indirectly, but nevertheless it was at the root of the trouble. 'How *could* you, Margaret?' she burst out. 'Have you no control at all?'

'What's control got to do with it?' Margaret said hotly. 'When strong emotions between a man and a woman are aroused, control goes out of the window.'

'And I thought you were a businesswoman.' Grace looked at her employer with something approaching contempt. 'Didn't you have any thought at all for me — for Elaine?'

'Frankly, no.' Margaret got to her feet. 'If you want to know, Grace, I think your attitude is very selfish. Not that I'm really surprised. I've always thought you a pretty cold fish. But I certainly don't feel I owe you anything. Who was it who helped you when Harry walked out and left you flat, eh? Who do you have to thank for all this?' She swept an arm around the room. 'Where would you have been if it hadn't been for me? Maybe it's time you stood on your own two feet for a change.'

'I've worked hard for you, Margaret,' Grace reminded her calmly. 'And, anyway, it was Bryan's money.'

Margaret's face turned an unbecoming shade of crimson. 'And do you think you'd have had so much as a smell of that if I hadn't been providing him with certain pleasures — filling the gaps in his rotten bloody marriage?' Her genteel accent had been slipping all evening but now it had disappeared completely. The nasal East End twang she'd spent years eradicating took over as she placed her two hands on the table to stare into Grace's face. 'It's all right for you, turning your toffee-nose up at my friendship with Bryan,' she said shrilly. 'But I'll tell you something: it's women like you — smug and sanctimonious, kidding yourself that all a man needs for perfect happiness is a clean shirt and a hot dinner — women like *you* who drive men into other women's arms.' Her eyes glinted with triumph at Grace's heightened colour. 'Do you think I didn't guess you were keeping poor Harry short? One look at your poor feller's face was enough to see that he wasn't getting it regular. No wonder he ran off with that sexy singer.'

Grace felt the hair on the back of her neck prickle and the hot blood rush to her cheeks. Slowly she rose to face Margaret, her knuckles white as she gripped the table's edge. 'Get out,' she said quietly. 'Get out of my flat.'

'Oh, that's right,' Margaret sneered. 'You've no need of me now, have you? Kick me out now I'm no use to you. And in case you've forgotten, it's not *your* flat.'

'While I live here it's my flat,' Grace said, standing her ground. 'I'll go when I'm given notice. You've been a good friend to me, Margaret. You're right to remind me of it. But I've given good value in return and I won't be spoken to like that.'

Trembling, Margaret straightened up. Grace's cool control bothered her far more than if she'd railed and screamed at her. 'All right then, I'll go. But you'll live to regret it,' she added darkly. At the door she turned. 'And I'll tell you something else. You'd better watch that girl of yours. She's far too attractive for *her* good or *your* peace of mind. She'll bring you a load of trouble before too long. Not all women see men like you do, Grace.'

Having delivered her parting shot Margaret left, slamming the door behind her. Grace sat for some minutes, staring at it, her heart beating dully in her breast. The bitter bile that had spilled out of Margaret's mouth still seemed to pollute the room, lingering acridly like smoke to taint the atmosphere. She got up and went to open a window, leaning out to breathe in the cool evening air. Surely it couldn't all come to an end just because Margaret and Bryan had had some silly row? All she had worked for, all her plans and ideas, the long hours she had put in — were they all to count for nothing? The shop and the flat were her life, all she lived for. Could it really all be taken from her because of something over which she had no control? She looked across at the books, laid out for Margaret's inspection. Well, whatever happened they must be attended to. Until she was told to go she was still in charge, so better get to work.

'It was marvellous, Mum. You wouldn't believe how real the puppets are. When you've been watching them for a while, you forget that they aren't real people.' Elaine stood in the doorway as her mother locked the shop door for the night. 'I'll make you something to eat, shall I? You look tired.'

Grace winced a little as she flexed her back. 'Thanks, love. I think I'll just have a quick bath before tea.'

Saturdays in the shop were always hectic. Normally Grace was delighted at the business she did but today her heart was heavy. She hadn't slept at all, worrying over Margaret's disturbing news. And now her head throbbed and her feet and back ached with tension and fatigue.

'Did you have any lunch?' Elaine asked, peering at her mother with grown-up concern. When Grace shook her head wearily she frowned. 'You know it's bad for you to go without. I should have

90

been here to get you something.' Grace slipped an arm around her daughter's shoulders. She was a good girl. How could Margaret say those nasty things about her? She was just jealous, that was all. Now that she'd lost Bryan she had no one of her own at all. Grace could almost feel sorry for her — until she remembered that it was Margaret's lack of emotional control that had landed them all in this mess.

Lying in the scented bathwater she felt the tension begin to seep out of her. The appetising aroma of the bacon and eggs Elaine was frying for their tea drifted under the bathroom door and she felt glad that she wasn't alone. Should she tell Elaine? she wondered. Should she warn her of the insecurity their future might once again hold? She decided against it. Elaine was about to begin her college course next term. She was happy here in Cambridge. She'd settled well and made friends in spite of the upheaval they'd had. Whatever happened, nothing must spoil her life.

When Grace emerged from her bath, refreshed and relaxed, she found the table neatly laid and tea on the table — eggs, bacon and chips. She attacked it with relish, realising how hungry she was.

'Tell me about the party,' she invited, aware that she had only half listened to Elaine's excited chatter. 'Did you have a nice time?'

Again, Elaine described the puppet play and the quaint barn theatre. She told about the buffet supper and the interesting new people she had met. But she didn't tell her mother about the glorious disorder of the Carnes' household, or the family's carefree, bohemian attitude to life, knowing instinctively that she would disapprove.

After the play was over they had gone back to the house for food and more drinks. By this time a lot more people had arrived and gradually they all seemed to pair off. Music from the record player provided a background and the air became thick with smoke and heavy with the strangely pungent perfume of the joss sticks that Red liked to burn in every corner. Couples sat on the stairs and in corners, wrapped around each other in blissful oblivion. A boy in a psychedelic shirt offered her a cigarette but Elaine shook her head.

'Thank you but I don't smoke,' she said politely. 'Tobacco makes me cough.'

The young man laughed. 'This'll do more than make you cough. Try it.'

She was hesitating, reluctant to look square and fuddy-duddy, when Patrick appeared and sent the boy away. She asked him why and he laughed softly.

91

'Because they're not for you,' he said. 'Harmless enough perhaps, but definitely not for little innocents like you.' He dropped an arm casually across her shoulders. 'Are you enjoying yourself?'

She nodded, although she wasn't really sure. It was all a bit confusing and she wasn't certain what to do. Even Alison seemed to have disappeared. At all the other parties she had ever been invited to they had played games — Sardines, Postman's Knock, Truth or Dare. 'It's a lovely party,' she said hopefully. Patrick laughed and gave her shoulders a little squeeze. 'Go on, tell the truth — you're hating it, aren't you?'

She blushed. 'Oh, no. I . . .'

'It's all right. You don't have to pretend. No one's going to be offended.'

'I loved the barn,' she told him. 'And the puppets.'

'Right.' He pulled her hand through his arm. 'That's where we're going. I'm sure you'd like to have a proper look round when no one is there.'

'Oh — *could* I?'

Once again he laughed, his blue eyes flashing. He'd never met a girl as sweetly innocent and as easily pleased as this one. They were as rare as rubies in this day and age. Where on earth had his cousin Alison found her? he wondered. She was deliciously flattering to the ego, and having his protective instincts aroused was something new and novel to Patrick.

He led her down the basement stairs, stepping over couples as they went. They crossed the yard and climbed the wooden staircase to the barn. Empty of people, it looked even more exciting to Elaine and she went excitedly from one curio to another, examining each item carefully, exclaiming and asking questions about them.

'I've never seen a place like this before,' she said, standing in the centre of the floor and looking round her. 'It's wonderful.'

Patrick draped himself over one of the divans. 'It's the most appalling fire risk,' he said. 'And I'm not at all sure that the floor is as sound as it might be. I'm always on at Red to have it looked at, but he puts it off.

Elaine looked at him. She'd noticed that both boys called their father by his Christian — or rather his nick-name. They were so free, so different from any other people she knew. Patrick smiled and held out his hand to her.

'Come and sit down. Tell me about yourself,' he invited lazily. 'Alison has certainly kept you quiet. Why have we never met you before?'

She sat on the edge of the divan, near his feet. 'I've been working

92

hard for my exams,' she told him. 'Alison and I start at college in September.'

'Really? What course are you taking?'

She pulled a face. 'Domestic science. Boring, isn't it?' She looked at him as he leaned back against the cushions. Everything about him was relaxed, from the long legs in their tight blue jeans to the romantically floppy fair hair. He had his father's loose-limbed ranginess and his mother's handsome looks, the blue eyes alight with lazy humour. Now he reached for her hand.

'Come on. You can sit a bit closer, you know. I won't eat you.'

She looked at his hand; broad, tanned and capable, with the long sensitive fingers of an artist. She put her own trustingly into it and allowed him to draw her nearer. 'Shall I see you at college?' she asked shyly.

'Afraid not. I'm going up to the Slade in September,' he told her. 'And if I do well, I'll follow it up with a year in Paris.' Elaine stared at him. 'Oh, you lucky thing. I've never been abroad.'

'Not on school trips?' Patrick's eyebrows rose. 'Haven't your parents taken you?'

'There's only my mother,' she told him. 'Daddy left some years ago. Mum has to work hard, so there's never any money or time for holidays abroad.'

'Are your parents divorced?'

Elaine shook her head. 'No. They didn't get along so they split up. Daddy is a musician. He's pianist-manager to Stella Rainbow, the singer.'

'No kidding? You know, I'm more and more surprised that Alison never mentioned you before.'

'I don't talk much about Daddy,' Elaine said. Avoiding his direct gaze she traced the pattern on the divan cover with one forefinger. 'I miss him though.'

'Don't you ever get to see him?'

'No. He's in America — with Stella. They live together, you see. I only hear from him on birthdays and at Christmas.'

He was still holding her hand and now he gave it a sympathetic squeeze. 'Poor kid. Can't you go over for a visit?'

'I haven't been asked.' She bit her lip, suddenly remembering the white lies she'd told Alison about her father. 'Don't tell Alison I said that though, will you? She thinks I have letters from him, inviting me over there. I don't know why I told her that, I wish I hadn't, but now I've started I can't very well stop.'

'But you don't — get letters, I mean?'

'No. Just cards.'

'Of course I won't say anything. It'll be our first secret together.' He let go her hand and swung his long legs to the floor. 'Tell you what — would you like to see backstage, and have a go with the puppets?'

Her eyes lit up like a child's. 'Oooh, can I really?'

Behind the tiny stage with its velvet curtains the space was incredibly small and cramped. Elaine wondered how on earth the four Carnes could possibly work in it. On the back wall the marionettes hung on pegs, their heads lolling. They looked dead and lifeless. Patrick took one down. It was the wizard, Caspar, from the play they'd seen this evening. His bushy orange hair and bright beady eyes instantly came to life when Patrick fingered the wooden control. He danced a little jig and held up his hand for Elaine to shake, looking up at her with a cheekily appealing expression.

Elaine laughed as she shook the small wooden hand in its white glove. 'Oh, isn't he sweet?'

'Here — have a go yourself,' Patrick invited. 'He has quite a simple control. See, you hold it here and this bar works his arms and legs.'

To Elaine's delight she found that after a few minutes' practice she could do it. Patrick gave her instructions in Caspar's squeaky voice: 'Phew, that's enough, Elaine. I'm not used to dancing so fast. I'm not getting any younger, you know. I'm worn out.'

Laughing, she handed the puppet back to him. 'I didn't realise it was you doing his voice.'

'We take a group of characters each,' he told her. 'We all try out to see who suits each character best when we're creating a new play.'

He showed her the tape deck and the library of tapes. There was the incidental music, labelled for each play, and the sound effects, mostly home made. Patrick made her laugh as he explained the odd ways in which some of them had been devised.

'This one, the sound of running water, was Tom's bathwater running, and this one — the dawn chorus — had me up at five a.m. hanging out of the window with a mike. It had to be in Toby's room because it faces the garden. I could only get the sound of the early morning lorries on the by-pass from mine.' He laughed. 'Toby wasn't best pleased, I can tell you, especially as he had his girlfriend staying for the weekend.' He broke off as he saw her blush. 'Come on, let's go and sit down again, shall we?'

Elaine was quiet as they sat side by side on the divan. She hated herself. It must look as though she disapproved. He would think her stuffy and naive — a silly kid. It was just that his remark had taken her by surprise and she didn't quite know how to react. She wished her mother had brought her up differently, wished she was more with it. Grace might look fashionable and sophisticated to her customers and to outsiders but when it came to keeping up with the modern way of thinking she was way behind the times.

'Are you all right?' Patrick took her hand again. 'Not tired?'

She shook her head. 'No. I'm fine, thanks.'

'You're fed up with my company, is that it? I don't want to keep you from the fun — from mixing with the others.'

'Oh, no,' she said, quickly turning her face to his. 'I'd rather be here with you than anywhere.'

His blue eyes smiled at her. 'What a nice compliment.' How fresh she was. As yet she hadn't learned to hide her feelings. Those expressive brown eyes revealed everything. It was like the feeling he got looking at a new, untouched canvas that challenged him to paint a masterpiece. In a year or two she'd have learned to keep her reactions to herself — to tease and flirt and play a man like a fish on a hook — especially with those eyes, those looks. But for now she was sheer delight. He felt his heart melt with tender anticipation.

'Do you have a regular boyfriend, Elaine?' he asked, taking her hand.

She shook her head. 'I've been too busy working.'

'I'm glad.' He smiled. 'How old did you tell me you were?'

She frowned. She didn't actually remember telling him. Seventeen sounded such a baby. 'Eighteen, umm, soon,' she said hopefully.

'Eighteen, eh? Just three years younger than me.' His voice was soft as his face came closer. Elaine could feel his breath on her cheek. She felt the anticipation of his kiss stir something, some magic, deep inside her.

'Just right.' His lips brushed hers experimentally and he felt her quiver. She was like a butterfly. So delicate and fragile; alive with vivid transient colour. He drew her closer. Her lips were soft and moist — almost childlike under his. Her arms wound softly around his neck and he felt her supple body curve instinctively against him. For a moment he held her, rubbing his cheek against the soft, springy hair, inhaling the sweet scent of her. Then he kissed her again.

'Hey, maybe we'd better go back now,' he said softly after a moment or two. 'People will be thinking I've spirited you away.' She was arousing him even more than he had anticipated and he knew instinctively that this one was not to be hurried.

Walking back through the yard, her hand swinging in Patrick's, Elaine thought she had never been so happy, but he'd said nothing about another meeting. Surely it wasn't going to end here? She must

95

see him again – she *must*. As he stepped in front of her to open the door she whispered: 'Patrick – when – when will I see you again?'

He stood looking down at her, resting his hands lightly on her shoulders. 'You really want to see me again?'

'Yes. Oh, yes, I do.'

He bent to kiss her lightly on the mouth. 'We have all summer ahead of us, sweetheart,' he whispered. 'And it's going to be the loveliest summer I've ever known. I can feel it in my bones.'

Elaine could feel it in hers too.

'I think there is some cake in the tin.'

Elaine was jerked out of her reminiscent dream by her mother's voice. 'Sorry. Cake?'

Grace was pushing her empty plate aside. 'In the tin. I think there's some left.'

'I'll get it.' Elaine fetched the cake tin and cut two slices. 'Did Mrs Bennett come last night?' she asked. 'If she stayed, you must have been quick changing my bed again.'

'She didn't stay,' Grace said shortly. 'She had to get back to Stanmore. An appointment or something.' She looked at her daughter thoughtfully. 'Elaine, you are happy here, aren't you? You don't still miss Stanmore?'

Elaine laughed. 'Good heavens, no. I love it here. I wouldn't change the flat or the shop or anything, not for the world. I'm looking forward to working with you in the shop in the holidays, like you said I could. I can, can't I?'

'Yes, love, of course.' Grace sighed. How long would it last, she wondered. What would next month – or even next week – bring?

As it happened Grace didn't have to wait long to discover whether she still had a job and a roof over her head. The following day when they had had their Sunday lunch Elaine announced that she and Alison were going for a walk, then back to Alison's house for tea afterwards. Grace was glad of a chance to put her feet up and look at the latest fashion magazines. She was just leafing through the August edition of *Vogue* when there was a ring at the flat bell. Sighing she put down the magazine and swung her feet to the floor, padding down the stairs in her stocking feet to answer the door. To her surprise Bryan Bostock stood on the step, an apologetic, almost hang-dog look on his face. 'Grace, my dear, I'm sorry to arrive unannounced like this. Can I have a word with you?'

96

She held the door open for him, her heart sinking. Now that the moment of truth had arrived she wasn't sure that she wanted to know. 'Come upstairs, Bryan,' she said, trying to sound cheerful. 'I was just going to make myself a cup of tea. I expect you'd like one too after your drive.'

'I would indeed.' He lumbered up the stairs after her, looking for all the world like a dejected bloodhound.

In the living room she poured tea and handed him a cup. He spooned three sugars into it and stirred morosely.

'What can I do for you, Bryan?' Grace prompted.

'Maybe you've seen Margaret,' he said, his eyes searching her face. 'Maybe she's already told you.'

'She was here on Friday for the monthly look at the books.'

'Say anything else, did she?' Bryan looked up at her with bloodshot eyes.

In spite of the sour note on which they had parted Grace still felt reluctant to break Margaret's confidence. Taking a deep breath she shook her head. 'No.'

'Well, you're bound to hear sooner or later. We've decided to go our separate ways,' Bryan looked up at her. 'I thought if she'd told you, you might be worrying about how you stood. That's why I'm here.'

Grace sighed. 'It was good of you to think of me. I'm sorry, Bryan.' She looked at him fearfully. 'What are you planning to do — about the shops, I mean?'

'As the sitting tenant, I shall give Margaret the chance to buy 'Margot's'. I imagine she'll take it. God knows she ought to have enough cash put away,' he added bitterly.

'And this one?'

'At the end of the present quarter the option to rent will be yours,' Bryan told her. 'If you want it, 'Style 'n' Grace' will be your business, with your name on the rent book from the beginning of the next quarter. But of course you're under no obligation. If your loyalty to Margaret will make things awkward for you, or you'd rather fit in with any plans she might have, I shall quite understand.'

Grace could feel herself turning pink with excitement. *Her* shop. Her *own* business. It was like a dream come true. She could almost have hugged Bryan. She took a deep breath, deciding to put her cards on the table and tell him the truth. 'As it happens, Bryan, Margaret and I have parted company too,' she said. 'I'll admit now that she did tell me briefly about your quarrel — though not in detail. She was in a very bad mood and she said some nasty things that I couldn't forgive.' She sighed. 'I'm afraid I had to ask her to leave. I've had a very worrying two days since then, Bryan.'

He reached across to pat her hand. 'I'm so sorry about it all, Grace. It's not fair that you should suffer because of the mess we've made of things. You've always been a good worker. You're bright – a good businesswoman. Between ourselves, I've always felt that Margaret underpaid you. She was on to a good thing with both of us, if you ask me.' He held her hand in his large fat paw, stroking its back absent-mindedly with his thumb. 'You deserve to get on and now's your chance. I'll rent the shop to you as reasonably as I can and the running of it will be up to you. I know you'll make a go of it.'

He would have stayed on, in fact he gave every indication of settling down for the evening, but Grace discouraged him by saying that she had to do some stock-taking. She felt mean for turning him out when he had driven over specially to take a load off her mind. He'd been so kind to her too, over the rent. But for a reason she couldn't quite name she never felt completely comfortable in Bryan's company, and being alone with him was a definite strain. As he was leaving he turned suddenly, almost bumping into her in the narrow passageway.

'Oh, I've just remembered. I've got tickets for a Sunday charity concert. It's next month, at the London Palladium. Dozens of stars appearing. I was going to take you, Margaret and Elaine as a little treat. Now there'll be a spare ticket. Would Elaine like to bring a little friend, do you think?'

Grace hesitated. His large face looked so pleased with the idea – so expectant – that she hadn't the heart to refuse. 'Thank you, Bryan,' she said. 'I'm sure we'd all love to go.'

Alison and Elaine sprawled on the rug in the sunshine on Parker's Piece.

'Come on then – give. I was too sleepy to prise anything out of you when we got to bed, and there were too many people milling around at breakfast yesterday.'

Elaine opened one eye and looked up at her friend. Alison was sitting up looking down at her expectantly. 'What do you mean – give?'

'Come off it. You know what I mean. You and Patrick, of course. Everyone noticed the two of you were missing – for absolutely *ages* too.'

'He was teaching me to work the puppets over in the barn.'

Alison snorted. 'Pull the other one − it's elastic. Come on, Ellie, I thought I was your best friend.'

'You are.'

'So . . .?'

Elaine sat up. 'Alison, what do you want me to tell you?'

'What happened, of course.' She gave her friend a sly glance. 'I must say, I never thought you had it in you. They say the quiet ones are the worst.'

'Nothing happened.'

'You've got to be kidding. You spent all that time alone in the barn − with Patrick − and you expect me to believe nothing happened?'

'I told you − he showed me the puppets and all the things backstage. He let me try one of them.'

Alison laughed. 'What else did he let you try? Don't tell me he didn't even try to kiss you . . .' Alison saw the faint flush that deepened Elaine's colour and pounced: 'Ah, he did. I'm right, aren't I?'

'Well, all right. One kiss. That's nothing, is it?'

Alison shook her head and threw herself down on the rug again. 'All right, if you're going to be cagey about it, I won't pry any more.' She closed her eyes, silent for a moment. Then she said: 'Do you fancy him?'

'He's nice.'

Alison rolled on to her stomach and gave Elaine a gentle punch on the shoulder. 'Elaine Wendover, you are the most irritating female I've ever known. *I* know Patrick is nice − *everyone* knows he's nice. That's not what I asked you.'

'I think he's good-looking too. Quite handsome, in fact.'

'Getting better. And what about when he kissed you? Did it give you butterflies?'

Elaine giggled in spite of herself. 'What do *you* think? Anyway how about you?' she countered. 'After we came back from seeing the play, you just vanished. Where were you?'

'That's no secret. Jake and I went upstairs to have a sneaky drag.' She looked at Elaine's puzzled expression and raised her eyes to the sky. 'Dear God, you're such an innocent − to smoke pot.'

'Is that what those cigarettes were made of − the ones that smelt funny?'

'What else?'

'Does your Aunt Zoe know?'

Alison shrugged. 'No idea. It's okay anyway. Perfectly harmless. All the kids smoke it. It makes you feel great.'

Elaine frowned. 'It's still — well — drugs, though, isn't it?'

'So what? You don't have to get addicted unless you're a stupid twit.' Alison breathed in deeply and spread her arms. 'It was a great party though, wasn't it?'

'Yes. Alison — you and this Jake, did you ...?'

'Of course.' Alison grinned up at her impishly. 'Oh, don't look so shocked. Not all the way — just snogging.' She shook her head at Elaine. 'You've got an awful lot of catching up to do, sweetie. Time you persuaded that mum of yours to let you off the lead a bit more.' She looked at her watch. 'Hey, look at the time. Mum said five o'clock and it's ten to already. No wonder I'm starving. Shall we go?'

As they walked back to Alison's house Elaine was silent, busy with her own thoughts. A lot of catching up to do. Alison had said. Sometimes her friend made her feel such a baby; years younger, slow and simple-minded. All the same, she wasn't sure she wanted to catch up with all of it too quickly. There was an awful lot she still didn't really understand. She couldn't ask her mother. She knew from experience that Grace found talking about such such things extremely distasteful. As for asking Alison, she'd die of shame rather than admit her ignorance; even though they were best friends.

'Are you seeing Patrick again?' Alison asked as she pushed open the front gate.

Elaine shrugged. 'I might,' she said. And her heartbeat quickened. It's going to be the loveliest summer I've ever known. The words sang inside her head like music. Suddenly the sky was bluer; the air sweeter; the sun warmer than it had ever been before. Happiness and the sheer joy of existence made her feel she could do anything — walk on water — sing like an angel — fly to the moon ...

'Come on, dreamy.' Alison grabbed her arm and pulled her inside. 'Mum's been baking. I can smell fresh bread and fruit cake. If we don't hurry up, the greedy pigs will have eaten the lot.'

Chapter Eight

Grace was serving a customer when the young man came into the shop. He stood by the door, a suitcase in his hand, looking as though he'd rather be anywhere than where he was. He was tall, almost six feet, with clear hazel eyes and a lightly tanned complexion. His tousled brown hair curled over the frayed collar of his blue denim jacket. Elaine stepped up to him.

'Can I help you?'

'I – er – I was rather hoping for a word with the owner, or – er – manageress.' His voice was soft and musical, with a hint of the Welsh hills in its vowels.

'That's my mother,' Elaine told him. 'If you'd like to wait, she's with a customer at the moment.' She looked at his case and immediately took him for a sales rep'. 'Perhaps you'd like to wait in the back?'

He nodded eagerly and smiled at her. The smile was disarming; it revealed strong white teeth and lit his rather ordinary face, completely transforming it. Picking up his case, he followed her through to the back room, eager as a stray puppy. Elained offered him a seat and, as an afterthought, asked if he would like a coffee.'

'Oh, thank you. That's really kind of you.'

He looked grateful, as though he needed that coffee badly, Elaine took the electric kettle and went through to the kitchen to fill it. The young man puzzled her. He was tall and well-built – quite good-looking in a way, especially when he smiled. But there was something about him – an odd vulnerability that sat incongruously on his broad shoulders. He was clean and well turned out and yet there was a slightly down-at-heel look about him. He looked as though he could use a good meal and someone to mother him.

'I forgot to ask your name,' she said, coming back into the room.

'It's Owen. Morgan Owen.'

Elaine put the cup of coffee on the table in front of him. 'I'll tell Mum you're here, Mr Owen,' she said.

Grace heaved a sigh of relief as she showed her customer out. There were certain women who only patronised 'Style 'N' Grace' during the sales, and although more often than not they tried on everything in the place and then bought nothing, Grace made sure that they were treated with the same courtesy as her regulars. Sometimes it wasn't easy to keep the smile glued to her face as they tossed aside garment after garment as though they were at a jumble sale. Out of the corner of her eye she had seen Elaine take the young man through to the back. He wasn't one of the regular reps. Maybe he was new − or a student, filling in during the vac'. Going through the curtained archway to the stockroom she nodded to Elaine.

'Take over for me for a while, will you, darling?' She looked enquiringly at the man sitting at the table. Can I help you, Mr − er . . .'

'This is Mr Owen, Mum,' Elaine told her.

Instantly Morgan was on his feet, taking the hand that Grace offered. 'Morgan − Morgan Owen.'

She smiled. 'I'm Grace Wendover. What can I do for you, Mr Owen? I don't think we've met before. Let's see now − you'd be from . . .?'

'From?' He looked puzzled. 'Oh, I see what you mean. No, I'm not *from* anywhere. I've got some − er − merchandise to show you.'

Grace's heart sank. He seemed such a nice young man. What on earth could he have in that case − and how was she to send him away without hurting his feelings?

'Please, may I show you?' He looked at her hopefully, lifting his case onto a chair.

'Well − all right.' Grace looked at her watch and wondered if Elaine was coping. But the next moment everything else was forgotten as Morgan Owen opened his case and drew out the most exquisite item of knitwear she had ever seen. It was a jacket, knitted in soft muted shades ranging from charcoal black through every shade of grey to cloudy white. The yarn was soft and whisper-light, and as he handed the jacket to Grace she impulsively held it to her cheek.

'Oh, it's beautiful. Where did you get it?'

'I made it,' he told her modestly. 'The colours are natural. The wool comes from the sheep on my father's farm in Wales.'

'You mean, *you* knitted this?' Grace stared at him in amazement.

'Well, yes.' He looked almost apologetic. 'I've got some more if you're interested. There are others in the natural wool shades and some made from yarn I've bleached and then dyed with various plant dyes and other things I've experimented with.'

Grace watched him bring three more garments out of the case; the most excitingly new and original items of clothing she'd ever seen. Not only were the yarns interestingly textured and the colours subtly different, but the designs were so astonishingly fresh and avant-garde.

'Where did you learn to do all this?' she asked him breathlessly.

'At art school, initially. But I dropped out. It was all too conservative for me and they certainly didn't hold with my radical way of thinking.' He smiled apologetically.

Grace looked at him with a new respect. Suddenly the rather hesitant young man who had stood before her a moment ago had changed into someone positive and knowledgeable. Some instinct told her with a sudden flash of intuition that she had made an important find.

'How many orders have you got?' she asked him.

'Here in Cambridge, you mean?'

'Yes − well, anywhere'

He sighed. 'None. Well, no firm ones yet. Lots of people are interested, but somehow they seem reluctant actually to commit themselves.'

Grace nodded. That would account for his lack of confidence. Was he perhaps asking too high a price? She fingered the jacket that had taken her fancy. 'How much is this one?'

'Have it on me − as a sample,' he said suddenly. 'The colours are perfect for you. Wear it in your shop perhaps, and see if your customers like it. I'll come back next week.'

'Oh, no. I *couldn't*.' But already he was fastening his case. 'Look, you can't just give your work away. I meant it. How much are you asking for your knitwear? I must know if I'm to order any.'

He looked at her, his assurance diminishing before her eyes. 'I'm no businessman, Mrs Wendover. I'll admit that I really haven't a clue what to ask. That's my trouble. I've been trying to get people to make me an offer.'

Grace laughed gently. 'Oh, dear. No wonder you're not doing very well.' She could hear voices in the shop now and peering through the curtain saw that several women had come into the shop and were raking through her rail of sale garments. She turned back to him. 'Look, Morgan − may I call you Morgan?' He nodded eagerly.

103

'Can you come back this evening after I've closed? We could do a little costing out and work out a proper price for you to charge. I'd have time to look at your things more closely then too.'

The radiant smile lit his face again. 'You mean you'd actually *help* me?'

Grace smiled, warming to him. 'I've an idea I'm going to be helping both of us, Morgan. Come at seven and have a bite to eat with us,' she added impulsively. His complexion was a little muddy and she suspected he lived out of tins and might welcome a home-cooked meal. 'I'm afraid I'll have to go right now.'

'That's all right. I'll see you later.'

He was going through the door when she remembered the jacket, still over her arm. 'Wait, you're going without this.'

He shook his head. 'I meant it. Wear it.' He gave her his radiant smile. 'Be my first model.'

Margaret slipped her arms into the sleeves of the jacket and stood for a moment before the stockroom mirror. He'd been right. The jacket suited her, its soft natural colours flattering her complexion; its wide, soft collar framing her face. As she walked into the shop one of her best customers stood waiting.

'Mrs Davies, I'm so sorry to keep you waiting,' she said. 'I had to speak to a rep ...' She broke off as she caught the woman's expression of rapt admiration.

'My dear, that's perfectly all right. But tell me, where did you get that delectable jacket?'

'This? It's part of a new exclusive collection I'm hoping to stock quite soon.' Margaret bluffed.

'Well, do let me know when you have them in stock,' Mrs Davies said. 'I just have to have one of those for the autumn.'

'I don't really have to stay, do I?' Elaine was laying the table whilst her mother cooked supper. 'Alison's cousin has asked us to go for a trip down the river in a punt. I've already said I'll go.'

Grace left her cooking to stand in the doorway, a slightly worried expression on her face. 'Her cousin — which one?'

'Patrick.' Elaine bent her head low over the table, pretending to adjust the small flower arrangement. If only she didn't blush so easily.

'Who else is going?' Grace asked.

'I told you, the four of us.' She longed to tell her mother that she was being taken out by Patrick alone for the first time, but she was so desperately afraid that Grace might do something to prevent her going.

104

Alison and both of her cousins?'

'Yes.'

'Oh, well, I suppose it's all right. But you won't lark about and fall in the water, will you?'

Elaine groaned. 'Oh, Mum. We're not children.'

'You're not far off it.' The sound of the door bell broke into her thoughts. 'That will be him now. Go down and let him in, there's a good girl.'

Morgan stood expectantly on the doorstep. His hair was brushed and slicked down; he looked neat and clean in flared jeans and a white shirt splashed with tiny blue flowers. Weighing him down was the largest suitcase Elaine had ever seen. It was so heavy and cumbersome that he had difficulty getting up the narrow stairs with it.

Grace had cooked a mixed grill, accompanied by fresh peas and new potatoes, and Morgan ate his meal with obvious enjoyment, remarking again and again how tasty and delicious everything was. Grace's suspicion that he lived out of tins was confirmed. The moment the meal was over Elaine looked appealingly at her mother.

'May I go now?'

'You'd better make your apologies to Mr Owen,' Grace said. But Morgan shook his head.

'Oh, please, don't worry on my account.'

'It's a previous engagement, you see, Mr Owen,' Elaine explained gravely. 'Please will you excuse me?'

'Of course.'

When Elaine had whisked eagerly out of the room, he smiled shyly at Grace. 'She's very pretty, isn't she? I expect there's a boyfriend in the offing.'

'Oh, no. Nothing of that sort.' Grace assured him. 'Elaine is only seventeen. Plenty of time for that. Now, show me what you've brought.'

The garments Morgan took out of the case and draped, one by one, over Grace's settee were like the contents of some magic box. As he shook them out he explained their origins.

'What I've tried to do is capture the colours and the textures of the countryside in Wales where I grew up. The hillsides, the rocks, the stone walls, the sky and the sea in all its varying moods. The wool comes from the sheep that live on the hills, and the dyes all come from natural plants that grow there. It's a natural projection, see? As natural as evolution. At least, that's what I'm aiming for.'

'It's a wonderful idea,' Grace told him. 'And very effective.'

He smiled, blushing with pleasure. 'I'm so glad you think so.'

'I hope you can give me some idea of what it costs you to make them,' she ventured.

'Oh, yes. I've jotted down some figures. I buy the raw wool from my father and a couple of uncles; I spin and dye it myself, see, so it doesn't really cost a lot,' he said. 'Especially as I do the knitting too.'

'Ah, but we must count it as though you pay someone else to do it,' Grace pointed out.

He stared at her. 'But I don't. Wouldn't that be dishonest?'

Grace was remembering the avid look on Mrs Davies' face when she had seen the jacket. 'Look, Morgan,' she said patiently. 'This could be big business for you. If your garments became popular you'd have to employ spinners and knitters and other workers too, so you must start the way you mean to go on. Besides,' she added, smiling wryly, 'people don't appreciate something they get for next to nothing. That's a piece of psychology I've learned for myself since I've been working in this business.'

Morgan shook his head bemusedly. 'I can see I've got an awful lot to learn.'

'Would you like me to make some enquiries?' she suggested. 'I can ring round some of my contacts in the trade and find out what the going rates are. Would you like me to do that?'

He looked unsure. 'Well, if you really think my work could be a success.'

'I do, Morgan. Oh yes, I do.' She smiled. 'In the meantime, why don't we have some coffee and you can tell me all about yourself?'

Zoe Carne put a large bowl of salad on the table and began to carve thick slices from the cold remains of a joint of beef.

'About time too,' Tom said, seating himself at the table and shaking out his napkin. 'Dinner in this house can be any time from six to nine thirty. You get worse, Ma.'

'I was busy. I didn't notice the time. Think yourself lucky to be getting dinner at all.' Zoe reached across to cuff his ear good-naturedly. 'So shut up and get on with it, brat.' She pushed a plate of meat towards him, the silver bangles on her wrist jangling. 'And I'll say again what I've said so many times before: I'm not the only person in this house with a pair of hands. One of you lot could just as easily make a meal.'

'That's right,' Red said, helping himself from a bowl of cold potatoes. 'Your mother's work is just as important as yours. More. She gets commissioned work.'

106

'Well, if I couldn't do better than this ...' Tom said scathingly, poking at the cold meat. 'Not exactly what you call gourmet grub, is it?'

'If it isn't good enough you know what to do, don't you?' Zoe seated herself at the end of the table and began to hack slices from the French loaf on a board beside her. She looked up as Patrick walked in.'Oh, there you are. We were beginning to wonder if it was something we'd said.'

Ignoring his mother's sarcasm, Patrick pulled out his chair, looking with disdain at the food on his plate. 'If I'd known it was going to be cold as well as late, I could have got myself something,' he said. 'I've got a date at seven.'

'Anyone we know?' Tom looked up cheekily.

'None of us would have objected if you'd prepared the meal yourself, seeing you were anxious for it to be on time,' Zoe put in. 'I was just saying — I don't know why you all have to wait for *me* to put food in front of you. Sometimes I think you'd all starve if I wasn't here.'

It was an old argument and went over Patrick's head as he applied himself to his food.

Tom repeated his question: 'I said, anyone we know?'

Patrick gave his younger brother a baleful look. 'Mind your own business.'

'Bet it's that friend of Alison's,' Tom said. 'You know she's still a school kid, don't you?'

Zoe looked up. 'She isn't, is she?'

Patrick sighed. 'No, she isn't. As a matter of fact, Elaine is almost eighteen and a student.'

'Ah, so it *is* her,' Tom said triumphantly. 'Mmm, jail bait if ever I saw it. Those quiet, mouse-like little creatures are always the worst, you know. Get them on their own and they burst into flames and singe the pants off you.'

'Tom ...' Red shot him a warning look. 'Eat your dinner and shut up.'

'That's right,' Zoe said. 'I will not have you speaking to each other in that disgusting way at the table. By the way, have you seen the state of that sodding kitchen?' She looked at her husband. 'You'll have to have a word with Toby. He wanders down for drinks and snacks at all hours of the day and night and leaves everything for some other bloody fool to wash up. It's like a pigsty in there. I don't know how many times I've asked you to speak to him.'

Red gave a short laugh. 'Come off it, Zoe. The lads are off to France next week and they won't be back until after the vac'.

107

Anyway, you know that one of *your* blistering lectures would be enough to make them all toe the line for at least a month. So why ask me to wield authority?'

'Because *you* are supposed to be the man of the house.' She threw down her napkin exasperatedly. 'Why is it that nothing ever gets done in this bloody house unless *I* do it?' she demanded. 'Why do I have to be the ogre as well as the flaming dog's-body around here? I'm an artist, damn it. Not a bloody seaside landlady.'

Tom chuckled through a mouthful of salad. 'Children, children.' He rapped the handle of his fork on the table. 'I will not have you speaking to each other in that disgusting way at the table.'

'Sorry, I'm off − late already.' Patrick rose from the table and made a hasty escape. No wonder the family only assembled to eat together once a day. It was more than enough for him. It was a wonder they didn't all suffer from chronic ulcers. He wondered about Elaine's home life. There was just her and her mother, he knew that much. Her mother ran the little boutique in Prince Regent Street; the one with the twee name: 'Style 'N' Grace'. He pictured the set-up; calm and quiet. A tidy well-ordered house, serene meal times with polite conversation. He sighed. What Elaine had found so romantic and fascinating about the Carne household, he didn't know. She should try living in it for a week or so.

He had surprised himself by feeling ridiculously pleased at the prospect of being with her again. After the party he'd hesitated about asking her out. She wasn't like the girls he was used to at college. He'd known somehow that the casual approach wasn't for her; she felt things deeply, he'd sensed that. A relationship would mean more to her than to most girls. She'd be easily hurt so she'd need careful handling. Could he cope with that? Did he really want to? He wondered too about her mother. Grace Wendover looked modern enough. He'd met her once in Red's shop, picking over the things in his bargain basket − looking for props for her window displays. She was a slender good-looking woman, and fashionably dressed. But there was a certain reserve about her that was reflected in Elaine and he wondered if she might perhaps be a little over-protective of her daughter. He'd still been wondering whether or not to ask Elaine out when he'd run into her in the town the day before yesterday. They'd had coffee together and he'd impulsively suggested a trip down the river. Her dark eyes had sparkled up at him radiantly as she'd accepted. Now he found his footsteps hastening towards their meeting place with more anticipation than he had felt for a long time over a girl.

108

Elaine lay back in the punt, watching Patrick. It was a warm evening and he had taken off his shirt, revealing a strong, tanned torso. He was broader and more muscular than he looked with his shirt on and as he propelled the punt expertly along she watched his rippling muscles with silent admiration. Since the party she'd wished and wished that he would telephone to ask her out and she'd almost given up hope when they met in town. For the first time she found that there was something she couldn't share with Alison. The other girl just would not have understood the way she felt about Patrick. She was so brash about boys, fancying someone different each week. And none of them seemed to mean any more to her than a casual fling. Elaine supposed that this was the way it should be. At seventeen one should be carefree. But somehow for her it didn't work that way. Since the first moment she'd seen Patrick she'd known she was destined to fall in love with him. Looking up at him, she could hardly believe that someone as sophisticated and worldly would actually want to take her out. Of course she had lied a little about her age, but even so ...

With older boys she always felt so gauche and tongue-tied, but Patrick managed to make her feel completely at ease. He laughed with her rather than at her, so that she didn't feel foolish; he informed, rather than corrected her so that she didn't feel she was being patronised. But the best of all was the way he looked at her – making her feel like a woman – an attractive, sophisticated, desirable woman. It was a heady feeling. It made her feel so happy, light as a bubble and high as a kite.

'Watch the branches.' Patrick crouched as the punt floated through a curtain of willow fronds and came to rest against the bank with a gentle bump. He tied up carefully and then, from under the seat, drew out the basket he had brought. He took out a bottle of wine, glasses and some biscuits.

'Shall we get out on to the bank? The grass is quite dry.'

He helped Elaine out and together they arranged the rug and cushions to make a comfortable place in which to take their refreshment.

Elaine looked around her. Under the willow tree the light was soft and muted. Dappled green and gold shadows danced on the grass. It was like a little private world all their own. She took the glass of wine Patrick poured for her and sipped. It was a little warm, but sweet and heady. Nothing had ever tasted quite so delicious. Patrick touched his glass to hers and smiled into her eyes.

'Here's to you, Elaine,' he said with a smile.

'No, to you. To your future.' She drank. 'London is a long way off,' she added wistfully. 'And The Slade sounds terribly grand.' She looked at him over the rim of her glass. 'I suppose you have to be very talented to get in there?'

'Oh, *very*.' He laughed. 'I did have to take an entrance exam,' he added. 'But it wasn't too much of a problem. London is no distance really. You can get there in no time on a fast train. Will you come up and see me?'

She felt the warm colour in her cheeks. 'You'll meet all sorts of people once you get there,' she said. 'You'll forget all about your Cambridge friends.'

'Maybe I will.' He took the half empty glass out of her hand and put it to one side. 'But you see I don't count you as one of my Cambridge friends. You're different – unique.'

Mesmerised by the fathomless blue eyes she slipped willingly into his arms. The skin of his cheek felt smooth against hers and she reached up to twine her fingers in the strong fair hair. His mouth was sweet on hers. He kissed her once briefly, then again, this time gently parting her lips with the tip of his tongue. For a moment Elaine stiffened slightly, but Patrick murmured against the corner of her mouth:

'Relax, darling. Let me kiss you properly.'

She did as he said, letting her lips part for him, allowing him to explore her mouth. She grew bolder, responding, finding a pleasure more intoxicating than she could ever have envisaged in the sensual intimacy of his mouth. A delicious, tingling sensation that began in the pit of her stomach, spread through her until every nerve in her body sang and vibrated with delight. They kissed for a while, then Patrick released her to pour more wine. She lay back against the cushions, dreamily trying to decide whether the heady feeling making her feel so marvellous was caused by the wine or his kisses.

They ate the biscuits. Elaine wasn't hungry but Patrick said she would get tipsy if she didn't eat something. He knows everything. He's wonderful, she told herself as she happily munched. They talked about everything under the sun. Elaine found that Patrick shared many of her own feelings about things. Opinions she'd never dared to express before in case people laughed. Patrick didn't laugh. He leaned over her, resting on one elbow, studying her face intently as she spoke. With one finger he traced the curve of her cheek, the line of her jaw, the slenderness of her neck. Her trusting naivety aroused and excited him far more than the flirtatious tricks most girls used. She wore a denim skirt and a white sleeveless top with tiny buttons down the front. Very slowly and carefully he began to undo them.

Morgan sat on the settee at the flat, looking relaxed. He'd had two glasses of Grace's best sherry and it had loosened his tongue in the way that she had hoped it might. If she were to work with this young man, she wanted to know more about him.

'So you come from a farming family?' she said.

He nodded. 'My father and his two brothers all farm. Near Cardigan Bay.'

'And you never wanted to follow in their footsteps?'

'No. I have three brothers and two sisters, all older than me. I'm twenty-six. They've all taken to the farming.' He glanced ruefully at her. 'I'm the odd one out.'

Grace nodded. 'I know how that feels. I was the eldest of five. I left home when I was seventeen.'

'When I announced that I wanted to take up art and design I might as well have confessed to a murder. My dad wouldn't hear of it, so I had to work on the farm until I'd saved enough money to see myself through.' Morgan fell silent, his face thoughtful. 'My mother always encouraged me, mind. But she died the year I left school,' he said quietly.

'My mother died young too,' Grace said sympathetically.

'My father is a lay preacher: Methodist.' Morgan looked up, forcing himself to laugh. 'You know the kind of thing – Hellfire and brimstone.'

Grace knew only too well. The mere word 'Methodist' made her heart begin to thud, but she said nothing.

'It's funny,' he went on. 'Religious people are supposed to be loving and forgiving, but my father couldn't forgive me.'

'For not farming?' Grace asked gently. 'Or for dropping out of college?'

'For anything. I told you, I was the odd one out. In more ways than one. The runt of the litter – the bad apple. It's only on sufferance that he lets me buy his wool.' He sighed. 'But you don't want to hear about me.'

'Yes I do. Where do you live?'

'Now, you mean? I've got this little bed-sit in Rowan Street,' he told her. 'It's not much. The only view is of the cemetery.' He laughed. 'That's a piece of irony that my dad would enjoy. But I have the use of the kitchen so food doesn't cost me much. As for the view – when I'm not out hawking my stuff around, I'm busy working, so it doesn't bother me too much.'

111

'How do you manage about your washing?' asked practical Grace.

'There's a bathroom that four of us share,' he said. 'I wash my smalls in there. Other things, I take to the launderette.' He shook his head. 'It's washing myself that's the problem. The bathroom's a lean-to affair and in winter the water freezes before you've finished filling the bath.'

Grace shuddered. 'It doesn't sound very comfortable. Can't you find anything better?'

Morgan shrugged. 'Nothing I could afford. You know how difficult it is to find accommodation here.'

They talked on till the summer evening light faded and Grace had to switch on the light and draw the curtains. She found that she liked Morgan Owen. He was one of the few men she felt easy with. In some strange indefinable way he reminded her of Harry as he had been when they first met – in the days when she had trusted him too; he reminded her of herself too. But when Grace had risen to switch on the light Morgan looked at his watch.

'Oh, dear. I hadn't noticed the time. I'm afraid I've outstayed my welcome. I'll say goodnight, Mrs Wendover. And many thanks for a pleasant evening.' He rose to leave, and it was only then that Grace remembered Elaine. It had been a little after seven when she'd left and it was now almost half-past ten. She'd been gone almost three and a half hours. Immediately visions of capsizing boats and thrashing figures filled her mind. Morgan saw the colour leave her face and asked: 'Is anything wrong?'

'It's Elaine,' she said, her voice trembling. 'I hadn't realised it was so late.'

'Can I do anything?'

Grace's heart was thudding with alarm. Elaine had never been out this late before. Surely they couldn't still be on the river at this hour?

'No – no, it's all right,' she said. 'I'll ring her friend's house. I expect the girls have been playing records and forgotten the time.'

Lugging his case downstairs Morgan said: 'Shall I get in touch again in about a week?'

'Yes, do that,' Grace said abstractedly, her mind still on Elaine.

As they reached the bottom of the stairs Morgan turned and saw the anxious look on her face. He laid a hand on her arm. 'Mrs Wendover, please let me help. I feel partly responsible. If it hadn't been for me, you'd have noticed how late it was getting. If you know where she might have gone I could look for her.'

Grace looked up into the concerned hazel eyes. He meant it. He

112

really wanted to help. But before she could reply they both heard the sound of running footsteps on the pavement outside. As Grace opened the door Elaine almost tumbled in.

'Where have you been?' Grace demanded.

Morgan cleared his throat. 'Well, I'll be off then. Goodnight, Mrs Wendover.'

Relief had turned Grace's anxiety into anger. 'Mr Owen here was just about to come and look for you. What have you been doing till this time of night?'

Elaine's face was crimson. 'It's only half-past ten,' she said. 'I'm not a child, Mum. All the other girls stay out much later.' She glanced at Morgan who was standing awkwardly by, shifting the heavy suitcase from one hand to the other. What did *he* want — standing there gawping at her humiliation?

'Please don't let us keep you, Mr Owen,' she said sharply.

Outraged by her daughter's rudeness, Grace shot Morgan an apologetic look and drew Elaine inside, closing the door firmly. 'How dare you speak to Mr Owen like that?' she demanded. 'And you haven't answered my question yet. Where have you been?'

'I told you — in a boat.' Elaine turned and clattered up the stairs, her eyes filling with tears. It had been a wonderful evening; the most perfect of her whole life. All she wanted to do was to shut herself in her room, lie on her bed with closed eyes and re-live every ecstatic moment of it. But now her mother was ruining it all.

'In a *boat* — till this time of night?'

'We had supper. We just didn't notice the time, that's all. It's summer anyway. It's hardly dark even now.'

'That's not the point. If you were going to be late, you could have telephoned.'

'Oh, yes. The river bank is *full* of telephone boxes.'

A chill gripped Grace's heart. There was something alarmingly different about Elaine tonight; a new brashness; a defiance she'd never displayed before. It frightened her. As she moved closer to her she could detect something on her breath too — the sweetness of alcohol. A bolt of pain shot through her as she remembered that terrible night, years ago when her father had smelt the whisky Harry had bought her on her breath. She remembered it all with such vivid clarity that the breath caught in her throat and her stomach tightened. It had all been so innocent, yet her father had suspected the worst; had beaten her within an inch of her life. She closed her eyes and swayed slightly as the horror of the frenzied attack assailed her as though it had happened only yesterday. Elaine's hand shot out, her eyes wide with alarm.

113

'Mummy, are you all right?'

'Yes, I'm fine.' Grace pulled herself together quickly. It was years since she had allowed that memory to invade her mind. 'I'm sorry I was cross, darling. I was worried about you, that's all. I know you'd never − I know − know you're sensible.'

Still shaking, she sat down suddenly on the settee. Elaine sank down beside her, taking her hand. 'Mummy, you look terribly pale. Let me make you a cup of tea.'

Grace waved her concern aside. 'No, I'm all right. It's a warm evening and Morgan − Mr Owen − and I have been talking. I may just be a little excited, because I think I've found a gem, darling. A real gem.'

Chapter Nine

Grace sat in the passenger seat of Bryan's car, moodily watching the flat fenland landscape as it flashed past.

He glanced at her. 'All right, my dear?' She'd hardly spoken a word since they set off for London twenty minutes ago and he was beginning to wonder if it was something he'd said.

'I'm so sorry about Elaine and her friend,' she said for the fourth time. 'I don't know what gets into young people these days. When I was her age a visit to a London theatre would have been a dream come true.'

Bryan shrugged good-naturedly. 'It doesn't matter a bit. You and I will have just as good a time on our own, eh?'

'That isn't the point. It's so rude,' Grace said. 'And after you've paid all that money for the seats.'

'Don't give it another thought. It's for a good cause,' Bryan said. 'When we get there I'll give the two spare tickets back. They might be able to raise more money on them. No harm done.'

Grace fell into an uneasy silence. Elaine's last minute refusal to accompany her and Bryan to the charity concert was completely beyond her. Some of her favourite pop stars would be appearing and Grace had been under the impression that she had been looking forward to it. She had even offered to let her choose a new dress from the last of the summer stock in the shop. Yet apparently she preferred to go to one of those puppet plays at the Carnes' tatty barn theatre instead. It didn't make any sense to her at all.

'But you know we may not be back till the small hours of the morning,' she'd warned when she'd realised she was losing the battle.

'That's all right. I can stay the night at Alison's.'

'Are you sure her mother doesn't mind? And what about Alison? Bryan invited her to the concert too. She might want to go.'

'She doesn't.'

Grace had shaken her head. 'Well, I don't know, I really don't. The chance of a lifetime. All your favourite stars — those that aren't appearing will probably be in the audience. Bryan had to move heaven and earth to get tickets. And you two turn it down as though it were some — some village hall concert or something.'

Elaine had sighed in the irritatingly arrogant way she'd acquired lately. 'Don't go *on* about it, Mum. What's the use of going when I'll hate every minute? Anyway, you know I can't stand Bryan. Neither can you if you're honest.'

'That isn't true. You and I owe Bryan a lot,' Grace admonished. 'If it weren't for him I don't know where we'd be today, so don't you talk about him like that.'

'Okay, so we owe him. That doesn't mean we have to *like* him, does it?' Elaine had replied.

Grace turned to look at Bryan. He had squeezed his portly figure into a dinner jacket for the occasion. At least that was better than the awful casuals he had taken to wearing lately. A man of his size in jeans — it was positively embarrassing. She had chosen a sleeveless shift in black chiffon for the occasion. It was embroidered with silver beads and sequins and was from one of her favourite fashion houses. Her hair was newly styled too, and she'd really been looking forward to this evening. What Elaine had said about Bryan was partly true, but he had been more than generous to her since the row with Margaret and she felt she owed it to him to co-operate and show her appreciation. If only Elaine hadn't been so awkward about it.

'The new agreement came from your solicitor on Friday,' she said to Bryan's profile.

He smiled. 'Good. I hope you've read it carefully. Mustn't sign anything you don't completely understand, my dear.'

'Yes, I read it carefully,' Grace assured him. She slightly resented the way he always treated her as though she were a 'little woman', incapable of understanding anything to do with business. 'I read it carefully, signed it and posted it back,' she said firmly. 'I'm very grateful to you, Bryan.'

One pudgy hand left the wheel to pat her bare arm damply. 'Not at all, my dear. My pleasure.'

'There are one or two changes I'd like to make at the shop — if that's all right. There's this young Welshman I've come across. He designs and makes wonderful knitwear. I know I haven't sold knitwear before but I believe he has a very bright future and I'd like to give him a start by selling his work.'

116

'Just as you like, my dear.' He glanced at her. 'I told you — nothing to do with me. The business is all yours now. I was never Margaret's actual partner, you know. More of a sleeping partner really.'

Grace shot a quick look at him to see if the double entendre had been intentional, but he went on unsmilingly: 'I have my own business to attend to. As far as I'm concerned I'm your landlord and nothing else.' He turned to bestow a benevolent smile on her. 'Except your friend, of course. I hope I'll always be that.'

'Naturally.' She shifted uneasily in the expensive leather seat, wishing that Elaine and Alison had come with them.

'And may I say how lovely you're looking this evening?'

Grace cringed slightly. It was the third time he'd said it. 'Thank you, Bryan. You look very nice yourself.'

They had just passed the sign that said: 'Bishop Stortford Welcomes Careful Drivers' when the car began to bump and swerve. Bryan slammed on the brakes, uttering a four letter expletive that made Grace colour in embarrassment. He pulled into the grass verge and switched off the engine.

'I'm afraid we've got a flat,' he said. 'I'll have to change the wheel. It's a damned nuisance when I'm dressed to go out for the evening, but it can't be helped.'

'Can I do anything?' she asked uncertainly.

He shook his head. 'Just sit tight. It shouldn't take a jiff.'

But it seemed to take an inordinately long time. Grace listened as Bryan fussed and fumed, muttering under his breath as he jacked up the car and unscrewed the bolts that held the wheel. Opening the boot he lifted out the spare wheel and trundled it round to the front. Then she heard him swear again. A moment later his face, crimson with exertion, appeared at her window.

'Bloo — blasted spare's flat too,' he said. 'I'll have to find a garage. Will you be all right while I look for a phone?'

'Of course.' Grace looked at her watch. They were going to be late. 'Are you sure I can't do anything?'

'No. Just you stay there. I'll ask at one of those houses over there if I can use the phone.'

It was the best part of an hour before a mechanic arrived in a van. He got out and assessed the situation gloomily.

'Nothing I can do here, sir. Have to take your spare down to the workshop and repair it there.'

'How long will that take?' Bryan asked.

The man scratched his head. 'Well now . . .'

'We're supposed to be in London for eight o'clock. A special

117

occasion as you can see.' He flicked a speck of dust off the lapel of his dinner jacket.

'Oh, ah?' The man seemed unimpressed.

Bryan extracted his wallet and extracted a five pound note, crinkling it pointedly.

The mechanic's face cleared. 'Well, shouldn't be too much of a problem, sir. Say an hour?'

'I'd rather say *half* an hour myself,' Bryan said. 'Still have best part of an hour's drive to do and then there's parking.'

Well, I dunno, sir,' the man said doubtfully. 'I'll do my best but with the best will in the world, I reckon you're going to be late now.'

Bryan sighed. 'Oh, all right then. We'll wait. Just do the best you can.' When the man had driven off with the offending wheel, Bryan looked at Grace. 'How about a drink and maybe a bite to eat while we're waiting? There's a nice little pub just down the road.'

Grace opened the car door and got out. Anything was better than being shut up in a car with Bryan for an hour.

Elaine lay on Patrick's bed staring at the ceiling. 'You can always come here whenever you want to,' he had said. 'It doesn't matter whether I'm here or not. The front door's always open.'

She found the Carnes' house with its clutter and dust, its unwritten laws of privacy, totally seductive. Here no one asked questions. The family and boarders came and went as they pleased, bringing in their individual friends, throwing impromptu parties, organising panic-stricken cramming sessions at the end of term. Anything was possible at the Carnes'. One of the nicest parts was that although there was always something going on, no one expected you to join in unless you felt like it. To Elaine it was sheer bliss — the epitome of freedom.

This evening she was waiting for Patrick. She knew he'd be home at seven and she wanted to surprise him. She'd thought long and hard about what he wanted her to do. She felt slightly ashamed of her initial reluctance. It was a tremendous compliment really. Patrick said she was still hide-bound by convention. He had gently teased her about that more than once. It was the kind of upbringing she'd had, she told herself. Her mother had never quite broken free of her Victorian background. But Elaine was trying hard to turn herself into a liberated young woman of the sixties with the freedom to do her own thing. And if anyone could help her do it, it was the Carnes and especially Patrick.

Already she felt far more sophisticated than when she'd first met

118

him. She still couldn't understand what he had seen in her then. She must have seemed such a child in her prissy little dresses and bubbly hairstyle. As she lay there lazily gazing at the abstract mural on the opposite wall she listened to the sounds of the house. It was quieter now that most of the boarders had gone off for the vac', but someone somewhere was playing records. The Beachboys; The Beatles; The Who. At the moment the soaring voice of Julie Andrews was proclaiming that the hills were alive with the sound of music. Elaine closed her eyes, smiling reminiscently. She loved that one. She and Alison had been to see the film and they had both wept buckets in the sad bits. Patrick's taste in music was more sophisticated. He liked the folk groups; the 'protest' songs of Joan Baez and Bob Dylan. The music stopped abruptly and she heard Tom's voice shouting down the stairs, demanding to know the whereabouts of his clean shirts. Zoe's voice floated stridently back: 'Find your own bloody shirts. I'm your mother, not your *slave*.'

Elaine smiled. Poor Zoe, always trying hard to establish her artistic status; constantly fighting a losing battle against domesticity.

Her eyelids grew heavy and she must have fallen asleep in the drowsy summer afternoon heat. That was how Patrick found her when he came home, lying on his bed, her tanned arms and legs spread, the thin cotton shift dress she wore making her look almost childlike. Her dark lashes fanned out on cheeks rosy with sleep and her mouth was soft and vulnerable. Very gently he sat down beside her and stroked her cheek with one fingertip. She woke instantly, the dark eyes dreamily unfocussed for a second as she looked up at him. Then a delighted smile lifted the corners of her mouth and she sat up and stretched luxuriously.

'Patrick, you're back.' She slid her arms around his neck.

Her trusting naivety never failed to touch him and he held her close, nuzzling his lips into her neck. 'What a nice surprise. So you didn't go to the charity concert?'

She held her head back to look at him. 'Do me a favour. Would *you* have done?'

He shrugged. 'I might. It did sound rather good.'

'You haven't met Bryan Bostock,' she told him, pulling a face. 'Mum might feel she has to butter him up, but I don't see why I should. Anyway, I'd much rather be with you.' She brushed her cheek against his. 'I've got something to tell you — I've decided.'

'Decided what?'

'You know — what you asked me. I've made up my mind. I'll do it.'

119

He held her away from him to look searchingly into her eyes. 'Elaine, that's great. But are you sure?'

'I told you, yes.'

'When?'

'Now if you like.'

He hugged her tightly to him and kissed her. 'Mmmm, you're marvellous. Did I ever tell you that before?' Getting up, he crossed the room and turned the key in the lock.

'I thought doors were never locked in this house,' she remarked.

Turning, he grinned at her. 'There are exceptions to every rule.'

She watched as he began to prepare. 'Shall I undress?' she asked.

It was almost nine-thirty by the time Grace and Bryan arrive at The Palladium. Their tickets were for front stalls and the usherette wouldn't allow them to take their seats until the act that was performing was finished. Standing in the aisle, Grace looked at the glittering assembly and wished they could have been on time. Ever since she had been to the local variety theatre with Harry all those years ago she had wanted to go to a West End theatre. Looking round she was sure she recognised one or two famous film stars. Bryan was muttering. His mood had deteriorated more and more since the business with the tyre.

While they were waiting they had eaten bar snacks in the pub, as it was becoming increasingly obvious that there wouldn't be time for the dinner Bryan had planned. Grace had felt embarrassingly conspicuous, sitting in the bar dressed in all her finery and eating chicken-in-the-basket. The locals had gazed at them curiously over frothing pint mugs, making her feel like some rare and exotic animal.

The mechanic had taken much longer than even he had estimated and when they had at last reached London there had been terrible difficulty in finding a parking space. They had finished up miles from the theatre, looking for a taxi to get them there.

'Now the blooming girl says there are no programmes left,' Bryan fumed beside her. 'I don't know, I don't really. This evening has been a damned disaster from start to finish.'

Grace patted his arm. 'None of it was your fault, Bryan. At least we're here now, so let's enjoy it. We don't need a programme. It'll be more of a surprise without.'

The troup of acrobats from the Moscow State Circus finished their routine with a daring balancing trick and left the stage to thunderous applause. Very hurriedly Grace and Bryan took

120

their seats. As the orchestra struck up again he leaned across to her.

'I got you a box of chocolates and now I've gone and left the bugg — left them in the car.'

She smiled. 'Don't worry. I'm fine. Just relax.'

The next act was a popular comedian, well known for his television programme. His patter soon had them both relaxing and Bryan laughed loudly and heartily at his jokes.

The comedian brought the first half of the show to a close. The curtain came down and the lights went up. Bryan looked at Grace.

'What about a drink? I don't know about you but I could do with one.'

The bar was crowded and Bryan had to shoulder his way through the crush to get served. When he returned with two lukewarm gin and tonics he was red in the face and his dress shirt collar clung limply to his perspiring neck. No sooner had they downed the drinks than the buzzer sounded for curtain up and the crowd began to wend its way back. Bryan looked at Grace.

'All bloody go, if you'll pardon my French,' he said, taking her empty glass. 'Better get back, I suppose — missed nearly half of it as it is.'

Most of the audience had returned to their seats by the time Grace and Bryan arrived back in the auditorium. Apologising, they picked their way along the row and settled down. The orchestra had already started to play the signature tune of the act opening the second half and now the curtain was rising on a stage empty but for a white grand piano backed by a single black satin drape. A man in evening dress sat at the piano and a beautiful girl with honey-gold skin stood beside him, one hand on his shoulder. She began to sing in her melodic, husky voice: 'Where Did Our Love Go?' Grace froze. Her heart thudded suffocatingly, filling her chest so that she couldn't breathe. The girl was Stella Rainbow, the man Harry.

'I'm getting a pain in my back.' Elaine shifted her position a fraction.

'Another couple of seconds, that's all.' Patrick looked up. 'You can come and look if you like.'

Elaine stretched her stiffening limbs and sighed. 'Phew! Thank goodness for that. I never thought posing would be such hard work.' Completely uninhibited now about her nakedness, she skipped across the room to look over Patrick's shoulder at the charcoal sketch on the easel.

'Oh, do I really look like that?'

'Does that mean you don't approve?' He turned to look up at her.

'No. It's lovely. But you've made me look so rounded. I'm skinny really, aren't I?'

He glanced up at her. She really had no idea of how attractive she was. In the short time he'd known her she'd matured – the coltish young body had filled out into curves that were, in their own particular way, voluptuous. He loved the small high breasts and the rounded curve of her hips; her tight little buttocks and gently moulded stomach. Finding her closeness irrestistible, he turned and put his arms round her, pressing his face into her waist.

'Haven't you looked at yourself in the mirror lately?' he asked softly. 'You're a woman, Elaine. A very lovely and desirable one at that.'

She twined her fingers in his hair. 'It was nice – being drawn. Apart from the back ache, that is.'

'It was nice drawing you. Will you let me carry on with it – turn it into a painting?'

She frowned, biting her lip with indecision. 'Then people would see it. They'd know ...'

'Okay. Anyway, we'll stop for now.'

'I'd better get dressed, hadn't I?'

When he looked up into her eyes he saw the tremulous invitation hovering there. She still hadn't acquired the knack of hiding her feelings. Had her decision to pose nude for him included another more exciting decision? He didn't reply. Instead he stood up, holding her eyes with his. Without a word he took her in his arms and kissed her; a long, slow, searching kiss. Her response told him all he wanted to know.

On his bed under the sloping ceiling in the dancing haze of the late summer afternoon he took her as gently as he could. At first she was tense and apprehensive, but slowly under the sensuous coaxing of his hand and lips her inhibitions melted away and she began to surprise and delight him with her burgeoning passion. Afterwards they lay together, her head in the hollow of his shoulder, dreamily watching the shadows on the ceiling. The minutes ticked by, then suddenly Elaine rolled over, leaning on her elbow to look down at him.

'Can we do it again, please?'

He laughed. 'Soon. Mustn't be greedy, must we?'

She bit her lip. 'It's just that I don't think I – not quite ... Maybe next time' She traced the outline of his lips with her forefinger. 'Patrick – was it all right? For you, I mean. Was I ...?'

122

'You were gorgeous.' He pulled her over him and kissed her.

'Patrick,' she said after a moment.

'Yes?'

'Can I stay the night?'

'What?' He opened his eyes wide to stare at her. 'What about your mother?'

'She's going to be late back. I told her I was staying at Alison's. I was going to, but we had a row.'

'That's not like you and Alison. What was it about?'

'The concert.' She pouted. 'I hadn't told her about it till it was too late, you see. I think — well, I *know* — she would have liked to go.'

'Oh, Elaine.' He rolled her over and looked down at her, shaking his head. 'What am I going to do with you? You're getting a very devious little thing, aren't you? Am I a bad influence on you?'

She giggled and began to stroke his thigh, her fingers fluttering up and down seductively. 'Yes, you are — and I *love* it.'

Her caressing soon aroused him again and they made love for a second time. This time they were both more relaxed and Elaine wished it could go on for ever. She knew now without the slightest shadow of doubt that she was in love with Patrick. He had said she was a woman — a desirable woman — and she wanted to prove him right. She wanted so much to please him, to make him want and need her as she needed him. Arching against him she moved instinctively. The first time had hurt, but now it was wonderful, as smooth and sensuous as silk. She could feel the excitement growing inside her. The blood seemed to sing in her veins and her heart raced. As Patrick's movements quickened her excitement grew, mounting until she felt it was almost more than she could bear. She clutched feverishly at his shoulders, arching her back convulsively and calling his name. Then suddenly, a great wave of sensation swept through her. It seemed to engulf her from top to toe, make her gasp and shudder with ecstasy. Feeling her climax Patrick thrust twice more, then lay still on top of her.

'Clever girl. You got there,' he whispered triumphantly. 'You came. Was it good?'

'Oh, yes — *yes*.' She turned her head to look at him as he rolled away from her. 'Oh, Patrick,' she whispered. 'I love you. I love you so *much*.'

In the taxi Grace shivered violently. Bryan didn't know what to do. He took off his jacket and put it round her shoulders.

'Are you all right? Do you think you ought to go to a hospital — see a doctor or something?' he asked anxiously.

She shook her head. 'No. Please don't fuss, Bryan. I'll be fine in a minute.' But in the darkness he could see the gleam of her eyes — like a frightened animal — and hear the uncontrollable chattering of her teeth.

'What is is though, love? Have you had one of these attacks before?'

She shook her head, turning away from him to stare out of the window. In her mind she could still see them, Harry and that woman. Stella had worn a skintight dress of flame-coloured silk; her shapely honey-coloured shoulders bare; her long dark hair caught back with a sparkling diamante clip. When she sang she had looked at Harry with a meaningful look in her eyes that was more than mere artistry. All Grace could think about was what they must do together when they were alone. The thought filled her with revulsion — strangely, for herself more than for them. Over the past five years her hate for the woman she had never met and her resentment of Harry had faded. She'd made a new life; a successful one. It didn't matter any more. Both she and Harry had got what they wanted and that was better than making each other miserable. She'd even wondered lately whether she ought to divorce him after all. But seeing him — seeing them together like that — so suddenly and unexpectedly, had been a terrible shock. All the old agonising trauma had re-surfaced with more power to hurt than ever before.

The taxi stopped and they got out. When Bryan had paid, they found the car and Grace climbed gratefully into the passenger seat. She took off Bryan's jacket and gave it back to him.

'Put this on, Bryan,' she said. 'You'll catch cold. I'll be all right with the heater on.'

Without a word he opened the glove compartment and took out a silver flask. Unscrewing the top he passed it to her. 'Go on, have a good swig. It'll make you feel better.'

'What is it?' She sniffed at the flask.

'Brandy.'

She drank a little. It made her splutter, but he was right; it did help, calming her raw nerves and slowing her rapid heartbeat.

As the powerful car ate up the miles on the almost empty roads she said nothing. Just stared out at the darkness trying to shut out the shameful images that tormented her. Bryan had been right when he'd said earlier that the whole evening was a disaster. Nothing had gone right from the beginning. The one thing she was grateful for was that Elaine hadn't been with them. She never mentioned her

124

father now. He sent cards at Christmas and birthdays, but other than that there was no communication between them at all. For that at least she was grateful.

It was after midnight when Bryan brought the Jaguar to a standstill in the little lane behind the shop. The very least she could do was ask him in for a nightcap, she told herself reluctantly. He had the drive home again to face.

'Come up and have a coffee, Bryan,' she said. 'I'll see if I can rustle up something to eat too if you're hungry.'

'I wouldn't dream of putting you to the trouble after your nasty little turn, my dear,' he said. But already he was getting out of the car.

Upstairs in the flat Grace switched on the lights and filled the kettle. 'If you don't mind, I think I'll just go and change,' she told him. 'I don't want to spill anything down this dress. Make yourself at home.'

By the time she re-emerged in her housecoat the kettle was boiling. She made coffee and quickly cut a ham sandwich for Byran. When she carried it through to the living room she saw that his jacket was draped across the back of the settee where he sat in his shirt sleeves. A wave of revulsion swept over her as she noticed the dark sweat stains under the arms.

'Are you quite sure you're all right now?' he asked, sipping the coffee.

Feeling she owed him an explanation she said: 'Perhaps I'd better tell you what happened, Bryan. Stella Rainbow's pianist is my husband. Until tonight I hadn't set eyes on him for the past five years.'

He stared at her, the ham sandwich halfway to his open mouth. 'Your *husband*? Well! I knew he'd gone off with some singer, of course, but I thought he was abroad.'

'So did I. But you know what these artists are − here today, the other side of the world tomorrow. If I'd known . . .'

'Oh, my dear. If *I'd* known, I'd never have taken you. It must have been a terrible shock.'

'It was.'

There was a pause, then he put down his cup and edged closer to her on the settee. 'It must be very difficult for a woman like yourself − managing without a man. I − er − I daresay you still miss him.'

She shook her head firmly. 'No. We're better apart. We didn't share the same interests.'

His large face sagged dolefully. 'Ah, I know so well what you

125

mean. It's the same with me and my wife. She's not the slightest interest in me as a man. It's been the great sadness of my life.' He reached for her hand and squeezed it. 'Now *you* – you're a very different kind of woman; sensitive, intelligent ...' He cast a coy glance in her direction. 'Beautiful too. Oh, yes ...' He took her shake of the head for modesty. 'Yes, you are. Margaret now ...' He pursed his lips. 'Good-hearted, I grant you, but she can be very crude at times. She hasn't your good taste, Grace. No, she can be very crude, can Margaret.'

Grace looked pointedly at her watch. 'It's very late, Bryan. I don't want to push you out but I'm thinking of your long drive home.'

'What have I to go home for?' he asked gloomily. 'My wife couldn't care less whether I'm there or not.'

'I'm sure that's not true.' Grace edged away but found herself trapped by the arm of the settee.

'I'm going to make a little confession to you, Grace.' Bryan slipped an arm around her shoulders and she caught a whiff of expensive talc mingled with male sweat from his shirt. It almost made her gag. 'I've always been very attracted to you, but seeing you so upset tonight, all trembling and helpless, brought out all the protective instincts in me. There's nothing I'd like better than to look after you, my dear. You know, right from the first moment I saw you, I knew that you and I had a lot in common.' He pulled her roughly against him, his other hand on her thigh. 'Come now, admit it. You felt the same, didn't you?'

Grace felt panic rising inside her. It was almost as stifling as the shock of seeing Harry. Trying to extricate herself from his claustrophobic embrace she said: 'Look, Bryan, I like and respect you very much. You're ...'

'There, I knew it.' He aimed a kiss in the direction of her mouth. It slipped off her cheek as she turned her head. 'Aw, come on, Grace. Don't be shy with me. I believe you're teasing?' he added archly. 'That's not fair, you know. You can't pull the wool over my eyes. You've been encouraging me all evening.' He leered into her face and the large hand closed over her thigh again, squeezing painfully. 'Come on now – do you think I didn't guess why you took your frock off?'

She dashed his hand away and broke free to stand up, trembling as she tried to swallow the disgust that rose like bile in her throat. 'Please go, Bryan,' she said shakily. 'I'm sorry if I've somehow managed to give you the wrong impression. But I'd really like you to go – *now*, please.'

126

Slowly he stood up and stood staring at her for a long moment, his eyes narrowed and his fleshy mouth pinched meanly. 'So ...' he said at last. 'Margaret was right about you. She always said you were a frigid bitch. I didn't believe it. I thought she was jealous because she knew I fancied you. You looked to me like a right little fireball. The cool, quiet ones usually are. Perhaps you would be for the right man. Perhaps you *are*, eh?' He leered at her unpleasantly. 'So who is he then? This man with the knitting needles? Sounds a right pansy, but perhaps that's what you fancy.'

She shuddered. This was the last straw. It was almost more than she could bear. Using every last shred of her control, she walked across the room and laid her hand pointedly on the telephone. 'Please go. I won't ask you again.'

'All right, I'm going.' He picked up his jacket and walked, scarlet-faced, to the door. When he reached it he turned. 'By the way – the new agreement on the shop. It's still quarterly, remember? That gives you till Christmas – unless you discover which side your bread is buttered before then.' Without waiting for her reply he left, slamming the door behind him.

Grace stood motionless, barely breathing as she listened to his footsteps going down the stairs. She heard the street door slam behind him and, a moment later, the Jaguar's engine starting up. Only when she heard the car roar angrily away did she unclench her fists and let out her breath. He'd gone. Thank God. It was only then that the frustrated anger pent up inside rose like a tidal wave to overwhelm her. A sound that was somewhere between a sob and a howl broke from her mouth and she screamed into the silence: '*You* brought me to all this, Harry Wendover. *I hate you. Oh God, I hate you.*' Picking up the glass paperweight she threw it with all her force at the door through which Bryan had just passed. It chipped the paint but it didn't break, merely falling to the floor with a dull thud. Sinking into a chair she sobbed till the tight coil of fury slowly unwound. But as she fumbled for a handkerchief and dabbed at her swollen eyes the words of Bryan's parting shot suddenly came back to her. 'That gives you till Christmas – unless you discover which side your bread is buttered before then.' It was only then that she recognised it as an ultimatum. He expected her to pay for his kindness by sleeping with him, as Margaret had done. If she failed to comply then she and Elaine would be out. Once again that deadly bargain. Once again she was expected to sacrifice herself to a man's revolting lust.

A vision of Stella, her hand on Harry's shoulder – of the intimate look that had passed between them – rose before her. She thought

127

of Bryan's flabby hand on her thigh — a hand so like another, long ago. She felt her flesh creep at the memory of those fingers on her skin. Her stomach heaved and clasping one hand over her mouth she scrambled to her feet and rushed to the bathroom to retch miserably into the toilet bowl. When the wave of nausea had subsided she felt exhausted but somehow cleansed. She splashed her burning face with cold water and walked on trembling legs into the kitchen to put the kettle on. A strong coffee was what she needed — coffee, and to think hard about the future. She drank it sweet, black and scalding hot, and began to feel stronger.

'Right,' she said aloud to the empty kitchen. 'We're really on our own now. It looks as though we're going to have to leave here. But we'll be all right. Somehow or other we'll be all right — because I'll never, ever, give a man the chance to ruin my life for me again. And that's a promise.'

In the room under the eaves in the silent house Elaine and Patrick slept as soundly as children, wrapped in each other's arms. The moonlight slanting down through the skylight turned their smooth young bodies to marble. On the easel the charcoal drawing of Elaine was already beginning to curl slightly at the edges. A light breeze stirred the humid air and Elaine shifted slightly, smiling in her sleep. 'I love you, Patrick,' she murmured.

Chapter Ten

'This is it, Morgan.' Grace drew the typed letter out of the pocket of her skirt and passed it across the table to him. They had finished dinner and she was pouring coffee.

'This is why I asked you to dinner this evening, while Elaine is out. I felt you should see it. It's what I've been dreading. Mr Bostock, my landlord, has decided to sell this shop.' She gave him an apologetic little smile. 'Not only the shop, but the business too.'

'Can he do that?'

'Apparently, yes. It seems that 'Style 'N' Grace' was registered in his name — a fact he conveniently forgot to mention to me. I thought I was renting the premises. It seems I was renting the business from him too.' She shook her head. 'The split with Margaret muddled everything up so. I suppose I should have read the small print more carefully. I'm sorry, Morgan.'

He read the solicitor's letter through twice, then looked up at her. 'They've given you three months' notice. And it says here that as sitting tenant you have first refusal to buy?'

'I know — but have you looked at the price he's asking?'

Morgan looked again at the letter. 'Mmm, I see what you mean?'

'He knows I don't have that kind of money.'

Morgan shook his head. 'I don't understand. Why would he do a thing like this to you? I thought you and he were old friends.'

Grace sipped her coffee thoughtfully. She was going to have to explain to Morgan. It was dreadfully embarrassing but it was only fair. It was four months since they had begun working together. After their first meeting Grace had obtained the information necessary for retailing Morgan's knitwear on a businesslike basis through acquaintances in the trade. She had also given him what advice she could. He had begun by advertising for out-workers to

129

knit his garments while he toured Wales, looking for further wool suppliers. Once he had found them he had come back to Cambridge and shut himself away to work on new designs. Meanwhile, Grace had put his garments on sale at 'Style 'N' Grace' and found them immediate best-sellers. Her customers just couldn't get enough of them and in no time at all she had sold out. As winter approached they had become even more popular. Her takings this Christmas, compared to other years, looked like trebling. Morgan now had ten out-workers and was working hard on new designs for a spring collection. When the letter had arrived from Bryan's solicitors they had been planning a fashion show to be presented in the New Year. Morgan Knitwear was to be the principal feature and Grace was sending invitations out to some of the leading fashion houses she bought from. She felt confident that they would be impressed enough to come up with orders. But with the arrival of the letter from Bryan's solicitors her hopes had crashed.

'And it's more than just the business, Morgan,' she said anxiously. 'This place had been both home and livelihood for Elaine and me for the past six years. It's going to be a wrench, leaving. Where we're going, and what I'm going to do about earning a living, I just don't know.'

Morgan raked his hand through his hair. 'I still can't understand his motive for doing a thing like this,' he said. 'The shop is doing well, so why close down? Do you think he's strapped for cash? Is he thinking of retiring maybe?'

Grace bit her lip. 'No. It's my fault,' she said quietly. 'Unfortunately, after Margaret went, Bryan developed — certain ideas about me. I can't imagine why, because God knows I never gave him any encouragement. When I made it clear that he was wrong, he gave me till Christmas to change my mind, threatening that something like this might happen if I didn't. I thought at the time that he might be bluffing. Now I know he wasn't.' She looked up at him. 'I'm sorry, Morgan.'

He was staring at her. 'Good God, Grace — if you're saying what I think you're saying you have nothing to apologise for. It's incredible. I thought that kind of thing only belonged in Victorian melodrama. I only hope you told him where to go.'

She smiled faintly. 'I did. It hasn't done us any good though, has it?'

'It might.' His face was beginning to brighten. 'Grace, how about you and me going into proper partnership — buying this place? What's to stop us?'

She smiled ruefully. 'At this price?' She tapped the letter.

'We could make him an offer — get a mortgage.'

Grace bit her lip. 'I don't know. It's a big step. You really should be trying for a bank loan of your own, to launch your business properly. You don't need me and the shop round your neck.'

'Round my neck?' He looked at her incredulously. 'Without you I'd never have got this far. We're a team, Grace. Look, why don't we make some enquiries? It couldn't hurt to ask.'

Grace hesitated. She had promised herself to stand on her own from now on; never to let another man into her life. If she went into partnership with Morgan and, at some future time, she wanted to get out of it, how could she? Over the past four months the two of them had become good friends. Morgan was the first man she had felt completely comfortable with since the early days with Harry. With him she never felt threatened or dominated. She warmed to his boyish charm — enjoyed mothering him. And she soon found that under the gentle vulnerability was a quiet, innate strength. But as the months passed and they spent more and more time together Grace felt increasingly worried that, in spite of the age difference, their closeness might one day lead Morgan to expect a relationship of a more intimate nature; something she dreaded, because quite apart from her revulsion against sex, she wanted very much for things to stay as they were. She looked up at him now. Aware that he was eagerly awaiting her reaction to his suggestion.

'We could enquire, I suppose.'

He reached across the table to touch her hand. 'Grace, what are you afraid of?'

'*Nothing*.' She snatched her hand away and, too late, heard the strident note of protest in her voice.

He smiled. 'You're afraid that I might be like old Bostock, aren't you. Might begin to consider the term "partnership" as something more personal. Is that it?' He saw the dull colour suffuse her face and gently covered her hand with his. 'Listen, Grace, I think it's only fair to put all our cards on the table. After all, I do owe my success so far to you.'

She smiled. 'It's worked both ways. I've made money too.'

But he brushed her protest aside. 'I've become very fond of you, Grace. You've become the family I've never really had. Because my own family turned against me — when they found out what I am.'

She looked up at him. 'What you are? What do you mean?'

He smiled gently. 'I think I told you before that I was the odd one out. In the eyes of the world I'm one of nature's oddities. I'm what they call "queer", "bent", and other nasty little euphemisms. Maybe

131

now you'll want to reject me too; on the other hand, knowing that might be reassuring to you.'

Very slowly Grace digested his words. Homosexuality was a grey area to her. It was something she knew very little about. But looking at Morgan's gentle, open face – knowing him as she did – she could not believe there was anything evil or wrong about it. Suddenly she began to see why she had felt such a strong affinity with him. She had instinctively identified with his isolation. He had suffered as she had. Not in quite the same way, maybe, but in the sense that they were both innocent and misunderstood. She looked at the sensitive, vulnerable face and saw the apprehension in his eyes. Suddenly her throat tightened.

'Oh, Morgan. Why didn't you tell me this before?'

He shrugged. 'It's hardly the kind of thing you introduce yourself with. There's still a stigma attached, even in the so-called swinging sixties. People think that we choose to be the way we are. They don't realise that we have no more control over it than over the colour of our eyes.'

'I know – I know. Do you have a – is there someone ...?' Grace asked tentatively.

He shook his head. 'Not now. There was someone at college but it ended – which was partly why I dropped out.' He looked up at her wistfully. 'We hurt just as badly as anyone else when things fall apart, you know. It's still love in every sense of the word. That's what most people can't, or won't, understand.' He shrugged. 'Since then there's been no one. And somehow, I don't think there ever will be.'

'I'm so sorry, Morgan,' she whispered. 'Believe me, I do know how you feel.'

'Of course. You're divorced, aren't you?'

'Not divorced – separated.' She licked her dry lips. He'd been honest with her. Now it was her turn. 'You know, you're lucky in a way. At least ...' She swallowed hard. 'At least you *know* what you are. In my case I – I couldn't respond – physically to my husband. I tried, but there was nothing I could do about it. It wasn't that I didn't love him. I did – very much. I just couldn't stand the intimate side. It got worse and worse. In the end he found someone else and left. As well as the hurt, it made me feel like some kind of freak.' She was faintly surprised at the ease with which she was able to say it to him, and at the tremendous relief talking about it brought her. It was as though a great weight had been lifted from her shoulders. Suddenly she felt light and free. Looking up at him, she added wryly: 'Maybe if I'd been more normal we wouldn't be in this mess now. Bryan was always kind to Elaine and me. Maybe I should have ...'

Instantly he was on his feet. Taking her by the elbows, he drew her up and put his arms protectively round her. 'Never let me hear you say a thing like that again, do you hear?' He held her away from him and looked into her eyes. 'Don't worry. It'll all work out for the best, I know it will. Look, Grace, now that we understand each other, now that everything is out in the open, how do you feel about a partnership? What do you say we find out whether we can get a loan and go from there?'

She looked up at him, a sudden sense of excitement and adventure lifting her heart. Here at last was someone who understood her – someone who would make no demands – someone she could even share her life with, because she wouldn't always have Elaine. 'Yes,' she said decisively. 'Yes, all right, Morgan. Let's do that.'

The Carnes' house was decked with evergreens and paper chains. The students had already left for the Christmas holidays but there was to be a party to celebrate Patrick's homecoming. Elaine hadn't seen him since half term when she, Alison and Tom had gone up to London for the day in Tom's newly acquired car – a battered pre-war, but still roadworthy Austin seven. The four of them had packed as much as they could into that one day. Patrick had taken them to Carnaby Street. It had been all the girls had imagined and more. They had treated themselves to a Union Jack tee-shirt each. In Kensington High Street all the young people had been dressed in up to the minute clothes that made them feel positively old fashioned. Here and there young men sweltered in vintage military uniforms, while, by contrast, some of the more daring girls wore see-through tops with no bras underneath. Elaine had specially wanted to visit Biba and she hadn't been disappointed. Its dark interior, with the black and gold decor, had thrilled her. She felt she could have stayed all day, listening to its throbbing pop heartbeat and looking at all the excitingly different ideas on offer.

Later they had gone to a Rolling Stones concert, then back to the flat Patrick shared with two other students in Earls Court. It was small and cramped; there was very little furniture and the walls were covered in avant-garde posters. Andy Warhol creations rubbed shoulders with Van Gogh, Monet and Renoir prints. Over the fireplace hung a framed abstract. It was made up of thousands of brightly coloured dots. Patrick came up behind Elaine as she stood looking at it.

'Like it?'

133

'I think I might go blind if I looked at it long enough,' she told him frankly.

He laughed. 'You'd better get used to it. It's here to stay. It's a Gino Severini,' he added proudly.

Elaine had never heard of Gino Severini but she loved the bright colours. She also loved the glorious disorder of the flat. It looked as though no one ever washed up or did any housework. The only thing wrong with it was that there were too many people in it. She hadn't been alone with Patrick once all day. A quick kiss when they set off for home was all she had to sustain her through the weeks that followed. That and the promise of letters and the time they would spend together at Christmas.

The eagerly awaited letters had been few and far between; full of excuses about long hours of study and lack of privacy. The weeks had dragged interminably till the end of term.

She had arrived early on the day of the party, ostensibly to help Zoe with the preparations, but really because she wanted to be there when Patrick arrived. Zoe had been busy working on a commission of two children's heads. They were to be a Christmas present for their grandparents, so it was essential for her to finish them, and stopping to prepare food for the party seemed to have put her in a bad mood. A cigarette hung from the corner of her mouth and her Indian silver bracelets jangled aggressively as she worked in the cluttered kitchen, snapping like a Jack Russell terrier at anyone who got in her way.

'Can I do anything?' Elaine ventured.

'Yes.' Zoe looked up from the pile of sandwiches she was cutting, her eyes squinting against the smoke rising from her cigarette. 'You can go and see where that lazy sod of a husband of mine is,' she said caustically, knowing perfectly well that Red was in the studio next door and could hear every word. He appeared now in the doorway, leaning against the jamb with folded arms, a negligent smile on his face. Winking at Elaine he asked: 'Did I hear someone tenderly whisper my name?'

'Yes, you bloody did,' Zoe said over her shoulder. 'I hope you've got the drinks organised.'

'Not to panic. Everything's done, blossom,' Red told her calmly. He called her 'blossom' to annoy her. It worked.

'Then take this sodding lot to the dining room.' She thrust the plate of sandwiches at him, 'And don't forget to cover them with a cloth. We don't want them curling up, do we?'

'I'll do it.' Elaine stepped forward and took the plate from Red. 'Er — what time are you expecting Patrick?'

134

Zoe shrugged. 'Who knows? He was planning to hitch a lift home. He could be here at any time.' When Elaine was out of earshot she said" 'Is Patrick sleeping with that child?'

Red looked startled. 'Good Lord, how should I know?'

'I though men were supposed to have an instinct for that kind of thing – especially where their sons were concerned,' she said, brushing crumbs from the table.

He laughed. 'I should think *sons* are the last thing any father has an instinct for,' he remarked. 'I haven't a clue what they're doing – either of them.'

'Maybe you should try to find out,' Zoe said thoughtfully. 'She's a nice girl, but terribly young. I wouldn't like to see her getting hurt – or worse still, pregnant.'

'Patrick's no fool.'

Zoe turned a baleful eye on her husband. 'Where women are concerned, all men are fools,' she said.

Alison arrived with an armful of records and she and Tom went off upstairs to sort them out. Elaine, finding that there was nothing much she could actually help with, found her way up to Patrick's room. Standing in the doorway she looked around. It looked oddly clean and un-lived in. Zoe had made up his bed with clean sheets. It looked unnaturally tidy and neat – almost clinical. She sat down carefully on the edge of it to wait.

Her first term at college had been quite enjoyable. She and Alison enjoyed most of the subjects, but while Alison was especially good at cookery, Elaine excelled more at sewing. To eke out her grant Grace had let her do alterations for the shop, which helped them both. But she had missed Patrick even more than she had expected to. His letters were scrappy and told her little. Sometimes she lay awake at night thinking about the girls he must have met. Wondering if there was anyone he liked better than her. Sometimes, especially when he didn't write, she was so convinced he had found someone else that she cried herself to sleep. There would never be anyone she loved more than Patrick. If only she could believe that he felt the same way about her.

Footsteps on the stairs brought her to her feet, her heart drumming. The door opened and there he stood in faded jeans and denim jacket, looking taller, fairer and more handsome than ever. He shrugged off his heavy back-pack, dumped it on the floor and held out his arms to her.

'Patrick!' She rushed into them, and the next moment he was kissing her as though he would never stop.

135

'God, I've missed you.' He hugged her so close she could scarcely breathe.

'I've missed you too. You didn't write much,' she admonished gently, looking up into his eyes.

'Writing isn't what I do best,' he said dismissively. 'I loved *your* letters though. Now if I could only send you pictures instead ...'

'Never mind. You're here now.' She looked up at him. 'You know there's a party for you?'

He laughed. 'I'd have been surprised and most offended if there hadn't been. God, I seem to have been on the road for ever. I suppose I'd better get out of these filthy clothes and have a bath.'

'Love me first.' She wound her arms around his neck. '*Please.*'

Laughing he encircled her waist with his hands and pulled her against him. 'There isn't really time,' he whispered, nuzzling his lips to her throat. 'But you're very hard to resist in this mood.'

She pressed close to him, her lips against his ear. 'I'm glad. We'll make time, won't we?' It's been so long, Patrick.'

She had slipped off her shoes and was twining one bare leg around his. He kissed her, his lips smiling against hers as he felt her eagerly undoing the buttons of his shirt.

Later, as she lay drowsily in his arms, she asked: 'How many other girls have you made love to since summer?'

He glanced at her. 'How would you feel if I asked you the same question?'

'I wouldn't mind. There hasn't been anyone, Patrick. There never will be.'

He hugged her close. 'There hasn't been for me either as it happens. But never's an awful long time, sweetheart.'

His words might have disturbed her but for a sudden hammering on the door. Tom's voice rang out, startling them both.

'Hey – why is this door locked? As if I didn't know. Folks are beginning to arrive for the party, just in case anyone in there is interested.' They heard his footsteps clatter away downstairs again and Patrick twisted his head to look at her.

'I suppose we'd better get dressed and go down.'

She sighed regretfully. 'I suppose we had.'

Grace and Morgan were shown into the bank manager's office, Grace bearing a briefcase containing a file of figures showing 'Style 'N' Grace's' takings for the past five years, plus a separate set of figures for the sale of Morgan Knitwear. Mr Fry, the manager, motioned them to two chairs opposite and peered at them over the

136

tops of his spectacles; a trick he had discovered was guaranteed to intimidate prospective borrowers.

'Ah – it's Mrs Wendover and Mr – er . . .' He looked at the notes on his desk. 'Mr Owen. Good morning. Now, what can I do for you?'

Briefly Grace explained that she and Morgan wished to buy the business trading as 'Style 'N' Grace' and go into partnership, selling Morgan's product. She showed him the figures, carefully pointing out the rise in her takings since she had been selling Morgan's knitwear.

Mr Fry peered at the figures before him and then up at the two expectant faces opposite him. 'Mmm. Mr Bostock seems to be asking an inordinately high price for the business.'

'We're hoping to make him a lower offer,' Morgan said.

Mr Fry looked doubtful. 'Are you quite sure you wish to purchase?'

'Of course,' Grace assured him.

'Mmm.' He looked at Morgan. 'This – er – venture of yours, what other orders have you apart from Mrs Wendover's, Mr Owen?'

Morgan glanced nervously at Grace. 'Well – none, as yet. But I have some sketches of my designs here if you're interested.' He produced his own briefcase, a brand new one Grace had advised him to invest in, and opened it. 'And here is a swatch of my newest shades.'

'Morgan Knitwear is very new. We were just about to launch it as a joint project,' Grace put in quickly. 'We're planning to have a fashion show and invite people from the fashion houses I deal with in London. But if I'm to lose my shop . . .'

Mr Fry was still looking somewhat sceptically at Morgan's sketches. At one point he even turned one of them upside down. 'Mmmm – don't you think perhaps you'd better see how that goes before you commit yourselves further?'

Grace bit back her impatience. 'But I've been given three months' notice to take effect when my quarterly rental agreement runs out in two weeks' time,' she said. 'I'd like to have a more secure future before I make any plans I might not be able to fulfil.'

He looked up at her in surprise. 'If I might say so, it seems rather odd of Mr Bostock to treat you so arbitrarily. Did he not warn you that he might be selling?'

'No, he did not,' Grace said crisply.

He peered at her over the spectacles again. 'If you don't mind my saying so, Mrs Wendover, there is something strange about all this. If you want my opinion you'd be better advised to seek the help of a solicitor at this stage.' He took another look at Morgan's sketches. 'Surely it would make better sense to find some other premises to rent?'

Grace sighed. It wasn't going at all as she'd visualised. 'Mr Fry, my business has taken almost six years to build. If I moved to another location − and traded under another name − as I would have to, I would lose many of my customers. 'Besides ...' She glanced at Morgan. 'I − we − want to buy. We feel that the time is right.'

There was a long pause during which Mr Fry looked at her thoughtfully. 'That may be so, Mrs Wendover, but in my opinion the right time to buy is when you have the necessary potential for success − and the wherewithal.'

Red-faced, Grace stood up. 'I see we are wasting our time and yours, Mr Fry, so we'll bid you good morning.' At the door she turned. 'I think you'll be sorry you didn't lend us the money. Morgan Knitwear is going to be a big name in the fashion world. A *very* big name indeed.'

Outside in the street Morgan looked at her. 'You were magnificent.'

'I didn't get us the loan though, did I?'

Morgan took her arm. 'He had a point about things looking fishy, you know. The more I think about it, the more I agree with him on that. There's something distinctly odd about Bostock deciding to sell up. I'm sure there's more behind it than the reason you gave. Maybe we should try to find out.'

They had left Elaine in charge of the shop and when they got back she was busy serving Lilian Davies, one of Grace's best customers and Morgan's greatest fan. The moment she saw Morgan her face lit up.

'Ah, I'm in luck. My favourite designer. I'm looking for a sweater as a Christmas present for my daughter-in-law and it seems you've sold out of her size. I suppose you wouldn't be an absolute angel and ...?'

Grace saw that Morgan was about to agree and put in quickly: 'Special orders do carry an extra charge, I'm afraid, Mrs Davies.'

'My dear, of course they do. I'd expect that.' Lilian smiled archly at Morgan. 'And if you could make it an exclusive ... After all, I was your very first customer, don't forget.'

'I've been working on some new designs,' Morgan told her eagerly. 'As a matter of fact I happen to have some of the sketches with me — and my newest colours. Would you like to have a preview?'

'Have you really? That would be marvellous.'

Elaine, who had been looking on with interest, said: 'Perhaps Mrs Davies would like a coffee? I've got the kettle on. I knew you'd both be dying for one after your battle with the bank manager.'

Grace winced inwardly as she saw the woman instantly pick up on the remark.

'Bank manager?' She looked from one to the other. 'I do hope everything is all right.'

'Oh, quite all right, thank you,' Grace said dismissively.

In the back room Lilian raved over Morgan's new designs and quickly chose one for her daughter-in-law. Elaine brought in coffee for the three of them and then went back into the shop.

'I do hope you're not thinking of heading for the bright lights now that you're becoming so successful,' Mrs Davies said, looking enquiringly at them over the rim of her coffee cup.

Grace made a quick decision. 'The fact is, Mrs Davies, that my landlord has put the shop and business up for sale,' she said. 'Morgan and I would like to buy it.'

'And as the sitting tenant, you should get it for a favourable price,' Mrs Davies remarked. Grace and Morgan exchanged glances, but Lilian was frowning. 'Just a minute though — surely . . .?' She shrugged. 'But it's none of my business, of course.' She picked up her bag and gloves. 'Thank you so much for the coffee and for the special order. I know Natalie will be thrilled with it. You'll ring me when it's ready, Grace?'

'Of course.'

It was later that evening, when Grace had washed up and Elaine had gone round to Alison's, that the street doorbell rang. Going downstairs, Grace was surprised to find Lilian Davies standing outside, her smart little red sports car parked at the kerb.'

'May I talk to you, my dear?'

'Of course.' Grace led the way up to the flat, wondering what on earth the woman wanted to see her about.

'I do hope you won't take this as interference,' Lilian said once she was seated on Grace's settee with a glass of sherry in her hand. 'It's just that I love your shop and Morgan's delicious knitwear so much. I do so admire your business flair and your courage and I'd hate to see you . . .' She broke off and took a thoughtful sip of her sherry. 'As you know, my husband is on the Council — he's chairman of the planning committee.' She bit her lip. 'Oh dear, I really *shouldn't* be

139

telling you this, although it's bound to be common knowledge quite soon anyway. The fact is, my dear, most of this street is scheduled for redevelopment.'

Grace stared at her, trying to take in all the implications of this piece of news. 'Really — when?'

'Oh, it may not be for some years yet. On the other hand the plans could go through much sooner. It depends on a number of things. The point is, that the compulsory purchase price would almost certainly be far less than whatever is being asked for it now.'

I see.' Grace's mind was working fast. Had Bryan known this all along? Had he meant her to buy and lose on the deal? Could he really be that vindictive? Suddenly she felt like giving up. Mrs Davies spoke of her business flair, but it was all very new and difficult — all so complicated that she wondered if she was up to coping with it. She looked up at Lilian. 'It's very good of you to tell me this, Mrs Davis. I don't know what to do now,' she said helplessly. 'I know my own business but when it comes to legal matters there seem to be so many snags — so many pitfalls.'

'Look — my husband is a solicitor,' Lilian said. 'Why don't you come and have a talk to him? He'll put you right. You'd better tell him you've heard a rumour about the redevelopment. He'd be furious if he knew I'd leaked it to you.'

'Why have you waited till now to tell me?' Morgan and Grace were in the kitchen at the flat. It was Christmas Eve and they were sharing the preparations for the following day. Morgan, wearing a blue and white striped butcher's apron, was peeling potatoes while Grace was preparing stuffing for the turkey.

'The trouble between Bryan and me is my problem,' she told him. 'I wanted to get it cleared up before I involved you.'

'So you've got your notice extended to six months? That certainly gives us a breathing space. But what then?'

Grace bit her lip. She'd been sworn to secrecy about the redevelopment, but how could she keep it from Morgan when it concerned him so much? She rinsed her hands under that tap and looked at him. 'Leave that a minute,' she said. 'I want to talk to you.'

He dried his hands, searching her face anxiously. 'All right. Tell me the worst.'

'It's good news really. Listen, on the same night we'd been to see the bank manager, Mrs Davies came round and told me a piece of news. It's classified information for the moment and she only told me because she could see we were about to be cheated out

140

of a lot of money. The fact is, most of this street is scheduled for redevelopment.'

Morgan stared at her. 'That means they'll be pulling the shop down, so how can Bostock sell it?'

'That's just the point. If I hadn't been warned off we might have paid what he was asking, only to have the place compulsorily purchased, maybe next year or the year after. We'd have lost a lot of money on it.'

Morgan let his breath out on a long, low whistle. 'So what happens next?'

'As I told you, I went to see Mrs Davies' husband, who happens to be a solicitor. I told him I'd heard a rumour about the redevelopment and asked his advice. He told me I was entitled to apply for another three months' notice and to threaten Bryan with a tribunal if he refused. He hinted that by then the news of the redevelopment would probably have broken and Bryan will be obliged to accept the Council's compulsory purchase.'

Morgan grinned. 'Serve him right. But where does that leave you — us?'

'Renting from the Council,' Grace told him triumphantly. 'Probably at a cheaper rent than I've been paying Bryan. And Mr Davies says that situation could last for quite some time. The actual redevelopment probably won't take place for five or six years yet. By that time we'll be on our feet and able to buy a place with a really good position somewhere.'

Morgan picked up his mug of coffee. 'Grace, you're a wonder. Here's to us.'

'To us.' Grace touched her mug to his. 'Us — and our bright future together.' She sipped her coffee then lowered her voice. 'Oh, by the way, I haven't mentioned this to Elaine. The fewer people who know, the better it will be for us.' She smiled at him. 'Oh, Morgan, I'd been dreading this Christmas. Now I can look forward to it.'

'It's certainly the best Christmas present you could have given me,' he agreed. 'By the way, are you really sure you want me spending it here with you? I know Elaine and you enjoy spending Christmas together and I don't want to intrude.'

'Of course you must spend it with us,' Grace assured him. 'You're part of the family now. Do you really think I could enjoy it, thinking of you alone in that horrid little room of yours?'

When Grace had first seen Morgan's room in Rowan Street she had been appalled. The tiny terraced house was in a cul-de-sac at the end of which was a cemetery. Morgan's one window looked out on to the narrow street and the moss-covered cemetery wall. The room was do dark that he couldn't work without the light on; the kitchen was disgusting and the sanitary arrangements primitive. It had reminded her painfully of the little room in Bow that she had occupied when Elaine was on the way.

'If only we had another room you could move in with us,' she said now.

Morgan looked doubtful. 'Somehow I don't think Elaine would care for that, even if you had room.'

He was right. Although Elaine had nothing against Morgan she resented the way her mother seemed to dote on him. Almost from their first meeting it had been Morgan this and Morgan that, till she was tired of hearing about his fabulous talent and his kind, gentle nature. There was something about the relationship she didn't understand. Morgan was years younger than her mother. Surely she couldn't be falling for him? She'd always said she'd never marry again. Anyway she was still married to her father so she couldn't. And yet the two seemed close — closer than most business colleagues — almost intimate. They always seemed to have their heads together about something. And lately they had taken to clamming up whenever she came into the room.

Standing outside the kitchen door she had been just in time to overhear her mother's remark: 'Oh, by the way, I haven't mentioned any of this to Elaine. The fewer people who know about it, the better it will be for us. Oh, Morgan, I was dreading this Christmas. Now I can look forward to it.'

And Morgan's reply: 'It's certainly the best Christmas present you could have given me.'

What could it mean? she wondered. What were they cooking up between them now? One thing at least was crystal clear: whatever it was, it didn't include her.

Up in her room Elaine locked the door and took out the card she had received the previous morning from her father. It usually came before this. She'd begun to wonder if he would send her one this year. And when it had arrived she had been surprised to see that it bore an English postmark. This time last year he and Stella had been in America. She had the impression they'd made their home there. Yet this year's card had been posted in Bournemouth. She took it out of the drawer and stared hard at it, as though by looking and concentrating it would tell her something.

She had been born in Bournemouth. Her father had been working there at the time. Her mother had told her the story so many times. Idyllic walks by the sea and in the gardens. The way the pine trees scented the air with their tangy perfume and the squirrels ate out of your hand. The endless blue skies, warm sands and golden sun. Harry had been working a summer season at the Pavilion. It seemed to have been a very happy time for them. She knew her mother had always wanted to go back — to live there. Even now she sometimes voiced her dream of some day going down and setting up in business there. Did her father feel the same nostalgia for the place? Had he gone there to relive those happy memories? Had he and Stella finally parted? If he and her mother met again, was it possible that they might get back together? Elaine knew that an uncertainty hung over the future of the shop and flat here. It was possible that Grace might lose the business. If she and her father were to meet again it could be the answer to everything.

As usual the card told her nothing. On the front was a colourful picture of a coach and horses. Inside under the printed greeting were the words: 'To Elaine, with love from Daddy.' She turned the envelope over and over. The postmark seemed to mock her. It must be possible to find him now that he knew which town he was in. It must — but how?

Christmas Day was not a success. Grace and Morgan were in a light-hearted mood. They cooked lunch together, laughing and teasing each other as they worked. Elaine stayed out of the kitchen. She felt like an intruder in her own home. Besides, there wasn't really room for three of them. They exchanged presents. Morgan had made them each an exclusive sweater, specially designed. Grace exclaimed over them, insisting on wearing hers, which was knitted in a soft black wool trimmed with white and suited her beautifully. Elaine's was moss green, a colour she didn't care for. She felt it made her complexion look sallow. She made an excuse and took it up to her room, pushing it to the back of a drawer.

Grace gave Morgan a watch to replace his old, unreliable one. It looked expensive and Elaine had a strong suspicion that there was an inscription on the back. It had clearly cost much more than the tiny heart-shaped locket which was her present from her mother. She felt guilty and mean for making the comparison and told herself sulkily that it was Morgan's fault. He brought out the worst in her.

She made an effort over lunch; pulling crackers with them and forcing herself to laugh at the corny mottoes, though she flatly refused to wear a paper hat. As soon as lunch was over and the washing up was done, she announced that she was going round to Alison's and might not be home for tea. Grace protested, but not too much. She didn't know what had got into Elaine lately. She used

143

to be a pleasure to have around. Now she was morose and sulky —
almost rude. She heard the street door downstairs slam behind her
daughter and gave a small sigh of relief. Now she and Morgan could
indulge in their favourite topic — their plans for the future.

Chapter Eleven

At Alison's house three generations had gathered for the festivities. When Elaine arrived they were all slumped in armchairs. Replete with turkey and plum pudding, they were all set to doze while they waited for the Queen's Christmas Message on TV. Alison nodded in the direction of her grandfather. Having undone the buttons of his waistcoat he had fallen asleep in the chair nearest to the fire, his mouth open and a green paper hat slipping over one eye. She raised her eyes to the ceiling.

'Zombies, all of them.' she pronounced. 'Christmas. Who needs it? Come on, let's go for a walk.'

They put on coats and scarves and set off at a brisk walk for Parker's Piece.

'Get anything good?' Alison asked.

Elaine fished inside her coat collar for the locket. 'This.'

Alison inspected it. 'Mmm, nice. Mum and Dad bought me a tranny so's I can listen to pop in my room without blasting their eardrums. I think they've forgotten Top of the Pops is still on telly though.'

Elaine sighed.'You're lucky. We still haven't even got a TV. Mum says it's a waste of time.'

'You can always come and look at ours whenever you want.'

'I know. Thanks.'

'What's up, Ellie. You seem a bit fed up.' Alison peered at her friend. 'Don't tell me Patrick's giving you the runaround.'

Elaine shook her head. 'It's not Patrick.'

'What then — or who?'

Elaine sighed. 'It's that Morgan Owen. He practically lives at our place these days. Mum seems to think the sun shines out of his ear holes.'

Alison giggled. 'Well, it's understandable, I suppose. He's quite good-looking in a soppy, poetic kind of way, and after all, she has been on her own for a long time, hasn't she?'

'She has *not*,' Elaine said hotly. 'She's had me.'

'Ah, but you're not a man, are you?' Alison said with a knowing wink.

Elaine felt slightly sick. 'Don't be so damned silly. As if Mum would do anything like that at her age – with *Morgan* of all people.'

'You might be surprised,' Alison told her in a matter-of-fact way. 'I thought my mum and dad were past it too till I walked into their room one Sunday morning and caught them at it.' She giggled. 'Thought I'd do them a favour and take them a cup of tea in bed. Instead of that it was red faces all round.' She peered at Elaine. 'I thought you'd have been more understanding by now. What about you and Patrick?'

'What about us?'

Alison nudged her. 'Come on, I don't have to spell it out, do I? Have you and he done it yet?'

Elaine's cheeks flushed hotly. 'I think that's a private matter, don't you?'

Alison's eyebrows rose. 'I thought I was your best friend. We always said we'd tell each other when it happened, didn't we?' Elaine was silent 'Oh, all right then – *be* like that.' She grinned. 'You do realise that your face is a dead giveaway though, don't you?' She gave Elaine a playful push. 'Oh, come on, cheer up, misery guts. I don't want to know the lurid details if you don't want to tell me. A plain yes or no would do. Tell you what, let's walk round town and look at the shop windows while it's quiet?' She took Elaine's arm determinedly.

Elaine allowed herself to be led back towards town and after a while the girls resumed their chatter. They peered at the festive displays in all the shop windows, inspecting the latest winter fashions and passing their opinions on them. Then, quite out of the blue, Alison asked: 'Heard from your dad this Christmas?'

The suddeness of the question was typical of Alison but nevertheless, it startled Elaine, making her blush again. 'Yes. I had a card yesterday. He's . . .' She was about to tell Alison that her father was in England again but stopped, almost in mid-sentence. She hadn't decided what to do about trying to find him yet and she wanted to think about it some more first.

'Go on – what did he say?'

'Say?'

'In his letter. There was a letter as usual, wasn't there?'

'Oh – no, not this time.' Somehow she no longer wanted to keep up the lie. It seemed childish and pointless now.

'Oh, poor old sausage. No wonder you're fed up. Maybe he was too busy. I expect he'll write in the New Year.'

'Yes. I expect so.'

'What are you doing tomorrow? We always go to the panto as you know. It's a kind of family tradition. Perhaps Dad could get another ticket if you'd like to come too.'

'It's all right, thanks. I'm invited to your Aunt Zoe's for the day.'

'Oh, great. It'll be heaps better fun at the Carnes'. I wish I was going to. The panto's a drag. We have to join in with all the daft songs and eat popcorn and stuff. It's dead boring, but Dad loves the whole dreary business. It's more for him than anyone else.'

Elaine was silent. She was wondering how it would be if her parents hadn't parted. Would they have gone to the pantomime every Boxing Day? Would they have been a real family like the Lintons? She'd never know now. Suddenly her resolve to find her father strengthened. She found herself wondering if he had changed; remembering all the things he used to like – things they shared together when she was little. Suddenly she wished she'd kept up her music so that she could have had something to surprise and impress him with.

Back at the Lintons' house everyone was seated round a table laden with salmon sandwiches and celery, sausage rolls, mince pies and trifle. In the centre, taking pride of place, was the massive fruit cake with the silver paper frill round it that Mrs Linton had made. Already a thick wedge had been cut from it, revealing its rich interior. Elaine looked at the thick marzipan and pink icing, and felt slightly nauseous.

'I'm not hungry, thank you,' she said when invited to sit down. 'We had a huge lunch. I really couldn't eat a thing. Would you mind if I went home now?'

Mrs Linton laid a hand on her forehead, her homely face anxious. 'Are you feeling all right, dear? You're looking a little peaky. There's a lot of 'flu about.'

'Oh, leave her alone. She's just in a mood, that's all,' Alison said helping herself to a large slice of cake. 'She'll get over it, won't you, Ellie?'

'Of course. I'm fine. I'll give you a ring after tomorrow, Alison.' Thanking Mrs Linton politely, she let herself out of the house and began to walk back to the flat. They didn't really want her there anyway, she told herself pityingly; any more than Mum and

Morgan wanted her. Did her father still miss her at Christmas? she wondered. As much as she missed him? She thought of that dreadful Christmas night when he had left. She'd been very young, but she'd felt the tension in the air all that day. Her throat tightened as she remembered saying goodbye to him. 'You'll always be my girl,' he'd said. Did *he* remember too, when Christmas came around each year?

Nearing the flat, she suddenly remembered Alison's remark about catching her parents 'at it' and slowed her steps. Suppose, just suppose, she were to walk in on her mother and Morgan in a similar situation? How awful. She'd never be able to look either of them in the face again. Better make good and sure they heard her coming when she let herself in.

Five minutes later, as she let herself in at the street door, Grace and Morgan sat at the dining table, papers spread out as they worked on their plans for the spring fashion show. Grace looked up as she heard the street door slam.

'That must be Elaine,' she said. 'I'll put the kettle on. I didn't realise it was so late.' She smiled. 'Oh, listen, she's singing. She must be feeling happier. Alison usually manages to cheer her up.'

Boxing Day at the Carnes' was something Elaine had looked forward to. She got up early and had a leisurely bath, then took her mother a cup of tea in bed.

'Come and have yours with me,' Grace invited, patting the bed. 'It seems ages ago since we had a talk.'

Going back to the kitchen for her own cup Elaine wondered if Grace might have something to tell her — something she didn't want to hear. When she got back to her mother's bedroom, Grace was sitting up. She looked happy, and younger than Elaine had seen her for a long time.

'I wanted to tell you something,' Grace began. 'Don't worry, darling. It's good news,' she added, seeing Elaine's expression. 'Morgan and I are going into partnership. I'm going to market and sell his knitwear.'

'Oh, but I thought you said we might have to move.'

'No. We'll be able to stay on here as tenants — at least for another couple of years — by which time I hope that Morgan and I will have made a success of things.' She smiled radiantly. 'Isn't it exciting?'

'Yes — great. I'm glad we won't have to leave.'

Grace put out her hand and took one of Elaine's. 'Darling, you do like Morgan, don't you?'

'Of course I do.' Elaine couldn't quite meet her mother's eyes.

148

'I know something is bothering you,' Grace went on quietly. 'Why don't you tell me what it is? We've never kept things from each other, have we?'

Elaine wanted to point out that she'd been the last to know about the partnership — and the fact that they didn't have to move. Her mind spun. Could she really tell her mother that the new relationship with Morgan made her feel left out? Dared she mention her father and her longing to find him again?

'I — you — aren't thinking of marrying again, are you?' she finally blurted out, merging the two worries together and yet voicing neither.

Grace looked surprised and a little shocked. '*Marrying*? You know I couldn't do that, even if I wanted to.'

'You could if you divorced Daddy.'

'Yes. And so could he.' Grace was silent for a moment. She'd always known of course that this subject would come up one day. Elaine was a child no longer. She was a grown woman and she had a right to ask.

'If your father were to ask me for a divorce now, I would probably agree,' she said slowly. 'If he is still with the woman he left me for, that is.'

Elaine searched her mother's face. 'Does that mean that you want to be free yourself?'

Grace smiled. 'I suppose it does, but not because I want to marry. I'd just like to be independent — stand on my own feet. For the first time in my life, I feel like a whole person.'

'Because of Morgan?'

It was a searching question. Grace considered for a moment, then answered it as truthfully as she could. 'Because of knowing him, yes. And because I believe we can help each other to achieve what we both want most in life. Do you understand that?'

Elaine nodded. 'I think so,' she said — not understanding at all.

'Good.' Grace drank the last of her tea and threw back the bedclothes. 'Now we'd both better get ready. You don't want to be late at the Carnes', and Morgan and I are lunching out. Do you know, I've been thinking — now that we don't have to lay out the money to buy the shop, we might invest in a car. We really do need one for the business, so we could claim for it on the tax returns. It would be nice for our free time too, wouldn't it? You and I could both take driving lessions. How about that?'

At the Carnes' the usual chaos reigned. Elaine walked in through the open door in the customary unceremonious way. She had chosen

149

to wear her new hipster jeans today, teamed, much to her mother's disapproaval, with a white shirt with huge bell-shaped sleeves — under which she wore no bra. She had changed her style a lot over the past year, growing her shoulder-length hair to a much longer length. It was cut in a spiky fringe that tangled with her eyebrows in front, while the rest tumbled halfway down her back.

As usual everyone was doing their own thing. From the basement came the mingled sounds and aromas of Zoe's cookery — helped by Red she was making an Indian meal. From the floor above came Tom's music. He had recently been converted to the new 'soul' music and as she mounted the stairs Elaine heard the husky voice of Otis Redding singing 'Loving You Too Long.' When she reached the top floor and opened Patrick's door she found him painting.

'Happy Christmas.' She took the flat parcel wrapped in red and gold paper out of her shoulder bag and held it out to him.

He unwrapped it eagerly. 'Hey, what is it?'

It was Bob Dylan's latest LP. As he stared down at it, she said, 'You don't like it?'

'It's not that. Tom gave me the same one. Sorry, sweetheart.'

'It's all right. The record shop girl said you could change it.' She was ridiculously disappointed. To her horror she felt her lower lip tremble. Patrick saw it.

'Hey, don't be upset. It doesn't matter, honestly. Come and look at your present.' He crossed the room to where his easel was covered with a cloth. With a flourish he whisked it off. Elaine gasped, her disappointment forgotten. On the easel was a large full-length oil painting of her.

'Oh, Patrick,' she breathed. 'It's lovely, but how ...?'

'From the sketch I did — and from memory.' He crossed the room and pulled her close. 'I should have plenty of that, shouldn't I?'

She wound her arms around his neck and the way she clung to him was tinged with a desperation that made him vaguely uneasy. He held her away from him to look into her eyes.

'What is it?'

She bit her lip. 'Patrick — will you help me? There's something I want to do.'

'Of course, if I can. Tell me about it.'

They sat down together on the bed. 'I had a card from my father. He's in England — Bournemouth. I want to find him.'

Patrick frowned. 'I don't quite see how I can help with that.'

'I don't know how to find out where he is.'

'He didn't put his address on the card?'

'No.'

150

'Well, do you think he might be on the phone?'

Her face brightened. 'Of course. Why didn't I think of that?'

'The directories for all the different towns are in the library. They should be open again next week.'

'Suppose he hasn't been there long enough to be listed?'

'Ring directory enquiries — though that might be difficult as you don't have the address.'

'It's a start. Thanks.'

He took her hand. 'Elaine, why do you want to do this? Is anything wrong?'

She shook her head. 'No — I don't know. It's just a feeling. Suddenly everything seems to be changing.' Turning to him she threw her arms impulsively around his neck. 'Oh, Patrick, I'm so glad I've got you. I love you so much. I don't know what I'd do without you. I wish you didn't have to go back to London.'

He held her close but his eyes were troubled. He hadn't told her yet that he was due to leave for Paris in the early spring — or that he was hoping to study there for two years.

Harry stood on the clifftop, looking out over a grey, choppy sea. 'What a way to spend Christmas morning,' he muttered to himself as he looked down at the deserted beach below. Stella had been asleep when he left the house. Asleep after another of her restless nights.

At first it had seemed to him a good idea to bring her to Bournemouth. Here in the peace and quiet she could rest and recover. Losing the baby had been a terrible blow for her — for them both.

It had been just after the charity show at the Palladium. She'd been just five months pregnant, and following her collapse and miscarriage she had been very ill indeed. For several days it had been touch and go. Finally the gynaecologist had decided that a hysterectomy was the only way to save her. Stella would make a complete recovery, Harry was told, but she would never have a child. Apparently there had been some kind of abnormality; it was amazing that she had conceived at all.

When she had first discovered that she was pregnant, Stella had been shocked. But as the weeks passed the idea had slowly begun to appeal to her. For his part, Harry had been delighted. He had never quite got over losing Elaine. He thought of her often, wondering how she was, what she looked like and how she had grown up. Once, quite recently, passing a group of teenage girls on the street, it had struck him that one of them could well be his daughter. It was quite possible that they could pass each other in the street now without

151

recognising each other. The thought had haunted him for days.

The child Stella carried had seemed like a second chance for him. His child — a new beginning. Together they made plans. They talked seriously about their future in a way they never had before.

With the advent of pop groups and the new wave in music, Stella's popularity had begun to fade. They had returned to the States where she still had a strong following from the musicals she had appeared in there. There had been recording contracts and she'd appeared on chat shows, gone on an exhausting concert tour. An Australian tour had followed and finally they had come home to do a short series for BBC TV. It had seemed promising, but it hadn't done too well in the ratings and the planned follow-up was abandoned.

Having foreseen the decline of her career well ahead, Harry had made sure that the money she earned was invested wisely. It brought them a good income, and there were still healthy royalties from her records. He worked out that she could comfortably retire. The past years had been punishingly hard and she deserved it. As for him, he could always put in the odd film session or do a bit of accompanist work. He hated the thought that he was living on her earnings.

At first Stella had gone along with it. She was exhausted from the overseas tours. Then came her pregnancy which seemed to set the seal on her retirement. There were just a few last bookings to honour before they retired to Bournemouth to await the baby's birth. Harry could hardly wait.

They had been lucky enought to meet some people who were going abroad for a year and were willing to let their house. It was snug and comfortably furnished, in a quiet road close to the Eastcliff. By the time the owners returned Stella would have decided whether she liked the place enought to look for a house of their own.

For his part, Harry loved the place. The relaxing sea air suited him. He felt well and at home there. Walking alone on the cliffs in the early mornings he remembered the year Grace and he had come for the summer season. They'd been happy then — reunited and looking forward to the birth of their first child. And when Elaine had been born ... He smiled reminiscently as he stared out to the misty horizon. That summer everything had seemed so full of promise. They'd been setting out together, the three of them, making a new start — their past troubles forgotten. They'd had so much love for each other, or so he had thought then.

The loss of Stella's baby and her subsequent illness had upset him far more than he would ever have admitted. His grief was spiked with anger and resentment. Why was he destined to have the things he loved snatched so cruelly from him? What had he done to deserve such rejection — such denial? All he had ever asked for was love, a home and family. Things other men took for granted. Now even Stella seemed to have turned against him. The doctor had said it was normal — that it would take time. She was suffering from a hormonal imbalance, it was explained; she'd been under a strain and the shock of losing the baby, plus a major operation ... They made him feel so selfish, so weak and inadequate. Their eyes seemed to reproach him in the same way that Grace's once had.

He shivered a little and turned up his coat collar as a drop of rain splashed off his cheek. The weather had been so warm when they first arrived; day after day of glorious sunshine. 'Halcyon days,' he said aloud to himself. Now it was cold. What a good thing they hadn't been able to see what the future held.

For in spite of the peace and quiet and fresh sea air, Stella couldn't settle. She missed the travelling, the excitement, the adulation. She felt useless and unwanted. And after her illness she resented the bad luck that had steered her away from her chosen course. For the first time in her life she began to worry about the future and security. She badgered Harry constantly about marriage.

'Why can't you ask Grace for a divorce?' she asked repeatedly. 'Surely after all this time she'd agree.'

Harry looked doubtful. 'I don't think so.'

'How can you possibly know if you don't ask her? Why are you so reluctant to try?' Stella asked accusingly. 'Is it that you don't *want* to marry me? Have I lost my attraction for you now that I can't make money any more? Or is it that I'm not a proper woman any more? Is that what's turning you off?'

He ignored the barbed remarks, wearily trying to assure her that he loved her as much as ever. But his passivity only seemed to anger her more.

'For God's sake, why don't you say it? I'm just a has-been, aren't I?' she demanded shrilly. I don't have a career any more. I can't have a child for you — can't do anything. I'm not even your real wife. I'm nothing — nobody.'

She had refused from the first to take the medication the doctor prescribed for her. She couldn't sleep and took little interest in her appearance. The once voluptuous figure had begun to thicken and her lustrous black hair was limp and dry. When he woke in the mornings Harry never knew what to expect. She was either silent and self-pitying, or waspish and demanding. Harry could do nothing right. If he stayed in he was fussing and getting on her nerves. If he went out he was neglecting her — couldn't bear to be in the same house with her.

'I hate it here,' she said one day. 'And there's only one reason why *you* wanted to come, don't think I don't know that. It's where you were happy once, isn't it? Happy with *her* — with your wife and child.'

Harry sighed. 'You and I could be happy here too if only you'd give the place a chance.'

'You complained enough about her, but at least she was able to give you a child, wasn't she?' Her mouth twisted. 'At least she was woman enough for that.'

'Stella, Stella, for God's sake stop torturing yourself. You're destroying everything we ever had. I fell in love with you. I still love you. Can't you be satisfied with that? Having children wasn't what we set out to do, was it? The baby was an accident.'

'An *accident*? Is that how you see it? Our child. You'd have asked her for a divorce if it had lived though, wouldn't you? You'd have done it to give our child a name. But you won't do it for me.'

Harry moaned softly. He'd heard the same argument day and night ever since he'd brought her home from the hospital. What did he have to do to convince her for God's sake? 'All right, I'll write and ask her,' he said resignedly.

For a moment triumph lit her dark eyes, then they narrowed suspiciously. 'You know her address?'

'Yes. She and Elaine live in Cambridge. Grace has a business there.'

'How do you know that?'

Harry's shoulders slumped defeatedly. 'You forget — I was sending maintenance for Elaine until quite recently.'

'I thought that was done through the solicitor.'

Harry raked his fingers through his hair exasperatedly. 'For God's sake, Stella. I have to know their address.'

She stared at him. 'Why?'

'In case of emergencies. In case anything happened — to Elaine. She is my daughter.'

'There's no need to rub it in. What else did you send?'

'Nothing.'

'Presents? Letters? You write letters — to your *daughter* — and to Grace.' He shook his head wearily. 'No, I don't.'

'Then how do you know she has a business?'

'The address: it's a shop — a dress shop.'

She sat down, suddenly quiet. 'You must think about them. Don't you wish you could see them? Do you wish you could turn the clock back, Harry? That you could be here in this nice little house with Grace and Elaine? That's what you'd really like, isn't it?'

154

'Be quiet, Stella! For Christ's sake, be quiet.' Harry was on his feet. 'Look, I understand that you're not yourself — that all you've been through has taken its toll. I've tried hard to be patient, but enough's enough. Do you think I haven't suffered too?' Seeing the tears well up in her eyes, he was instantly sorry for his outburst. He sat down beside her and took her hands in his. 'Look, we'll go away somewhere — Paris maybe. Just for a few days — just the two of us. How's that?'

But she shook her head. 'I want to work again, Harry,' she said softly. 'All I want is to work again. It's the only thing that'll make me feel like a real person.' She raised the dark tortured eyes to his. 'And I want to be your wife, Harry. Oh, Harry, *please*.'

'All right. I'll write and ask Grace for a divorce,' he promised. 'And I'll go up to Town in the New Year and see what I can do about getting us some bookings. But only if you'll promise to take your tablets and try hard to get fit again. You're not going to be up to working until you're well again.'

Elaine's attempts to find her father's telephone number both from the directory and from directory enquiries drew blanks. What she didn't know was that the number of the owner of the house Harry was renting was ex-directory and Harry had seen no reason to reverse the situation. It was only when she was going through her box of cherished cards late one night that she found Gerry Sylvester's card, now yellow and dog-eared at the bottom of the box. She turned it over thoughtfully in her hand. Mr Sylvester had retired, she knew that. But the agency was still in business. At least, it had been that time she tried to ring Gerry. It was possible that Harry was still a client. It was certainly worth a try.

She rang the following morning from the Carnes' house when Zoe and Red were out, holding tightly to Patrick's hand, her heart thudding in her chest as she listened to the phone ringing out at the other end of the line.

'Good morning, Sylvester Agency. Can I help you?' The woman's voice was clipped and businesslike.'

Elaine swallowed hard. Her tongue seemed to have stuck to the roof of her mouth. 'Hello. I — er — can you tell me if Mr Harry Wendover is still a client of yours?'

'Who's enquiring please?'

'I'm — er, it's a personal matter.'

'I'm sorry, but we're not allowed to give out private information about our clientele over the telephone.'

Patrick leaned closer. 'That means he *is*,' he whispered encouragingly. 'Go on. Don't give up.'

'As a matter of fact, I'm his daughter,' Elaine said.

'If you're his daughter you must surely know whether or not he is on our books?' the voice said suspiciously.

'I — we haven't seen him for some years,' Elaine said. 'He and my mother parted some years ago. But now it's desperately important — *urgent* — that I get in touch with him. For family reasons.' She was even ready to lie now — invent some family crisis in order to trace him. She couldn't get this far and then fail. She couldn't.

'Just one moment, please.'

Elaine squeezed Patrick's hand tightly and held her breath. It seemed an eternity before the woman spoke again.

'I've just had a word with Mr Rose,' she said. 'We do have a Mr Harry Wendover on our books. His address is Fern Lodge, Manorfield Road, Eastcliff, Bournemouth.'

'Thank you.' Elaine scribbled the address on the scrap of paper Patrick pushed towards her. 'And the telephone number?'

'I'm sorry, I can't give you that. It's ex-directory.' There was a click and the line went dead. Elaine hung up and turned to look at Patrick with shining eyes. 'I got his address.'

He smiled. 'I know.'

'The phone number if ex-directory though.' She paused, chewing her lip. 'So what shall I do now?'

'Write, I suppose.'

'I wish I could go down there — surprise him.'

Patrick looked doubtful. 'Don't you think it might be more of a shock after all these years? Better prepare him first with a letter.'

She nodded thoughtfully. 'There's Stella too — if he's still with her. I don't want to make any trouble.'

Patrick picked up her hand and tucked it through his arm. 'Come upstairs. There's something I want to talk to you about.'

In the studio bedroom at the top of the house Patrick closed the door and turned the key in the lock. Elaine giggled.

'Patrick! At this time of the morning?'

He shook his head. 'I don't want anyone barging in, that's all.' He sat down beside her on the edge of the bed and the look in his eyes sent a sudden chill running down her spine.

'Patrick, what is it?' she asked quietly. 'Is something wrong?'

'Not exactly. It's just that I've got some news.'

She frowned. 'I'm not going to like it, am I?'

'I'm afraid not.' He took her hand and looked down at it, stroking

156

the fingers one by one. 'Elaine — you know I told you I was going to Paris?'

'Yes. After you've done your time at the Slade.'

'It's been brought forward. I don't feel I'm getting as much out of studying in London as I'd hoped. So I'm going to Paris in the spring.'

'*This* spring?'

'Yes. In March.'

'After Easter.'

He looked into her eyes. 'No, darling, before Easter. As soon as next term finishes.'

She felt her heart turn cold as she digested this piece of news. 'But what about me?' she asked in a small hurt voice. 'I'll have to wait till the summer holidays to see you.'

Patrick shook his head. 'I won't be coming home in the summer, love. I'll have to work, you see, to pay my way. And I want to learn the language fluently too.'

'Are you saying that we won't see each other again — not for the whole two years?' Tears began to well up in her eyes and he pulled her close.

'Oh, darling, don't. Look, we've had a marvellous time together but we knew it couldn't last forever, didn't we?'

Elaine was silent. She hadn't known anything of the kind. If she'd thought about it at all, she'd imagined them staying together till the end of time.

Patrick went on: 'We're both young. You have your career to think of too. Believe me, there'll be other fellows — plenty of them. They'll be falling over themselves. You get lovelier every time I see you.'

His words stabbed her to the heart. To think that he wouldn't care about all these other boys he spoke of. She felt as though her chest would burst with the pain. Although she tried hard to hold them back, the tears welled up and ran down her cheeks. 'Oh, Patrick, there won't be anyone else — not ever,' she whispered. 'I don't think I can bear it. How can I live for two whole years without seeing you?'

He drew her close, pressing her head onto his shoulder, soothing her like a child. 'You'll be surprised at how quickly you'll forget me.'

'No — never.' Her voice was muffled against his neck. 'I love you, Patrick. I'll never love anyone else. I — I thought you loved me too.'

He sighed. He hadn't been prepared for the depth of her hurt. 'I

157

do, darling, I do. And I always will — in a way.' He held her away from him to look into her eyes. 'Listen, it's only for a couple of years. It'll go really quickly, you'll see. When I come back I'll get a job; teach maybe, or take a job with some advertising company — just until I make my name. If our love really is strong enough, it won't die. But it's my guess you'll be married by then to some upright fellow with a steady job. Not a layabout artist like me.'

She shook her head. 'How can you say that? I won't. I know I won't.' She looked at him with pleading, tear-filled eyes. 'We'll keep in touch, won't we?'

'Of course — if you like.' Patrick winced inwardly. He'd meant to be so strong, so positive. Make a clean break so that they could both be free. It was all going wrong. In a minute she'd be offering to go with him, then what would he do? Already her eyes had brightened with a terrible transparent hope.

'Perhaps, if I save up hard, I could come over and visit you,' she said.

He shook his head awkwardly. 'I expect to be moving around a bit — not staying in Paris all the time.' Seeing her crestfallen expression he relented. 'Look, tell you what: you could come up to Town at the end of term. We could spend a couple of days together while the flat is empty, before I go.'

She threw her arms round his neck. 'Oh, Patrick, that would be marvellous — something to look forward to all this term.'

'That's if your mother will let you come.'

Her chin lifted. 'She can't stop me if I want to, can she? Anyway, she's far too involved with Morgan and his bloody knitting to bother about what I'm doing.' They laughed together and the tension eased. 'How will I exist till March though?' She laid her head against his chest.

'You've got the reunion with your father to look forward to as well,' he reminded her. 'The time will go so fast you won't notice it. Once I'm gone you'll hardly give me a thought.' But even as he said it he knew it wasn't true. He only wished it were.

Chapter Twelve

'It's a Hillman Hunter. Isn't it lovely? Grace rubbed at a speck of dust on the car's immaculate paintwork and looked at Elaine for approval. 'Two years old and only one lady owner. Wasn't Morgan clever to find it?'

'Brilliant,' Elaine muttered between clenched teeth. She had found her mother standing at the kerb, admiring the car when she'd arrived home from college. Looking at the dark blue estate car she had to admit that it looked as new as the day it drove out of the showroom. Of course it would have to be Morgan clever-clogs who found it, she told herself.

'There's plenty of room in the back for transporting stock,' Grace said excitedly, opening one of the doors. 'The back seat folds down, see? We might even be able to go up to the warehouses at weekends and bring back our own stock. That way we'd reduce delivery costs. Morgan's going to start teaching me to drive this very weekend,' she went on. 'I shall have to put in for a test at once. There's always a long waiting list, he says.'

'Yes. I know.'

'He'll give you some lessons if you want. You do want to drive, don't you? You're old enough for a licence now, you know.'

'Mother, I can drive already,' Elaine told her coolly. Grace stared at her.

'Don't be silly, dear, of course you can't.'

'I can. Tom's been teaching me.'

'*Tom*? In that terrible old jallopy of his? You might have been killed. Anyway, it's against the law.'

'No, it isn't. I've got a provisional licence. So far I've had ...' Elaine counted on her fingers. ' ... six lessons. And my test date came through last week. It's at the end of next month. Tom says I should pass first time.'

She was rewarded by her mother's shocked silence. When she recovered her breath Grace asked: 'But − when did all this happen? You never said a word about it.'

Elaine smiled apologetically. 'I'm sorry, Mum. It was meant to be a surprise. I've been going in the lunch break and sometimes after college. There's no need to worry. Tom's a really good teacher.'

'Well, it's certainly a surprise, I'll say that. I do wish you'd mentioned it to me first, though if I'd known what you were up to I'd have been worried out of my mind.'

'That's exactly why I didn't tell you,' Elaine laughed. 'Tom's been teaching Alison too. She didn't tell her mum either.'

Grace looked at her daughter with grudging admiration. 'Well − I hope I take to it as easily as you obviously have. I'm so pleased with the car though. We've got it just in time for the fashion show next week. Oh, I really feel that things are looking up for us, don't you?' She linked her arm through Elaine's as they walked back into the shop and began to climb the stairs to the flat.

'By the way, darling, I haven't told you. I had a bit of luck this morning − I found Morgan a new room.'

'That's good.' Elaine went through to the kitchen and began to fill the kettle.

'Yes. I went into Mr Carne's shop when I was passing − just to see if he'd got anything new and to have a chat. He's such a charming man. I happened to be talking about Morgan and the show and everything . . .'

'When *aren't* you?' Elaine mumbled under her breath.

Oblivious to the remark, Grace went on: 'He said what a shame it was that an artist of Morgan's calibre should have to work in such soul-destroying surroundings. Then he mentioned that they have a spare room as Patrick is about to go to France for two years.' She glanced at Elaine. 'Well, you're friendly with them all so I expect you know that.'

'Yes.' Elaine's heart began to beat dully in her chest.

'So I said I was sure that Morgan would be more than grateful for a room like that. I rang Mrs Carne as soon as I got back and it's all settled. Morgan can move in as soon as he likes. She said she'd been looking for someone artistic to let the room to. They don't like to have just anyone. Well, you can't blame them, can you?'

Elaine wanted to scream. Morgan in Patrick's room − sleeping in his bed; the bed where they'd made love. The thought made her feel sick. 'Look, Mum, I've got some preparation to do for college tomorrow,' she said 'I won't stop for tea now. I'll go up and get on with it.'

In spite of her mother's protestations she escaped to her room. Closing the door behind her she threw herself full-length on the bed and closed her eyes. Patrick had been gone three weeks now and she missed him more with every passing day. Much to her disappointment he had gone back to London before the term started. To clean the flat and get ready for the new term, he had said. She wanted to believe him when he said he loved her and that he would miss her too. But if it were really true how could he bear to go away and leave her days before he needed to? How could he face the thought of two whole years in France without her? She squeezed her eyes shut in a concentrated effort to block out the doubts that tormented her. Instead, she levelled her thoughts on the weekend they were to share at the end of term. Seven weeks away. How was she to exist till then? And then there was her mother to persuade. It wouldn't be easy to convince her that she must go, but somehow she would do it. At the back of her mind a dark thought lurked. Had Patrick suggested the weekend as a sop — something to keep her quiet — and not because he wanted to see her at all? She closed her mind against the thought, determined to shut it out.

Swinging her legs over the side of the bed, she opened the bottom drawer of her dressing table and took out the box of cards from her father. At the bottom was the scrap of paper on which she had scribbled his address. Ever since the New Year she had been trying to write to him a letter, but she had torn up all her attempts in disgust. They sounded so false; so fatuous. She wanted him to know that she hadn't changed, and yet show him she was a grown woman too. Did she address him as 'Daddy', 'Father' or even 'Harry'? Did she write as a woman or as a child? She had tried both ways and found them forced and unreal. Sometimes she wondered despairingly whether they had anything to say to each other any more. If only they could meet. She took out the faded snapshot of him and sat looking at it, wondering how much he would have had changed. If she saw him in the street, would she recognise him? She peered at herself in the mirror, comparing her reflection to the framed photograph of her mother and herself on her dressing table, taken soon after they moved to Cambridge. She was sure that he wouldn't know her. She had altered out of all recognition even in the five years since it was taken.

She fetched a pen and notepaper from her desk and tried once more, driven by a sudden sense of urgency. If she didn't send a letter

161

soon he might move away again and she'd have lost the chance to get in touch again.

'Dear Daddy' ...' Yes, Daddy was still how she thought of him. Better to write as she felt.

I expect this letter will come as a surprise to you. I've always been so pleased to hear from you but lately I've been wishing so much that we could meet again and tell each other all our news. So much has happened since last we saw each other ...'

She went on to tell him about school and her 'O' levels; how she was studying domestic science at college; about Alison and her friends the Carnes; about Red's puppet theatre – she was sure he would love that. She told him how much she regretted giving up her music – about her driving lessons. In fact once she got into her stride she found herself covering page after page. Being herself – writing straight from the heart – was the answer. And once she got into her stride, it came easily, as easily as it had when she had written to him during the fateful world cruise six years ago. The significance of the fact that she hadn't mentioned her mother, the shop or Morgan never even occurred to her.

When she had finished the letter she read it through carefully. Then she folded it and slipped it into an evelope, carefully printing the address on the front.

'If he likes it, he likes it,' she told herself philosophically as she sealed the envelope. 'If he wants to see me, he'll let me know. If not – well, then I'll know not to try again.'

David Rose looked up as Harry took a seat on the opposite side of his desk. He'd retained the name of the agency when he'd bought Gerry Sylvester out, but sometimes he wondered if he wouldn't have done better building a completely new image for the outfit. Some of the clients he had taken over from Gerry were undeniably dead wood. The singer Stella Rainbow and her pianist-arranger, Harry Wendover were among them in his opinion. Over the hill was how he privately thought of them. Profitable enough in their time, granted, but fit only for the end of the pier or opening village fêtes now. These were the sixties. The dawning of the Age of Aquarius, as the song said: a time of revolutionary social change. Groups were what everyone wanted now; something excitingly different. New music, new songs with up to the minute lyrics expressing modern ideas. Double acts were

162

old hat — dead as a doornail. Most of David's out-of-office time was spent travelling up and down the country, searching the clubs and pubs, the small-town theatres and discotheques, looking for talent. Young people with that special something that today's public craved; finding a group to succeed the Beatles, that was what David dreamed of for his agency, not acting as a crutch for a bunch of has-beens.

'Are you sure Miss Rainbow is fit enough to work again?' he asked abstractedly, leafing through his morning post.

'She will be,' Harry assured him. 'We've been rehearsing and her voice is as good as ever. I thought perhaps a summer season. By the end of May I'll have her back in shape again.'

David looked up with a faintly amused expression in his quick brown eyes. 'You sound more like a football coach than a musician,' he remarked.

Harry flushed. 'She's still popular, you know. People are still buying her records. The last royalty statement . . .'

'People are still buying Gracie Fields' records, Harry,' David interrupted tetchily. 'But that doesn't mean they still stand in line to see her. Bums on seats is what it's all about, Harry boy — bums on seats.' He opened a drawer and pulled out a file. 'Most of the summer shows are already booked, but I might be able to offer you a season at a holiday camp.'

Harry's heart sank. 'I had thought perhaps a cruise. It would really set Stella up.'

David lit a cigar, more to hide his irritation than from a desire to smoke. What did they think he was in business for? What was he? Some kind of benevolent society — a rest home for washed-up singers?

'The cruise ships are all looking for something a bit more with it nowadays,' he said, with brutal frankness. 'Younger artists with a bit more chutzpah — pzazz — a more sexy image.'

'Stella's only thirty,' Harry said defensively. 'She's still a great looking girl.'

David looked doubtful. The last time he had seen Stella he'd thought she was running to fat. 'Thirty's over the hill, Harry,' he said, leaning forward earnestly. 'Today's punters are the kids — fourteen to twenty, that's your sixties public. They don't want to see folks who look like their mums and dads standing up there singing golden oldies. They want someone they can identify with — someone to idolise, scream and drool over.'

Harry bit his lip hard to stop himself telling this brash young man what he thought of his insulting remarks. If he'd had his way

163

he wouldn't be here at all. After all, he and Stella didn't have to work any more. They could afford to retire. But if he didn't go home with an engagement of some kind, Stella would fall back into her depression again. 'Okay then,' he said. 'Where's the holiday camp?'

David looked down at the file again.'With a bit of luck I could do you Skegness,' he said hopefully.

'*Skegness*?'

'Yes. Lucky to get it too. The act they'd booked let them down − got a better offer last week and backed out.'

Harry didn't blame them. He turned the fiery protest that rose to his lips into a cough. 'David, in case you don't remember, only five years ago Stella was starring in a Broadway musical.'

David spread his hands. 'I know − I *know*. It never made it over here though, did it? Even the hit number didn't get into the charts in the UK.' He shrugged. 'I don't have to tell an old stager like you, Harry. Five years in this business might as well be five hundred. Stella's been out of the public eye too long. You know what people are. Today, they love you − tomorrow they can't even remember your name. Well . . .?' He waited, drumming his fingers as Harry struggled to make a decision. 'Do I book you for Skegness or don't I?'

Harry sighed. 'Pencil us in. I'll see what Stella says.'

David pursed his lips. 'I warn you, the offer won't stay open long.'

Harry stood up. His temper was shortening dangerously. If he didn't get the hell out of here soon, he'd be unable to resist telling David Rose what he could do with his holiday camp − Redcoats and all.

'I've got another appointment in ten minutes,' he lied. 'I'll have to be going. I'll be in touch.' He was already halfway out through the door.

As he went through the door to the outer office he almost collided with a secretary on her way in with a sheaf of letters for David to sign. She looked over her shoulder as she came into David's office.

'Wasn't that Harry Wendover?'

'Yeah.' David nodded, taking the letters from her.

'Did you tell him his daughter rang a couple of weeks ago?'

He looked up at her with a frown. 'Didn't know he had a daughter.'

The girl nodded. 'From a previous marriage, apparently. Don't you remember, I asked your permission to give her his address?'

164

'Yes, I remember now you mention it.' David shrugged. 'Sounds dodgy to me. Doesn't do to get involved in their private affairs, Lyn. If they drop themselves in the shit we don't want the name of the agency linked with theirs in the papers.' He rolled the cigar from one side of his mouth to the other. 'Anyone else rings asking personal stuff about those two, just hang up.'

Still seething, Harry bought himself a sandwich at a nearby coffee bar and sat wondering what to do. Stella might be pleased just to be working again. On the other hand, when she heard what the offer was ... One could never tell with Stella nowadays. If only Gerry were still his agent, he'd have come up with something. Gerry really cared about his clients; treated them more like his family. But Gerry was the last of a dying breed. Harry looked at his watch. It was still early. He'd made an early start this morning.

An idea struck him: if he got a fast train he could be in Cambridge by mid afternoon. He had the address in his pocket. He could see Grace and talk to her face to face. Surely all the old bitterness would be gone by now. And it shouldn't be too difficult for them to get a divorce. After all this time she could divorce him for desertion. And if he could go home with the promise of his freedom it would more than make up to Stella for the lack of exciting offers. Feeling more cheerful he paid for his sandwich and set off determinedly for King's Cross Station.

'Hey, watch it. You nearly hit that cyclist.' Tom glowered. 'Look, Ellie, you're just not concentrating. Better call it a day. This old crate may be on her last legs but I don't want to write her off just yet.'

'Sorry, Tom.' Elaine drew the car into the kerb and stopped. She'd carried the letter to her father around in her pocket for days, finally posting it yesterday. But ever since the moment she dropped it into the postbox her thoughts had been in turmoil. Should she have told her mother what she'd done? Would he reply? Maybe the letter would cause him trouble. She didn't wish that for him. More and more she felt that she shouldn't have written at all. Patrick had encouraged her, but on reflection, maybe he had merely welcomed a diverson that would take her mind off his departure.

She turned to Tom. 'Look, I've got something on my mind, Tom. I shouldn't really have come out with you today.'

'You can say that again.' He let his breath out in a relieved sigh and grinned at her. 'Okay − out you get. I'll take over now. It's beginning to get dark anyway.' They changed places and as he took

165

the driving seat he glanced at her pensive face. 'Is it Patrick?'

'No.' She looked at him. There was no fooling Tom. He was quite sensitive underneath all that devil-may-care brashness. 'Yes, I suppose it is, partly.'

'Look, kid, we all wanted to warn you when we saw how keen you were getting. Patrick's restless. He always has been and I reckon he always will be. He does think a lot of you − in his way. But Patrick is like Red. He's got itchy feet.'

Elaine swallowed hard. It was horrible, having people sorry for you. 'But your father settled down,' she argued. 'Look at him now.'

He laughed. 'Call that settling down? Anyway it took him long enough. Sometimes I think he only did it for us − for Zoe, Patrick and me. And because Grandad left him the house and the business.'

'So you don't think Patrick ever will − even if he has a family too?'

'Let's face it, love, a wife and family would be like a millstone round Patrick's neck.' Tom slipped an arm around her shoulders. 'Look, Ellie, you're just a kid. You don't want to hang around till you're old on the off-chance he might change, do you? You've got your life ahead of you, love. There's a great big beautiful world out there. Go and grab yourself a piece of it.'

She nodded, sniffing back the tears. Tom and she had become good friends over the past months. He was like the brother she had never had. What he said made good sense, yet it sounded so heart-breakingly final. She just couldn't accept that it was over between them. She thought of her father. If things had been different, if he'd still been around, *he* would have told her what to do. He'd have understood. It was no use asking her mother. She'd just get all pink in the face and warn her that no man was worth it. She'd heard her say things like that before. She'd wait till their weekend together, she told herself desperately. No one, not even Alison, knew about that. It would be her last chance to prove to Patrick just how much he loved and needed her.

'Come on, love. Don't look so despondent. We'll try again tomorrow.' Tom was looking at her.

'What? Oh, driving? Yes, all right, Tom. We'll try again tomorrow. I'll concentrate better then, I promise.'

'That's the spirit.' He gave her shoulder a final squeeze and started the car again, edging it into the traffic.

'It's the fashion show this evening,' Elaine said, dragging her

166

thoughts back to the present. 'I said I'd help behind the scenes. It's time I was getting back anyway.'

'That Morgan of yours has started moving some of his gear in,' Tom said conversationally as he drove.

Elaine gave a little shrug. 'Don't call him *my* Morgan. He's Mum's if he's anybody's.'

He glanced at her curiously. 'Is she fond of him? I mean − you know, in *that* way?'

Again Elaine shrugged. 'I don't know. And what's more I don't want to know.'

He laughed. 'Don't fancy him as a new dad then?'

'God forbid.'

'I don't think you need to worry too much on that score,' Tom steered the car into Prince Regent Street. 'He's as queer as the proverbial clockwork, but surely you realised that?'

Elaine turned to stare at him, her mouth dropping open. 'Are you *sure*?'

'Sure as I can be. He's not one of your flamboyantly obvious types, but the signs are there all the same.'

Elaine was silent. *Morgan.* Odd, it had never occurred to her before. She wondered if her mother knew? And if not, what would her reaction be when she found out?'

It was almost five o'clock and growing dark by the time Harry found Prince Regent Street. He'd never been to Cambridge before and all the people he asked for directions seemed to be strangers.

He spotted the shop from the other side of the street. Small and exclusive; very different from the shabby little drapery store where Grace had worked when they first moved to Stanmore. It seemed to be half closing day and Harry stepped into the doorway of a chemist's shop opposite, using the cover the shadow gave him to observe for a moment.

In the window of 'Style 'N' Grace' was a low table with a large Chinese vase of chrysanthemums on it. A brightly coloured scarf was draped from the mouth of the vase and across the table to trail on to the grey carpet. It looked very effective, as though the colour from the flowers were spilling over. In the opposite corner of the window an elegant black chiffon evening dress was displayed, its finely pleated skirt romantically fanned out. It had a single diagonal diamante shoulder strap and looked very expensive. It was the kind of dress Stella had worn in the days before she had started to put on weight.

Suddenly the shop door opened and Harry leaned back out of

sight as a woman came out, her arms full of garments. He stepped forward slightly to get a better view. Was it − could it really be Grace? There was a street lamp outside the shop and it illuminated her like a spotlight as she opened the tailgate of a blue estate car parked at the kerb. Her glossy dark hair was cut in a short fashionable style and her face was expertly made up; the fine dark eyes accentuated with shadow and mascara. Slim as ever, she wore a classically cut black suit with a crimson scarf at the neck. The skirt was fashionably short, revealing shapely legs in sheer black stockings and high-heeled shoes.

He watched, riveted, as she loaded the garments into the car. It *was* Grace − and yet it wasn't. At least not the Grace he had married. This woman was a stranger and he felt hesitant and suddenly unsure of himself. But he had come a long way and if he was going to speak to her he must pluck up his courage and do it now.

He moved forward out of the doorway, but as he did so a young man followed Grace out of the shop, carrying another armful of clothes. He was tall and good-looking and, Harry guessed, younger than Grace by some ten years. But as she turned to smile up at him it was immediately clear to Harry that there was a closeness − perhaps even an intimacy − between them. The young man said something and Grace laughed up into his face. Her eyes sparkled as they once had for him and Harry knew a moment of sharp and unexpected pain.

The letter had come by the first post, shortly after Harry had left to catch the London train. The feminine writing and the Cambridge postmark had taunted Stella all morning as it lay there on the hall table. When Harry hadn't returned by half-past four her patience ran out. She dialled the number of the Sylvester Agency and asked the girl who answered if Harry had been in. She was told he had left at eleven-thirty.

Angrily she paced the room. Where was he? What could have kept him till now? For the hundredth time she walked into the hall and picked up the envelope, turning it over in her hands. Had he already written to Grace to ask for a divorce without telling her? Could this be her reply? The same questions and speculations had haunted her all day and now she could bear the uncertainty no longer. It concerned her too, so why shouldn't she open the letter and find out? It wasn't her fault that Harry was so late after all.

Making up her mind, she took the letter into the dining room and ripped it open eagerly. Sitting down at the table she spread the letter out before her and began to read, her eyes widening as they took in the words. He had *lied*. Harry had lied to her. He'd never actually lost touch with his daughter at all, and now here she was, writing him a chatty letter and asking to see him again. If she hadn't opened this letter he might never have mentioned it. Perhaps he had started seeing his wife and child again secretly. He might even be planning to go back to them − arranging it all at this very minute. She glanced at the clock. It was now almost six o'clock. Seven and a half hours since he left the agency. Her heart quickened with a sudden stifling panic. Perhaps he wasn't coming back at all. Perhaps he had already left her.

She went upstairs and stood looking at herself in the bedroom mirror. She still wore the crumpled slacks and sweater she'd put on this morning. She was a mess. Even she could see it now. She'd begun to put on weight with her pregnancy, and after the hysterectomy the weight-gain had accelerated. The doctor had said it was something to do with her hormones. He had advised her about healthy dieting and given her some tablets but they made her feel sick so she stopped taking them. As for dieting − food was her only comfort. She'd already lost so much that made life bearable.

Going to a drawer she took out the album she'd kept ever since her singing career had begun. All her publicity pictures and her press cuttings were in it. Stella Rainbow on a world cruise. The lovely Stella Rainbow enjoying a joke at a first night party. And one of Harry and her, looking radiantly happy as they toasted each other. The caption under that one read: 'Broadway Starlight Shines on Stella.' She looked so slender and glamorous. Could they really have been taken such a short time ago? Tears of self-pity trickled down her cheeks as she threw the album into a corner and lowered her head despairingly on to folded arms. All that hard work − all that promise − just to end up like this; washed up at thirty, looking like a fat old woman. Living with a man who wasn't even hers. Anger and resentment began to burn inside her. Had she slaved just to earn money for Harry to send to his wife and daughter? Had he been keeping in touch with them behind her back? And now that he'd had the best out of her, did he intend to throw her over and go back to them? It was so unfair − so bloody unfair. How could he betray her like this? She looked up at her tearstained reflection in the mirror and suddenly she felt afraid. 'I don't want to be alone,' she said aloud to the dowdy woman staring tearfully back at her through the glass. 'I couldn't bear it if he left me now.' It's up to you, a voice seemed to answer inside her head It's up to you Stella. So get off your backside and do something about it.

169

Elaine was ready to go. Her mother and Morgan had taken the first load of stock round to the hall where the fashion show was taking place. When they returned for the second load she would accompany them, squeezed reluctantly between the two of them on the bench seat in front. She stood at her bedroom window with her coat on, looking down into the street, waiting for the car to return. In the doorway of the chemist's shop opposite she suddenly spotted a man standing in the shadows. He wore a light-coloured raincoat with the collar turned up. She frowned. There was something vaguely familiar about him. She rubbed the patch of mist her breath had made on the glass and knelt on the window seat to get a better look. Who was he? What was he doing, lurking there in the doorway? The shops were all closed and there were few people about. Was he up to no good? She was still watching when he suddenly stepped out onto the pavement into the full light of the street lamp. She pressed her face against the window, but at that moment a bus passed, obscuring him from her view. It stopped at the bus stop opposite to let down passengers. By the time it had driven off he was gone.

The fashion show had been a great success. All the tickets had been sold and the hall was packed to capacity. Grace had hired a professional actress to compere for them; a sophisticated blonde with a beautiful voice who, although not exactly well known, had brought a touch of glamour and class to the occasion. Most of the models were professional too, though Grace had invited some of her customers − mainly those with fuller figures − to model the larger sizes. Without exception, they had all agreed, flattered and pleased at being chosen. Among these was Lilian Davies, Morgan's greatest fan. Grace felt that having Lilian in the show was a coup. It mean that all her friends would come and she numbered among them some of the town's most influential and well-heeled women.

Morgan had arranged the lighting and music as well as the decor and the evening had gone off exceptionally well, exceeding all Grace's expectations. After the main part of the show was over she mingled with the audience as they sipped wine and nibbled canapes. She was delighted to see that several of the London buyers to whom she had sent invitations had come, and they all enthused over Morgan's designs, promising to get in touch with her over the next few days.

Eyes sparkling and flushed with her success, she was just about to go in search of Morgan himself when she felt a hand on her arm and

170

turned to see Lilian Davies standing at her elbow, a small, elegant blue-rinsed lady in tow.

'Grace, I'd like to introduce you to Mrs Mary Kingston. She enjoyed the show so much and would like to meet you.'

Grace took the soft hand the woman offered her. 'How do you do? I'm so glad you liked the show.'

'Oh, I did. I have to confess that I'm not a customer of yours, my dear, but I certainly shall be in future. Up until now I've always gone up to London for all my things — or had them made. But it gets a little more tiring with each passing year, and now that I see what we have here in our own town ...' She smiled, her bright eyes darting round the room. 'Mr Owen — the young man who designs the knitwear — is he a relation of yours?'

Grace smiled back. 'No, just someone I'm proud to have discovered. He's so talented.'

'I'm sure he'll go a long way,' Mary Kingston agreed. She peered around her. 'I'd love to meet him too if he's about anywhere.'

'I'm afraid he's rather shy.' Grace led her towards the rows of specially hired gilt chairs, now vacated. 'But if you'd like to have a seat for a few minutes? People are beginning to drift away. I might persuade him to come out now that it's less crowded. Let me get you another glass of wine and some of the smoked salmon sandwiches.'

Mary Kingston simpered. 'Thank you, I think I will. I admit I have a weakness for smoked salmon and those little sandwiches were delicious.'

It was fifteen minutes later when Grace returned with Morgan and a reluctant Elaine. She found Mary Kingston still waiting quite happily, the plate that had been full of miniature sandwiches now empty on the chair beside her, along with her empty wine glass.

'This is Morgan Owen, Mrs Kingston,' she said smilingly. 'And this is my daughter, Elaine.'

The elderly woman looked Elaine up and down with razor-sharp blue eyes that beamed approval. 'What a pretty girl. How do you do, my dear?' She turned her attention to Morgan. 'And this is the talented designer I've been hearing so much about. Do tell me — do you really knit the prototypes yourself?' She simpered at Morgan, paying him effusive compliments about his work and asking him all kinds of questions about his background. Standing back, Grace privately thought some of them a little impertinent, but the woman looked like being a good customer, so she kept the smile firmly glued to her face. Finally Mrs Kingston stood up.

'My son is collecting me,' she said. 'He's probably waiting outside

171

at this very moment, thinking I've got lost or eloped or something.' She smiled coyly at Morgan. 'Chance would be a fine thing at my age, eh?' She looked at Grace, her simpering smile suddenly replaced by a determined stare. 'Mrs Wendover, may I come and see you next week? I've a little business proposition I'd like to discuss with you.'

Grace tried not to look surprised. 'Yes, of course you may. Come and see the shop too. I'm always there. Maybe if you came close to closing time, then we wouldn't be disturbed.'

'I'll do that.' Mrs Kingston raised her arm to wave to a tall young man standing at the back of the now almost empty hall. 'There's Paul, my son. Come and meet him.' She glanced round for Elaine. 'I'm sure you and he would get on like a house on fire, my dear.' Reaching out, she grasped Elaine's arm firmly, her small soft hand amazingly strong. 'Come and be introduced. I'm always telling him he should meet more young women.'

Paul Kingston was tall and willowy. He had blue eyes like his mother. But where hers were sharp and perceptive, his were wary and guarded. Although he was only in his early thirties his brown hair was already receding and he wore a small military moustache that sat somewhat incongruously above his slightly weak mouth.

'This is Ellen Wendover, Paul,' Mrs Kingston said.

'*Elaine*, actually.' Elaine offered her hand to the young man who touched it briefly with his fingertips, looking acutely uncomfortable.

'My son is assistant headmaster at St Jasper's boys' school,' Mrs Kingston said. 'My late husband, Paul's father, was a don at the University, but Paul didn't quite aspire to that, did you, darling?'

The young man blushed and Elaine felt sorry for him. Why didn't he stand up to the old battle-axe? She might look small and frail but she obviously had a will of iron. She smiled at Paul sympathetically.

'Is your school in Cambridge?'

He looked slightly startled. 'Yes − er, no. It's in a village on the outskirts. It's a private school.'

'Do you live in?

'No. I live at home − with Mother.'

'Oh, I see.'

Grace shook hands politely with Paul Kingston, then said: 'I hope you'll excuse us if we go and pack up now, Mrs Kingston. There's an awful lot to do and we have to be out of the hall by eleven.'

'Of course, my dear. You mustn't let us stop you. Is there anything Paul here can do to help you?'

Grace shook her head, slightly embarrassed. 'Oh, no – thank you all the same.'

'Perhaps we can give Ellen here a lift to save space in your car?'

'Oh, no. Mum will need my help too,' Elaine put in quickly. But to her dismay her mother was smiling at her encouragingly.

'How kind. You've worked really hard all evening, darling, and you do have college in the morning. No, you run along with Mr Kingston. Morgan and I can probably manage in one trip with only the two of us.'

The Kingstons' car was a stately Rover, large, elderly and comfortable. Mrs Kingston insisted Elaine should ride in front with Paul, whilst she sat in the back. 'Where is it you live, dear?' she asked Elaine.

'Prince Regent Street. In the flat over the shop.'

'I see. Well, as we live in the opposite direction, Paul had better drop me off first,' she said decisively. 'Then you can take your time taking Ellen home, Paul.'

He flushed dully in the darkness. He was a careful driver. He delivered his mother to the door of a Victorian house near Jesus Green and after he had seen her safely indoors and resumed his seat beside Elaine, she immediately felt a change in him. His mother's presence obviously oppressed and inhibited him. He turned to look at Elaine, and for the first time he smiled.

'I'm sorry about that. Mother has a way of organising people. You'd probably much rather have stayed on and helped with the clearing up.'

'Oh, no. It's quite nice to get out of it really,' Elaine lied. She felt rather sorry for Paul. Unless she was very much mistaken his mother had undermined his confidence so much that he had a pretty low opinion of himself. Why on earth didn't he get out and find a place of his own? she wondered. Surely a man of his age shouldn't still be tied to his mother's apron strings.

'You'll have to tell me when we get to your place,' he was saying. 'I'm not very familiar with this part of town.'

'Yes, I will.' She glanced at his profile. He was quite nice-looking in a hungry, raddled sort of way. He looked as though he could do with a good meal. 'I like your car,' she said chattily. 'It's very comfy.'

'She's getting old now, but Mother would hate to part with her,' he said. 'I'd like to trade her in for one of the new 2,000 models.'

Elaine glanced at him. Why did he have to do everything his

173

mother told him? Why didn't he get his own car? She was sure she would in his position.

'I'm having driving lessons,' she told him. 'I take my test in a few weeks' time.'

He glanced at her. 'Really? Good luck.'

They drove for a moment in a silence that felt to Elaine like a thread, drawing tighter. To break the tension she said: 'I expect you enjoy your job.'

'Yes.'

'Assistant Head sounds terribly grand. You must be very clever.

He gave a dry little laugh. 'Not at all. It isn't a very prestigious school. When the last deputy was promoted to Head they had trouble replacing him.'

Why did he have to be so brutally honest? 'Your mother is obviously very proud of you,' she said. 'But mothers usually are, aren't they?'

For a moment he was silent, then he said: 'I'm afraid I was a bit of a disappointment to her. Father was an academic, but my brother was the one who took after him, not me. Richard was quite a bit older. He was killed near the end of the war.'

'Oh, I'm sorry.'

'Mother never got over it. He had a dazzling career ahead of him. He was working in London at the time. It was a stray flying bomb.'

Elaine bit her lip, unsure of what to say next. 'Oh, look ...' She peered out of the window with some relief. 'This is where we live. You can drop me here.'

As he opened the car door for her he asked suddenly. 'Elaine — can I see you again?'

She paused, startled at the unexpectedness of the question. 'Oh — I — er — don't know.'

'Perhaps I could ring you sometime?'

'Yes, I suppose you could.'

'Right. Goodnight then, Elaine.'

'Goodnight. And thank you for the lift — Paul.' She watched as the Rover drove away. What a strange man. Too old for her. Too stuffy too, though he had loosened up a little after his mother left. As for seeing him again ... She giggled, wondering what Alison and Tom would make of Paul Kingston. Anyone with less in common with them would be hard to find.

When Harry got home it was late and he was bone weary. He'd had a long walk from the station and he dreaded telling Stella that he had achieved nothing.

He let himself into the quiet house. It was dark. There were no lights on at all on the ground floor. His hopes rose. With a bit of luck she would have gone to bed and fallen asleep. He'd get the chance to postpone the confrontation until the morning.

He hung up his raincoat on the hallstand and tiptoed softly towards the staircase. At the foot he hesitated, then slipped off his shoes. Better leave nothing to chance. Very softly he ascended, relying on the moonlight coming through the landing window to light the way. At the bedroom door he paused to listen. No sound came from within. Turning the handle gently he pushed open the door, but immediately he saw that the bedside lamp was on. His heart sank. She was awake after all.

Stella lay on top of the bed. She wore a black négligée made of chiffon and lace over a scarlet satin nightdress. It was low-cut and revealing and made her body look voluptuous and full of promise. Her face was carefully made up and her hair was freshly shampooed and brushed till it hung around her shoulders like a shining black curtain. When she saw him her eyes lit up.

'Harry, there you are at last. You've been so long. I've missed you so much.'

Her voice held no hint of reproach. He stared at her, hardly able to believe his eyes. 'Stella, you look wonderful.' He sat on the edge of the bed and took her hand. 'Are you feeling better, love?'

She sighed. 'I took a good look at myself today, Harry. I realised just how much I've let myself go since my illness. Poor Harry. Have I given you a very hard time? Darling, you look so tired. I was beginning to get quite worried. Come to bed.'

He undressed hurriedly and stretched out beside her. 'I'm afraid I didn't get very far today, love,' he said, anxious to get the bad news over with. 'David Rose isn't like old Gerry. He didn't have anything very exciting to offer. Then I had a thought: I got the train and went to Cambridge. I thought I might talk to Grace about a divorce.'

She leaned on one elbow to look into his eyes. 'You did?'

'Yes, but she was out. I didn't even get anywhere with that. It's been a wasted day, love. I'm sorry.'

'No it hasn't.' Sitting up she slipped her arms out of the négligée and pulled the scarlet nightdress over her head. Although her body was plumper now, it seemed to Harry that she was more beautiful, more sexy and desirable than ever before. She leaned over him till the brown nipples brushed his chest, hard and tantalising. Taking his face between her hands she kissed him lingeringly, her tongue darted teasingly into his mouth. 'Because you're home again,' she whispered. 'You've come back to me. That's something I didn't

175

really deserve. We're still together, darling. That's all that really matters.' She ran one hand down the length of his body and found to her satisfaction that he had hardened for her. 'Oh, Harry,' she breathed urgently. 'Make love to me. I want you so much.'

His weariness left him as she began to caress him in the old ways that had delighted him in the past. Somewhere in the back of his mind he wondered what could have happened to bring about such a miraculous change in her, but soon he was too aroused by her eager lips and hands to care. Passion mounted between them in a way he had feared was gone for ever and soon they were making love with a desperate urgency wrought by the past weeks of abstinence. The climax came for both of them at the same moment. It was explosive. Like the birth of a star, Stella told herself ecstatically.

Much later, as they lay in each other's arms, sated and still drowsy, she said: 'I never asked you — what *did* David offer us?'

Harry held his breath, glancing down at the gloriously tangled black hair spread across his chest. 'A summer season in a — holiday camp.'

'Oh, where?'

'Skegness.'

Stella sat up and looked down at him. 'You're joking.'

'No.'

For a moment she stared at him, her dark eyes round and expressionless, then she began to laugh: the deep infectious throaty chuckle that Harry hadn't heard in months, her golden breasts bouncing with the vibration. Soon he was laughing too. Clasping her shoulders he pulled her down on top of him and they rolled over together on the rumpled bed, helpless with mirth.

'*Skegness*! The cheeky bastard. Oh, Harry.' She kissed him hard. 'I love you so much. What the hell does it matter where we are or where we work, just so long as we're together and we love each other?'

Later, just as he was falling asleep, Harry had a sudden thought. 'By the way,' he asked sleepily, 'was there any mail today?'

Stella sighed and snuggled closer to him. 'No, love. No letters. Nothing at all.'

In her mind's eye she saw the little pile of ashes in the dining-room fireplace. She remembered thinking as she burned the letter, how odd it was that something so fragile, so transitory, could have caused her to make the biggest, the wisest decision of her life.

176

Chapter Thirteen

Excitement quickened Elaine's heartbeat as green fields began to give way to the rows of grimy houses that made up the outskirts of the city. She would see him soon — see him soon — see him soon. The train wheels seemed to repeat it joyously and her body tensed as she sat forward to look out of the window. In less than an hour she and Patrick would be alone together in his flat, for two whole days. She sighed, wishing it could have been for longer. It seemed so long since the New Year when he had left. In her last letter she'd asked him to meet the four-thirty train, but she had managed to get away in time to catch the two o'clock. How surprised he would be when she turned up at the flat early. She closed her eyes and tried to visualise his delighted expression.

She had so much to tell him. During the last few weeks a lot had happened and she'd been saving it all up. The most exciting thing was that she had passed her driving test. She'd thought at one point that it would have to be postponed. Just two weeks before she was due to take it, Tom's old car had broken down during one of Alison's driving lessions. It turned out to have something quite serious wrong with it. So serious and expensive that Tom couldn't afford to have it done until he'd saved up enough money. Alison had cancelled her test with good-natured resignation, relieved that it hadn't been her driving that had caused the problem. Elaine had been about to cancel hers when she had run into Paul Kingston one Saturday morning in town.

He'd telephoned her twice since the fashion show to ask her out but each time she'd made an excuse. But coming face to face with him in W H Smith's that Saturday she could hardly refuse when he asked her to have coffee with him.

Over it she'd told him about Tom's car and how she was going to have to put off her test.

'There's no need, you can borrow *my* car,' he said suddenly. 'I'll take you for a couple of practice drives first too, if you like.'

She stared at him, her eyes round. 'Oh, I couldn't.'

'Why not?'

She'd been about to suggest that his mother might not like the idea and the fact that she'd stopped herself only just in time made her blush. 'Well, if you're really sure . . .' She so wanted to be able to surprise Patrick with the news that she'd passed. 'It's very kind of you, thanks.'

'Not at all.' He glanced at his watch. 'No time like the present. We could go for a drive now, if you like? I've got an hour to spare.'

Paul had proved himself a good teacher, cool-headed and calm; encouraging her when she felt unsure and offering good advice. The result had been that two days ago, on the first day of the Easter holidays, she had passed her test with flying colours.

Paul had been waiting for her at the test centre on her return. He smiled indulgently when she waved the slip triumphantly at him. 'Congratulations. What did I tell you? I knew you'd do it.'

Impulsively she stood on tiptoe and kissed his cheek. 'I couldn't have done it without your help. Thanks, Paul.'

He flushed, turning quickly away to the car. 'Nonsense, the credit's all yours.'

Alison pretended to be sick with envy. 'Jammy pig. I'll tell Patrick next time I see him that you've been going out with another bloke. You might have asked if he'd let your best friend borrow his posh car.' She pulled a face. 'Toffee-nosed little cow. It'll be fourpence to speak to you now. Just you wait till *I* pass. I'm going to make Dad buy me a Mini and I shan't let you borrow it. You'll be jealous of *me* then.'

Elaine laughed, all too familiar with the good-natured schoolgirlish banter they still lapsed into. She knew there was no real envy or malice in Alison.

The other thing that had happened was that Mrs Kingston, Paul's mother, had offered to sponsor Morgan. After the show he'd been inundated with orders, some of them from London shops. Initially he and Grace had been over the moon, then they began to worry that they wouldn't be able to meet the demand and might have to pass up some of the precious orders. Mary Kingston's little 'business proposition' had seemed like a stroke of real luck. She had some money to invest, she told them. She was bored with the stock market and wanted something she could take a personal interest in. She offered to put up the money for Morgan to take a lease on a small factory and employ a team of full time knitters. Mary Kingston had

178

'joined the team', as Elaine put it to herself. She wasn't sure that she liked the idea. There was something about the old woman that gave her the creeps, and since her arrival on the scene Grace had been busier with her business interests than before.

In a way all this worked in Elaine's favour. With her mother so preoccupied it hadn't been too hard to convince her that a weekend trip to London was necessary for her studies. Visiting the British Museum where there was an exhibition of Tudor costumes and embroidery was a must for serious students of needlework, Elaine had assured her. There was an invitation to stay with a friend from college too. They'd been given tickets for a show on the Saturday evening, so she'd stay up in London till Sunday evening.

It had been ridiculously easy. So easy that Elaine had been stricken with guilt. She'd never lied seriously to her mother before. She wouldn't have now if it hadn't been so desperately important to her.

The train slowed as it began the long pull into King's Cross Station and Elaine stood up to pull her weekend case down from the rack. Patrick wouldn't be there to meet her and she regretted that. She'd looked forward to catching the first glimpse of him standing at the barrier − of running into his outstretched arms. Still, it would be fun to surprise him, and it wouldn't take long to get to the flat. She'd looked up the Underground map and knew where to change and everything.

When the train drew into the station and came to a halt she was waiting impatiently by the door, unable to keep the smile of anticipation off her face.

Tom had been on his way through the hall, about to go out, when the telephone rang. He was enjoying what was left of his freedom. There would be precious little of it these holidays. On Monday morning he was to begin working in his father's shop to help earn the money to pay for his car repairs. The telephone rang just as he was passing it. Reaching out one long arm he picked up the receiver and assumed a high, falsetto voice.

'Mill House home for the terminally bewildered. To whom would you speak?'

'Shut up, idiot, it's me. Listen, I've only got a minute.'

'Patrick?'

'Yes. Look, I've got a problem. You probably don't know this, but Elaine was supposed to be coming up today for the weekend.'

'Well, I'm not surprised. I always knew you were a vile seducer of innocent virgins.'

179

'Oh, for God's sake, stop being flippant and listen.'

'Okay. Go on.'

'I want you to go round there and stop her from coming. She's supposed to be catching the four-thirty, so there's still plenty of time.'

Tom frowned. 'Hang on, she's going to be pretty disappointed, isn't she? I hope you've got a bloody good reason.'

'Of course I have. Look, Ann-Marie, the French girl I told you about who was here last term, has suddenly turned up.'

'And I'm to tell Ellie that, am I?'

'Of course not. Tell her I've been asked to go on a weekend school – anything you like.'

Tom winced. 'It's a bit rough, isn't it? Can't you get rid of this French bird? You said you were fed up with the way she threw herself at you last term.'

'Look, just do as I say and put Elaine off, will you?' Patrick sounded impatient. 'If you must know, I want to stay on the right side of Ann-Marie. She's got a flat in Paris and if I play my cards right she'll let me move in with her. Think of the cash I'll save.'

'If you ask me, I think you're being a bit of a shit.'

'Nobody did ask you. Anyway, since when have *you* been an upholder of morals? Look, are you going to do it, or aren't you? Someone else is waiting to use this phone.'

Tom toyed with the idea of telling Patrick to do his own dirty work, then he thought better of it. 'All right, all right. I'll go round there now.' If she was going to be hurt it might as well be his shoulder she cried on, he told himself.

'Good.' Patrick hung up abruptly without thanking him.

Tom held the buzzing receiver away from him and stared at it. 'Cretin,' he said explosively as he dropped it back onto its rest. 'Must want your head examining.' This French bird must be quite something if she was worth ditching Ellie for. Turning, he came face to face with Morgan. He clapped one hand over his chest. 'Gawd, you made me jump.'

Morgan looked embarrassed. 'I'm sorry, Look, I heard the phone ring and thought it might be for me. I didn't mean to eavesdrop, but you were shouting at each other.'

'Patrick was phoning from the call box. You have to yell because of the traffic.'

'Yes, well, I'm going round to the shop now. Do you want me to give Elaine the message?'

Tom shook his head. 'No. I'll see it through. It's always the younger brother who gets the shitty end of the stick, but there it is, I suppose.'

'Her mother thinks she's staying with a friend,' Morgan said reproachfully.

Tom nodded. 'She is — or rather, *was*.'

'Well, it's nothing to do with me, of course, but I wouldn't like to see Elaine, or Grace get hurt.'

Tom turned to look at him. 'Believe me, neither would I,' he said seriously. 'You might think I'm a bit of a clown, Morgan, but I am fond of Elaine, which is why I'm going to pass this message on to her personally.' He fixed Morgan with a steely look. 'It's also why I hope no one is going to blow the whistle on her, right?'

'You don't have to worry. I won't say anything.' Morgan looked at his watch. 'But if you're going to stop her catching the four o'clock train you'd better let me give you a lift round there now. It's half-two. She's probably started packing by now.'

It was almost half-past four when Elaine finally arrived at the flat. She'd got a little bit lost on the Underground, but in the end she managed to get on to the right train. The flat was one of three, over a men's outfitters and reached by a side entrance. Beside the door was a row of bells with cards beside them. She rang the one with Patrick's name and waited. When there was no reply her heart sank. Surely he wouldn't have left this early to meet her train? She picked up her case and was just turning away when she heard movement in the narrow passage on the other side of the door. A moment later it opened and Patrick's astonished face peered out at her.

'Elaine!'

She laughed uncertainly. 'Yes, I know I'm early, but I thought you wouldn't mind. I caught the two o'clock train.' She frowned. 'It is all right, isn't it? I mean, you were expecting me this weekend?'

'Of course.' He recovered, reaching out to take her case. 'Come on in.' He closed the door and then turned to look at her. 'It's just — look, someone has arrived unexpectedly. She's from France — a student who was on an exchange last term. The boys and I made friends with her. She's over for a visit and she just sort of turned up at lunchtime. I could hardly chuck her out, could I?'

He looked harassed and not at all pleased to see her. He hadn't even kissed her. Elaine's heart plummeted. 'You mean, she's staying here?' she asked.

He laughed. 'Oh, good Lord, no. She just looked in for a chat — didn't realise the others had gone home for the holidays. Look, come up and meet her.' He led the way up the stairs but Elaine

181

noticed that he pushed her case surreptitiously into a cupboard on the landing before opening the living room door.

'Ann-Marie – this is Elaine,' he said, his voice loud and unnaturally jovial. 'She's an old friend of my family from Cambridge – from home.'

Ann-Marie was taller than Elaine and seemed to tower over her in her long black dress. She inspected rather than looked at her, with sloe-dark eyes skilfully accentuated with heavy black liner. Her thick black hair hung around her like a glossy cloak and silver chains jangled at her neck and wrists. She held out one long, white, heavily ringed hand and smiled with her blood-red mouth.

''ow do you do?' Her voice was low and richly accented. Elaine felt intimidated.

'How nice to meet you. Are you staying long?' She blushed. 'I mean in England, of course.'

'Ann-Marie is over for a couple of weeks, visiting friends,' Patrick put in.

'Zees is right.' Ann-Marie gave Patrick an enigmatic smile. Then she said, as though on cue: 'I 'ave to go now, Patreek. I see you again before you leave, eh? You 'ave ze number I geev to you? You let me know about ze apartment?'

Patrick took her arm, steering her towards the door. 'Yes, I'll be in touch. I'll come down and see you out.' He looked over his shoulder at Elaine. 'Make yourself at home. I won't be long.'

But it seemed to Elaine that he was an inordinately long time. Very firmly she closed her mind to the thoughts and suspicions that chased each other through it. She bit her lip hard, despising herself – wishing she didn't mind so much – that she trusted Patrick more. After all, he had never given her any reason not to. When he came back he was smiling brightly as though nothing had happened.

'Sorry about that. Now, what can I get you? You must be dying for a drink of some sort.'

'Who is she?'

He looked at her, his brows coming together with a twinge of annoyance. 'What do you mean, who is she? She's Ann-Marie Labeque. I introduced her, didn't I?'

'I mean what is she to you, Patrick. You know perfectly well what I mean.'

'She's just another art student.'

'From France.'

'Yes. From Reims as a matter of fact. She was over here last term on an exchange.'

182

'I see. She must like you a lot to have come back to see you.'

'I told you, she came to see us all. I happened to be the only one here.'

'What did she mean about an apartment?'

'She knows of one I might rent in Paris.'

'I see.' She walked to the window to stare down unseeingly into the busy street. 'What a disappointment it must have been when I turned up.' She turned to look at him, her cheeks pink and her eyes bright. 'Maybe it was for *you* too?'

He sighed, then crossed the room to her. 'Oh, Ellie. Are you going to let it spoil our weekend? If you'd come on the train you said you were catching, she'd have been gone by the time you got here. I'd have been at the station to meet you, and you ...'

'Would never have known. Is that what you were going to say?'

He reached out to rest his hands on her shoulders. 'Whether you knew about her or not is immaterial. She's just a friend. Lots of friends pass through this flat. Sometimes it's like Piccadilly Circus.' He drew her gently towards him. 'Ellie, you're not jealous, are you?'

Her lip quivered. '*No*. It's just ...'

'Just what?' His arms were round her now and his lips were brushing her cheek.

'Just – oh, Patrick ...' She swallowed hard at the lump in her throat. 'I've been looking forward to seeing you so much. Arriving early was meant to be a surprise and – and ...'

'And what?'

'And ...' His closeness – the touch of his hands was beginning to turn her knees to water and sending the familiar shivers up and down her spine. She was finding it difficult to concentrate. She felt his hand slide down her back to draw her closer. Very gently he tipped up her chin, lifting her face so that he could look into her eyes.

'Yes. *And* ...?'

'And, you haven't even kissed me yet.'

He chuckled softly. 'Ah, is *that* all? Well, we can soon do something about that ...'

Her lips parted for him and she closed her eyes, her heart quickening as she tasted the familiar longed for taste of him. Her arms wound tightly around his neck and she pressed close to him, her heart quickening as her softness moulded against the hard muscle of his body. She had waited so long for this moment.

Their mouths were still joined as he slid an arm beneath her legs and lifted her into his arms. Shouldering open the door of his bedroom he deposited her on the bed and began to undress.

'We've got a lot of catching up to do,' he whispered as he lay down beside her and began to unbutton her shirt.

As she felt the breathless thrill of his naked skin against hers, the last doubt in her mind evaporated and she gave herself up to his lovemaking. When he held her like this, when their limbs entwined and the rhythm of their movements matched the beat of their hearts, nothing else in the world seemed to matter. She moaned, arching her body eagerly for him. He *did* love her. He couldn't make love to her like this if he didn't, could he?

Much later they went out to dinner. Patrick took her to a little Italian restaurant in what had once been a cellar. All around the whitewashed walls were photographs of well-known actors, musicians and artists. They sat at tables with red checked table cloths and little candle lamps and ate the best spaghetti Bolognese Elaine had ever tasted. They also drank a lot of red wine. They walked back to the flat under a velvet sky studded with stars, climbed the dark stairs hand-in-hand and fell eagerly back into the tumbled bed to make love till dawn began to bleach the sky.

'But why did Tom want to speak to Elaine,?'

Morgan shrugged. 'I think he had some kind of message for her.'

'But he seemed so taken aback when I said she'd gone. He turned quite pale.'

Morgan laughed. 'Tom? Turn pale? That'll be the day.'

Grace frowned. There was something here she didn't quite understand. 'What was this message he had for her? You brought him round here in the car. He must have told you.'

Morgan frowned. 'He had a call — from the friend Elaine was staying with, I think.'

'But why would she telephone the Carnes'? She must have known our number.' She touched Morgan's arm. 'What was the message? It must have been urgent for him to come haring round here like that. Morgan, there's nothing wrong, is there?'

Morgan was in a spot. He was no good at telling lies, especially to people he was fond of. 'No. Nothing like that. The friend wanted her to catch another train. I — think something had come up and she wasn't going to be able to meet Elaine. That's all.'

Grace frowned. 'This friend — it isn't Patrick, is it?'

'Patrick?' He felt stupid and inadequate. Once again he felt the warm colour creeping up his neck. His collar suddenly felt as though it had shrunk and he longed to loosen it.

184

'I know she was seeing him. And he's going away for two years,' Grace said half to herself. 'She's been so preoccupied lately. I put it down to the driving test ...' She turned to him. 'You don't think she'd be foolish enough to let him persuade her to spend a last weekend with him, do you?'

Morgan coughed to clear his constricted throat. 'What, Elaine? I'm sure she wouldn't.' To his relief Grace let the matter drop. As soon as he got back to the Carnes' that evening, he went up to Tom's room.

'Did you manage to contact Patrick and let him know Elaine had already left?' he asked.

Tom shook his head. 'No, I couldn't. They're not on the phone at the flat. They have to use a call box just outside in the street.'

'So she would have turned up unexpectedly?'

'Yes.'

For a moment they stared at each other, each picturing the scene in his own way.

'There's nothing either of us can do about it now,' Tom said at last. 'We'll just have to hope it worked out okay.'

It was the following morning when Morgan arrived at the shop that Grace faced him with the direct question: 'It *is* Patrick she's gone to, isn't it?'

He hedged: 'Who?'

'Elaine, of course. Come on, Morgan. I'm her mother. If you know anything, you owe it to me to tell me. She's only seventeen, you know.'

He looked at his feet. 'Grace — don't. I gave my word.'

'Gave your word? Who to — to Elaine? She confided in you?'

He shook his head. 'No, Tom. Patrick rang yesterday afternoon to try to put her off. That was the message.'

'But she'd already left.'

'I know.'

'*Morgan*,' She grasped his arm. 'Why didn't you tell me then? I could have gone and brought her back. They've been together all night now. Do you realise what that means?' She was almost hysterical and he took her shoulders firmly and pressed her into a chair.

'Look, Grace, Elaine isn't a child any more. She's a woman. Things are different from when you were — well, they're different now. I really don't believe there's anything you could have done.'

But Grace was silent, her mind seething with loathsome pictures. She was remembering things she'd tried not to think about for a long time. Suddenly she could hear her father's wheedling voice

185

again and her flesh crawled as she felt his large soft hands touching her skin. She recalled with vivid clarity the day she came back to the flat in Hackney and found Harry in bed with that girl — writhing — their naked limbs entwined. Her heart began to race and the breath caught in her throat. Suddenly she felt suffocated. The room began to swim dizzily in front of her eyes.

'Grace — *Grace*.' Morgan was pushing her head down between her knees. 'Hold on, I'll get you a glass of water.'

With a great effort she controlled her panic. 'I'm — I'll be all right. Just give me a moment.' She sat very still, her face ashen, forcing herself to breathe slowly and deeply. Looking up at Morgan she dimly registered his anxious expression and she attempted a reassuring smile.

'Don't worry. I'll be fine.'

'Are you ill? Do you need a doctor?'

'No, no. I'd love a cup of tea though.'

'I'll make it. Will you be okay on your own?'

'Yes, yes. I'm fine now.'

When he'd gone she leaned back in the chair and closed her eyes. She'd tried not to think about this — about Elaine's emergence into real womanhood — her first love affair. Somehow she'd visualised her only as a virginal bride, all in white, floating down the aisle towards some shadowy ideal man who would love, honour and cherish her for ever without laying so much as a finger on her. As in her own case all those years ago, she was incapable of equating love with what she considered vile, dirty and corrupt.

It was only as the shock began to subside that she became aware of Elaine's deceitfulness. Anger flared up hotly inside her, to be replaced almost at once by pain and guilt. Was it her fault? Had she been such a bad mother that her child could not confide in her? Had she been too full of business these past months — not seen that Elaine needed her? And even if she had seen, what good would she have been? As Morgan came back into the room she blinked back the tears.

'Here we are. You'll feel better after this.' He set the tray down and smiled at her, relieved to see that some of the colour had come back into her cheeks. 'There's still half an hour before you open the shop. Try to relax. And don't worry. Everything will be all right. You'll see.'

They had to run for the train. Patrick bundled her on to it just as the guard was blowing his whistle.

'I'll let you have my address as soon as I can.' He thrust her weekend case in after her, and handed her the large flat parcel containing his Gino Severini picture.

Elaine leaned out of the window. 'I'll write. You will try to write back, won't you?' Her eyes searched his. It was almost over. Oh God, how was she going to bear it?

'I'll try — but you know what I'm like with letters.'

The train began to move. 'Thank you for a lovely weekend — and for the Severini. I'll cherish it.' Patrick stepped back and raised his arm.

'Goodbye.'

'Goodbye.' It sounded so final. She wanted to beg him not to forget her — to come back again soon. All weekend she'd prayed for a miracle. How wonderful if he'd changed his mind and didn't go to France after all. In her favourite fantasy he broke down and confessed that he couldn't live without her — begged her to run away to France with him. But deep in her heart she'd known all along it wouldn't happen.

Now he was just a small figure in the distance, getting smaller and smaller as he stood there on the platform with all the other ordinary little people. She had to lean out of the window quite perilously to see him at all. Then the train rounded the bend and she lost sight of him altogether.

Her heart leaden, she sat down on the seat, unable now to prevent reality from crowding in. She thought of going back to college, of the shop and her mother, of Morgan and the Kingstons and wondered how she would bear going back to the sheer mundaneness of everyday life again. It was all too dreary for words. It seemed to her that everything she had lived for these past months was gone. Patrick would forget her. Deep down she knew that. This morning, after they had made love for the last time, he had almost said as much. Leaning on one elbow to look down at her he had said: 'No regrets?'

She turned her head from side to side on the pillow. 'No regrets. I love you, Patrick. How could I regret anything?'

'Shhh.' He kissed her gently. 'Darling, you don't really love me, you know. You're very young. There'll be dozens of others before you find the one you can really say that to.'

She stared up at him, tears stinging her eyes. 'What are you saying, Patrick?'

'Just that I'm setting you free. It's the best parting gift I can give you. We've had a wonderful time together. I'll always think of you lovingly. But that's all either of us should feel. You mustn't care too much, love. I don't want you to be hurt. Understand?'

187

She rolled over to bury her face in the pillow so that he wouldn't see her quick hot tears. How could he imagine she could escape the hurt of loving him? How could he not see that it was already too late to tell her not to care too much?

'I shouldn't have come this weekend,' she mumbled into the pillow.

He turned her over and looked into her eyes. 'I'll tell you now. I tried to stop you. I rang Tom. If you hadn't caught an early train you wouldn't be here now.'

'Then I'm glad I did.' She reached up to pull him down to her. 'I'm *so glad* I did, Patrick.'

The journey seemed interminable, but at last she was stepping down from the train, thankful that the flat was within easy walking distance of the station. She let herself in through the street door with her own key and climbed the stairs, hoping for once that her mother would be busy with Morgan, working out some new scheme, so that she wouldn't be expected to talk about her fictitious weekend and the show she was supposed to have seen. All she wanted to do was climb into bed and be alone with her own misery.

But Grace was waiting for her at the top of the stairs, her face strained and pale.

'So you're back.'

'Yes.' Elaine reached the landing and put down her case and the wrapped picture. 'Is the water hot? I'd like a bath.'

Grace's face was stiff and unsmiling. 'I'd like to talk to you first.'

Elaine tried to push past, all her senses suddenly alert. 'Do we have to? I'd rather ...'

'Up in your room. *Now.*'

Elaine stared at her mother. She'd never heard her use that tone before. Without arguing she walked up the stairs and into her room. Turning she faced her mother defensively.'Right, what is it you want to talk about?'

Grace slammed the door behind her. 'How *could* you?' she demanded.

'How could I what?'

'You know what I'm talking about. How could you make yourself so cheap? How could you lie and cheat just to go to him — to *sleep* with him? You make me feel sick.'

Elaine's heart was beating fast. She must keep calm. She'd told no one, so how could her mother possibly know where she'd been? 'I don't know what you're talking about.' She looked round the room, suddenly aware that things had been disturbed. Things from

188

the drawers lay strewn on the bed — including the contents of the box of souvenirs of her father. She swung round angrily.

'You've been prying into my things. Those are Daddy's cards.'

'Yes. You're your father's daughter all right. Perhaps you'd like to explain *this*?' Grace strode across the room and reversed a stretched canvas that had been leaning against the wall. Elaine froze. It was the nude painting Patrick had done of her; her Christmas present. Ever since he'd given it to her it had been hidden at the back of her wardrobe.

'Patrick painted it. It's me,' she said defiantly.

'I can see it's you, you disgraceful, shameless girl. What decent man do you think will ever want you now? Because *he* won't, I'll tell you that. I wouldn't mind betting you'll never hear from him again, once he leaves for France.'

The truth hit her like a blunt instrument, but she weathered the blow. Swallowing hard she said: 'These are the sixties, Mum. In case you've forgotten, it's Elizabeth on the throne, not Victoria. *You* may have grown up in a vicarage, but that doesn't ...' She stopped speaking to cry out as Grace picked up a pair of scissors from the dressing table, and slashed the canvas of the picture from top to bottom.

'Oh, *no*. Don't. Please don't. It's mine. You've no right.'

'Don't tell me my rights.' Grace was trembling with rage. 'I was so proud of my daughter. I thought I'd brought you up to be decent and good. Now I find that you're nothing but a little slut. I wish you'd never met those Carnes. When I think of what must have been happening — under my very nose. Why, if it hadn't been for Morgan ...'

Elaine had been crying quietly, on her knees as she held the ripped edges of the canvas together. Now she stopped, tears streaming down her face to stare at her mother. '*Morgan*? How did he know?'

'There was a telephone message for you at the Carnes'. Your wonderful Patrick tried to stop you from going at the last minute. Unfortunately he was too late. Morgan happened to be there at the time.'

Elaine rose slowly to her feet. 'And he ratted on me? He told you?'

'He was concerned for us both. At least *he* has a sense of what's right and wrong.'

'Oh, yes? That's why he's queer, I suppose?' Elaine was almost beside herself with rage now. The injustice — the betrayal — was almost more than she could bear. She took a step towards her mother, her eyes blazing. 'Or are you so naive you don't know

189

what that means?' She threw back her head. 'You think Morgan is God's gift, don't you? Maybe you even think he's in love with you. Didn't you know that your precious boy is as bent as a hairpin? I expect you think *he* doesn't do all those *nasty* things you find so disgusting? Well, I can tell you that he *does* − only in his case it's with other ...' The sentence ended in a cry of pain as Grace's hand struck her a ringing blow that made her ear sing and sent her reeling across the room to tumble on to the littered bed.

For a shocked second Grace stood staring numbly at the sobbing girl. It was the first time she had ever laid a hand on Elaine in anger. And all because of a man − and sex; the root of all evil; the reason for all the misery, all the turmoil in her life. Now it had come between her and her child. Instantly she was on her knees beside the bed, gathering Elaine into her arms, tears of shame and remorse streaming down her cheeks.

'Darling, I'm sorry. Oh, Elaine − my baby, I didn't mean it.'

'Neither did I. Oh, Mummy, I'm sorry.' Elaine allowed herself to be comforted, sobbing against her mother's shoulder as though her heart would break. 'It wasn't the way you made it sound, Mum. I love him, I really do. I don't think I can bear it now that he's gone. Oh, Mummy − what am I going to do without him?'

Grace hugged her daughter close, angry and fiercely protective. She knew all too well what her daughter was feeling. That bleak sense of loneliness and abandonment. 'It'll be all right,' she whispered. 'The hurt will fade and heal, I promise it will. When your father left me, I went through hell.'

Elaine swallowed her tears to peer into her mother's face. She could imagine now what she must have been through. She thought about the letter she had written to her father and felt like a traitor. Suddenly she was glad he hadn't replied. She knew now that she never wanted to see him again. She touched her mother's tearstained cheek. 'Oh, Mummy, if I'd only known then. Listen − I didn't mean what I said about Morgan. It isn't true.'

To her surprise Grace smiled calmly. 'Yes it is. It's all right, I already knew. Morgan told me a long time ago.' She stroked Elaine's hair. 'He knows all about love and rejection too. He lost his family because of the person he loved. Then that person broke his heart and left him. It makes no difference who or what you are, Elaine, the emotion − the hurt − goes just as deep. You can't call yourself a human being till you can understand that.'

'Then why couldn't *you* understand − about me and Patrick?' Elaine asked.

Grace looked down at her own hands, tightly clenched in her lap.

'You're my daughter,' she said quietly. 'I want the best for you. Happiness and contentment; a successful marriage; a good life. If you'd told me, I could have warned you that Patrick Carne wasn't the kind to give you those things.'

Elaine frowned. 'But if you love someone . . .'

Grace's face hardened. 'Love is a trap — a *cheat*,' she said vehemently. 'It's hard but it's the truth, Elaine. It's like the golden unicorn in the old story — a mythical beast, a half-truth. It demands everything — takes all you have and leaves you with *nothing*. Not even your pride.'

Elaine shivered, bewildered at the bitterness she saw in her mother's eyes. Then Grace turned suddenly and kissed her on the cheek, smilingly herself again.

'Come down and have your bath, darling. I'll have supper ready by the time you've finished.'

191

Chapter Fourteen

Mary Kingston's dinner party had been arranged for the evening of Easter Monday. Since she had insinuated herself into their lives, Grace and Morgan had both come to realise that she was a force to be reckoned with. It was no use trying to wriggle out of her invitations. If she wanted you to be present at one of her little parties she wouldn't take no for an answer. But when Grace had broken the news to Elaine that she was expected to attend too, she had been dismayed.

'Why me? I've got nothing to do with the business.'

'Come just this once, darling,' Grace said. 'I think she's inviting you because you're a friend of Paul's. If you refuse you'll probably upset her numbers.'

'A friend of Paul's? What gave her that idea?'

'Well, he did help you with your driving test, didn't he?'

Elaine shrugged resignedly. She supposed she might as well go. After all, she had nothing else to do. Alison had gone to France with her family for the whole of the Easter holidays and Tom was busy helping his father. Besides, she didn't particularly want to go to the Carnes' house. There were too many hurtful memories there.

On the morning after she had returned from her weekend with Patrick, Morgan had sought her out. Her mother was busy in the shop downstairs and she was making coffee in the kitchen when she heard his step on the stairs. He stood hesitantly in the kitchen doorway for a moment, then he said: 'I've come to say I'm sorry.'

Elaine didn't turn round. 'What for?'

'For spilling the beans about your weekend. I didn't mean to, believe me.'

'Don't worry about it, Morgan.'

'But I *do*.' He came into the kitchen. 'It happens to be important

192

to me not to break confidences. I just wish that Tom and I could have been in time to stop you going.'

'Don't wish that.'

'If you want my opinion – and I'm sure you don't – you're better off without him.'

She sighed and spooned instant coffee into the cups. 'Well, you would think that, wouldn't you – being on Mum's side?'

'I'm not on anyone's side really. I just wish there was something I could do.'

'Well, there isn't.' She turned to look at him. 'Do you want any coffee?'

'Yes, please.' He gave her a tentative smile. 'I meant what I said about Patrick, Elaine. I think it was despicable, asking you up there and then trying to put you off at the last minute because this French girl had turned up and ...' he saw the colour drain from her face and winced. 'Oh, *Christ*, I've done it again. You didn't know.'

'Yes, I did.' She held her chin hight as she poured boiling water onto the coffee. 'Her name is Ann-Marie Labeque and she's an exchange student from France. She arrived unexpectedly – and I know Patrick tried to stop me going.' She didn't tell him that he had carefully avoided telling her that he'd tried to stop her going to London *because* of Ann Marie. Small remembered things dropped into her mind like pebbles into a pond. The apartment Ann-Marie had mentioned. Her intimate, enigmatic little smile and the mysterious way she'd promised to see Patrick again before he left. Then there was the length of time Patrick had spent with her downstairs, no doubt explaining Elaine's presence. He'd have made up some convincing story – lied about her to suit himself. She took a bottle of milk from the fridge and slammed the door.

'Black or white?' she asked him, with flashing eyes.

'White, please. Look, Elaine, I know it hurts but it's better you know the truth about him. It might not seem that way now, but it is, I promise you.'

She took a long, deep breath. 'Isn't it marvellous that so many people are so concerned for my good?' She pushed a cup of coffee at him across the worktop, slopping it into the saucer.

'I do understand, Elaine, really. Look, if you ever need anyone to talk to ... Oh, I know I messed things up for you this time, but Grace would have found out anyway. It's that intuition of hers. It's uncanny at times.'

'Morgan,'

'Yes?'

'Do stop talking crap, will you?'

193

He stared at her with startled eyes. 'Oh — right.'

For a moment they stood looking at each other, then he laughed. After a moment Elaine joined in, releasing her pent-up tension.

'I'd like us to be friends,' he said simply. 'I expect you know that I'm, well — I'm sure you know. What I mean is that you don't have to worry about me having — well, designs on you.'

'Thanks, I won't. Worry, I mean.' She looked at the gentle eyes and the wide, mobile mouth and suddenly found herself liking him. He really meant what he said. He was offering her unconditional friendship and she had never needed an unbiased friend as much as she did now. She smiled and held out her hand. 'Friends,' she said.

He took her hand between both of his and pressed it warmly. 'Friends.'

Langmere Lodge was the Kingstons' family home. Mary's husband, Henry, had been born there and it was to this house, newly inherited from his parents, that he had first brought his new bride in 1930. Both their sons had been born there and since Henry's death in 1955 Mary had lived there with Paul and Edna, an impoverished cousin who served as housekeeper in return for a home. In all the years the house had changed very little. The rooms were still furnished with the heavy mahogany furniture that had belonged to Henry's parents. In the hall Henry's father's hunting trophies still held pride of place: the stag's head with its doleful expression adorned the wall at the foot of the stairs, flanked by a fox's mask and the head of a motheaten wildcat, wearing a cynical snarl. Beside the front door with its stained glass panels stood an elephant's foot umbrella stand with its collection of walking sticks and umbrellas at the ready.

On the evening of the dinner party Mary made sure she was ready early. She wore her royal blue velvet and the pearls Henry had given her on their last wedding anniversary before he died. Her hair was newly set in the rigid style she had worn for the past twenty years, the rows of little curls glinting like steel wool. First she went into the dining room to check the table; straightening a knife here, tweaking a flower petal there. Then she went into the kitchen to make sure that Edna had the meal under control and wasn't indulging in one of her hysterical flaps.

'You can serve the consommé chilled with slices of cucumber,' she said. 'And the sweet is cold too, so there's no reason for you to panic. Cheese and fruit will be served at the end, after the sweet and before coffee. Please try to remember that. We don't want everything dumped in front of us at once. Last time you made the

194

table look like a bring and buy sale. Now — are you sure you've remembered everything?'

Edna, a whisp of a woman with a perpetually harassed expression, pushed a strand of damp grey hair out of her eyes and counted off the items on her fingers. 'The wine is chilling in the fridge, the chicken is done and the vegetables are just going on now. I'm quite sure I've remembered everything, Mary.' She bit her lip. 'At least, I think I have.'

'And don't call me Mary in front of the guests. I know we're related — distantly — but it doesn't sound right when you're waiting at table.'

'No, I'll remember this time.'

'Have you called Paul?'

'I thought you . . .'

'Really, Edna, I can't do everything myself. You know how carried away he gets with all that marking he brings home. You'd better go up now and make sure he's out of the bath. No . . .' She held up her hand. 'You stay here and make sure you haven't forgotten anything. I'll go myself.' She left the perspiring Edna and climbed the stairs again to rap smartly on Paul's door.

'I hope you're ready. Our guests will be here soon.'

'Yes, Mother.'

'Have you managed to tie your tie without making it look like a dish rag?' She laid her ear to the door, straining to hear his mumbled reply. 'Oh, look, I can't hear a word. I'm coming in.' She opened the door and strode in. Paul was in his shirt sleeves, struggling to tie his evening dress bow tie. He looked at his mother with a sigh.

'Do we really have to get ourselves up like this? It's only a few people coming for dinner.'

Mary tweaked savagely at the tie. 'The slack way people behave would make your father turn in his grave. There's no reason why we should drop our standards too. We should set an example.'

'Did you make it clear to Mrs Wendover that she was expected to dress formally?'

'I certainly did. I want this to be a memorable occasion — to seal our partnership.'

Paul winced. 'Mother, you're only lending this Owen chap some cash. That's not a partnership, you know. And I still think it's a bit rash of you. How do you know he won't lose the lot?'

'Because he's got Grace Wendover behind him. That's how I know.' Mary smiled. 'Behind every successful man there's a strong woman. Anyway, you don't know dear Morgan. He's a true artist — brilliantly clever with those designs of his. With his talent and

Grace's business sense he's going a long way, mark my words. I've always admired creativity and enterprise.' She gave his tie a final tweak and brushed a speck of fluff from the dinner jacket. 'There's another reason for this dinner party. I particularly want us all to become good friends.' She peered over his shoulder at him in the mirror. 'Especially you and Elaine,' she added with a sly smile. 'You do like Elaine, don't you?'

'Yes. Very much.' He opened a drawer and took out a clean handkerchief.

'That was a good move of yours – helping her pass her driving test. Now you know what I told you?'

He turned to look at her. 'Look, Mother, she's a very nice girl but I doubt if she ...'

'Oh really, Paul,' Mary's eyes snapped at him. 'You're so negative. If you hadn't let the Phipps girl slip through your fingers, you'd have got the headship last time.' She flicked at his hair. 'You're not a bad catch, and Elaine is young. She's an impressionable little thing. Show off a bit, can't you? Or is that totally beyond your capabilities?' She looked back from the door, her blue eyes glinting a warning. 'Don't mess this one up, Paul. I shan't always be here to see to everything for you, you know. Now – come down as soon as you can. I need you to play host.' She shot him a final exasperated look. 'And do *try* to look a little more affable. Really, I believe this household would fall apart if I weren't here to prop you all up.'

Paul watched as his mother sailed out of the room and disappeared down the stairs. Why did he let her rule his life? He'd asked himself the question so many times but there never seemed to be a satisfactory answer. Because it was easy just to go along with what she said? Because making decisions wasn't his strong suit? Because to stand up to her hardly seemed worth the trouble? Maybe the latter was closer to the truth.

He stared critically at his reflection in the mirror. He supposed he wasn't bad-looking. Tall and slim, perhaps a little serious? Did women find him attractive? It was a question he'd never asked himself. He certainly had no evidence that they did. He wasn't all that keen on women to tell the truth. Although most of his life had been spent among them he couldn't say he came anywhere near understanding them, or even wanting to. Marjorie Phipps, the woman his mother had accused him of allowing to slip through his fingers, had been a young widow of about his own age. His mother had thought her the perfect choice, but she had terrified him. Her rather horsy, intelligent looks had disguised a sexually avid nature whose appetites had intimidated Paul and sent him running for cover at the earliest opportunity. He counted himself lucky that Marjorie had quickly become bored with his ineptitude and turned her attentions elsewhere.

Since the death of his brother and his father, Paul's mother seemed to have taken over his life. She bought his clothes, organised his meals, even chose his friends for him. She had made it clear that she intended him to form a close relationship with Elaine with a view to marriage. That had been her intention when she had introduced him to Marjorie, and, as she was quick to point out, it was entirely for his own good. But *he* was the one expected to make a lifetime commitment. How did he feel about it? He stared at his reflection as though expecting it to tell him the answer.

Elaine was a pleasant girl, pretty and intelligent. It was true that if he were to apply for the headship when it came up next time he would stand a better chance as a married man. But would a girl like Elaine ever consider marrying him? For one thing he was thirty and that was at least twelve years her senior. She was bright and vivacious, while he was − well, what was he? Dull, he supposed. He had no real interests outside school. He couldn't dance and he didn't care much for sport or for the theatre or cinema. The only thing he really liked was motor racing and that wasn't likely to arouse much interest in a young girl. Besides he hadn't the vaguest idea of how to go about courting a young woman. His mother had assured him that it would come naturally when he met someone he could care for. He sincerely hoped it would. He had no wish to make a complete ass of himself again. One read and heard so much nowadays about the permissive society − the sexual revolution. What did girls expect of a man? If Marjorie was anything to go by, a great deal. Perhaps that was the advantage of taking out a girl as young as Elaine. At least she wouldn't be experienced.

Grace had chosen to wear the black embroidered shift she'd worn when Bryan Bostock took her to London. It hadn't been out of the wardrobe since that fateful night and even as she put it on she wondered anxiously if there was a jinx on it. Elaine wore a geranium red dress with bell sleeves and a horseshoe neckline. Its vibrant colour helped to brighten her pale face.

It was a week now since she had said goodbye to Patrick and if anything, the pain was worse. She hadn't slept all week. There seemed to be no escape. She thought about him constantly. Tossing and turning through the nights, she re-lived over and over every second of their time together, asking herself where she could have gone wrong − if he had ever really loved her as she loved him. She tortured herself with thoughts of what he would do in France − saw

197

him walking hand in hand with Ann-Marie along the boulevards, stopping to kiss her in some leafy, shadowy place by the Seine, making love to her in her apartment, their naked bodies bathed in milky moonlight. Every time she closed her eyes the vision of Ann-Marie haunted her: the secret smile in her dark, enigmatic eyes; the sexy, scarlet mouth; the long dark hair and willowy figure. Patrick had warned her last Christmas that their relationship was over, but she hadn't accepted it. Perhaps even then he had been in love with Ann-Marie. In the mornings she rose exhausted, her eyes puffy and her head aching, to drag herself through another day; wondering how long the aching misery would last and if she would ever feel happy again.

Going for dinner at Langmere Lodge was the last thing she wanted to do and she had put on the red dress that evening in a gesture of defiance. It was very short and she wore matching tights. Mary's quickly suppressed flash of disapproval when she removed her coat gave her a little stab of triumph.

From the moment they arrived Mary made it clear that Morgan was the guest of honour. She flattered and flirted with him outrageously; telling him how handsome he looked in his dinner jacket and fussing round him like a mother hen, eager to anticipate his slightest whim. Paul poured drinks for them all, but before Elaine could take a sip of hers, Mary said: 'Paul, why don't you show Elaine the garden? I'm sure she'd like to see the daffodils. And it's such a warm evening. You won't even need a coat.' Taking Elaine's arm she ushered her determinedly towards the French windows and opened them.

'Ah, just take a breath of that air,' she said, breathing in noisily. 'You can smell the spring, can't you? Don't you think that spring is quite the most romantic time of year?' She turned to look for Paul, a glint of impatience in her steely eyes. '*Do* come along, dear,' she said briskly, 'Elaine is waiting.'

They strolled along the path in silence for a while, both embarrassed by Mary's heavy-handed attempt to throw them together. At last Elaine said: 'It's a very big garden, isn't it? Do you do all the work?'

'Good heavens, no. Mother does some of it and there's a man who comes in twice a week for the heavy digging and so on.'

'It's very beautiful.' In the fading light the pale yellow drifts of daffodils looked almost luminous. A huge old cherry tree, its boughs heavy with double white blossoms, stood at the end of the lawn, filling the air with its sweet fragrance.'

'I wish we had a garden. It must be nice to sit out on summer evenings.'

'Yes – yes, it is,' said Paul, who never sat out on summer evenings or at any other time. She was very attractive. That red suited her and her hair was beautiful, thick and curly. He wondered briefly how it would feel to run one's hands through it. She turned and caught his eye and he felt the warm colour mount his cheeks. He cleared his throat.

'How is the driving?'

She shrugged. 'I haven't had a chance to do much yet.'

'That's a pity. Er – Elaine, I wondered – there's a concert at school a week on Wednesday. Would you like to go?'

'What kind of concert?'

'Oh – er, just a concert. The boys put it on every year. St Jasper's goes in for music in quite a big way. Some of the boys go on to the Guildhall – take it up professionally when they leave.'

'Really? That sounds interesting.'

He heaved a sigh of relief. At least the idea didn't bore her. He was acutely aware of the fact that his mother had sent him out here to arrange a date with Elaine. She would be furious if he didn't accomplish it.

'I love music,' she said. 'Are you musical?'

'No, not really. Classics is my subject.'

'Did you know that my father was a musician?'

'No, I didn't.' He peered at her. 'Is he – I mean, did he ...?'

'Die? No. He and my mother are separated.'

'Oh, I'm sorry.' Paul wondered what his mother would make of that.

'It all happened a long time ago. When I was eleven.'

'You must miss him.'

'Not really. I hardly remember him.' Elaine made a sudden defiant decision. Her father and Patrick – they weren't worth her tears. She'd forget them. They'd both let her down. Maybe it was as her mother said; maybe the men you loved always did that. Maybe it was safer to stick to friendship, such as she and Tom had – such as Morgan had offered. Patrick had left for France four days ago, without contacting her – even to say a final goodbye. He was probably with Ann-Marie at this moment. So why shouldn't she accept an invitation too? Paul had been kind to her over the driving test and he was quite nice. A light breeze stirred the air and she shivered. Paul noticed at once.

'You're cold. Shall we go in?'

199

She smiled at him. 'Thank you for showing me the garden. It's lovely, but I would like to go in now.'

Reaching out, he tentatively took her arm. The feel of her soft, warm flesh through the thin material made him swallow hard. She didn't pull away though. 'You'll come then – to the concert?'

She smiled. 'Yes. I'd like to.'

'Good. I'll pick you up at seven then.' He had a sudden flash of inspiration. 'And I'll tell you what – you can drive us there.'

He was rewarded with her most radiant smile. Oh, Paul. Can I really?'

'Paul Kingston? The bloke who lent you his car for the driving test? Well, things *have* been buzzing since I've been away. Right on top of going up to London for a dirty weekend with Patrick too.'

'It wasn't like that.'

'So what was it like?'

'It was a distaster, if you want to know. First we had a row, then Mum found out and there was hell to pay when I got home.'

'Wow!' Alison's eyes were round. 'What did you have the row about – you and Patrick, I mean?'

Elaine shrugged noncommitally. 'Oh, things.'

They were having lunch in the college canteen. It was the first day of term and they hadn't seen each other for the past three weeks.

'He'll be away for two years,' Elaine said, staring at her hands. 'He isn't even coming home for the holidays. Says he has to work to pay his way.'

'So you've really split up then?'

Elaine looked up. 'You could say that. Anyway, there's another girl.'

'But if he's going away ...'

'A *French* girl.'

Alison pulled a face. 'Ah, I see. The dirty rat! In that case I don't blame you for going out with Paul Kingston.' She peered at her friend. 'Are you cheesed off about it?'

Elaine's face was closed. She shrugged. 'Not particularly. Not now I'm going out with Paul.'

'Oh, that's all right then.' Alison looked doubtful. 'Isn't he a bit old for you though?'

'No. Anyway, I like mature men. The young ones all seems so – so juvenile.'

Alison leaned forward, her face eager. 'So he took you to this concert? Come on then, what's he like?'

'He's all right. Anyway, you know what he's like.'

'Come off it, you know what I mean. Did he kiss you?'

'Do you *have* to know all the details of my dates, Alison?'

'I tell you all the details of mine.'

'But I don't ask for them. That's the difference,' Elaine pointed out.

'All right – *be* stuffy about it. See if I care.' She looked piqued. 'You haven't even asked me about my holiday. Sometimes, Elaine Wendover, I wonder if you're only interested in yourself.'

Elaine sighed. 'Sorry, Ali. I do want to hear about it – really. Go on, did you have a good time?'

Alison's face brightened instantly. 'Better than good. We met this American family – Mum, Dad and two sweet little kids. And guess what? They've invited me to go over and spend a year with them in the States.

'A year? What for?'

'They're starting up in business and they need someone to look after the kids while they get it going. They don't start school for another year, you see. And it seems they're mad about English nannies over there.'

Elaine's heart sank. Was she about to lose her best friend too? 'Are you going?'

'What do you think? Mum and Dad weren't keen at first, but the Railtons managed to twist their arms. I'm off in August. This'll be my last term. And that's not all. They live in California and they have this gorgeous house with a swimming pool and everything. I've seen the photographs. I'll have the use of a car and my own self-contained flat.'

'It sounds wonderful. I'll miss you.' Elaine tried hard to keep the stiff smile glued to her face.

'Maybe you could come over for a holiday,' Alison said excitedly. 'I'm sure they wouldn't mind. Hey, you could even see your Dad while you're there.'

'Yes, who knows?' Elaine pushed her plate away from her and stood up. 'Look, I want to go to the shops before the afternoon lecture,' she said. 'I'll see you later.'

Alison looked taken aback. 'Oh, okay. See you then.'

Elaine collected her coat and walked out into the spring sunshine. She and Alison seemed to be drifting further and further apart. There had been a time when she could have confided her feelings to her friend, but what she felt at the moment went much too deep to confide to anyone. She felt isolated and depressed.

The school concert at St Jasper's had been very good. The standard had been high and Elaine had enjoyed it. Just for a couple

201

of hours she had actually managed not to think of Patrick. Paul had allowed her to drive the Rover both there and back afterwards. He had also asked her for another date — which she had accepted. It had been the fumbling goodnight kiss that had disturbed and upset her. Paul had been nervous and inept. His lips had felt slack and damp against hers and memories of Patrick had flooded back like pain after an anaesthetic, making her feel as though her heart were being torn apart. When she had drawn back from him he had apologised profusely.

'I'm sorry. Maybe I shouldn't ... You're not offended, are you?'

'No, of course not.' She'd felt perversely angry with him. Why couldn't he be more positive — take the initiative? That at least would have made up for his inexpert fumblings.

'Are you going to say you don't want to see me again?' He peered at her and just for a moment she had the oddest feeling that he'd had been relieved if she'd said yes.

'Do you really want to see me again, Paul?' she asked.

'Oh, yes. I just thought ...' He broke off. 'Elaine, I'd like us to see each other regularly — what's the expression — go steady?' He looked at her. 'Is there any reason — I mean, are you seeing anyone else?'

'No.'

'Oh, good. Then ...?'

'Shall we just wait and see how things go?'

'Yes, if you say so. I'll pick you up on Friday then. We'll go out for dinner. Is that all right?' At least with food they would be on common ground, he told himself.

Lying in bed later Elaine wished with all her heart that she could find him more attractive. He was kind and considerate; he wasn't bad-looking either. It would help so much if she could fall even a little bit in love with someone else. But there was something about Paul — she didn't know what. Except of course that he simply wasn't Patrick. When her mother had tactfully enquired about her evening she'd confided these feelings to her. Grace had echoed her own thoughts.

'You're still upset about Patrick. It's early days. For a long time no one else will make you feel as happy, that's only natural. But give it time, darling. Just give it time.'

So she'd decided to do just that. But as for confiding in Alison about Paul's goodnight kiss ... There was a time when they would have laughed over it together. But now talking or even thinking about it brought her a feeling of despondency. Would she ever

202

be able to laugh again? she asked herself. Would she ever feel the heady excitement she had known with Patrick? Could she ever feel the same about anyone else? She doubted it.

In the weeks that followed the relationship between Elaine and Paul became easier and more relaxed. In spite of his misgivings they found some common ground, discovering that they both enjoyed reading the same detective thrillers. And Elaine found a new interest in motor racing, introduced to her by Paul. He was very knowledgeable about the Cambridge colleges too and took her to see his father's old set. They walked around the ancient buildings in the spring sunshine and Paul told her about their history and traditions.

She hardly saw her other friends. Alison and she drifted even further apart. There were no outings with friends and no parties. And she never saw the Carnes at all, until one Saturday morning she ran into Tom. He was coming out of his father's shop and they almost collided as she hurried past on her way to town.

'Hi there.' Tom caught her by the shoulders. 'Long time no see.'

She coloured. 'Hello, Tom. How are you?'

'I'm fine. You?'

'I'm fine too.'

'I hear you're dating some new bloke?' When she didn't reply he shook her gently. 'Hey, don't look like that. I'm glad. You don't want to waste time agonising over my brother, you know.'

'No, I'm not.'

'We had a postcard from him last week. Seems he's having a whale of a time,' Tom went on. He peered at her. 'Look, love, I'm sorry about what happened that weekend.'

'It's all right.'

'Morgan told me about your mother finding out. Did you have any trouble?'

'No. Look, Tom, I've got to go. I have an appointment.'

'No hard feelings?'

'Of course not. It's all over and done with.'

'That's good then. Look, there's a party at our house tonight. Why don't you come? Bring your new bloke.'

Elaine had a sudden vision of Paul at the Carnes' house and would have laughed if she hadn't been almost overcome with nostalgia. 'I'm sorry, Tom. I can't,' she said.

He nodded. 'Pity. We've all missed you. We must meet some time – have a drink.'

'Yes.' She watched with a heavy heart as he walked away down the road, his hands in the pockets of his leather jacket, whistling a carefree tune. With all her heart she wished she could call him back. She badly needed to talk to someone. But who? Alison wouldn't understand; Elaine felt suddenly much older than Alison. It was as though she had left her behind in the carefree world of youth. Talking to her mother about what was on her mind was out of the question. Morgan . . . he had said she could trust him, but she still wasn't sure. Tom would have been the perfect choice. She felt sure he'd have known what she should do − if only he wasn't Patrick's brother. She walked on, peering unseeingly into shop windows as she went. No, there was no one. She had never felt so alone in her life. Maybe it would all go away. Maybe she was worrying over nothing. She passed a travel agent's and thought about Patrick in France, having a whale of a time − with Ann-Marie, no doubt. She hated them both with all the bitterness the past weeks had wrought in her. It was so unfair. So desperately unfair.

Paul knew the city of Norwich well and when he suggested to Elaine that they might spend a Saturday there she had agreed. He'd taken her to Cobb Hill with its quaint cobbled streets and medieval houses and shops. They'd walked round the beautiful cathedral and had lunch in a nearby restaurant. Afterwards they had taken a leisurely stroll round the shops, pausing outside a jeweller's window.

'Do you like jewellery?' he asked suddenly.

Elaine laughed. 'Only the kind I could never afford to buy.'

'How about that ring?' He pointed to one with three diamonds.

'It's beautiful.

'Would you wear it for me?'

Startled, she turned to look at him. 'For you?'

He took her hand. 'Elaine, I want to talk to you. Let's go back to the car.'

The Rover was parked in the cathedral close. As Elaine settled herself in the passenger seat her heart was beating fast, half with apprehension, half with hope, Paul turned to her at once.

'I know we haven't been going out together all that long, Elaine. And I know I'm a few years older than you. But I do think an awful lot of you and I'd − I'd like you to become my wife.'

She was silent. It was the moment every girl dreamed and fantasised over. The proposal. She had never visualised hers like this. 'I see,' she said.

'Well, how do you feel about it?' He was looking at her hopefully. 'You might think this is a bit sudden, but you see, Elaine, I've been tipped the wink that the headship at St Jasper's is coming up again

shortly. I'd stand a pretty good chance of getting it as a married —
even an engaged — man. If you fancy the idea we could go back
now and get that ring.'

She took a deep breath. 'Thank you, Paul. I'd like that.'

For a moment he stared at her unbelievingly. He hadn't really
believed his mother when she said Elaine would jump at the chance
of marrying him. It was uncanny how often she was right.

'That's wonderful,' he said. 'Come on then, let's go.'

Elaine opened the door and got out of the car. She felt empty and
totally devoid of feeling. There had been no passionate declaration
of love — no kisses. Not that she would have welcomed them. She
had welcomed Paul's proposal though. In fact it had come like an
answer to her prayers. Her second period was ten days overdue now,
and although she hadn't seen the doctor she knew instinctively that
she was pregnant.

They stood side by side on the pavement outside the register office,
the wind catching at the brim of Elaine's hat. It was all over except
for the photographs. Paul, tall and upright in a dark suit at her side,
was her husband. She was Mrs Kingston. Mrs Elaine Kingston. The
words drummed meaninglessly inside her head.

'Smile please.' The photographer snapped them once more and at
last they were free to get into the car and drive to Langmere Lodge
for the reception.

In the car Paul smiled at her. 'Happy?'

She smiled back. 'Of course.'

It had been easy to persuade everyone that a quick marriage
was best. For one thing Alison, her best friend, would be gone
by the end of July. Then there was Paul's application for the
headship. If he was already married when he applied it would
surely make all the difference. No one could argue with that.
Both Grace and Mrs Kingston were happy — at least over the
date. After that the disagreements began. Mary wanted to hold
the reception at Langmere Lodge — Grace would have preferred
a hotel. Mary would have liked a church wedding, whilst Grace was
dead against it.

'Are you an atheist?' Mary had asked her suspiciously.

'Not exactly. I just think the church is filled with hypocrisy,'
Grace told her bluntly. 'And I should know. My own father was
a Methodist minister.'

Mary was silenced by this. There was also the fact that the girl's
parents were estranged. She would have no father to give her away.
That might take some explaining. Maybe it would be better all round

to make it a quiet register office affair. But having given in over that, Mary felt justified in pressing her wish to hold the reception at home.

Oddly enough, the only person to express misgivings had been Morgan. Finding himself alone with Elaine one evening he'd asked: 'You do really want to marry Paul, don't you?'

'Of course.' Elaine had coloured hotly.

'It isn't just a rebound thing after Patrick?' He looked at her with some concern. 'It isn't too late to back out, you know. Marriage is an awfully big step and you're still very young.'

'It's all right, Morgan. I'm quite sure.' She looked away quickly from his questioning, too perceptive eyes. Not too late, he'd said. But it was too late. Much too late.

Grace had insisted on taking Elaine up to London to choose her wedding outfit straight from the fashion house. She had gone along with it and together they had chosen a softly pleated dress in palest pink with a matching picture hat. But it didn't end there. There was the fuss over flowers, the wrangling about menus, the invitations — who to invite and who to leave out — till she thought her head would burst. The four weeks between engagement and wedding seemed interminable. All she could think of was the date. By the time she was married she would be ten weeks pregnant. So far no one knew. Even her mother hadn't guessed. She'd been lucky. There had been no physical sickness in the mornings and she had coped with the feelings of nausea, hiding her revulsion for certain foods and keeping out of the way at breakfast times. Grace was always too rushed to notice at that time of the morning anyway. The thought of telling Paul worried her. She didn't want to deceive him. At some stage he would have to know. She dreaded that.

Somehow she got through the reception. She and Paul went up to the room that was to be theirs and changed. In a shower of confetti they drove away and two hours later were in their hotel room in London where they were to spend a brief honeymoon. As she showered in the adjoining bathroom Elaine closed her eyes and prayed: 'Please let me learn to love him — please let him understand about the baby. Oh *please* let it all work out.'

Much later as they lay stiffly side by side in the double bed, Paul apologised for the third time.

'I'm sorry. I don't know what went wrong. Maybe we're tired — all the fuss.'

'Yes, perhaps that's it.' Elained swallowed hard at the lump in her throat.

'I'm sure it'll be better next time.'

'Of course. It doesn't matter.' But as she turned over and stared into the darkness, all she could think of was that they were no more than a mile away from the flat she and Patrick had occupied just a few weeks ago, sharing the kind of love she would never know again. Her heart felt as though it would burst with longing and it took a gigantic effort not to cry out with the pain of it. She closed her eyes tightly and clamped her teeth so tightly over her lower lip that she tasted blood mingled with her tears.

'Oh God, what have I done?' she whispered.

'I thought I was being clever, going to the States, but you went one better — as usual.' They were in their favourite coffee bar one afternoon after college, the week after the wedding.

'The wedding was an absolute knockout, wasn't it? You looked fabulous of course and so did your mum, but I thought I'd die of laughing at your ma-in-law's hat. It looked like a giant blob of whipped cream. And that funny old aunt — Edna, is it? She was wearing some sort of tapestry bucket on her head.' Alison leaned forward. 'You haven't told me about the honeymoon yet. Was it blissful?'

Elaine forced a smile. 'Naturally.'

'Is he a marvellous lover.'

'Brilliant.'

Alison sighed. 'You are lucky. I bet I never meet anyone half passable in bed and here you are on your second.'

Elaine flushed, looking round. 'I wish you wouldn't say things like that. You never know who might be listening.'

Alison laughed. 'Come off it, you old square. This is 1968. No one's still a virgin when they marry nowadays. I hope I'm not. I'd consider myself a dismal failure if I was.' She looked at her watch. 'I suppose I'd better be getting home. Mum will have tea on the table.'

Suddenly the thought of Alison going home to the comfort of her mother's kitchen brought a lump to Elaine's throat. In the three weeks since she and Paul had been married they'd been living with his mother at Langmere Lodge. It had been sheer hell. Mary Kingston watched her every move and Elaine was sure she suspected something. She was always asking her if she felt all right, pressing plates of greasy food or cream cakes on her and remarking that she looked peaky. When she wasn't prying she was picking her up on every single thing she did, from laying the table to washing up. Mary criticised her clothes in an oblique, bitchy way and Elaine was pretty sure she told tales to Paul when he came home. The moment he came through the front door his mother would call out from the room at the front where she sat watching for him, and he would be closetted with her for half an hour or more, hearing, no doubt, all about her new daughter-in-law's shortcomings. Being in the same house as his mother inhibited Paul in the bedroom too. Although they had been married almost a month their marriage had barely been consummated. Elaine's constant worry was what his reaction would be when she dropped the bombshell about her pregnancy.

'Hey – are you all right?' Alison was peering at her.

'What?' Elaine pulled herself out of her reverie. 'Oh yes, I'm ...' To her horror tears filled her eyes and began to trickle down her cheeks.

'Ellie!' Alison's face was filled with concern. 'Ellie, what's the matter?'

Elaine wanted to howl like a baby. She wanted to lay her head on Alison's shoulder and pour out all her troubles. Instead she swallowed hard and gathered up her things. 'I'm fine. Take no notice of me. I was just thinking that you'll be gone soon. I seem to be losing all my friends. I'll miss you.'

'Oh, is that all, you silly old thing?' Alison patted her arm affectionately. 'The year'll go as quick as a flash, just you wait and see. Before you know it I'll be home again.'

And what will I be doing a year from now? Elaine asked herself despairingly. What will have become of me?

'Paul, close the door. There's something I want to say to you.'

He did as she asked, his face puzzled. 'Can't it wait? Mother says dinner is ...'

'No. It can't wait. I want a place of our own to live.'

He looked startled. 'But there's plenty of room here. It seems a shame ...'

'I can't live in the same house with your mother any longer.'

'But you're at college all day. I thought it would be nice for you not to have to bother with housekeeping. And, anyway, where would we go?'

'I don't care – just as long as it's somewhere where we can be on our own.'

Paul looked slightly mollified. 'Well, of course it would be nice, darling. But I really don't know how ...'

'There's another reason.' Her heart began to thump. She'd been rehearsing this all afternoon and she was determined not to weaken, but now that the moment had come her knees were trembling. Her nervousness made her sound slightly shrill as she said: 'There's something I have to tell you, Paul.'

'Yes?'

'I'll have to give up college at the end of this term. I'm going to have a baby.'

He stared at her, too stunned to speak for a moment. A baby? He wouldn't really have thought it possible and yet ... 'Elaine! Darling, are you sure?'

'The doctor seems to be. And so you see we shall need a place of our own.' She had meant − *really* meant − to tell him the truth. But the look of astonished delight on his face had taken her by surprise. The words seemed to stick in her throat and she watched as he groped for a chair and lowered himself into it.

It was amazing news. And of course it changed everything. Truth to tell, he felt his mother was beginning to feel the strain too. She wasn't used to sharing her home. It hadn't been easy for him either, trying to be loyal to two women at once. Maybe his mother would be cheered by the news that she was about to become a grandmother. At least it would give them a good excuse to move out.

'Wait till Mother hears about this,' he said.

'Paul, if you don't mind I'd rather we kept it to ourselves for the time being,' she said.

Much to Mary Kingston's displeasure, they found a small house to rent quite close to St Jasper's. At the end of the term Paul was interviewed for the post of headmaster. Two weeks later he heard that he had been appointed.

It was on Christmas Eve when they were all having dinner at Langmere Lodge that Elaine went into labour. She'd had niggling pains all day but by seven o'clock she could keep them to herself no longer.

Grace was worried. 'Paul, you must get her to hospital at once, dear. The baby mustn't be born yet. It isn't time.'

But Mary, watching with narrowed eyes from the other side of the table, said nothing. She wasn't so sure that the baby was premature. She remembered the nausea Elaine had tried to hide when she first moved in, just two days after the wedding. She'd insisted once or twice on giving her a fried breakfast and watched with satisfaction as the girl had left the table, ashen-faced. There'd been other little signs too. The way she'd slyly engineered the house move before her pregnancy began to show. And the fact that they'd kept it secret for so long. As for Paul being responsible − it was about as likely as Edna winning the Miss World title. She'd mulled all these things over to herself during the past months, but after long consideration she'd decided to bide her time and say nothing. She'd achieved her ambition to get her son married and it had had the desired effect and gained him the headship. One couldn't have everything, she supposed. Besides, there might come a time when what she knew would provide her with useful ammunition. One never knew.

Rising from the table, her face a mask of assumed concern, she said: 'Grace is right. You must take good care of her. Drive very carefully.'

For two days Elaine drifted in and out of pain, hardly knowing whether it was day or night. Doctors and midwives appeared periodically to examine her. People came and looked at her; spoke her name: Paul, her mother, once Mary Kingston, or so she thought. Then the pain became even worse. She dreamed she was in a circus ring, being torn apart by lions. They had sharp teeth and claws but their faces were human. One of them looked like her mother-in-law; another had a blood red mouth like Ann-Marie Labeque. She heard her own cries as though from a long way off. She knew that she called for her father, and once or twice she thought she called out for Patrick but afterwards she couldn't be sure. All she knew for certain was that she was going to die.

At last, after what seemed weeks of torture, she was loaded on to a trolley and rushed along a corridor. There was a dizzying view of the ceiling until they arrived at a small room where a masked doctor was waiting. He placed something over her face that finally — mercifully — took away the pain and put out the light.

When she came round she could hear a baby's cry. Someone asked: 'Do you hear that, Mrs Kingston? Can you hear your daughter?' A nurse put a closely wrapped bundle into her arms and she looked down in numb astonishment at a tiny face with enormous dark blue eyes and a fuzzy halo of blonde hair. Sunlight flooded the room and she realised that the nightmare lions and the pain had gone at last, to be replaced by this tiny perfect being and a wonderful feeling of peace. She hadn't died after all. It was like a miracle.

'Is she all right?' she asked, examining one of the minute hands.

The nurse smiled. 'She's rather small. Only five and a half pounds, and she was delivered by forceps which is why she has those little marks on her head. But apart from that she's a fine, healthy baby. She's beautiful, isn't she? What will you call her?'

Elaine looked down wonderingly at the little face of her child — hers and Patrick's.

'Patricia,' she said firmly, hugging her daughter close. 'She's going to be called Patricia.'

Chapter Fifteen

1975

Anyone observing the two women having tea together at the corner table of the Old Cottage Tea Room would have been forgiven for taking them for sisters. The elder of the two looked much younger than her forty-three years; delicately built and still slender, she wore an elegant classic grey suit. Her dark hair, now attractively streaked with silver, was dressed in a sleek French pleat. The younger woman was taller and looked more mature than twenty-five. Her hair, cut short and softly curling, was a lighter shade of brown, and she wore a stylish jacket in the fashionable long length over a tweed skirt.

'More tea?' Grace asked, her hand on the teapot.

Elaine looked at her watch. 'I think I've just got time. I mustn't be late at Paul's mother's. You know what she's like.'

'What does she want to see you about?' Grace asked, pouring the tea.

Elaine sighed. 'I don't know, but you can bet it won't be to my advantage.' She drank her tea quickly and gathered up her bag and gloves. 'I'll have to go. I have to pick Tricia up from school first and take her for a music lesson.'

Grace smiled fondly at the mention of her granddaughter. 'Isn't it strange, the way she's inherited your father's talent for music?'

Elaine looked wistful. 'Yes. You know, I've never said so before but I've always regretted giving up my own music. That's why I encouraged Tricia as soon as she showed an interest in it.'

'I still think the violin is an unusual instrument for a little girl to choose. Easy to transport though.' Grace smiled reminiscently. 'I always remember your father saying he wished he could carry his own instrument around with him. Pianists have to make do with whatever is provided.'

Later, as Elaine drove to the school, she thought about what her mother had said. It was odd how much she spoke lately about her ex-husband. It seemed that Tricia's interest in music had refreshed her memories of him — softened the bitterness of their parting and revived only the good times. Or maybe it was that she had more time to reminisce now that she had given up the shop.

Four years ago Morgan had received an offer from a group of London designers. He had moved to the city to work at their London studios, where he had quickly risen to become a well-known and respected name in the fashion world. He now had a smart flat in Mayfair and a villa in Majorca, but he still returned to spend occasional weekends with Grace.

As his move had coincided with the expiry of her lease she had given up the shop and taken on the running of his Cambridge factory where Morgan Knitwear were still produced, buying a small house on the outskirts of the town and settling down to partial retirement.

It was almost eight years now since Elaines's marriage to Paul. To the casual observer it was an ideal match. They were a good-looking couple; they attended all the school functions at St Jasper's, and seemed, outwardly at least to be devoted to one another. In actual fact it was not a marriage at all. Since soon after Tricia's birth they had occupied separate bedrooms — at Paul's request. He said that he was unable to sleep in a shared room and suffered severe headaches as a consequence. Elaine hadn't complained. Their sex life had been practically non-existent from the beginning. She threw all her emotional energy into caring for her small daughter. It was enough. For her, physical love and passion had ceased to exist when Patrick had walked out of her life. She had long since acknowledged the fact that there could never be any other man for her.

For the past four years, since Mary Kingston's cousin Edna had died, Paul, Elaine and Tricia had lived at Langmere Lodge. Left on her own, Mary Kingston had found the place too large for her and moved into a small flat, closer to the centre of town. Although Elaine had been glad to leave the pokey little house in Fenchester, she hated the rambling Victorian mansion — especially as Mary insisted that they changed nothing, keeping the rooms furnished exactly as they were and refusing to allow any redecoration. The house was still in her name and she refused to allow Paul to buy it from her. Elaine's one consolation was the garden, which she loved and had made into a relaxing hobby. When Mary's old gardener had finally retired she had taken it over herself. Working in the early days until she thought her back would break, she had re-designed the layout, planted, seeded and mowed. Now her labours were rewarded with velvet green lawns, and borders ablaze with colour.

At seven, Tricia had grown into a beautiful, independent child. She was tall for her age and could charm the hardest heart with her engaging smile and bright blue eyes. She had shown an aptitude for music before the age of five and now, after two years of study her teacher was already encouraging her to play in public. At first Elaine had been afraid that the child might become precocious but although she was spirited, with a strong individual character, Tricia had shown no sign of conceit, being too engrossed in her music to notice any flattery or admiration she might receive.

Elaine arrived at the school gates with a few minutes to spare. She had bought a local paper and now, as she waited, she took it out of the glove compartment and opened it. On page two a small headline near the bottom of the page caught her eye: *Sudden Death Of Bank Manager*. Reading on she saw that the deceased was George Linton, Alison's father. She made a mental note to send a card to Mrs. Linton and to attend the funeral if she could.

To her regret she had lost touch with Alison, who had stayed on in America after her initial term of employment had ended. As far as Elaine knew, she had been there ever since. After leaving the Railtons, for whom she had gone to work, she had moved to San Francisco. She had written to Elaine once or twice from a commune she had joined and once she had sent a photograph of herself in a long ethnic-style dress, beads around her neck and flowers in her hair, which now fell to below her waist. In the photograph she wore ugly wire-rimmed spectacles and Elaine hardly recognised her. In her letters she'd mentioned a man called Luke, who it seemed had asked her to marry him. But whether the marriage actually took place Elaine never found out. Soon after the letter with the photograph had arrived the correspondence had ceased abruptly, and although she had written several times, Elaine had heard nothing more since. Reading the report of George Linton's death, she wondered if Alison knew, or if she had lost touch with her family too.

'Mummy – *Mummy*. Wake up. I've got to be at Miss Hazel's at a quarter past four.' Tricia was climbing into the passenger seat beside her, clutching her violin case. Her cheeks were pink from the fresh March wind and her long flaxen hair was escaping in cobwebby strands from its pony-tail.

'Here, let me tidy your hair first,' Elaine took a comb out of her bag. 'Can't have you turning up for your music lesson looking like a ragamuffin.'

214

Tricia submitted to the combing and re-tying of ribbons, fidgeting impatiently. 'Oh, hurry *up*, Mummy. I want Miss Hazel to hear my new piece. I can play it without making one mistake now.'

Elaine dropped her daughter off a Miss Hazel's house, then drove to the block of flats where her mother-in-law lived. As she parked the car in the car park at the rear her heart was filled with apprehension. Mary had called her early that morning, soon after Tricia and Paul had left.

'Elaine, can you come round this afternoon? There's something I want to talk to you about.'

'I'm afraid I'm rather tied up this afternoon, Mother.'

There was an irritated intake of breath at the other end of the line and Mary said: 'I'm sure there's nothing you can't rearrange, Elaine. What I have to say is rather important. What is it you're doing?'

'I promised to go shopping and have tea with my mother.'

'Well, come after that if you must go, though I'd have thought you could have seen your mother any time.'

'I have to pick Tricia up from school and take her to her music lesson.'

'Well then, come while she's having it. I know it won't give you long but I suppose it'll have to do. You can't possibly put your mother off, of course.'

The implication was clear and Elaine clenched her teeth. 'No, I can't. She has to come into town today to go to the factory.'

'I'll see you around four then.' Mary rang off abruptly, making it clear that she wasn't best pleased with the arrangement. Now, on her way up in the lift, Elaine wondered what it was her mother-in-law had to say to her.

Mary had aged considerably since Edna's sudden death four years previously. Although she still took care of herself and paid attention to her appearance, she seemed to have diminished in size since she'd been living alone. The pink and white complexion was wrinkled and papery and the blue-rinsed hair, cut and set meticulously each week, looked sparse and dry.

'I've got tea ready,' she said as she opened the door. 'You'll only have about half an hour, I suppose.'

'That's right.' Elaine sighed. She'd already told her mother-in-law that she was having tea with her mother, but she knew from experience that Mary would be deeply offended if she didn't eat anything. She followed her through to the living room and slipped off her jacket. 'I hope you're well, Mother.'

Mary looked at her sharply. 'No, I'm not. And that's what I

wanted to talk to you about.' She eased herself into her chair and began to pour tea into bone china cups. 'I've been having these dizzy spells lately and the doctor says I shouldn't be living here all alone on the fourth floor. One of these days I'm going to have a bad fall.'

Elaine refused the cucumber sandwiches and shortbread. Mary looked disapproving.

'I suppose you're dieting.' She sniffed and looked her daughter-in-law up and down. 'Tell me to mind my own business if you like, but I've never yet met a man who liked a skinny woman.' She helped herself to a sandwich and began to eat. 'I suppose you're going to refuse a cup of tea as well?'

'Of course not, Mother.' Reluctantly, Elaine took the tea and sipped it thoughtfully. She had a terrible premonition about what was coming next but nevertheless felt obliged to ask: 'What was it you were saying?'

'Just that I think the time has come for me to move again.'

'I see. Where to?'

Mary bridled. 'Where *to*? Why, back to my own house, of course.'

'You mean, you're asking to move in with us?'

'Not asking — *telling*.' Mary put down her cup with a clatter. 'After all, it is my house and you've lived in it rent free for four years.'

Elaine bit back the retort that was bursting to be made. 'Does Paul know about your decision?' The prospect of having Mary to live with them — of being at her beck and call all day long — was daunting to say the least.

'Of course he knows. I spoke to him about it last week.' Mary helped herself to a piece of shortbread and munched determinedly.

'Then why didn't he discuss it with me?' Elaine said, half to herself.

'Perhaps because there really isn't anything to discuss. After all, I am his mother,' Mary said, her eyes glinting. 'He knows his father would have expected him to care for me in my declining years. Paul may have his shortcomings but at least he's never shirked his duty.'

Elaine looked at the clock on the mantelpiece. 'Oh dear. Is that clock right?'

Mary gave an exasperated little cough. 'Naturally it's right. I can't think why it is, Elaine, but you always seem to have one eye on the clock when you come to see me.'

'I did tell you, Mother. I have to collect Tricia.'

Mary grunted. 'Huh. If you ask me that child is spoiled. She'll

216

grow up to be a conceited little baggage, you mark my words. Too big for her own boots.'

'She's musically talented. She takes after my father,' Elaine said stiffly.

'Oh?' Mary sniffed. 'Well, we'll have to take your word for that, won't we — seeing that we've never had the pleasure of meeting the man?' She got to her feet. 'I'll wait to hear from you then.' As she opened the door she delivered the trump card: 'Oh, by the way, I've already given my notice in here. The flat is re-let from the end of the month. So perhaps you'll be kind enough to let me know when it's convenient for me to move in.'

That evening Elaine had two things to talk to Paul about. She waited until Tricia was asleep and took a cup of coffee to his study where he had been working since dinner. Sitting down in the chair by the window, she began diplomatically with the good news.

'Miss Hazel feels that Tricia should try for a musical scholarship at St Jasper's at the end of this year, Paul. What do you think?'

He looked up from his desk. 'But I'm the headmaster. She can't.'

'Why not?'

'It wouldn't look right. It would smack of nepotism.'

'Don't be absurd, Paul. You don't judge the music scholar-ships.'

'Nevertheless, I don't feel it would look right.'

'But she's talented.'

'If she's talented she won't need St Jasper's help to get on, will she?' He lowered his head, returning to his work as though the subject were closed.

Elaine seethed. 'The only alternative is a boarding school and I hate the idea of that.'

'I can't see why. I went to one and it didn't harm me.'

'That's a matter of opinion,' Elaine muttered under her breath. Paul had never taken much interest in Tricia. As a baby he had made no secret of the fact that he found her messy and disruptive, and since she had grown older he seemed at a loss in her company; unsure of what to say or how to treat her. It was almost as though she belonged to some strange unfamiliar species from another planet. Swallowing her annoyance at his arbitrary dismissal, Elaine went on: 'Paul, there's something else — quite unrelated.'

A frown of annoyance at the further interruption to his work wrinkled Paul's brow and he sighed as he looked up. 'Oh dear, is there? What is it now?'

217

'Your mother asked me to go over there this afternoon. She says she intends to come back here to live. She tells me she mentioned it to you a week ago.'

'That's right.'

'And you didn't think to pass the news on to me?'

He shrugged. 'I don't see that it need affect you.'

She sprang angrily to her feet. 'Not affect me Paul? — you know she and I don't see eye to eye. She was utterly impossible last time we shared the house and I'm sure she hasn't mellowed with age. She's already rubbing it in that she's let us live here rent free and that it's her house.'

'Mother's a little eccentric. You know she means well.'

'I know nothing of the kind! She was making remarks about Tricia being spoilt too. It'll be terrible having her here, Paul. Can't we find somewhere of our own?'

He laid down his pen with a sigh and looked at her. 'That would defeat the object surely? You know as well as I do that what Mother needs is company. She misses Edna. She's lonely. She just needs her family around her.'

'She just needs someone to dance attendance on her night and day, you mean.'

'Suppose we just give it a try?' he said cajolingly.

'Why do you always fall in with everything she wants?' Elaine demanded exasperatedly. 'She does nothing but criticise you and compare you unfavorably with your brother.'

'Mother has had a very hard life. We should make allowances. We'll give it six months, eh?' He took off his glasses and looked at her. 'I'm sure she's really very fond of you, Elaine.'

'Oh, Paul, do we really have to?' She sat down again and suddenly there were tears behind her eyelids. Most of the time she could live with the monotony of her life, the lack of physical love and the absence of excitement. But the prospect of having her mother-in-law to live with them at Langmere Lodge, constantly complaining and reminding them that it was her house, was enough to tip the delicate balance of her emotional state.

He got up and came round to perch on the front of his desk. 'Look, Elaine. You often say you're bored and that you'd like to take some kind of job. This could be your chance.'

'Let your mother keep house for us?' She laughed. 'Can you see her agreeing to that? Somehow I don't think it's quite what she has in mind.'

'You never know until you ask,' he said, adding unrealistically: 'She might even jump at the idea.'

218

'What kind of work could I get anyway?'she asked despairingly. 'I've never had a job – except working with my mother in the shop.'

'There's always voluntary work,' Paul suggested tentatively.

'Pushing a trolleyful of chocolate bars round the hospital? No, I'd rather have a proper job – something in fashion perhaps, as I did before.'

'Well, find another job like that,' he suggested. The actual idea of his wife working in a dress shop was anathema to him. He only suggested it because he didn't believe for a moment that anyone would employ her.

Privately, Elaine shared his view. At twenty-five she saw herself as on the scrap-heap; not much use for anything, except bringing up her child and looking after a house. It wasn't even her house either. And pretty soon she would have her mother-in-law laying down the law and telling her what to do. The thought was deeply depressing.

Lying in bed that night, sleepless as she so often was, she thought about her life, wondering just how she had drifted into her present situation and what was to become of her. She had grown up in what were known as the swinging sixties, yet she had seen very little of them. He mother had tended to be over-protective. She'd had only a brief glimpse of what real life could be like through Patrick. When she had been going out with him life had seemed so vivid, so brightly coloured, exciting and vital. And now that they were into a new decade all one heard about was Women's Liberation. It seemed she was to miss out again. The whole thing seemed to her very much a no-win situation. One must first be free in order to take advantage of these trends.

In the early years of her marriage she had worried about the lack of physical contact between herself and Paul. Once she had even tried to speak to her mother about it. Grace had been embarrassed. Pressed for an opinion she had indicated that a lack of physical love was, to her way of thinking, a definite advantage – something to be thankful for. It made Elaine wonder for the first time if it might have been this attitude that had been responsible for her parents' break-up.

As well as being mean with his affections Paul was tight with money, keeping her so short that at times she had difficulty in making ends meet. He and Elaine had little in common. Sometimes she had been so desperately unhappy and unfulfilled in her marriage that she had thought of ending it. But if she left Paul, what would she do? She was incapable of earning enough money to keep herself

219

and Tricia and she knew Paul well enough to know that he would never agree to a divorce. The stigma would be too great and he would consider it harmful to his position as headmaster. Besides, there was Tricia to be considered. None of it was her fault. The child was talented; she deserved the best music teachers and all the chances available. Although she would miss her dreadfully, Elaine would even agree to sending her to a boarding school if that were the only way she could obtain the best musical education for her. She remembered what life had been like for herself and Grace after her father had left. The emotional trauma had been hard for her, and she was fairly certain that it hadn't felt like liberation for her mother. No. She had been glad enough to marry Paul and there was nothing for it but to stay married to him. If only for Tricia's sake.

The day of George Linton's funeral was bleak and cold. A vicious March wind whipped across the churchyard, bending the elm trees and tingeing the already pale faces of the mourners with blue. Elaine kept a respectful distance as the family followed the coffin to the grave. She'd arrived in the church at the last minute. It had been packed and she had stood at the back, unable to see who occupied the front pews. Now she watched as Mrs Linton, her brother and assorted relatives grouped themselves around the grave for the final farewell.

It was only as they turned to go after the interment that Elaine saw Alison. She walked alone behind the rest of the family, wearing a black suit that looked too thin for such cold weather. Her hair was cut in a short spiky style that made her eyes look huge and gave her thin face a gamin look. Elaine barely recognised her. Picking her way across the churchyard she touched her arm.

'Alison.'

The other girl stared at her for a moment, then her face broke into a smile of delighted recognition. '*Ellie*. Oh, how lovely to see you.' She threw her arms around Elaine and pressed a cold cheek against hers. 'God, you're like a ray of sunshine on a day like this.' As she drew her head back Elaine saw the tears glistening in her eyes. 'Are you coming back to the house for tea? Oh, please say you'll come, for God's sake. It's about the only way I'll be able to get through it.'

'Of course I'll come.' Elaine slipped her arm through Alison's and they were girls again. It was as though the past seven years had melted away.

*

'Tell me everything. I want to hear it all.' Alison looked better now. The glass of sherry had brought the colour back to her cheeks and the sparkle to her eyes. But there was still an oddly pinched look about her face. The rounded teenage plumpness was gone, replaced by a gaunt, worldly, look. And Elaine thought she could see hurt reflected in the lovely hazel eyes. She was thin too. Far too thin. The black suit hung loosely on her angular frame, and the rounded bosom and hips that Elaine had so envied when they were growing up had been whittled down almost to nothing.

The two sat on the window seat in the front room of the Lintons' house apart from the feasting mourners. Alison leaned forward eagerly, pouring herself a second glass of sherry with tense, trembling fingers. 'Come on – give. How's Paul? And that baby of yours – she must be positively ancient by now. And your mother – how's your mother? Does she still have the shop? And Morgan. I've heard all about him, of course. He made quite a name for himself, didn't he?'

Elaine laughed. 'Which one would you like me to answer first? Anyway, I want to know what you've been doing with your life. I'm sure it's far more interesting than mine.'

The smile left Alison's eyes for a moment. 'No, it's not fair, I asked first.'

Elaine briefly outlined the events of the past few years, concentrating on Tricia and touching only lightly on the relationship between herself and Paul.

'And your ma-in-law – is she still friendly with your mother?'

Elaine smiled wryly. 'No. As soon as he could Morgan paid her back the money she lent him to start his company. She showed every sign of trying to run it for him and he flatly refused to allow her to be involved in Morgan Knitwear any more.'

'Good for him,' Alison laughed.

'She blamed Mum for the whole thing of course and they've barely spoken since.'

'And what about all the old chums? Do you still see the Carnes?'

'Not often. I believe that Tom is teaching in the Midlands some-where, but apart from that I hardly ever see any of them.'

'They were in church, you know. At least, Zoe and Red were.'

'Were they? I didn't see them. But then there were so many people.'

'So you don't go to their parties any more?'

'No.' Elaine looked down at her hands. 'Ever since Patrick ...'

'Don't tell me you're still carrying a torch for him?' Alison leaned forward to peer into Elaine's face, the old teasing look in her eyes.

'Of course not. It was just a teenage romance.'

'He's married now, so Zoe tells me,' Alison said lightly, unaware of the effect the news had on Elaine. 'An actress, Cathryn Harte. No one's ever heard of her, of course. It seems Patrick met her when he did some set designs for a West End show a couple of years ago. He thought he was made when he landed the job, apparently, but the show folded and the company went into liquidation, so nothing came of it for either of them. Now she's touring and Patrick's working for some advertising company or other in London.'

'Really?' Elaine swallowed hard. 'And you? Last time I heard for you you were living in a commune.'

Alison gave a brittle little laugh. 'Oh, that. My hippy phase. That soon passed.'

'And what about what's-his-name – Luke? Did you marry him?'

The smile faded from Alison's face. 'Oh, yes, I married him,' she said. '*That* passed even sooner. The least said about it, the better. I'm into feminism now. There's nothing like being independent - financially *and* emotionally.'

'I know what you mean,' Elaine said wistfully. 'How long are you home for?'

Alisone looked thoughtful. 'I haven't decided. I might stay on for a bit.' Suddenly she put down her glass to hug her friend warmly. 'Oh, Ellie, I *have* missed you. I can't tell you how lovely it is to see you again. We must get together soon. It's going to take days to catch up with all our news.'

Elaine left soon after that, taking her leave of Mrs Linton and promising Alison that they would meet again soon. As she drove to the school to pick up Tricia, thoughts of Patrick filled her mind. So he had married? And to an actress. She might have known he would choose someone with an exotic career like that. Cathryn Harte. She said the name aloud to herself. It had a glamorous ring to it. She tried to imagine what she would be like; beautiful, intelligent, intellectual? Totally unlike the dull housewife she herself had become.

Mary Kingston moved back to her old home the following week. Elaine had prepared the first floor back bedroom for her. It got all the early morning sun and overlooked the garden. Elaine had thought her mother-in-law would be pleased. She was wrong.

'I'm sorry, Elaine, but I know I wouldn't sleep a wink in here. It used to be poor Edna's room and it would bring back too many memories.'

'Which room *would* you like then, Mother?' Elaine asked patiently.

'The one at the front, over the porch.'

'But that's my room.'

Mary assumed a long suffering expression. 'Oh, I see. Well, of course, I don't want to put you out ...'

'I'll move my things,' Elaine said resignedly.

'I'd have thought that room was far too small for two,' Mary observed on her way downstairs.

'It would be. I sleep there alone. Paul has the room next to the bathroom.'

Mary stopped in her tracks to stare at her. 'You mean you've turned Paul out of his own bed?'

'No. It was Paul's own choice. He's a very light sleeper and ...'

But Mary was screwing up her face as though she were eating a lemon. 'It's a big mistake,' she pronounced. 'Henry snored quite dreadfully. I never *ever* got a good night's sleep. But I wouldn't have dreamed of asking him to leave the marital bed. It's extremely unwise and I'm afraid I find it rather shocking.'

'And *I'm* afraid I feel that it's a private matter between Paul and me,' Elaine said crisply.

It was the pattern for what was to come. In the days that followed Mary objected to practically everything that made up the Kingstons' daily routine. She complained about Tricia's practising, disagreed with the times Elaine served meals and insisted that the television set was moved from the living room to Paul's study.

'But he works in there most evenings,' Elaine said. 'It means that no one will be able to look at it.'

'And a good thing too if you ask me. That child watches far too much television. It'll ruin her eyesight.'

Elaine soon felt the strain. Mary had taken over the house again as though it was hers alone. She announced that she had arranged for three friends to visit her twice a week to play bridge. She told Elaine that they would be needing the drawing room on those afternoons and gave orders for what refreshments they would require. She asked for the furniture to be rearranged and complained about the alterations Elaine had made to the garden. As days went by, Elaine realised to her horror that she was slowly stepping into the role Edna had vacated. She knew that she must do something to stop it before it was too late.

223

She told all this to Alison when they met for lunch a couple of weeks after George Linton's funeral.

'But why do you put up with it?' her friend demanded. 'Why can't you and Paul buy a house of your own?'

'Because his mother doesn't want to live at Langmere Lodge by herself.'

Alison gave a snort of annoyance. 'Then tell her to move into one of those up-market old people's homes. She can boss people about there to her heart's content.'

'She wouldn't go. Langmere Lodge is still her house. There's nothing I can do about it, and nothing that Paul *will*. He just keeps out of the way and leaves it all to me.'

'You've got more patience than I have,' Alison said. 'If it were me I'd tell the bossy old cow to take a running jump.' She leaned across the table. 'Why don't you get a job? At least it'd get you out from under her feet for most of the time.'

'Let's face it, there's nothing I can do,' Elaine said with a sigh. 'All the training I ever did was a domestic science course and I never even finished that.'

'What of it? I did the same.'

'Ali, why did you stop writing to me?' Elaine asked. It was something that had been nagging at her ever since the day of the funeral.

Alison was silent for a moment, then she looked up at Elaine with pain-filled eyes. 'I fell into some rather bad ways. I didn't want anyone to know.'

'What kind of bad ways?'

'Dope, to name but a few.' She gave an ironic little laugh, searching her friend's eyes for signs of disapproval. 'It was Luke. He started me off. Well, I'd smoked a bit of pot here and there ever since school. Everyone did it in those days.' She glanced at Elaine. 'Well, everyone but you, that is. Anyway, it never seemed to do me any harm.'

'But you became addicted?'

'I got into the harder stuff.' Alison's fingers nervously pleated the edge of the tablecloth. 'Luke was quite a bit older than me. He'd served in the army − been in Vietnam. After he came out he went a bit wild − kicked around a lot. I knew all this when I said I'd marry him, but I was young and it seemed rather romantic.' She smiled wryly. 'I suppose I had some mad idea that I could reform him. He said he wanted to settle down and have a family.'

Elaine waited, but when Alison didn't go on she asked: 'And did you?'

'Almost. Our baby son was still-born. Afterwards I was very depressed, especially when the doctor said I wouldn't be able to have any more. Luke lost interest in me then. He got bored with having a weeping female around all the time so he introduced me to the stuff to keep me quiet. It was sheer bliss in the beginning. It seemed like the answer to everything — till I got hooked and it all got out of hand. That was when he finally walked out and left me to it.'

'Oh, Alison.' Elaine reached across the table to cover the thin restless hand with hers. Now she knew the reason for the change in Alison; the gauntness and the haunted look. Just for a moment she was tempted to share her own unhappiness; to tell Alison about her heartbreak over Patrick — the truth about Tricia. But something stopped her. Instead she said: 'Darling, I'm so sorry. Did you love him very much?'

'When I first met him I was completely bowled over. I'd never met anyone like him before. But falling for Luke was a bit like driving a car off the roof of a skyscraper. For a while it felt like flying - then I hit the ground.'

Elaine nodded. 'I know what you mean.'

'Do you?' Alison looked up. 'I doubt it. After he left I knew it was a question of pick myself up or sink. At first it didn't seem to matter much either way, then someone put me in touch with an organisation that helps addicts. The drying out process was sheer hell. There were times when I wished I could just die.'

'But you beat it in the end?'

'Eventually. Afterwards I went back to California to work for the Railtons again. They were wonderful to me. They took me into the business and taught me everything.'

'What kind of business was it?'

'They ran a bridal service.' Alison laughed dryly. 'Funny, the irony of it never occured to me at the time. They did everything — dress hire, marquee hire, floral displays, catering, cars — right down to the printing and the press announcements.'

Elaine smiled. 'That sounds really interesting.'

'It saved my life, I can tell you.'

'So why did you leave?'

Alison shrugged. 'Homesickness mainly. I just woke up one morning and longed to be home; to feel good old English rain trickling down my neck and taste a British Rail sandwich again.' Her smile faded. 'Then, while I was still thinking about it, the cable came to say Dad had died. Funny how fate has a way of stepping in to make up your mind for you.'

225

'So you'll stay?'

Alison nodded. 'I think so, yes. If I can find something interesting to do.' She looked up. 'By the way, no one else knows any of what I've just told you, apart from the divorce. So keep it to yourself eh?'

'Naturally.'

'Actually, I've been wondering if I could start a bridal service here. I've been doing a bit of research and there doesn't seem to be anything of that sort for miles around. I worked with the Railtons for almost two years so I know how the business works.'

'It sounds exciting. Would you do it on your own?'

'Not if I could help it.' Alison looked up at her, a ghost of the old mischievous gleam back in her eyes. 'Actually, I'd thought of asking a certain old school friend to go into partnership with me.' She grinned. 'How about it, Ellie — are you game?'

For a moment Elaine stared at her. 'Are you serious?'

'Yes. I think we could work together, don't you?'

'Of course I do. But ...' Elaine's mind was racing ahead. 'Wouldn't we need money?'

Alison laughed. 'It would help, yes.'

'But — I haven't got any. There's no way I could put any money into your scheme, Ali. Maybe you should ask someone who has some cash to invest.'

'Would Paul help?'

Elaine shook her head. 'I can't see him financing any business I had anything to do with.'

Her friend grinned and suddenly the old Alison looked out from the hazel eyes. 'Don't worry. We'll do it somehow. We'll start on a shoestring. Where there's a will there's a way. We'll *make* it go — you just see.'

Her enthusiasm was infectious and Elaine felt her heart lift. A new excitement stirred inside her. Life was beginning to open up again for her. She could feel it in her bones.

Chapter Sixteen

Now that Mary was living at Langmere Lodge it was almost impossible for Elaine to find the privacy to speak to Paul alone. She chose her moment, after Mary had gone up to her room. Making coffee she carried the tray through to Paul in his study. As she poured it she glanced at him as he sat at his desk, glasses perched on the end of his nose as he worked on a pile of exercise books.

'If you could spare a moment, Paul, there's something I'd like to talk to you about.'

He pushed the books aside and took off his glasses, accepting the cup of coffee she passed him. 'What is it? Tricia again? I've sent for a prospectus from a school in Hertfordshire. They specialise in musical education. It looks very good actually. I was rather impressed.' He drew the folder out of a drawer and passed it to her. She glanced at it briefly.

'She'd have to board.'

'Of course.'

'But Paul, she's only seven.'

'She'd be almost eight by the time she started there. They take them at that age. It'll do her the world of good.'

'I don't know.'

'You baby her too much,' he said tersely. 'Mother was only saying so the other day. Too much cosseting is bad for a child. You'll make her too dependent on you.'

She swallowed her resentment. She'd no wish to start an argument with him about his mother's interference just now. 'I suppose we could ask her,' she said.

'*Ask* her?' Paul snorted. 'How can you expect a seven-year-old child to know what's best for her? There's an open day next month. I suggest we all go over and have a look. Then of course she'd have to pass the entrance exam.' He finished his coffee and put on his glasses again in preparation for continuing his work.

'Paul, I didn't come to talk to you about Tricia,' Elaine said.

He looked up. 'Oh? Then what?'

She took a deep breath. 'I had lunch with Alison today. She and I want to go into business together.'

He looked incredulous. 'Into business? Doing what, may I ask?'

His scathing tone brought the blood rushing to her cheeks. 'Alison has been working for some people who run a bridal service in the States. We'd like to start one here.'

'*Bridle* service? But you don't know the first thing about horses.'

She stared at him for a moment, then laughed. 'Not bridle – bri*dal*, as in weddings. The idea is to organise the whole thing – dress hire, catering, cars, flowers ...'

'Is there any call for that kind of thing?' he asked. 'In the States, yes, but here in England I thought families rather liked doing all that for themselves.'

'We believe it would go well,' Elaine said positively. 'Anyway, we'd like to give it a try.' She looked at him. 'You did suggest I got a job, Paul. And if Tricia is going away to school ...'

'Yes, yes. You're going to be bored, I know.' He pulled off his glasses again to frown at her impatiently. 'You're very naive about these things, Elaine. What business knowledge do you have? And how do you think you're going to start up a business like that – without money?'

She cleared her throat. 'Alison has the business experience, and as for the money – well – that's what I wanted to talk to you about. I wondered if we might ...' She stopped, her heart sinking as she saw his expression.

'Put good money into a hare-brained scheme like that?' he laughed dryly. 'Not me, Elaine. My money is much too hard-earned to throw it down the drain. And believe me, that's what it would be.' He sighed with exaggerated tolerance. 'Why not do as I suggested, Elaine – volunteer your services for the Friends of the Hospital or something? I'm sure they'd be delighted to have you. And now, I really must get on with this, if you don't mind.'

Elaine picked up the tray and left the room, closing the door behind her. So that was that. Well, she hadn't really held out much hope of getting any support from Paul anyway. In the kitchen she washed up the cups and put them away. She was just hanging up the teacloth when a voice behind her startled her.

'Elaine – I couldn't help overhearing ...'

228

She spun round in alarm. 'Mother! You made me jump. I thought you were in bed.'

'I came down for a hot water bottle. I felt chilly. I couldn't help overhearing what you were discussing with Paul as I passed the study.'

Elaine bit back a tart remark. The doors of the old house were so thick that Mary would have had to press her ear to the door of Paul's study in order to overhear.

'I think your idea sounds very interesting,' Mary went on with a smile. 'I'm more than tempted to put some money into the scheme myself. I'd have to hear more details, of course. But I'm sure I could help you a lot with ideas as well as money. After all, I haven't lived for sixty-eight years without gaining a little experience.' She smiled expectantly at Elaine.

'No, thank you, Mother.'

The smile evaporated. 'What do you mean — no, thank you?'

'Just what I say. At present we want to try to do it by ourselves.'

'But you were asking Paul for money.'

'Paul is my husband.'

'And I'm nothing to you, is that it?'

Elaine looked at her mother-in-law's glinting eyes and reddening face and knew she must stand her ground firmly. 'It's very kind of you to offer,' she said evenly, 'but I'm not alone in this. There's Alison to consider too.'

'Then why don't you ask her what *she* thinks?'

'Because I know what her answer will be. We want to make a go of it on our own.'

'Very well.' Mary turned and flounced towards the door. 'But Paul won't change his mind, I can assure you, and you'll soon find that floating a business without money is a non-starter. If you go to the bank you'll find yourself paying back all your profits in interest, whereas my loan would be almost interest-free.' At the door she paused. 'You don't deserve it, but I'll keep the offer open for you. But if you change your mind, you'll have to come to me and ask.'

Elaine let out her breath as the door closed on her mother-in-law. 'I'd have to be desperate before I'd come to you,' she muttered under her breath. But where her share of the money was to come from to start the business she didn't know. As she made her way upstairs her heart was heavy. It seemed she was doomed to be cooped up in this Victorian mausoleum at Mary's beck and call for ever.

She was almost asleep when the idea dropped into her mind. Instantly she was wide awake. Sitting up in bed she switched on

229

the light. Of course! Why hadn't she thought of it before? All the time the answer to her problem had been literally staring her in the face. She sat looking at the Severini on the opposite wall. It had been hanging there in Edna's old room for so long that she barely saw it any more. It held too many painful memories for her ever to have become over-fond of it, yet because it had been Patrick's parting gift she had never been able to bring herself to give it away.

She stared at the dazzling mass of coloured dots and wondered for the first time if it were worth anything. Might she realise enough on it to make her contribution to the business? Who did she know who could tell her? There was one name that sprang immediately to mind. The prospect of approaching him brought her mixed feelings, but if she wanted an honest appraisal of the picture she must do it.

'Elaine, my dear girl.' Red Carne seemed genuinely delighted to see her. He hadn't changed much since the last time they'd met except that he had grown a beard, a luxuriant ginger affair that jutted assertively from his chin. He peered at her more closely.

'It *is* Elaine, isn't it?'

She laughed. 'Yes, it is. How are you, Red?'

'I'm fine thanks. How are you? It's been ages. Where have you been hiding yourself all these years?'

'Oh, I've been around. Busy, you know.'

'I do hear news of you from time to time when your mother pops into the shop.' He rubbed his hands, smiling delightedly. 'So what can I do for you?'

'I've got a picture I want to sell. Oh, I'm not asking you to buy it,' she added hurriedly, 'but I thought you might give me an idea of how much it's worth. I haven't a clue.'

Red stroked his beard thoughtfully. 'Mmm, you were wise to come to me in that case. There are some very unscrupulous people around. I wouldn't like to see you getting ripped off. What kind of picture is it?'

'A modern one. A Severini.'

His eyebrows rose. 'A Severini, eh? How did you happen to come by that?'

Elaine blushed. 'It was a present.'

He smiled. 'From someone who obviously thought a great deal of you. I hope you won't think me inquisitive, Elaine, but why do you want to sell? It'd pay you to hang on to it. A picture like that is likely to increase in value.'

'I want to go into business and I need the money.'

'Well, that's an honest, straightforward answer. Do you have it with you?'

'Yes. It's in the car. I'll get it.'

In the room at the back of the shop, Red studied the picture for a long time. 'It's a very nice example,' he said a last. 'Very nice indeed. And naughty of you never to have had it insured. Of course, it's very "sixties"; not everyone's cup of tea. I think your best bet would be to approach one of the museums.' He looked at her, noting her doubtful expression. 'Would you like me to handle it for you?'

'I was rather hoping you'd say that. It would be marvellous of course but ...'

He smiled. 'You're worried about what I'll charge you. Don't worry, I don't sting old friends. It's an interesting painting. I'll be curious to see how it goes myself. Let's call it quits.'

'Oh, Red, I couldn't.'

'Well, I'll tell you what − bring that small daughter of yours to see us one of these days. Zoe is always talking about you. She's missed having you around.'

It was just three days later that he rang her.

'Elaine, I've got some news for you.'

'The picture?' She held the receiver tightly, hardly daring to hope for a sale.

'After you'd gone the other day I remembered a chap I know − a collector of modern art. I gave him a ring and he's been in to see the Severini. He's fallen head over heels in love with it.'

Elaine held her breath. 'He's made an offer?'

'He certainly has.' He named a figure that almost took Elaine's breath away.

'Red,' she breathed, 'it can't be worth all that.'

He chuckled at the other end of the line. 'Clearly it is to him. He's besotted with that particular school. I've got the cheque here now. I had it made out to you. So any time you'd like to come and collect ...'

'Oh, Red, I can't thank you enough. It means a great deal to me. And I must insist that you let me settle with you.'

'Nonsense. All I did was make one phone call. Just remember your promise to come and see us.'

'I will. Thanks again, Red. I'll see you soon.'

Just before she dropped the receiver back on to its rest she heard a tiny clink. She'd heard it before at the end of her telephone calls and she knew only too well what it was. Mary had been listening in on the extension in Paul's study.

*

231

Alison was amazed at Elaine's windfall.

'You must invest it at once,' she said as they sat over tea in her old room at the Lintons' house. 'We'll only use what's absolutely necessary. With what I can put in too we should be fine until we get on our feet. Now listen, things are moving. Mum has suggested we use a room here at home as our temporary headquarters. She's got the house to herself now and she'd be glad to have us around all day. We could turn the morning room into an office. She says her contribution will be to make us endless cups of coffee and hot dinners to keep up our strength.'

'My mother will help too,' Elaine said excitedly. 'She still has her contacts in the fashion world. She's been on to someone who'll let us have some dresses at cost price to start us off.' She looked uncertainly at Alison. 'I did think I might make some too. If you think my work would be good enough.'

Alison shook her head. 'One thing you're going to have to ditch is that inferiority complex. Of course your dresses will be good enough. You always were clever with design and your needle. Now ...' She opened a businesslike-looking notebook. 'First, the groundwork. I suggest that we start by making a tour of the following places. The idea is to get favourable terms in exchange for putting business their way. Of course we'll do it all ourselves once we're established and can afford to employ people, but for now we'll have to hire outside help.'

The list she put in front of Elaine included florists, car-hire firms, printers and photographers. 'We can do the catering ourselves, of course,' she said confidently.

Elaine looked at her. 'We can?'

'Of course we can. Our training has got to be good for something. It'll be a doddle, and anyway I had some experience of catering in the States. Mum will let us have the use of the kitchen here. She has a huge freezer we can use, so we can keep stock of all the freezable things. She's even offered to help with some of the cooking too.' Unable to contain herself, Alison got up and did a little dance. 'Oh, Ellie, it's all going to be *fabulous*, I know it is . A couple of years from now we'll be famous. We'll have a fleet of white Rolls-Royces and our elegant society weddings will be the talk of the county.'

'I suppose I should tell you, I had another offer of help,' Elaine confessed. 'But I'm afraid I turned it down.'

Alison stared at her. 'You turned down an offer – why, for heaven's sake?'

'It was from Paul's mother. She helped Morgan start his business,

232

if you remember, but he and Mum paid the price and we would have too. She made life intolerable for Morgan. He had the devil's own job shaking her off. She tried to run him and his firm as well.'

'Ah, I see.' Alison looked wistful. 'Still — it must have been tempting.'

Elaine shook her head. 'You wouldn't say that if you knew Mary as I do. Much better for us to be independent, even if we take longer to get off the ground.'

Alison nodded. 'Fair enough. You know best. So what are we going to call ourselves?'

They sat for an hour with pencil and paper, arguing good-naturedly as they had in the old days, racking their brains for ideas, some serious, some so frivolous that they collapsed with laughter. Finally Elaine came up with something that satisfied them both.

'Let's call it "Happy Ever After",' she said.

Alison snapped her fingers. 'That's it.' She smiled ruefully. 'There's a sort of delicious irony about me running something with a name like that?' She looked at Elaine. 'I've just had a thought. You won't go and start another baby just as we get ourselves off the ground, will you?'

Before she could stop herself, Elaine had said vehemently: 'That's extremely unlikely.'

Alison regarded her friend for a moment in silence, then she said quietly: 'You know, ever since I came home I've known there was something. Want to talk about it?'

Elaine lifted her shoulders resignedly. 'Oh, it's nothing much. Put it down to having my mother-in-law living with us.'

'No, you can't fob me off with that. There's more, isn't there?'

There was a pause, then Elaine said: 'Paul and I have what the Victorian novels used to call a "marriage in name only".'

Alison frowned. 'You mean he doesn't — you never ...?'

'We've had separate rooms for ages now. I don't think it will ever change.'

'Is there any special reason?'

Elaine shrugged. 'Paul says it's because he's a light sleeper. I keep him awake. He gets head-aches.'

'You poor love.' Alison looked concerned. 'But things must have been all right once. You had Tricia, after all.' Elaine was silent and Alison wondered if she'd said too much. 'Is it hard for you, love?' she asked gently. 'Maybe there's some sort of counselling you could have.'

'No. Paul would never agree to that. Anyway, I don't really want things to be any different now.'

'You mean you don't love him any more?'

'I mean I never really have.' Elaine twisted her fingers together in her lap. 'Sometimes I feel this is a kind of punishment. I should never have married Paul. Perhaps I was unfair to him.'

'Then why did you?' When Elaine made no reply she asked: 'Have you thought of calling it a day? After all, you're only young. You can't go through life like this, Ellie – tied to a man you don't love, and who doesn't seem to want you either. From what you say it shouldn't be too difficult to get a divorce.'

Elaine shook her head. 'It doesn't really bother me any more. And Tricia needs security. Better to leave things as they are.'

But Alison was really disturbed by Elaine's attitude. 'Ellie, you can't let yourself be dependent on a man who neglects you. Then there's his awful mother. Suppose you met someone else? Come on, love, surely you'd rather be independent?'

Elaine looked up at her friend, suddenly seeing the width of the gulf that had grown between them. Alison had done so much – true, much of her experience had been painful, but nevertheless she had tasted life, she had lived. She had seen something of the world outside; fought and overcome tragedy and freed herself to begin again – whilst she, Elaine, had let the pain of her first rejected love bring her life to a close, almost before it had begun. She forced herself to smile.

'Of course I'd rather be independent. It's what I've always dreamed of. But as for meeting another man – I won't, Ali, because I don't want to. With a bit of luck my independence starts here, thanks to you.'

'No.' Alison shook her head firmly. 'Don't thank me. You're putting your share into the business. We're partners in every way. It's up to both of us to pull our weight if we want it to work. And we will, won't we?'

Elaine reached out to grasp Alison's hand, her heart lifting. 'Yes, we will.'

St Cecilia's School was housed in a lovely mellow red brick Georgian house on the fringe of a Hertfordshire village. It stood in its own wooded grounds and as far as Elaine could see there were no drawbacks at all. The staff were pleasant, the pupils seemed charming and well behaved, and the standard of music was quite impressive. Tricia sat her academic entrance exam in the morning, after which she was free to look around the school with her parents. After lunch the musical auditions were held, at which parents were allowed to be present.

Privately Elaine thought Tricia had never played better. She performed the set piece, which she had been practising at home, and managed the sight-reading without any problems. The theory questions she answered correctly and without hesitation. The music mistress seemed delighted.

Tea was taken on the lawn along with all the other prospective pupils and their parents, then it was time for each child to see the headmistress individually. Finally it was time for the parents to receive her verdict. Paul and Elaine were ushered into her study, where Miss Gaynor, the Head, invited them to take a seat.

'Patricia is extremely talented,' she pronounced. 'Musically she is quite outstanding for her age, and she has a pleasing personality.' She pursed her lips. 'Academically she is not *quite* so gifted, but one can't have everything and she is still very young. I'm sure she will improve with individual attention.' She smiled. 'All in all, we should be delighted to enrol her at St Cecilia's in September. She is just a little under age, but with her outgoing personality I feel sure she will cope.'

Tricia chattered excitedly all the way home in the car. She had loved everything about St Cecilia's and had already made friends with several of the pupils.

'Did you see the hall where they have the concerts? You'll be able to come to those,' she said. 'And I'm going to learn to play a wind instrument too. I think I'll choose the saxophone,' she said thoughtfully. 'Then I could get a job in a band and play jazz too.'

Paul glanced disapprovingly at Elaine and asked: 'Why do you want to play jazz? I thought you were all for the classics.'

'My grandfather played jazz music,' Tricia said solemnly. 'Granny Grace told me all about it. He played with some of the best bands there were, in the olden days when Granny was young.' She leaned forward in the car to slip her arms around Elaine's neck. 'I wish I could see him, Mummy. Why does he never come to see us? Does he know about me?'

Elaine turned to look at her small daughter. 'He and Granny decided not to live together a long time ago, darling. They don't see each other any more.'

'Don't they even write letters to each other?'

'No.'

'I wish he did know about me,' Tricia said wistfully. 'We could talk about music together, couldn't we?'

Since Mary had moved into Langmere Lodge and complained

about Tricia's practising, Grace had offered to let the child practise at her house for an hour after school each evening. The two had always been close, but the practice sessions seemed to have drawn them even closer. Elaine discovered that they talked a lot about her father over tea before Grace brought Tricia home. Later Paul brought the subject up again.

'Why is your mother filling the child's head with fanciful half-truths about your father?' he asked as they sat over a late cup of coffee after Tricia had gone to bed.

'I don't know that they're half-truths,' Elaine said defensively. 'He did play with some well-known bands, and when he and Stella Rainbow ...'

'It's all rather unsavoury,' Paul interrupted with a look of distaste. 'The man was obviously an inveterate womaniser. I don't think I want Tricia going about mentioning that she's connected with him or that singer woman. It's just possible that someone might remember the name and connect us with the scandal. Perhaps you'd have a word with your mother next time you see her.'

'No, I won't.' Elaine said hotly. 'He was — and still is — my father, and as far as I'm concerned he was never anything but a good musician and a kind man.'

'So *kind* that he walked out on you,' Paul sneered. 'I can't see what your mother's got to be so proud of.'

Anger rose like a ball of fire in Elaine's chest. 'At least he was normal,' she said.

Colour flooded Paul's face and his eyes glinted as he stared at her. 'And just what is that supposed to mean?'

Elaine rose on trembling legs. 'It means what it says,' she said. 'I've never known what happened between my parents to cause the failure of their marriage but I do know that my father was a normal, affectionate man. At least my mother was never starved of love. He never shut her out.'

He rose to face her, his face flushing. For a moment she thought he was about to say something, then his eyes slid away from hers and he turned and walked out of the room.

It was the next morning after breakfast that Mary brought up the subject of the Severini. Paul and Tricia had left for school and Elaine had begun to clear the table when Mary said: 'Your bedroom door was open yesterday. I couldn't help noticing that that picture had gone. You know, that one with all the colours.'

Elaine didn't look up as she loaded dishes on to her tray. 'Really?'

236

'Yes. Have you put it away? Don't you and Paul like it any more?'

Elaine met her mother-in-law's eyes. 'As you know quite well, Mother, I've sold the picture. I'm sure you even know the price it fetched.'

Mary's face turned a dull red. 'Are you accusing me of evesdropping.'

Elaine lifted the tray and walked towards the door. 'No, Mother. I'm just stating a fact. You were listening on the extension when I got the call. I heard you hang up.'

She was unloading the tray in the kitchen when Mary, silent on her slippered feet, appeared at her elbow. 'It happened that I was about to make a call myself,' she said. 'I heard your conversation quite by accident.'

Elaine ran hot water into the sink. 'Really?'

'Does Paul know?'

'*I* haven't told him.' Elaine said pointedly.

'Well, *I* certainly haven't.' Mary paused, watching thoughtfully as Elaine began to wash up; making no attempt to help. 'I know he's against you going into business,' she said at last. 'What would he say about your selling the picture behind his back in order to do it, I wonder?'

'The picture happens to be mine,' Elaine told her. 'It was a present, given to me before Paul and I were married. It was mine to sell and I sold it.'

'A very special kind of present. Who could have given you that, I wonder?' Mary's eyes glinted provocatively, but when Elaine did not rise to the bait she went on: 'When you have a windfall like that it hardly seems fair to let poor Paul pay for that expensive boarding school for Patricia. I'm surprised that you don't want to contribute.'

Elaine rounded on her. 'As he chose to send her there it's only fair that he should bear the cost,' she said. 'I didn't want her to go away from home, especially so young. She could have got a scholarship to St Jasper's but Paul wouldn't hear of it. Anyway, I daresay you'll be relieved to have her out of your house too.'

Her slight emphasis on the word 'your' brought the colour to Mary's face again. 'That's a downright wicked thing to say.'

'Is it? She isn't even allowed to practise her music at home now. I have to send her to my mother's.'

Mary frowned. 'Your mother is younger than me. Maybe she can stand all that endless sawing and wailing. I have to think of my nerves.'

237

Elaine laughed. 'You have nerves of reinforced steel, Mother. And since you're so upset at the thought of my going into business when Paul is against it, why did you offer to lend me money yourself?'

Mary's eyes bulged with rage. 'Well ...' she spluttered. 'I like that. I allow you to live here rent free, I offer to lend you money in spite of all the inconveniences I have to suffer, and all I get are accusations and abuse.' She pressed her lips into a tight line. 'I shall speak to Paul about this, you can depend on it.'

'As always, I daresay you'll do exactly what suits you,' Elaine said wearily. 'I can't stop you, can I?'

Elaine often reflected that the house her mother had bought for her retirement was very like the one they had lived in Stanmore. When she collected Tricia on the following Friday afternoon the thought struck her yet again as she pushed open the front gate. The leaded bay windows at the front looked out on to a neat front garden, bright with spring flowers, and the white-painted garage doors enclosed the smart little sports car which was a recent acquisition. Grace answered her ring at the doorbell, her face wreathed in smiles.

'Go through. Tricia's helping me with tea in the kitchen. You will stay, won't you? Morgan's here.'

Elaine nodded. 'I'd love to. Paul is staying on at school for a staff meeting.'

She found Morgan sitting in his favourite armchair in the living room; a very different Morgan from the shabby, gangling young man who'd walked into their lives eight years before. Now his clothes were exquisitely cut and his shoes hand-made. The once unruly mop of hair was now elegantly styled by a fashionable London coiffeur. He rose when she came into the room and held out his arms to give her an affectionate hug.

'Elaine, it's good to see you.'

'You too. Are you here for the weekend?'

'Yes, and a much needed rest. I've been over to Switzerland finalising some new outlets there.'

'How exciting. What kind of outlets?'

'Mainly apres-ski wear – you know the kind of thing. The Swiss love good knitwear.'

Elaine settled herself in a chair opposite him. 'I thought you had high-powered business people to do all that for you nowadays.'

He smiled. 'I do, but I'm in the process of buying a little place over there, so I thought I'd combine business with pleasure. It helps to make personal contact too, I always think. The house is in Davos. I fell in love with the place a first sight. You'd love it too, Elaine.'

She sighed wistfully. 'I'm sure I would. Paul hates holidays abroad. He says he gets enough of them, going over with the school party each year.'

Morgan frowned. He'd never liked Paul. He had formed opinions of his own about him long ago, but had never confided them to anyone.

'In that case you must bring Tricia over in the holidays,' he said. 'Maybe Grace will go with you. Have the place for as long as you like.'

'That's very generous of you, Morgan. Maybe we'll take you up on it.'

He leaned forward. 'I hear from Grace that you have the pleasure of Mary's company again.'

She sighed. 'Pleasure is hardly the word.'

'No need to elaborate.' He smiled sympathetically. 'Tricia played for me. She's coming along well, isn't she? I heard all about her new school. She's so excited.'

'I'm grateful and relieved that she's looking forward to it, of course, but ...'

'You'll miss her? But you'll be busy with your new venture soon.'

She laughed. 'I can see that Mum has stolen all my thunder. Is there anything left for me to tell you?'

He looked searchingly into her eyes. 'You can tell me if you're happy, Elaine.'

His eyes held hers until she dragged them away to stare down at her hands. 'I daresay I'm as happy as I deserve to be, Morgan. No one's life is a bed of roses, is it?'

'I think life is what we make it,' he said carefully. 'Sometimes it's all too easy to drift along, but life is too short to waste. We should take opportunities when they come along. I haven't forgotten what Grace did for me. I wouldn't be where I am today if it weren't for her.'

'Nonsense. You had talent and flair.'

'But Grace had the drive and the business head I was sadly lacking. If it hadn't been for her I'd still have been hawking my hand-knits from door to door and living in that awful dingy room with the view of the cemetery.'

Elaine laughed. 'I don't think I quite believe that, but I do get the message.'

'Good. Basically I'm wishing you luck. And if I can help you and Alison in any way, you know where I am,' he said. 'I've got plenty of good contacts now. Maybe you'll need some good publicity

239

pictures — a feature in one of the glossy fashion mags. One good turn deserves another. Remember, I mean it, Elaine. Anything you want, just get in touch.'

She smiled at him. 'Thanks, Morgan. I will.'

For a whole week Elaine and Alison walked round the town, armed with a street map and a directory of businesses. They talked to car-hire firms, florists, printers and photographers. Besides the firms they had listed, they found a place that hired out marquees and another where a horse and carriage could be rented for the occasion. They talked to hairdressers and beauty salons. At the end of it all their limbs ached, they had blisters on their feet and their throats were hoarse from talking. But if their energy was flagging, their spirits certainly weren't. Some of the firms they had approached had reservations but most thought their ideas made sense. They agreed that it was much better to co-ordinate and work together, and they seemed happy to put the organisation into the hands of the two enthusiastic young women trading under the name of 'Happy Ever After'.

The following week they made the trip up to London to look at the dresses Grace had laid on for them at one of the fashion houses she once did business with. They chose twelve to begin with, in assorted sized. Then they went on to a fabric warehouse where Elaine chose materials for those she intended to make herself. Fingering the beautiful silks and satins, laces and tulles, she felt excitement tingling through her veins. What had seemed like an improbable dream was really going to happen. She and Alison were going to create something worthwhile — something that would be theirs alone. She couldn't wait to begin.

The list of pupils' uniform and requirements arrived from St Cecilia's in the same post as the invitation for Paul to attend the head teachers' conference. He left for Harrogate on the following Friday evening and on Saturday Elaine took Tricia into town to order her new uniform and buy all the things she would need. As a special treat they had lunch at The Old Cottage. Tricia chattered excitedly over her favourite fish and chips, followed by ice-cream. She seemed to be looking forward so much to the new school that Elaine felt a little twinge of hurt at her eagerness to be off.

When they came out of the restaurant it had started to rain and Elaine drew Tricia back into the doorway while she opened her umbrella. They had just stepped out onto the pavement when a car drew up at the kerb close by.

240

'Hi there. Want a lift?' A hand reached across to open the door and a curly head looked out at them. Elaine stared in disbelief.

'Tom! Where did you spring from?'

He laughed. 'Never mind that. Get in the pair of you, you're getting soaked.'

As they piled in he introduced himself to Tricia in characteristic fashion: 'Hello, shrimp. I'm Tom Carne. What's your name?'

Tricia eyed him solemnly. 'Patricia Anne Kingston.'

He reached into the back of the car and shook her small hand. 'Well, Patricia Anne Kingston, I knew your mummy long before you were born and yet this is the first time I've set eyes on you. How about that?'

Elaine settled herself in the passenger seat. 'This is very good of you, Tom. If you could just run us round to the long-stay car park, I'd be very grateful.'

Tom revved the car noisily. 'Your wish is my command, madam.' As he negotiated the busy Saturday traffic he told her he was home for one of his rare weekend visits.

'I'm teaching in the Midlands − well, it's almost into Derbyshire really. It's a fair old drive and I have so much weekend work to do I hardly ever get home. But I do try to make an effort for one of Red's parties.' he told her. He glanced in the mirror at Tricia who was sitting sedately in the middle of the back seat. 'I like your sprog. She's a real little cracker, isn't she?'

Elaine laughed. 'And not just a pretty face − talented too. She's just got herself a place at St Cecilia's school. It's well known for its specialisation in music.'

He raised his eyebrows at her in elaborate surprise. 'Hey, you don't say. What does she play?'

'Violin,' came the piping voice from the back. 'And I'm going to learn the saxophone too, so's I can play jazz.'

Tom laughed. 'Good for you, kid.' He looked at Elaine. 'Have you seen the folks lately?'

'I saw Red. He helped me out recently with a bit of business. Actually, I feel a bit guilty. I promised I'd take Tricia to see him and Zoe, but I seem to have been too busy to get round to it.'

'Yes, I bumped into Alison this morning. She told me you and she are starting up some kind of business together. I'd love to hear more about it. Look, if you're not doing anything special this evening, why don't you come to the party? Alison's promised to come.'

'Oh − I don't think I could. Paul's away this weekend and Tricia ...'

'Bring Tricia too,' he said. 'Most of the old gang have got kids now and they all bring them along. They love the barn shows and Zoe loves having them around.'

'Well ...'

He saw her wistful expression and seized on it. 'Oh, come on, Ellie. It'll be like old times, and you did say you'd promised to call on the folks. Tell you what, I won't say anything to them. Turn up if you can and we'll keep it as a surprise.'

Tom's infectious exuberance was working its old magic and Elaine laughed aloud, feeling suddenly light-hearted and free. 'All right then, you're on,' She turned to look at Tricia. 'You'd like to go to a party, wouldn't you?'

Tricia looked thoughtful. 'Will there be jelly?'

'There'll be terrible trouble from me if there isn't,' Tom said gravely.

Tricia giggled. 'Goody.' Then, remembering her manners: 'Thank you for inviting me. I'd like to come.'

Mary clearly disapproved of Elaine and Tricia going out for the evening.

'Surely you don't expect me to stay in this great house by myself all evening?' she said when Elaine told her their plans.

'We shan't be late. And you've got the television.'

Mary looked at her askance. 'You know I hate that thing. Just how late will you be? It's nothing to do with me but I'd have thought that keeping a child of Patricia's age up late ...'

'You have no need to worry about Tricia,' Elaine said firmly. 'It's Saturday and there's no school tomorrow. Anyway there are plenty of rooms at the Carnes' house. I daresay I could put her to bed if she got sleepy.'

Mary sniffed and folded her arms tightly across her bosom. 'I'm sure I don't know what Paul would say about such Bohemian goings on.'

'Well, when he comes home, perhaps you could ask him,' Elaine said tartly. As she went out of the room she reflected that her tongue was becoming almost as sharp as Mary's.

The Carnes' house was unchanged. It seemed strange to Elaine to be going in at the front door instead of down the basement steps to help Zoe with the food as in the old days, and she couldn't shake off the feeling that she shouldn't really be here. She stood for several minutes on the pavement outside, till Tricia tugged at her hand and asked:

'Aren't we going in, Mummy?'

She smiled down into the anxious blue eyes. 'Of course we are.'

242

Walking firmly up the steps she reached out to knock on the door — and found, as she might have expected, that it was off the latch. Once inside the familiar informal party atmosphere was just as she remembered. For a moment she stood there, absorbing the babble of voices mingled with taped music. A feeling of almost overwhelming nostalgia engulfed her. The door of the living room was open and people were already spilling into the hall. She was still standing there uncertainly when Zoe came through the door at the back of the stairway — the door that led down to the basement. She had put on weight since Elaine had last seen her and her hair was a little greyer, but apart from that she looked the same. She wore a red and gold Indian print kaftan and the familiar silver bangles jingled musically on her wrists. For a moment she stared at them, her eyes wide, then she gave a delighted little cry of delight and came to meet them, arms outstretched.

'Elaine, my dear child. What a lovely surprise. It's been so long.' She enveloped her in a warm hug. 'Red said you'd promised to come and see us.'

Elaine smiled, touched by Zoe's warm welcome. 'I saw Tom in town this morning. He invited us to the party. He said he would keep it as a surprise.'

'Well, it's certainly that all right.' Zoe laughed her deep throaty laugh. 'And it couldn't be a more pleasant one. Just wait till Red sees you. We've heard news of you from time to time through Morgan.'

'Morgan?' Elaine asked in surprise.

Zoe nodded. 'Yes. He always pops in to see us when he's over for a visit with your mother. He really has done well, hasn't he?'

Elaine was silent. She felt guilty. Even Morgan had kept in touch with the Carnes. But then, he didn't have her memories, did he?'

'And this is your little girl.' Zoe bent to frame Tricia's face with her hands. 'Oh, she's quite lovely. You must let me do a head of her for you. She has the most perfect bone structure.' She took Tricia's hand. 'Come and meet everyone, though I'm sure you know most of them.'

The lights were muted in the large living room and at first it was hard to make out who was there. Then Elaine saw Alison. She stood in the opposite corner, talking to Toby Fisher, who had been one of the Carnes' tenants when he was an undergraduate. During the next few minutes she learned that Toby was now a successful solicitor, practising in Manchester, but that he was in Cambridge for a weekend seminar. She also met several other old acquaintences. Someone put a drink into her hand and soon she found herself relaxing and beginning to enjoy herself, happily reminiscing about old times.

While they were talking Zoe had taken Tricia off to another room where a group of children were playing separately. Elaine noticed with some satisfaction that she went quite happily. Alison laughed as she watched her go, chatting amiably to Zoe.

'She's not shy, is she?'

'No. She can't wait to go off to her new school,' Elaine said. 'Of course, I'm very glad,' She sipped her drink and looked around. 'I haven't seen Tom or Red anywhere. Where are they?'

'Getting the barn show ready,' Alison said. 'And actually I think they're ready for us to go over. I can see Zoe making signals over there for someone to turn the music off.'

Tricia was enchanted with the barn theatre. She sat with her mother and Alison in the cushioned seat at the back known as the Royal Box. From the moment the miniature velvet curtains parted she sat enthralled, her round blue eyes fixed on the stage where the marionettes played out their magical fantasy. After the final curtain Red appeared with the customary flourish of his cloak. He thanked them all for being such a good audience, then held out his hand and asked for a round of applause for his team as they stepped out from behind the curtain to join him.

Elaine looked down at Tricia who was clapping enthusiastically.

'Did you enjoy it darling?'

'Yes, it was lovely.' Tricia smiled up at her happily. Elaine turned her eyes once more to the front. Then she saw him and her heart seemed to freeze. Standing between his mother and Tom was Patrick. He was a little heavier — broader of shoulder; more mature. The blond hair had darkened to a deep honey colour and his skin was tanned a rich gold from a recent trip abroad. Apart from that he looked just as she remembered as he stood there smiling at the applause.

It was almost as though she had no part in what was happening, as though she were dreaming or seeing it all from afar. So often, lying awake at night, she had wondered what her reaction would be if she were to see him again. No day had passed in the last seven years that she had not thought of him. But sometimes she told herself that she had built a romantic image, that the man who haunted her memory had never really existed. Surely he could not have been so attractive — so desirable? She was an adult now. Not the starry-eyed teenager she had been then. Surely after all this time he could never again have

244

the power to lay siege to her heart as he had when she was seventeen.

But now, as she sat there in the hot, cramped little theatre, with Patrick's child at her side, she knew the answers to all these. Knew them as certainly as she knew her own name.

Chapter Seventeen

Just for a moment she was filled with a wild panic. I must get out of here — go before he sees me. She looked around for some way she could escape without being noticed and knew it was impossible.

'Mummy, you're not *listening*.'

Elaine took a deep breath to steady the thudding of her heart and brought the focus of her attention to the child sitting beside her. 'Sorry, darling. What did you say?'

'I said, can I go?'

'Go where?'

Tricia sighed. 'I said you weren't listening. Mr Carne and Tom are going to show us the puppets and how they work.'

'Oh — yes, of course you can go.' She watched as Tricia scrambled down from her seat and followed the other children to the curtained backstage area. Alison looked at her.

'Are you all right?'

'Yes — yes, of course I am.'

'Well, you don't look it. You've gone as white as a sheet.'

'I'm fine. It's warm in here that's all. You go back to the house with the others. I'll wait here for Tricia.'

'You're sure you're all right?'

'I've told you, haven't I? I'm fine.' Elaine bit her lip. 'Sorry, I didn't mean to snap.'

Alison grinned at her good-naturedly and gave her arm a squeeze. 'Okay. You know best.' She got up and made her way out of the barn with the other guests.

Elaine sat watching dazedly as they all filtered out through the narrow door. Patrick was nowhere to be seen now and she was relieved. It gave her time to gather her thoughts. Then, as the last of the guests disappeared through the door he came out from the backstage area and came towards her with a smile.

'It's good to see you, Elaine. I didn't know you were coming.'

Suddenly she thought she knew why Tom had invited her tonight – and why he had said he'd keep it as a surprise.

'It's good to see you too,' she said shakily.

'How are you?'

'I'm fine – and you?'

'Great.' He smiled the smile she remembered so well and her heart gave a painful flip.

She swallowed hard. 'I hear you're married. Congratulations.'

'Thanks – to you too. Look, I'm dying to hear all your news. Shall we go back to the house and get a drink? I could do with one after being cooped up in there.'

'It must have felt like old times, helping with the show.'

'It did: hot, stuffy and frenetic.' He laughed. 'It's ages since I helped out with a barn show. I don't get home very often.' He nodded towards the door. 'Shall we go?'

She looked uncertain. 'Tricia – my little girl is in there.'

He laughed. 'Don't worry. Tom will look after her. He loves kids. Teaching really suits him. I keep telling him he should get married and have a brood of his own.'

They walked back across the yard to the house and Patrick got them both a drink. Handing her the glass he said: 'Right, now you can tell me all your news.'

She shrugged. 'There's nothing much to tell. I daresay you're the one with the interesting life.'

'Not as interesting as I'd like it to be.'

'We could all say that.'

He looked at her over the rim of his glass. 'You're the first of us to become a parent. That's interesting for starters. Tom introduced me to your daughter. She's lovely. Zoe is very taken with her.'

'Thank you.'

'She looks like you.'

Elaine shook her head impatiently. Her nerves were stretched to snapping point. Just how long could she stand here making polite small talk about the child they had created together? 'She isn't at *all* like me, Patrick.' She looked at her watch. 'And I think perhaps I should take her home now. It's way past her bedtime.' She made to move but his hand reached out and took her arm firmly.

'I've obviously said something to upset you. I don't know what, but I'm sorry. Look, Elaine, you don't really have to go. Your daughter is enjoying herself and it isn't all that late. Am I embarrassing you, is that it? Do you want to leave because of me?'

She swallowed hard. 'No, of course not. Why should you embarrass me?'

'I wish I knew.' Someone passing jogged his elbow and he almost spilled his drink. 'Look, we can't talk here. Let's find a quiet corner somewhere. We've got an awful lot of catching up to do. Wait here a minute. I'll be back.' He disappeared into the crowd and Elaine stood sipping her drink and wondering what to do. Everything in her that was still sane was telling her to leave now, to find Tricia and run, but her feet refused to move. It was as though she were rooted to the spot. Go now. In a minute he'll come back and it will be too late, her head told her. She half turned. She would find Tricia and ...

'Here, grab one of these.'

She turned back to see Patrick struggling with two plates of food. He had a bottle of wine tucked perilously under one arm. Very carefully she took one of the plates and followed as he led the way.

'Where are we going?'

'Upstairs,' he said over his shoulder. 'Somewhere where we can hear ourselves think.'

Patrick's old room at the top of the house hadn't changed much. A new wardrobe stood where the bookcase had once been and the room now boasted two armchairs. He pulled a small table up between them and put down the bottle of wine. Then he went over to the record player and put on a record. A moment later the haunting melody of 'Clouds' filled the room. Patrick smiled at her.

'Remember this one? It used to make you cry.'

She nodded. 'I remember.'

'Have a seat,' he invited. 'At least we can talk uninterrupted in here.' He looked at her hesitant expression and amusement tugged at the corners of his mouth. 'Am I compromising you, Mrs Kingston? Would you like me to leave the door open?'

She blushed. 'Of course not. I might be a headmaster's wife but I haven't become as stuffy and conventional as that.'

He poured the wine, looking at her speculatively as he did so. 'I'm not so sure. There's a certain settled look about you. Maybe it comes with motherhood.'

The remark stung her, even though she knew he was joking. She swallowed the hurt and said: 'Patrick, before we go any further I have a confession to make.'

'Really? What can you have done? I can't wait to hear it.'

'I'm serious. Remember the picture you gave me — the Severini? I sold it.'

248

'I know.'

'You know? Oh, I suppose Red told you?'

'He told me you'd been to him with a Severini painting – and that he'd been able to dispose of it successfully for you. I didn't tell him I gave it to you.'

'Were you angry?'

'Angry? Why should I be angry? I gave the picture to you. It was yours to do as you liked with.'

'I needed the money to finance the business Alison and I are starting. I wanted to be independent.'

He smiled. 'Fine. I'm all for that. Good luck to you both.' He refilled her glass. 'Now – tell me about this husband of yours. Are you happy?'

She frowned. 'I'm surprised you have to ask. You seem to know so much about me already.'

'I see Morgan Owen from time to time.' He sipped his wine thoughtfully, turning the glass in his hand. 'The firm I'm with handles the advertising for the designers he works with. I heard from him that you were married. He raised an enquiring eyebrow at her. 'But you haven't answered my question. Are you happy?'

She avoided his eyes. 'Naturally. Are you?'

He lifted his shoulders. 'If Cathy and I saw more of each other, I might be able to answer that. As it is, with her away on tour so much and me stuck in a nine-to-five job in London, the marriage hasn't had much of a chance as yet.'

'You must miss her.'

'Yes.' He looked at her. 'I've missed you too, Elaine.' He said the words so softly that just at first she wasn't sure that she'd heard him right. 'When I first went to France, I hated it. I was actually homesick, would you believe? That was something totally unexpected. I missed all my friends, Tom and the folks, but most of all – I missed you.'

She looked up at him, her heart squeezed so tightly in her chest that she could hardly breathe. 'You could have written,' she whispered.

He shook his head. 'No. It wouldn't have been fair. You had to be allowed to live your own life.'

'But you could have *asked* me – given me the choice.'

He smiled gently. 'You were so young. You didn't know what you wanted in those days, love. You only thought you did.'

'And you knew better? You thought you'd make up my mind for me, did you?' She heard her voice shaking as she rose to her feet, her heart thumping painfully in her breast. Suddenly she was so angry

249

that she wanted to scream and it was only with a real effort that she kept her voice level as she said: 'You'll never know what you did to me, Patrick — walking out of my life like that? Did you think about it at all? Did you even *care*? No. Until you felt homesick you never even gave it a thought, did you?' Her face was pale and her eyes looked huge and luminous. She made an impulsive move towards the door but he reached out to grasp her arm.

'Don't go, Elaine. Not like that. I really didn't know you felt so deeply. I thought it was just a teenage crush — that you'd soon get over it.'

She swung round to face him. 'Don't insult me by lying. Patrick. You were bored. You couldn't wait to get away — to France and to Anne-Marie or whatever her name was.'

He held on to her arm, looking down into her eyes. 'Elaine, it's all so long ago. You can't still be angry about it after all this time.'

She shook her arm free of his grasp, trying hard to control the tears that tore agonisingly at her throat. 'I wish I hadn't come tonight,' she said thickly. 'I wish we hadn't met again. I wish it with all my heart.'

'You don't mean that.' He drew her towards him, cupping her chin with his other hand. 'Elaine, you don't really mean that, do you?' For a long moment he looked into her eyes, seeing the hurt she had hidden from everyone for so long. 'Oh, Elaine,' he murmured. 'Oh, my love, I didn't know, I promise you. I thought it was all just fun — learning about life. I never guessed.' He drew her close, encircling her with his arms, one hand cradling her head. 'I did love you, you know,' he said softly. 'In my way. It was just that we both had so much living to do. We needed to get out into the world and try our wings.' He tipped up her chin to look into her face and saw that her cheeks were wet with tears. He felt his own chest constrict as he bent his head to kiss them away. His lips brushed her eyelids, her cheeks - finally they found her mouth. For a moment he held its tremulous softness with his lips, then, as he felt her lips part for him he crushed her close, kissing her with all the passion and hunger she remembered so well; as she had longed to be kissed all these years - as no one but Patrick had ever kissed her, either before or since.

The depth of their passion left them both shaken. When they drew apart Elaine stood for a moment within the circle of his arms, her head against his chest and her heart aching as he held her close.

'I should go,' she said at last, her lips moving against his neck. 'It must be getting late. I must go, Patrick.' She began to push him gently away.

He dropped his arms to his sides but his eyes did not release her. 'I'll be at home for another couple of days. Can we meet?'

'I don't think so.'

He took a step towards her. 'We must. We have to talk.'

'There isn't anything to say.' Her voice shook and she turned away, tearing her eyes from his, her hand on the door. 'It's all too late, Patrick. Nothing can alter that — nothing can change the way things are.'

He crossed the room and took her hand, turning her back towards him. 'You're wrong. I want to — to understand what it was we threw away ... Please, Elaine. We can't just leave it at this.'

We could. We must, she wanted to say. But she couldn't find sufficient strength to say the words, let alone mean them. She pulled the door open and stepped through, then she turned to look back at him. 'Ring me if you like,' she heard herself say. 'Tomorrow morning. The number's in the book.'

Elaine slept late the following morning. When she woke the memory of what had happened the previous evening sprang instantly into her mind and she lay there, thinking, her mind in turmoil. Why had she asked Patrick to ring her? It was madness. All it could bring her was more unhappiness. Maybe he would see that too in the clear light of day. Perhaps after all he would let it go and not ring. But half of her — the half she despised and tried so hard to ignore — hoped that he would.

She got up and showered. She had promised to have tea with her mother that afternoon. Tricia wanted to take her new school uniform to show her. She was standing in front of the wardrobe, wondering what to wear when the telephone beside her bed rang, startling her. She snatched up the receiver quickly.

'Hello?'

'Elaine. It's me.'

She sank down on the bed, the receiver cradled in both hands. 'Patrick. Look — maybe this wasn't a good idea after all. I ...'

'I'll pick you up at twelve,' he interrupted. 'Just tell me where.'

'No, I can't. I have to go to my mother's this afternoon.'

'That's all right. I'll see that you're back in time for that. We'll have lunch at a place I know. You needn't worry. It's off the beaten track.'

'Well — I don't know ...'

'I can't go back to London without seeing you again. Drive out to Little Hinton. Do you know how to get there?'

'Yes, but I ...'

251

'I'll meet you at the pub on the green — The Queen's Head. Twelve o'clock in the car park. Right?'

'Well, all right.' Before she had time to think clearly about what she was doing he had rung off. She sat there on the bed for a long while, staring at the telephone, wondering just what she had started. Then suddenly she remembered that she had promised to take Tricia to church this morning. There was a special service to celebrate the school's anniversary. She couldn't ask Mary to take her.

She lifted the phone again and dialled her mother's number. Grace answered almost at once.

'Mum, I wondered if you'd do me a favour,' Elaine said. 'Would you take Tricia to church for me this morning? It's the school's fiftieth anniversary service and I promised we'd go, but I have someone to see.'

'Of course I will,' Grace said. 'After all, business is business, even on Sundays.'

'And could she stay for lunch with you afterwards?'

'Of course.' Grace laughed. 'You don't have to ask. You know how I love to have her.'

'Oh thanks, Mum. I'll join you later for tea, as planned. See you in about half an hour then.' She replaced the receiver with a sigh. She hated herself for letting her mother believe it was a business appointment. How many more half-truths would it be necessary to tell before this day was over? If only Tom hadn't invited her to the party last night. If only she'd had the strength to say no to Patrick. If only . . . .

The church clock was striking twelve as she drove into the village of Little Hinton. She wore a black trouser suit with a bright yellow shirt and had taken special care over her hair, shampooing and brushing it till it curled around her face in a shining halo. She refused to admit that she wanted to look her best for Patrick, telling herself that she wouldn't have him thinking that she turned into a dowdy provincial housewife.

He was waiting for her when she drove into the car park at the rear of the pub. She saw him at once, sitting in the driving seat of a dark green Triumph Stag. He spotted her too and got out of the car.

Seated by the fireplace in the old inn they ordered drinks and their meal. Then the practicalities over, they looked at each other. Elaine said bluntly: 'This is all wrong, Patrick. We shouldn't have come.'

He laughed wryly. 'That's a good start.' He covered her hand with his. 'Two old friends meeting for a drink and a bite to

252

eat, in broad daylight in a village pub. What could be more innocent?'

She looked at him. 'But what's the point, Patrick? We're both happily married. I have a child. There's nothing to be gained.'

'Do old friends meet in order to *gain* anything? I told you, I want to hear all your news.'

'But there's nothing to know that you haven't already heard from Morgan.'

'Don't you want to know about me?'

She looked up and met his eyes. Of course she wanted to know about him - *all* about him — with one part of her. The other half knew that to know would be to suffer. 'No,' she said firmly.

'Then why did you come?'

'Look, Patrick, tomorrow you'll be gone again, back to London; to your job, your home and your wife.'

'Not my wife,' he corrected. 'Hardly ever my wife.'

'That's your business, Patrick. Not mine. I have my life to live now and I think you should leave me to get on with it, the way you did before.'

He winced. 'I suppose I asked for that.'

She picked up the glass of sherry in front of her and put it down quickly when she realised how much her hands were trembling. 'Why did you ask me out today anyway?'

'Why did you come?' He watched as she shook her head helplessly.

'I wanted to know why you married him so soon after,' he went on quietly. 'I wanted to know why you're so unhappy.'

Her eyes snapped up to meet his.

'Well, are you going to deny it? You are unhappy, aren't you?' he insisted.

Colour flooded her cheeks. 'Mind your own bloody business,' she snapped. 'Christ, but you've got a nerve. You go away. You make up your mind what's best for me. Then you come back years later and calmly demand to know about my emotional state. Why should you care? Why should I tell you anything?'

'All right.' He laid a restraining hand on her arm. 'I put it badly. I'm concerned for you, Elaine. That's all. I feel partly responsible for you.'

'Then don't. I suppose I'm as happy as I deserve to be. Can any of us expect more than that?'

'That's not what I asked.'

'Look, Patrick. Everyone I grew up with has a worthwhile, satisfying life. I'm just the one who stayed at home. I'm a dull, boring housewife. I've been nowhere — done nothing. There's absolutely no reason why anyone should be interested in me.' She looked up at him. 'There — are you satisfied?'

He shook his head. 'What's the matter? You're so defensive. You weren't like this last night.'

'Last night I'd been drinking. I'm not used to it. I'm not in the habit of throwing myself into the arms of every man I meet. Sorry to disappoint you.'

He smiled at her, refusing to rise to the bait. 'You married Paul Kingston so quickly after we — after we said goodbye.'

'So? He swept me off my feet.' She tossed back her drink and stared at him. 'Did you think it was on the rebound? You always did have a high opinion of yourself, didn't you?'

The landlord brought their food and they ate in silence. From time to time Patrick glanced at her, noting the firm set of her mouth, the resentment glittering in her eyes. When they'd finished he said: 'Let's get out of here, shall we?'

She shrugged. 'Why not? Nothing to stay for.'

In the car park he took her arm. 'Sit in the car with me for a while. There's plenty of time.'

She wanted to scream. This was agony. Why couldn't she just shake him off — tell him to go to hell and drive back to town, to the warmth and safety of her mother's house, to her child? Against her better judgement, she allowed him to propel her towards the car. she got in, despising herself for her weakness.

He turned to look at her, his eyes dark as they looked into hers. 'Would it soften that hard heart of yours to know that I've never, for one minute of one day, forgotten you, Elaine? Would it help to know that I've never really stopped loving you?'

She gave a stifled cry of exasperation. 'Stop it. For God's sake leave me alone, Patrick.' She wrenched open the car door and jumped out, sprinting across the car park. Switching on the ignition with fumbling fingers, she revved the engine wildly, then with a squeal of tyres and a shower of gravel she sped out on to the road, willing herself not to look at Patrick as she passed. She drove fast, much too fast, looking from time to time in the rearview mirror to make sure he wasn't following.

254

After a few miles she eased her foot off the accelerator and turned off the road into a quiet lane. Stopping the car, she wound down the window and forced herself to breathe the fresh air quietly and deeply to steady her raw nerves. She had been so close to giving in. It would have been so easy – so blissful – just to cave in, fall into his arms again and tell him everything: that Tricia was his child; that she had never stopped loving him and probably never would. But she hadn't done those things. And now, thank God, she never would. Patrick was bored again. He regretted his marriage and saw her as an amusing and safely married diversion. At least now she was adult enough to recognise that much. No, Tricia was hers and hers alone as she always had been. The child was her life – all she had and all she wanted. The one thing she could be really sure of. She'd never let anything or anyone alter that.

Grace stood at the window, waving as Elaine and Tricia drove away. She'd enjoyed having her granddaughter for the day. On the weekends when Morgan didn't come she was often lonely, even though she had her garden to enjoy and sometimes paperwork from the factory to catch up with. Truth to tell she missed the shop. When Elaine had told her about the new venture that she and Alison were starting she had caught some of their excitement. It had been all she could do not to ask to be allowed to help, but she had restrained herself, knowing that the girls wanted the venture to be all their own, just as she would have at their age. It had reminded her of the time when she and Margaret had turned the shabby little drapery shop in Stanmore into a boutique. She'd contented herself by offering the girls an introduction to some of her contacts and advice, if and when they needed it, and forced herself to take a back seat.

But this evening loneliness wasn't troubling her. She had plenty to think about as she drew the curtains on the darkening spring evening and set about tidying the room. Elaine had been in a strange mood when she arrived for tea. She seemed nervy and on edge. When spoken to she seemed miles away. Grace wondered if it was the worry of the new business. She'd mentioned that she'd been to see someone about it that morning. But Elaine wasn't her prime concern at that moment. She had something much more immediate to think about. And a special visitor to see.

Grace had taken Tricia to church. Attending a service was something she rarely did. Since her childhood she had avoided so-called places of worship. The memories and associations connected with church were far too painful. But this morning, with the spring sunshine slanting through the stained glass windows, the church decorated with bright spring flowers and filled with children's voices, the occasion had been pleasant.

She and Tricia had taken up their position in a pew about halfway down the nave and Tricia had chattered happily, pointing out her friends and teachers as they arrived. The church was almost full when a tall slim woman wearing a smart grey suit had come in. Tricia nudged her grandmother.

'Granny, look. That's Miss Troughton, my teacher, and she's brought a friend who's staying with her. They were at college together. She told us.'

Grace looked at the woman standing beside Harriet Troughton and her heart seemed to miss a beat. Rachel! She was sure it was her sister, Rachel.

After that she found it impossible to concentrate on the service. Her eyes kept straying to the pew across the aisle where the woman sat with members of the teaching staff. Rachel had always been a plain child and she was still plain, but she had made the most of what good features she had with careful, tasteful make-up and good clothes. Her figure was good, and her hair, thick and dark like Grace's, was arranged in a soft style that suited her rather sharp features. She still wore glasses, but becomingly shaped frames made them a fashion accessory rather than a disadvantage.

Grace was in a quandary. Should she make herself known or not? The last time they had met, Rachel had sent her away. But she had been little more than a child then, bitter and resentful at what she saw as her elder sister's abandoning her, knowing nothing of the reason for it. Clearly she had made good in spite of having to take over the upbringing of their three younger sisters. Grace was relieved. She had always felt guilty about her sister's disrupted education. She found herself longing to make her peace with her. And most of all to hear news of the other girls: Sarah and the little ones, Christine and Victoria, who must now be grown women. And her father . . .? Although she had deliberately put him out of her thoughts long ago, her heart lurched sickeningly at the memory. How was he? she wondered. Was he still alive? And there was that other thought — the one that had haunted her — that she had never quite been able to erase: had he abused the others in the way he had abused her? If he had, could she ever forgive herself for leaving them? The impotent, helpless anger she thought she had laid to rest churned anew in the pit of her stomach and quickened her heartbeat. For a moment her surroundings swam dizzily before her eyes and her knees buckled. She glanced at the child beside her, Tricia, with her wide blue eyes and cornsilk hair. She mustn't let her down – mustn't faint and make a scene. With an enormous effort she forced her mind to concentrate on the words of the hymn they were singing. *'All things bright and beautiful. All creatures great and small. All things wise and wonderful, The Lord God made them all.'* At her side Tricia sang. Her sweet young voice reached Grace's ears and soothed her tortured mind.

The service ended and they all filed out of church. Ahead of her, Grace could see Rachel as she walked out of church, smiling and confident, talking with her friend. She knew then that she could not approach her. She could not risk another rebuff, could not risk hearing the news she dreaded to hear. She was just turning away when she felt a hand on her arm and a voice said: 'It's Mrs Wendover, isn't it?'

She turned to see Harriet Troughton, Tricia's teacher, smiling at her.

'We're all so proud of Tricia's success at St Cecilia's.'

Grace smiled. 'So are we.'

'I'd like you to meet a friend of mine from college days. I've been telling her all about our star pupil.' Before Grace had time to think she had called out: 'Rachel, do come and meet Tricia's grandmother.'

Rachel left the others and walked across. She held out her hand and smiled into Grace's eyes without a flicker of recognition. 'How do you do? Does your granddaughter get her musical talent from you?'

'No. From her grandfather, I think.' Grace held a gloved hand in hers and looked into the other woman's eyes. Tricia had skipped ahead with two of her friends and Miss Troughton had moved on to speak to some other parents. Rachel's eyes narrowed slightly and clouded with uncertainty.

'Haven't we met before, Mrs ... I'm sorry, what did Harriet say your name was?'

'Wendover. Grace Wendover.' Grace smiled. 'Don't you remember me, Rachel?'

The brown eyes widened and Rachel's mouth opened in an 'O' of surprise. '*Grace*,' she breathed. 'My God, it's you. It's really you.' She shook her head bemusedly. 'But how ... when ...?' She laughed. 'I don't know where to start. Look, can we meet? How about lunch? I'm sure Harriet would understand.'

'I can't. I'm looking after Tricia for the day. My daughter is picking her up later and staying for tea. If you're not busy, why

not come this evening? We can talk then. I'll give you my address.'
She opened her bag and found a business card. Rachel looked at it
and smiled, her eyes misty.

'Oh, Grace, it's wonderful, finding you again like this. I can
hardly believe it. There's so much to tell you. And I want to know
all about you too.'

Grace had just had time to make coffee, comb her hair and put
on fresh lipstick when a ring at the door told her that Rachel
had arrived. Her heart beating with apprehension, she hurried to
open it.

At first they were both a little uneasy. Grace brought in the coffee
and they sat making polite small talk for a few minutes, both of them
reluctant to break the ice, a little shy of each other. Grace lifted a
plate of biscuits and offered it to her sister.

'Do have one of these. I made them myself. Tricia loves them.'

Rachel shook her head. 'Nothing to eat, thank you.' She smiled.
'Grace - we're getting nowhere, are we? We have so much to say to
each other. How are you, Grace − really, I mean? Have you been
happy? Was Harry worth leaving home for?'

Grace bit her lip. 'My marriage didn't last. It was over many
years ago, Rachel.' She smiled. 'But I have a lovely daughter and
granddaughter. I had a good career too − for a woman with only a
basic education.' She went on to tell Rachel about 'Style 'N' Grace'
and about how she had discovered Morgan and helped him take the
first important steps towards his own career.

Rachel was impressed. 'I've heard of Morgan Knitwear, of course.
I'm glad you've been happy and successful.' She smiled ruefully.
'You know, I hated you for leaving at the time. But later I saw
how selfish I was. I've had a good career. I'm headmistress of a
girl's school in Yorkshire now. No marriage or children, but one
can't have everything.'

Grace poured two more cups of coffee, her eyes on the cups.
'And what about the others? How are they − Sarah and the
little ones?'

Rachel laughed. 'Sarah is a nurse − a sister. She went to Australia
five years ago. The "little ones" as you call them are both married
- Vicki to a doctor and Christine to an architect. They have two
children each. Three boys and a girl.'

Grace avoided her sister's eyes as she asked: 'And − and
Father?'

The smile left Rachel's face. 'Father died twelve years ago. I'm
sorry to have to tell you that he took his own life, Grace.'

258

She paused. 'There was a scandal. It was terrible for us all at the time.'

'Go on.' Grace steeled herself for what was to come.

'There was a young girl in the choir at church. She made — certain accusations against Father. Her parents went to the police and he was charged with ...' She glanced at Grace and swallowed hard. 'With indecent assault on an under-age girl.' She shook her head. 'It was terrible — and ridiculous of course. We all knew he was innocent. But the girl stuck to her story and for some reason he refused to defend himself — wouldn't answer any questions or even talk about it. Then, on the night before he was to have appeared in court, he took an overdose of sleeping tablets. I — I found him the next morning.'

'Oh, my God. Poor Rachel. How terrible for you.' Grace reached for her sister's hand and squeezed it tightly.

'I know he was hard on you, Grace,' Rachel went on, her eyes full of tears. 'There were times — later — when he spoke of you to me. He often seemed troubled. He confessed to me that he'd thrashed you that time when you went to the theatre without telling him. But I know he was convinced it was for your own good. He was always so determined to bring us up to be God-fearing Christian women. After you left he was kindness itself to the rest of us. He even engaged a housekeeper eventually, so that I could go back to school. It must have been a terrible struggle for him to afford it, but he did it — for me. I'll always be grateful to him for that.'

'Of course you will.' Waves of relief were washing over Grace like a refreshing balm. It was as though a weight had been lifted from her shoulders; one she had carried with her for a long, long time. Now it was really over. her worst fears were unfounded. Now there would never be any need to tell anyone what had happened all those years ago. She need feel no more guilt. It was like an exorcism.

Rachel looked at her. 'Did the break up of your marriage make you unhappy, Grace?'

'Yes, at the time. But I've had plenty to occupy me since — plenty to help me to forget.'

'When did you last see him?'

'Years ago ...' Grace broke off, remembering the traumatic night when Bryan Bostock had taken her to the charity concert at the London Palladium. 'It must be almost ten years ago,' she said. 'And even then it was only from a distance.'

'How long since your divorce?'

'We're still married,' Grace said. 'Harry left me for someone else

259

— a singer. She became quite well known. I said I'd never give him a divorce. And I haven't.'

Rachel looked surprised. 'Have you ever regretted it?'

Grace considered carefully before she replied: 'I regret losing Harry. I loved him very much, you see. But it was my fault that he left, and I suppose it was unfair of me to refuse him his freedom. As for me I think I've made the best of what I had left, though there are times ...'

Rachel nodded understandingly. 'It isn't possible to go through life without regrets and mistakes. It's what we learn from them that counts.'

They parted soon after, clinging to each other and promising to keep in touch, though both knew in their hearts that they had grown too far apart to have anything in common. Grace stood at the gate waving as Rachel drove away. The spring evening smelt earthy and fragrant with bruised grass and blossoms. She breathed it in deeply, feeling her heart lift within her. 'New life,' she whispered to herself. 'Now I can begin a new life.' She felt light and cleansed and free.

But although she went to bed in a peaceful frame of mind, she found sleep impossible. In her mind she went over and over all that Rachel had told her, her mind churning with a bewildering mixture of emotions. She was so thankful that her younger sisters had not suffered in the way that she had, but her feelings for her father hovered between revulsion and pity. There was anger too. She still could not find it in her heart to forgive him for her wasted life, for the failure of her marriage, for all the misery and unhappiness he had caused — to her and to others. She thought of Elaine. Because of her own experience she had been too protective of her, kept her on too tight a rein when she was growing up. Afraid that she might join the new 'permissive society', she'd been over-anxious to see her safely married and encouraged her to marry Paul. She'd clearly been wrong in that. It was obvious from the first that the marriage wasn't happy. Elaine had come to her once, asking advice about it. And she had let her down once again, brought down the shutters between them as she had done so often in the past.

Finally she thought of Harry, wondering what the years had done to him. He would be getting on for fifty now, she calculated. Since Tricia's birth she had thought of him more and more. She had spoken to her little granddaughter about him far more freely than she had ever talked of him with Elaine. Lying there in the darkness she tried to analyse why. Perhaps it was because Tricia had inherited his musical talent. She felt free to fantasise a little to the child, describing Harry as the debonair young man she had known when they first met — talented, light-hearted and kind. Her romantic saviour; a knight in shining armour. The Harry she had loved so much — before they had married and *she* had spoilt it all. Yes, she could face the truth of it now.

Had he really been the way she remembered him? she asked herself as she lay there. Or had she created a romantic, idealised image, designed to soften the guilt and the painful memories of her own failure?

'It isn't possible to go through life without regrets and mistakes,' Rachel had said. 'It's what we learn from them that counts.'

Chapter Eighteen

Over the weeks that followed Elaine and Alison worked very hard on the promotion of 'Happy Ever After'. Morgan had put in a word for them with a friend who was editor of the women's page of one of the national newspapers. She had sent a journalist and a photographer along to interview them for a series she was planning on enterprising women. When the edition carrying the article came out, it created a lot of interest. The local paper had also given them a centre page spread soon afterwards, featuring photographs of models wearing some of their bridal gowns and sketches of Elaine's designs.

Each in their own way, Elaine and Alison were glad of the hard work, and before the month was out their appointments book was filling up nicely and their first wedding assignment was well under way.

The bride-to-be had chosen one of the dresses Elaine herself had designed, and would be buying rather than hiring her dress, which was a big boost to their finances as well as to Elaine's confidence. She spent every spare minute at her mother's house, working away on the sewing machine in the spare bedroom. She had intended to turn one of the spare rooms at Langmere Lodge into a sewing room but Mary had objected. The room was next to hers and she insisted that the whirring of the electric machine would disturb her rest. Since Elaine had turned down her offer of financial help she had done everything she could to throw obstacles in the way of the success of the venture, including pointing out to Paul that Elaine's housekeeping standards were slipping. She chipped away constantly at everyone's nerves until at last things came to a head one evening over dinner. After toying with her food she finally pushed her plate away.

'It's no good. I can't eat all these convenience foods, Elaine,' she said. 'You know they give me indigestion, and yet we never seem to have anything else nowadays. When I was a young housewife I used to take such pleasure in preparing fresh food for my family.' She looked at Paul with a wan smile. 'There are sacrifices to be made in having a career woman for a wife, I'm afraid, Paul.'

He flushed but said nothing.

'There's the garden too,' Mary went on. 'You used to take such a pride in it, Elaine. Now it looks more like one of those nature reserves.'

Elaine looked up. 'As I remember, you didn't like what I was doing to the garden. Perhaps if you were to get a man in ...?'

'I'm sure I didn't mean you to let it go to seed,' Mary said indignantly. 'But if you can't take a little constructive criticism ...'

'It didn't sound very constructive to me.' Elaine avoided her mother-in-law's eye as she applied herself to her food.

Paul said nothing until later in the evening, after his mother had announced that she would have an early night, having first made a great show of mixing herself a large bicarbonate of soda. The moment the door had closed behind her, he looked up from his evening paper.

'Perhaps you could arrange to spend less time with your − er − partner, and more time in your own home,' he said stiffly. 'I understand that Tricia even goes to your mother's after school now.'

Elaine looked up. 'We wouldn't have to spend any time there at all if your mother didn't object to our disturbing her.'

He laid the paper down, frowning at her over the tops of his reading glasses. 'What do you mean, disturbing her?'

'She objects to the noise my sewing machine makes. She objects to Tricia's practising. And she never stops reminding me that this is her house.'

'And so it is.'

'Then she can hardly complain if we let her have it to herself, can she?'

'Elaine, we do live here rent-free,' he reminded her. 'Mother has been very good to us. I think she has a right to expect a little consideration. I believe she even offered you money to help you start your business and you rejected it out of hand.'

'Alison and I want to stand on our own feet.'

'So you sold a picture − for a very high price, I understand.' He shook his head at her. 'Why is it that you never discuss these things with me? Can you imagine how embarrassing it is, having to learn them through a third person?'

Elaine swallowed her resentment. 'I did ask your advice about

263

starting the business, Paul. And the painting was mine. I had every right to sell it.'

'You asked me for money as I remember — not advice,' he pointed out. 'Had you asked me, I would have advised you not to go to that Carne man. Mother tells me that you went to a party there, by the way. The weekend I was away at the conference — and took Tricia with you. From what I hear they're a rather dubious family. I'd rather you didn't mix with them in future.'

Elaine sprang to her feet. 'There's nothing dubious about the Carnes. They're old friends of mine,' she said hotly. 'And I won't be told what to do and who I may or may not be friendly with, Paul. There is no privacy in this house. Your mother constantly spies on me.'

He gave a dry, dismissive laugh, rustling the pages of his newspaper. 'What nonsense.'

'She does. She listens in to telephone conversations all the time — on the extension in your study. How else do you think she knows things I haven't told her? It's becoming intolerable.'

'Mother is lonely,' he said, laying his paper down, 'Perhaps she'd appreciate a little more of your company — a bit of attention and consideration. This food business, for instance. You must admit that the meals have been somewhat — well, scrappy lately.'

'Then I suggest that she takes them over,' Elaine said. 'She's got nothing else to do and she's perfectly capable of doing a little cooking. She's always telling me about the marvellous meals she used to produce. Perhaps you'll tell her in future dinner will be in her hands? Or would you like *me* to tell her?'

Paul got to his feet and pulled off his glasses, his face reddening. 'As long as we share this house with my mother, you will treat her with respect and consideration,' he said.

'But that's just it. I don't *want* to share a house with her, Paul. Please — can't we find somewhere of our own?'

'You know that is out of the question.'

'But why?'

'Mother needs us. She can't be alone. She isn't well enough.'

'Rubbish! She isn't all that old, and she's as fit as you are. We could compromise if you want to stay here. She could have a little flat of her own — here in the house. It wouldn't be too hard to convert the top floor. We'd still be here but living separate lives.' But Paul's face had assumed the closed look he always wore when he didn't want to discuss anything further.

'I'm sure you know what Mother would think of being virtually put away in the attic,' he said. 'Now, can we please drop the subject?

264

Since you've developed this *partnership*, as you call it, you've become very sharp-tongued – almost shrewish. Alison Linton doesn't seem to be a very good influence on you. Sometimes I think I should have put my foot down right at the beginning.'

Elaine stared at him, her cheeks blazing. 'Put your foot down? About what?'

'About starting this ridiculous bridal business,' he told her calmly. 'And I warn you now – if it's going to result in all this squabbling with Mother, and your cavalier attitude towards your household duties, I may even yet.'

Elaine stared at him for a long moment, her heart thudding with resentment at the bitter injustice of it all. 'I don't think you will, Paul,' she said at last.

Something about her quiet, even tone made him look up from his newspaper.

'I don't think you will,' she repeated, her voice beginning to shake. 'Because to wield the power of a husband, you first have to *be* one. And you're no more a husband to me that you're an effective father to Tricia.' She saw the dull flush colour his face and waited, her eyes holding his, for him to take up her challenge. For a moment he seemed about to say something, then he shrugged and turned his attention to his newspaper. Was he being dismissive, or simply hiding from her? Filled with disgust and resentment, she turned on her heel and walked out of the room.

In the kitchen Mary was filling her hot water bottle. She shot Elaine a look full of bogus pathos.

'I do hope I didn't cause any trouble,' she said in a whining, placatory tone. 'The last thing I want to do is upset Paul. He works so hard, poor boy.'

Unable to trust herself to reply, Elaine turned and went upstairs. Mary watched her from the kitchen doorway, a look of smug satisfaction on her face.

As the time approached for Tricia to go away to school, Elaine grew more and more apprehensive about her going.

'Suppose she changes,' she said to Alison one day as the worked. 'I've heard people say that boarding schools turn out a very hardboiled, self-sufficient sort of child. Tricia's so sweet and affectionate. I don't want her any different.'

Alison laughed. 'She has to grow up, Elaine. And that's what you're really afraid of, isn't it? You're afraid of losing your baby. And I can't say I blame you.'

Elaine was working on an embroidered panel for the dress she was making, whilst Alison was busy with pencil and paper, costing out the buffet for the coming wedding. She pushed her reading glasses on to her forehead and turned to Elaine.

'Did I tell you I've got a ticket for that new cash and carry place?' she asked. 'We'll save a lot, buying our stuff there.' She saw Elaine's wistful expression and said: 'Oh, don't worry, love. Tricia and you have always had such a good relationship. She won't change. She'll always be your daughter. Look, Aunt Zoe tells me she's offered to do a head of her for you. Why don't you let her? It would be a lovely thing to have when she's away. Tactile — three-dimensional. Much better than a photograph.'

Zoe was delighted when Elaine rang and asked if she could take her up on her offer. She suggested that they went round the following day and she did some sketches of Tricia then and there. It was arranged that Elaine would take her again for regular sittings after school.

Tricia herself was intrigued at the prospect of seeing the puppets again, thrilled at the thought of looking around the little theatre, this time on her own. She liked the Carnes with their free and easy manners and their big untidy house.

Zoe found her newest subject fascinating. The child's face was so mobile and elusive. Just when she thought she had caught her, another facet would reveal itself. She never seemed the same child two days running. She could look angelic, almost ethereal one day, and piquant and mischievous the next. She had abandoned her work several times before she caught the essence of Tricia that she wanted to portray.

When Zoe worked she talked to her young subjects, usually finding that once she found the topic that interested them most, the desired expression came naturally. But with Tricia it was not a topic, but a picture, that brought about the required touch of magic.

The picture was one that Patrick had done years ago when he was still at college. Zoe had found it at the back of a cupboard on one of her rare spring-cleaning sessions and decided to hang it in her studio. It was a quasi-abstract impression of a waterfall. The technique was brash and naive, but it had an impetuous, youthful style, and a joyous freedom of movement that was appealing. The moment Tricia saw it her face broke into a delighted smile. Zoe followed her eyes.

'You like that picture?'

'Oh, *yes*.'

Zoe began to work, her strong sculptor's fingers quickly moulding the clay as the child gazed raptly up at the picture. 'Tell me about it,' she invited. 'Tell me what you see.'

'Well − it's got sunshine,' Tricia said, looking up with her head slightly on one side. 'Sunshine and leaves and the wind and splashing water. It's *fun*.'

Zoe looked up with a smile, and at that moment she caught something in the child's face that took her breath away. Tricia looked exactly as Patrick had looked at that age. The same wide blue eyes and flaxen hair; the same wiry strength and grace of movement; the same look of deceptive fragility and innocence. She caught her lip between her teeth. You're his, she said wonderingly to herself. You're my grandchild. And in the same instant everything fell into place − Elaine's hasty marriage, so soon after Patrick left for France; the way she had broken off all contact with them. Poor child! Suddenly Zoe knew that she must keep her discovery to herself. Too many people could get hurt. She could tell no one. Not even Red; not Patrick himself. If it ever emerged it must not be through her.

The first wedding organised by 'Happy Ever After' was to take place at the end of August. Alison and Elaine grew nervous as the time drew near. Each day there seemed to be a new panic. So much depended on this, their first job, and there seemed so many pitfalls − so many things that could go disastrously wrong. Everything depended on the cooperation of the firms working with them; people whose reliability was, as yet, untried. Also they were painfully aware that their whole future depended on the smooth running and the recommendations − or otherwise − that would come from this first wedding.

The reception was to take place in a marquee in the garden of the bride's home. Alison was doing the catering and was up to her neck in white icing and lucky horseshoes; constantly worrying about the availability of fresh salmon and whether she had chosen the best butcher and the greengrocer with the freshest fruit and salads.

Elaine was pleased with the dress she had made. She was expecting the bride for her final fitting on the day that Tricia was to have her final sitting with Zoe. Grace had offered to take her along and to collect her again later in the afternoon.

Elaine worked on at the Lintons' house after the bride had left, doing the final small handsewing jobs on the dress, then driving round to deliver it personally in its polythene shroud to the bride's house. On her way home she looked in at the church to check that the florists had done their work as arranged. She finally arrived home at about half-past five. Paul had gone into school for the usual pre-term staff meeting that afternoon. He had said he'd be home around six, so she would just have time to get the evening meal started.

Dumping her things in the hall, she went straight through to the kitchen and began to prepare the meal. She was just putting the casserole into the oven when the back door opened. Out of the corner of her eye she glimpsed Tricia and said, without turning, 'If you're hungry there are some apples on the dresser. I don't want you to start nibbling at biscuits.'

'Can I have one too?'

She spun round, her heart jumping at the familiar male voice, and found herself face to face with Patrick. 'Oh — hello.' She glanced guiltily at Tricia who stood by the table, smiling.

'I brought Tricia home,' he said. 'I hope it's all right. Your mother does know about it. She had some shopping to do so I said ...'

'Why are you here? I mean — I thought you hardly ever came home.' She felt the hot colour creeping up her neck and wished there were something she could do to stop it. Any minute now Paul would be home. Not that it mattered. There was no earthly reason why Patrick should not be here — and yet ...

He was smiling at her. 'That's a nice welcome, I must say. I was at a loose end this week — thought I'd come home.'

'Don't you join your wife when you get a free weekend?'

'Not always.' He shrugged. 'She's gone up to Edinburgh to rehearse for a Festival thing. It's a long way just for a weekend, besides they seem to work through Saturdays and Sundays at this stage. It's one of those things where the re-writing is being done as they go along.' He pulled a face. 'It sounds chaotic. I don't really think they welcome visitors.'

'I see.' Elaine glanced at Tricia. 'Has Zoe finished with you now?'

Tricia nodded. 'Yes. Can I go out to play now, Mummy?'

'Of course.'

The child took an apple from the bowl on the dresser and skipped out through the back door into the garden.

'Zoe has finished the head,' Patrick told her. 'It's rather good. She asked me to tell you that you can have it cast in a metal of some kind, or she can do it in some other new material she's rather keen on. Maybe you could look in some time and see what you think.'

'Yes, I will.' She didn't look at him but concentrated on clearing away the knife and chopping board, meticulously wiping

268

the worktop, all the time acutely aware of his eyes on her. 'Why are you here, Patrick?'

'Why do you think? I wanted to see you. Bringing Tricia home seemed a good opportunity.'

'You shouldn't have come. Please go.'

He crossed the kitchen to her, frowning. 'What's wrong? You're as jumpy as a kitten.'

'What good can it do – coming here – seeing each other? It was all over eight years ago. We're both married now, and ...' She broke off abruptly as the door opened and Mary came into the kitchen.

'Elaine, I thought I heard you come in. I – oh ...' She stopped abruptly, looking from one to the other. 'I'm sorry. I didn't know you had a visitor.'

'This is Mr Carne,' Elaine said hurriedly. 'He brought Tricia home.'

'How do you do?' Mary's sharp eyes swept over Patrick from head to foot, assessing him, sniffing the atmosphere in the kitchen like a gun dog; quickly sensing the feeling of tension and guilt emanating from her daughter-in-law. That, coupled with what she had heard as she stood on the other side of the kitchen door, excited her in a way that nothing else could.

'What is it, Mother?' Elaine said, her stretched nerves in her voice.

'What? Oh, there was a telephone message from Paul,' Mary said, dragging her eyes away from Patrick's face. 'The staff meeting is taking longer than he thought, so he'll be a little late. I told him I didn't think it would matter. You've only just come in yourself, haven't you?'

She smiled sweetly at Patrick. 'My daughter-in-law works very hard. Am I to take it that you're old friends?'

'Very,' Patrick said with a smile. 'Childhood sweethearts, you might almost say.'

'How nice. Well ...' Mary backed towards the door. 'I'll leave you to – er – chat. I daresay you have a great deal to say to each other.'

As the door closed behind her Elaine winced. *'Damn!* That's all I needed. Why did you have to make that stupid remark?'

'Oh, come on. If there was anything going on we'd hardly get up to it here in your own kitchen, would we?'

'You don't know what she's like, Patrick,' she whispered. 'It's no laughing matter. Oh, why can't you leave me alone? Can't you see what you're doing?'

269

He took her shoulders and turned her towards him, surprised by the brightness in her eyes. 'You're really scared, aren't you? Surely you don't have to live like this. Do you let that old battle-axe run your life? This is 1975, for God's sake.'

'Just mind your own business and go, Patrick. You don't understand. Forget all about me. It's best.'

'Do you mean that? Do you really want me to go — not to see me again?'

'*Yes.* We've managed without seeing each other for the past eight years. Why start again now?' She wrenched herself free and turned away. 'Go now, Patrick. And don't come back.'

He didn't move. When she turned round he was still there, his eyes troubled as he looked at her. 'There's something here I don't understand,' he said quietly. 'You were right about that. But I mean to, Elaine. I certainly mean to.' He turned and walked out through the back door. Looking out of the window, she saw him wave to Tricia. Jumping off her swing the child came running up the garden to him and the look on her face brought a lump to Elaine's throat. She turned away abruptly, busying herself with preparing the vegetables, forcing her mind on to tomorrow's routine.

Alison was slightly breathless as she joined Elaine and the two bridesmaids in the church porch.

'I only just made it,' she whispered. 'Didn't want to steal the bride's limelight by arriving at the same minute, but I just *had* to be here to see her walk down the aisle in your fabulous dress.'

Together they watched as the car drew up at the lytch gate and Elaine went forward to help lift the train so that it didn't snag or soil on the pavement. In the porch she smoothed, tweaked and carefully arranged the gown she had created, then with a smile and a whispered 'Good luck' to the bride she slipped into one of the back pews along with Alison.

'Everything all right at your end?' she enquired. Alison nodded, holding up two pairs of crossed fingers. 'I really believe I've thought of everything. I hadn't bargained for quite such a hot day, but I think the champagne will be chilled enough. And that toastmaster the agency have sent — *c'est formidable.*' She pulled a face. 'He's bound to go down a bomb. He scared the pants off me.'

Elaine smothered a giggle and together they stood to sing the first hymn. The church was cool and fragrant with the scent of flowers. Elaine thought the ceremony moving and beautiful; so very different to the brief register office ceremony she and Paul had gone through. As she sat watching the two young figures standing at the alter, she

270

couldn't help wondering what her life might have been like if things had been different. Just for a moment she pictured herself and Patrick standing in place of the bride and groom, making vows, looking at each other like these two, with so much love in their eyes. Then she pulled herself together sharply. That could never be now. And the sooner she stopped thinking about it, the better. If only Patrick hadn't come back to torture her with what might have been. And to prove to her that what she had felt for him all those years ago hadn't died.

'Are you all right, Ellie?' Alison was looking at her anxiously.

She forced a smile and brushed a single tear from the corner of her eye. 'Of course I am. Don't you cry at weddings?'

Alison leaned closer. 'As long as they pay the bill promptly, *I* shan't be shedding any tears,' she whispered.

'Paul, I want to talk to you.' Mary stood in the doorway, a tray of tea in her hands. He groaned inwardly. He was watching cricket on television.

'Can't it wait, Mother?'

'I'm afraid it can't.' She put the tray down on the coffee table and seated herself between her son and the TV set, obscuring his vision. 'It's very worrying. I wanted to speak to you while we were alone.'

With a resigned sigh, Paul got up and switched off the set. 'Very well then. I suppose you'd better get it off your chest. What is it this time?'

Mary poured two cups of tea and handed Paul a plate of biscuits. He shook his head irritably.'

'Are you going to get to the point or aren't you, Mother?'

'I think you should put your foot down about this business Elaine has got herself involved with.'

He sighed. 'And how do you propose that I should do that?'

'It's simple. Get her pregnant again.'

Paul almost dropped his cup. 'What on earth are you talking about?'

'Well, why not? It's a mistake to have only one child anyway, and when Tricia goes off the school in September Elaine will miss her. She'll be spending even more time away from the house if you're not careful, working with this friend of hers. But if she were to find herself pregnant, she'd have something else to occupy her mind, wouldn't she?'

'Elaine and I have no plans to increase our family,' Paul said dismissively. But Mary was not to be put off as easily as that.

'Why are you so against having more children?'

'We just don't want any more, Mother.' He got up and switched on the television set again, but Mary ignored the pointed hint.

'You would tell me if there was anything wrong between you, wouldn't you, Paul?' she said wheedlingly.

'There is nothing wrong. And I'd like to watch the cricket if you don't ...'

'Of course, I can't help knowing that you don't share a room,' Mary interrupted. 'Why is that, Paul? Is Elaine frigid?'

A dull flush began to creep up Paul's neck. He kept his eyes on the television set as he said: 'Not as far as I know.'

'It's you then?' Mary shook her head. 'There's no need to look at me like that. I'm your mother, not some stranger. Elaine is still very young, Paul. You should be a proper husband to her if you want to keep her. You don't want her to start looking around at other men, getting ideas about divorce, do you? That wouldn't do your position at school any good.'

'You can safely leave my marriage problems with me, Mother.'

'Ah, so there *are* problems. I was right.' Mary's eyes glinted triumphantly.

'There are no problems as far as *I'm* concerned,' Paul said, his tone carefully controlled.

'But there are as far as Elaine is concerned? And that's where the danger lies.' She shook her head. 'Can't you see that you're asking for trouble?'

With a resigned sigh he went across and switched off the television again. 'All right, if you're determined to give me your views on the subject, I suppose you'd better get them off your chest,' he said.

Mary edged forward until she was sitting on the edge of her chair. 'Well – and remember, I'm only telling you this to help save your marriage – I have reason to believe that Elaine is – well – *seeing* someone.'

'Oh, really?' Paul's face remained impassive. 'Who?'

Mary frowned. 'I must say you don't seem very put out.'

'Mother, are you really trying to help? Or is it just sensation you're after?'

She bridled. 'How dare you accuse me of trying to make trouble? That's the last thing I've ever wanted to do. I'm just telling you so that you can do something about it before it's too late.'

'Very kind of you. And what do you suggest I do?'

'Surely that's up to you? Most men would at least be concerned – furious, even. Doesn't it make you angry at all?'

'Do you have any evidence to back up this accusation?' Paul asked.

'As a matter of fact, I do. I've heard them talking on the telephone ...' She glanced at him. 'Accidentally, of course. And yesterday he was actually here in the house.'

He laughed dryly. 'You think Elaine would be foolish enough to entertain a lover here − with *you* liable to pop into the room at any minute?'

Mary sprang to her feet, her face crimson. 'Oh, you're such a stupid complacent fool, Paul. You never did have any imagination − any *go* in you. That child Patricia − she isn't *yours*, of course. Anyone but a fool would have tumbled to that years ago.' Before he could open his mouth to respond she went on: 'You've only got to look at her colouring. Where do you think she got that blond hair from, and those eyes? Not from you − or from Elaine's side of the family either. And she certainly wasn't the premature baby everyone was led to believe. I always suspected it, right from the first. Oh, no. Elaine and her mother saw *you* coming all right. You walked right into their hands, like a lamb to the slaughter.'

She only just stopped herself from telling him of her other suspicion - that Patrick Carne was the child's father. The conversation she had overheard between him and Elaine yesterday afternoon had all but confirmed it, but if she were wrong and it came out that she had said it ...

Paul's mouth tightened and a muscle began to twitch in his cheek. 'if you knew this right from the beginning, as you say, why the hell didn't you tell me?'

She sat down again, eyeing him with a scornful expression. 'Why? Because I was only too glad to get you married off, of course. If you believed the child was yours, then you must have had reason to. That in itself was a relief to me. At least it proved you were a man. It meant that other disgraceful business was over and done with. Then I was thinking of your career; you needed a wife to get you the post of headmaster. By that time, quite frankly, Paul, I didn't much care who she was or how you got her.'

'I see. Thank you.' His face was now deathly pale. 'So what do you suggest I do about this suspicion of yours? Clearly you're against divorce − so what should I do? Come on now, Mother. Don't tell me you're stumped for ideas about that.'

'There's no need to be sarcastic. I've already made a sensible suggestion. Do you really want me to tell you how to control your own wife? It's not my place.'

'Exactly. So there's no more to be said, is there?' Paul picked up a book that lay on the table at his side. He opened it and began to read. After a few moments Mary got up with and exasperated little snort and left the room.

The wedding reception was a great success. Everyone admired the bride's dress and Alison and Elaine circulated among the guests, their ears open for remarks, eager to learn of their mistakes as well as their successes.

From the other side of the marquee, Elaine watched Alison as she talked animatedly with a middle-aged woman. She wore an attractive dress in a shade of blue that suited her colouring perfectly and Elaine thought that she was looking so much better than when she first came home. She had put on weight, the haunted look had gone from her eyes and she was clearly more relaxed. Their new venture was obviously helping her to readjust. Elaine only wished it could do the same for her.

'Penny for them.'

She turned, surprised and more than a little dismayed to see Patrick standing at her elbow. 'Patrick! What . . .?'

'Am I doing here?' He finished the sentence for her. 'And why didn't I tell you yesterday that I was coming? The answers are that I didn't want to add to your anxieties, and I didn't want to risk having you spend the afternoon avoiding me.' He smiled apologetically. 'I promise you it wasn't contrived. I was officially invited. It happens that I was at school with the bridegroom. Sorry.'

'Don't be. You have a perfect right to be here.' She turned and helped herself from the buffet table.

'Am I allowed to congratulate you on the wedding?' he asked. 'Everything seems to have gone like clockwork.'

'It's a joint effort,' she told him. 'Alison did all this.' She indicated the buffet table. 'It looks beautiful, doesn't it?'

'And so do you.' His eyes swept over her admiringly. 'That shade of peach is wonderful with your colouring and the hat gives you a Renoir look. I don't think I've ever seen you in a hat before.'

'Haven't you?' She looked around for an excuse to escape, acutely aware of the colour in her cheeks.

He touched her arm. 'Elaine, don't run off again. Look, couldn't we meet? Can't you come up to Town? I want to see you so much. Ever since we met again at the party, I haven't been able to get you out of my mind.'

'No.' She shook her head. If he only knew how she had lain awake night after night since the party, remembering his kiss; if he could know the terrible aching joy being in he arms again had

274

brought her. She took a deep breath. 'What possible good could it do? There's no future in it, Patrick. There never was any future in our relationship. I was too young to realise it all those years ago, but I'm older and wiser now. I don't want to be unhappy.'

'But you *are* unhappy. I can see it in your eyes. It's written in every look, every gesture. If we could find the happiness we had it would be worth it, wouldn't it? Even if it were only for a little while.'

She shrugged. 'A little while? And for what? No, Patrick, I'm not a naive child any more. You're being unfair — cruel, even. Please don't ask me again.'

'Is that your last word?' His eyes searched hers and she was aware of an electric tingling in her arm as his fingers closed round it.

It was with an effort she made herself say: 'Yes. It's my last word.'

She drew her arm away from his grasp and turned to walk away. 'Goodbye, Patrick.'

On the other side of the marquee Alison turned with shining eyes as Elaine touched her sleeve. 'Hey, guess what? I've just had three enquiries and a firm booking. The bride and her mother are coming round on ...' She broke off, seeing the look in Elaine's eyes. 'Ellie - you're upset.' She sucked in her breath sharply. 'Damn! It's Patrick, isn't it? I knew it meant trouble when I saw you talking to him at Red and Zoe's party that night.' She frowned angrily. 'Honestly, men. Who needs them?' Taking Elaine by the arm, she said firmly: 'Forget him, Ellie. Look, see that pretty blonde girl over there? She's been enquiring about the wedding dress. She adored it, and when I told her you made it she asked if you could design one for her. Naturally I said you could. Come and meet your next client. You've got work to do, my girl'

When Elaine went to collect Tricia from her mother's house she found the two of them in the middle of a game of Ludo. Tricia looked up in dismay.

'Oh, Mummy, it can't be time to go home yet. Can't I stay the night?' she begged.

'Well ...' Elaine looked doubtful.

'Oh, please let me, Mummy. Granny says we could have breakfast in the garden and then go down to the river and feed the swans. They've go some babies and they're ever so sweet.'

Elaine looked at her mother and saw the mute appeal in her eyes. She knew that Grace was often lonely at weekends and felt guilty about it, but she couldn't invite her to the house with Mary there. The two hadn't spoken since Morgan had insisted on repaying Mary's loan.'

She laughed. 'I get the feeling this is a conspiracy. You're ganging up on me. Mum, are you sure she isn't too much trouble?'

Grace looked at her reprovingly. 'How can you ask me that? She'll be off to school in a couple of weeks' time and then I shan't see her for ages. Let her stay.'

Elaine laughed. 'All right then, if you're sure.'

'I'm sure. Now – you'll stay for a cup of tea, won't you?' Grace asked. 'I'm dying to hear all about the wedding.'

It was nine o'clock by the time Elaine got home. The house was quiet as she let herself in. Upstairs, as she changed out of her wedding outfit, she heard Mary's radio playing in her room. She was listening to the Saturday night play – obviously having an early night. That at least was a relief. Downstairs she found the living room empty. She crossed the hall and looked into Paul's study. He was working at his desk.

'Hello, I'm home. Tricia is staying the night at Mum's. Did you have the cold meal I left out for you?'

'Yes.' He didn't look up.

'Your mother having an early night, is she?'

'As far as I know.' She turned to go out of the room when he suddenly laid down his pen and said brusquely: 'Elaine, come in and close the door. I want to talk to you.'

Something in his tone made her hesitate. Closing the door carefully she turned to look at him. 'What is it? Is something wrong?'

He stood up and came round the desk. 'I'm going to ask you something. I'll ask you just this once and I want you to answer truthfully.'

'Yes?'

He paused. 'Is Patricia my child?'

Her heart missed a beat and it was as though something cold and heavy had replaced her stomach. 'Your child? She . . .'

He shook his head, holding up his hand as though warding her off. 'Don't try to fob me off with platitudes. My *natural* child, I mean.'

His face was white and pinched, his eyes cold and almost colourless as he came towards her. 'You tricked me, didn't you? Admit it.'

She backed away. She'd never seen him this angry before. 'Paul – listen – I . . .'

'Don't insult my intelligence by making up feeble excuses. Just answer me, yes or no. Am I Patricia's natural father?'

He was facing her now, no more than a couple of feet away, and she could see that he meant it when he said he wanted the truth. In spite of the thudding of her heart, she met his eyes.

'No, Paul. You're not. And I admit I should have told you at the time, but if you'll only listen I'll ...' She got not further. Raising his hand he slapped her hard on either cheek, first with the flat of his hand, then with the back of it. 'Whore!' He breathed the word venomously, his eyes glittering with fury. 'All the cheap innuendoes I've put up with from you, when all the time you were nothing but a dirty cheating little whore. All these years you've let me believe ...'

'You would have believed anything,' she said, stung into retaliation. 'Don't be a hypocrite, Paul. You needed a wife quickly – or at least a woman to play the role of wife. You asked me and I said yes. Our marriage was a matter of convenience, as much to you as to me, so don't pretend it wasn't. I didn't do *all* the cheating. And if you think I haven't paid for my deception, you're wrong. I've had almost eight years of emptiness. A travesty of a marriage.' She turned away from his. 'I'll pack and leave tomorrow.' But he caught her arm and pulled her round to face him again.

'Oh no you won't. You're married to me and that's the way it's going to stay.'

'And if I don't want to stay?' She stared up at him, her eyes dark with dislike.

'You'll still stay. And I'll tell you why. You'll want to keep your good name now that you've started this so called business of yours. An unsavoury scandal and a broken marriage would hardly be the kind of publicity to set you on your feet, would it?'

'I daresay we'd live it down. We're not living in the dark ages now, Paul.'

His mouth twisted with cynical triumph as he played his trump card. 'Perhaps not. Perhaps you're thick-skinned enough to brazen it out as you say. But you're forgetting something. If I divorced you on the grounds that you deceived me into thinking I was the father of another man's child, I could hardly be expected to pay maintenance, could I? That would be the end of the expensive musical education you're looking forward to giving her. It would also be the end of your child's name too. Because I'd insist that she no longer bore mine.' Elaine's heart plummeted as they stared at each other for a long, breathless minute.

'Well, what is it to be?' he challenged. 'Either have your lies rebound on your daughter – have her name and yours dragged

277

through the courts and the newspapers — or stay here, carry on the charade you've been living.' He pushed his face close to hers. 'You've managed to bring it off with praiseworthy aplomb for the past eight years, so it shouldn't be too difficult to continue, should it?'

Chapter Nineteen

For Elaine, the worst part was not being able to talk to anyone. Apart from Paul no one else knew the truth about Tricia's parentage. Thinking about it, she felt that Paul must have had his suspicions all along. At the time of their marriage she had been young and naive. She had taken things at face value, assuming that as he never questioned it, Paul believed the child was his. But he was older and more mature. Surely he must have wondered about Tricia's early birth? The strange thing was, why had he waited eight years to mention it? What had triggered off his sudden demand for the truth that night? Perhaps he was afraid of her impending independence — looking for a sure way to hold her. Because he still needed her to play the role of headmaster's wife, to bolster his public image, if nothing else.

In one way it was a relief to have it out in the open. Lying in bed that night she had asked herself if Paul could have been bluffing. If she were to leave, would her really do as he threatened? St Jasper's was an old-fashioned school. A scandal would damage his career too. She had faced him with this the following day, but he had laughed in her face.

'I'd simply leave the country,' he told her. 'Get a job abroad. So don't think you can hold that over my head.'

The days that followed were tense and difficult. She had tried hard to put on a show for Tricia's sake, but it hadn't been easy. Just a few more days and she would have gone to her new school. After that Elaine would work out what must be done.

It was halfway through the week when she went to see Zoe. Tricia had gone to Miss Hazel's for her final music lesson and Elaine had dropped in at the Carnes' house on the way back. She found Zoe busy at work in her studio, the house empty for once. Welcoming

279

her warmly, Zoe invited her into the studio and put the kettle on for coffee.

'I hope I'm not disturbing you,' Elaine said.

'You know me, always glad of an excuse to knock off for coffee.'

Zoe took the head of Tricia out of the cupboard where it had been drying and placed it on the table between them. 'There, it's finished, and I must say I'm rather pleased with it. Is there any particular medium you want me to cast it in, or will you leave it to me?' She turned her head round slowly. 'Well, do you like it?'

Elaine caught her breath. 'Oh, Zoe, it's beautiful. And I'm happy to leave the final choice to you.'

'I think it lends itself to something pale and light. If you're happy to leave it with me, I think I know just the material.'

Elaine reached out one finger and gently touched the face of the model. 'It's uncanny. I could almost believe it's really her. It'll be lovely to have when she's gone.' Suddenly her voice broke and her eyes filled with tears. 'Oh, Zoe, I'm going to miss her so.'

'When does she go?'

'At the weekend.' Elaine swallowed hard and fumbled in her bag for her handkerchief. 'Sorry. You must think me horribly sentimental.'

'Not a bit of it,' Zoe said gruffly. 'I wept buckets when the boys left home for the first time — made sure no one saw me doing it, but nevertheless . . .' She peered at Elaine as she spooned instant coffee into two mugs. 'People think I'm a hard nut. I'm not really, you know.'

Elaine smiled. 'I know.'

'It's a bit more than just Tricia though, isn't it? You're looking distinctly peaky.' She put a mug of coffee down in front of Elaine. 'Tell me to mind my own bloody business if you like, but if you want to talk about it, I've got a broad shoulder . . .' She smiled ruefully. 'And a narrow mouth — if that bothers you.'

Elaine laughed shakily as she put away her handkerchief. 'Thanks, Zoe. I know you're discreet.' She took a deep breath. 'It's just that things are — well — difficult between Paul and me.'

'I thought as much. Is it serious?'

'Oh, I daresay we'll sort it out — in time.'

'That doesn't answer my question.'

Elaine sighed. She might have known there was no fooling Zoe. There was no one she could talk to about the real cause of the trouble between them. Her mother would be profoundly shocked; Alison was somehow too close, and besides, she had trouble enough of her

280

own. Pouring out as much as she dared to Zoe was overwhelmingly tempting.

'I suppose the real trouble is that I should never have married Paul,' she said.

'So why did you? You were very young. You had your whole life before you.' Zoe sipped her coffee thoughtfully. 'Could it have had anything to do with Patrick?'

Elaine looked up sharply, but the older woman's face revealed nothing. 'I did love Patrick. You knew that, of course. When he went away to France I was − I thought I was heartbroken. Paul came along ...'

'And you married him under pressure from both mothers,' Zoe said gently. 'And for all the wrong reasons?'

Once more Elaine searched Zoe's face but found it impassive. She sighed. 'That's about it. Everyone seemed to want it. I knew that Paul needed a wife to get the job he was after but, to be fair, he did seem fond of me − at the time.' She sighed. 'Perhaps it's my fault. Perhaps I've never really tried hard enough to make it work. It wasn't too bad at the beginning.'

'"Not too bad" isn't enough to make a good and lasting marriage though, is it?' Zoe looked at her. 'Elaine, do you want to tell me the truth?'

Their eyes met across the exquisite head of Tricia, and for the first time the relationship between the three of them struck Elaine. She opened her mouth.

'Tricia's ...' she began − then changed her mind. Telling Zoe would open up a whole set of new complications. It would be putting unfair responsibilities on her. In spite of her promise to keep Elaine's confidence, she might feel obliged to tell Patrick. Elaine shook her head.

'Oh, I don't know. I'd like to leave Paul. I'm so tired of everything - living in the same house as his mother; putting up with her interference; keeping house for two people who often seem positively to dislike me; never having a real home of my own. I can't let Tricia see how I feel, though she's growing up fast − she must feel the tension. I can't tell my mother. She'd only worry over something she couldn't help with. Oh, Zoe, I just don't know what to do.'

Privately, Zoe felt that most women would have walked out long ago. But then most women didn't have Grace Wendover with her Victorian values for a mother. Grace, nice, hard-working woman though she was, was most probably at the root of Elaine's trouble, in her opinion.

281

'Why don't you go away for a while?' she suggested. 'Right away, I mean?'

Elaine sighed. 'It sounds bliss.'

'Morgan would let you have his place in Davos. Red and I went over for a few days soon after he bought it. It's beautiful, Elaine. So peaceful. It might help you to get things into perspective.'

'He did offer to let me go there.'

'Then what are you waiting for? Ring him — take up the offer. Go as soon as Tricia's settled in her new school. And go alone. Give yourself some space — some time to think, where you won't be influenced by anyone else.' She reached across the table to lay a hand on Elaine's arm. 'Do it, love,' she urged. 'You owe it to yourself. Do it before you make yourself ill.'

When the weekend arrived Paul announced that he was too busy to accompany Elaine and Tricia to St Cecilia's. Elaine was relieved. She'd been dreading the journey home closeted in the car alone with Paul.

Tricia chattered excitedly all the way there. They stopped off for lunch as a special treat at a motorway restaurant and as she picked unenthusiastically at a sandwich, Elaine watched as her daughter demolished burgers, beans and chips, followed by a double banana split.

At the school Tricia renewed her acquaintance with the friends she had made at her interview and Elaine was relieved to see that she had no anxieties about being left. It was only when the time came for them to say goodbye that she gave any indication of emotion. Hugging her mother fiercely she whispered: 'Will you be all right, Mummy?'

Swallowing the lump in her throat, Elaine said, 'Of course I will, darling. Just you settle down and enjoy it all. And don't forget to write, will you?'

'We're only allowed to write one letter a week,' Tricia said solemnly. 'But I'll write a little bit every night after music practice, then it'll be a nice long letter.'

'Lovely. I'll do the same,' Elaine promised. A quick last hug and Tricia, apparently reassured, waved her mother off happily.

Elaine stopped at the first filling station she came to. While the car was being filled with petrol she went into the forecourt phone booth and dialled Morgan's number. As she waited for him to answer her heart was beating fast.

'Morgan?' She quickly inserted her money as she heard his voice. 'It's Elaine.'

'Hello. Nice to hear from you.'

'I've just taken Tricia to her new school.'

'Quite a milestone. Feeling a bit down?'

It was just the lead she required. 'That would be an understatement. Right at this moment it feels like the end of the world. Morgan – you remember you offered me your Swiss chalet a while ago?'

'Of course I remember. Any time you like.'

'I'd like to go now – well, soon, if that's all right. As soon as I'm happy that Tricia is settled.'

'Fine. Just ring and let me have the date and I'll lay it on for you. There's a local couple who look after things for me at that end. They'll open up and see that everything's ready.' He paused. 'Will Paul be going with you?'

'No.'

'I see.'

'I need some time to myself, Morgan. Things are – well, difficult.'

'Do you want to talk?'

'Not at the moment. Maybe later.'

'Are you sure going off to Davos is the answer?' He sounded concerned. 'All alone – in a strange place?'

'I'm sure, Morgan. Really. I need some time and space to work things out for myself. It's important to be on my own for a while.' She tried to sound positive and in charge, and she must have succeeded because he sounded reassured.

'Okay then. You know best. Just ring and give me your date. I'll meet your train and drive you to the airport. I take it you'll let me do that?'

He sounded slightly whimsical and she laughed. 'Thanks, Morgan. I'd be grateful if you would. Thanks – for everything.'

When she got back into the car she felt much better. She'd done something positive – made the first step. The first step towards just what, she would work out later.

She told Alison first. She'd worried about taking time off just when they were getting their business under way, but she needn't have done. Alison was delighted.

'Great. Just what you need. You've been looking really tired lately. Are you sure you're all right?'

'I'm fine – just missing Tricia, that's all. I hate leaving you with everything.'

Alison laughed. 'You're only going for a few days and our next wedding is months away. I *think* I can just about cope without you.

283

Don't start getting the idea you're indispensable. Look, if it'll make you feel any better, you can make enquiries about Swiss laces and anything else that takes your fancy while you're there. Try and do some deals. It'll help you to shift gear from motherhood to business woman.'

The idea appealed to Elaine. It would give her a legitimate reason for going — and a definite purpose when she got there. And it was this reason that she gave to her mother. Grace was pleased.

'I'd come with you, only I'm expecting Morgan's accountant up to go through the books with me.' She smiled. 'Maybe we can go again together in the holidays — when Tricia can come too.'

'Yes, Mum. Maybe we can.' She longed to tell her mother everything, but it was impossible. Grace would never understand. They were close and yet there were so many secrets, so many differences, between them. Better to leave things as they were.

When she told Paul he showed little interest.

'Do what the hell you like,' he said brusquely. 'It doesn't matter to me whether you're here or not.'

But to her surprise, when she broke the news to her mother-in-law, Mary seemed more anxious than disapproving. She'd been surprisingly affable since the night Paul had challenged her about Tricia, and when she learned that Elaine was to have a few days away on her own, a look of apprehension came into her eyes.

'We shall miss you,' she said. 'Elaine — I hope it isn't anything I've done that's driving you away?'

'No. I just need a rest,' Elaine said guardedly. 'And to get used to not having Tricia around. If I leave it till later, Alison and I will be too busy for me to have a break.'

'It's a pity you have to go alone,' Mary said. 'Maybe Paul could get his deputy to take over for a week, then he could go with you.'

'No,' Elaine said, a little too quickly. 'One of the things I'm going over there for is to buy materials — maybe set up a deal or two. Better if I go alone.'

'Of course. I understand.' But privately Mary was seriously worried. Maybe she had said too much. The atmosphere in the house had been very strained since the night she'd talked to Paul. She sensed that if Elaine were to leave, Paul wouldn't stay on with her at Langmere Lodge. What would become of her then? She couldn't manage the house on her own. It was something she hadn't foreseen.

The trip loomed in front of Elaine like an adventure. She had never been abroad before, never flown, and as the time drew near she found herself growing more nervous and apprehensive by the minute.

Morgan met her train at King's Cross and drove her to the flat where she was to stay overnight, catching her plane early the following morning.

As a surprise he'd booked seats for a show that evening. They saw Godspell at Wyndham's and had dinner afterwards at a quaint little restaurant in Greek Street, where Elaine enjoyed spotting celebrities.

Morgan looked well, and very prosperous. He seemed to have an impressively large circle of friends. Many people greeted him warmly as they passed their table and Elaine vaguely recognised some of them. There was a news-reader from television with a middle-aged character actress, and two very glamorous models, both of who she'd seen often in fashion magazines.

Morgan asked about Tricia and her new school, and about Grace, expressing regret that she wouldn't come up more often to spend time with him in London.

'She's still basically a very shy person,' he said affectionately. 'But I'm working on getting her to spend a holiday in Switzerland with me soon. I'm relying on you to go back and excite her curiosity about the place.' He paused, breaking a bread stick into tiny pieces. 'Did she tell you I'd been trying to persuade her to come up here and share my flat?'

'No.' Elaine was surprised. 'She hasn't mentioned it to me.'

He smiled ruefully. 'She says she's got too many ties in Cambridge and that she enjoys seeing Tricia and you often. But I think it's that dogged independence of hers.' He looked up at her. 'I still miss her, you know. Grace is a wonderful, warm person. I owe her so much and I'd like to give her something back.'

Elaine laid a hand on his arm. 'But you have, Morgan. You're a success. That's all she's ever wanted from you.'

He shook his head. 'It's a pity she had to give up the shop. She's too young and too energetic to retire, and keeping an eye on the factory isn't enough of a challenge for her.'

'You needn't worry about that,' Elaine laughed. 'Alison and I will be needing as much of her help as she's prepared to give if we take off as we're hoping.'

He smiled. 'It's good to hear you say that. Between you and me, I think she's afraid to offer in case you think she's interfering.'

He wanted to know all about 'Happy Ever After' and their first wedding, and was full of helpful suggestions. He also gave her a letter of introduction to a Swiss designer friend who lived in Davos and would show her where to look for the best embroidery and lace. To her relief he didn't mention Paul at all.

Next morning at the airport she tried hard to look like a seasoned traveller. On the plane she sat next to a smartly dressed woman who turned out to be an orthodontist, going to a dental convention in Zurich. It amazed Elaine that what seemed to her like an exciting journey into another world was taken for granted by people who did it every day of the week.

At the airport a bus was waiting to take her to the railway station and then began an enchanting journey through the most magnificent scenery she had ever seen. She made two changes at tiny stations from which the little train climbed higher and higher into the mountains. Sitting by the window she looked out, entranced by the richness of colour and the chalets precariously perched on the hillsides. Cows with bells around their necks grazed serenely on the lush green grass under laden apple trees and farmers drove their tractors up and down impossibly sloping fields. She began to see the magic that had captivated Morgan.

At Davos Dorf Station a small dapper man with thinning fair hair stepped forward and asked politely if she were Frau Kingston. When she told him she was, he beamed a welcome and introduced himself as Carl Kleber. Taking her suitcase from her, he led the way to a car, telling her as they went in his almost perfect English that his wife Krista had everything ready for her.

As they drove Elaine sat in the back of the car looking out at the little town that seemed to have been hewn out of the mountain side, the streets built like terraces, one above the other. Smart little shops lined the gleamingly spotless streets. Restaurants and pavement cafes beckoned invitingly, their coloured umbrellas fluttering like a crop of bright flowers. Elaine longed to explore. As they drove she admired the fascinating mixture of new and old architecture, leaning forward to peer at the older houses and hotels, built in the traditional Swiss style, with timbered gables and painted shutters. Some boasted murals painted in bright colours on their white walls. And over all, dominating the town like benign, protective giants, towered the mountains, their craggy peaks still capped with snow that gleamed and sparkled like crystal against the azure backdrop of the sky. Who could ever have dreamed that such a magic place as this existed?

Morgan's chalet was on the fringe of the town on a road that climbed steeply. It was built high up on the lower slope of the mountain, and part of the first floor was actually cantilevered out over the mountainside, giving it a magnificent view of the town and the valley. Krista had prepared one of the rooms on that side of the house for Elaine. It was a spacious room with a rose pink carpet. The furniture was of natural golden pine, richly carved with flower and heart-shapes. The bed was huge, and covered by the traditional fat duvet. It had a half-tester from which hung white lace drapes, caught back with rose pink ties. Adjoining the bedroom was a pink and white bathroom, which Krista proudly displayed.

'Here is *das badezimmer*,' she said, hesitating and wrinkling her brow. Then, pointing to each of the taps in turn: 'See – *heiss* – *kalt*.' She shook her head, explaining haltingly that her English was not as good as that of her husband, who had worked as a chef in a London hotel for five years. She managed to covey to Elaine that she had prepared a meal of schnitzel, which was waiting in the oven in the gleaming modern kitchen downstairs, and that she would come in each evening if required, to prepare the main meal of the day. Then, with many smiles and good wishes, she left, wishing Elaine, '*Guten abend*.'

It seemed to Elaine that the magic of Switzerland waited round every corner to surprise and delight her. The sun wakened her early in the mornings and she would get out of bed to open the shutters and watch it rise over the mountain tops, the majestic blue-grey peaks turning first pink and then golden. The spectacle of the early morning sun spreading pale fingers to light and transform every rock and crevice never failed to thrill her. When the sun was fully up she would dress in jeans and an anorak and set off to cross the bridges that led from street to street and climb the lower slopes of the mountain. There a little church, like a child's toy, on a plateau looking out over the most beautiful view she had ever seen. Here she would rest awhile on the little wooden seat, listening to the bells whose sound echoed, round and golden through the valley, waiting until she had regained enough breath to make the descent again. Once the priest, a tall, slim West Indian man in a black soutane, joined her and they chatted like old friends until it was time for him to celebrate early mass.

Slowly, as the days went by, she began to unwind, enthusiastically exploring the town with its smart shops and the surrounding valley. When she looked in the mirror she began to see a more serene, more relaxed face. The worry lines around her mouth and eyes began to smoothe out and her skin took on the golden glow that only mountain air and sun can provide. She visited Morgan's friend and found him hospitable and friendly. He took her to his favourite suppliers and she spent a fascinating day examining their

287

fine fabrics and watching the manufacture of lace and embroidery. In the evenings she ate Krista's delicious food, then read or watched television. Though she could not understand the language, the sound of human voices took away the loneliness and put off the moment when she must put out the light. Then came bed and darkness and the time for thinking. But always, before she could apply her mind to the problem, pushed away during the day into the darkest corner of her mind, she fell mercifully asleep, tired by exercise and intoxicated by the heady mountain air.

It was on the fourth day, when she returned in the early evening from a coach ride over the mountain passes to Lichtenstein, that Krista met her at the door, a slightly worried look on her face.

'Frau Kingston, there is a visitor for you.'

'For me?' Elaine shook her head. 'For Herr Owen, surely?'

But the woman shook her head. '*Nein*. He ask for Mrs Kingston. He is coming much hours ago.' She shook her head, holding out her hand as she did so to indicate that the visitor was in the large room to the right of the hall. 'I make tea, but he is, I think ...' She gave up and relapsed into her native German: '*Er ist des wartens mude.*' She shook her head and disappeared in the direction of the kitchen.

With a heavy heart Elaine walked towards the double doors that stood ajar. Paul. It could only be him. He had come to invade her little haven of peace − to make her go home again. The thought sliced through her mind like a scythe through grass. Nothing was resolved. There was no escape. Perhaps there never would be.

Pushing one of the doors open she stood in the doorway. On the opposite side of the room the sliding glass doors that gave on to the balcony were open and he stood with his back towards her, looking out at the view. The fiery evening sun shone on his hair, turning it to a halo of spun gold. Her heart leapt dizzily with shock and disbelief.

'*Patrick.*'

He turned and began to walk towards her, hands outstretched, face alight with pleasure. 'Hello, Elaine.'

Her mind spun like a top. How did he know she was here? Why had he come? Had Zoe spoken to him? She voiced none of these thoughts, but as he took her hands he read the confused questions in her eyes.

'I ran into Morgan,' he explained. 'He'd just driven you to Heathrow. I couldn't get it out of my mind that you were here alone, Elaine. I knew there must be something wrong. I just *felt* that you needed me. I had to come.'

288

She said nothing, just laid her head against his chest. His arms closed around her. It felt so good to be in his arms. After a moment he said against her hair: 'It's no use, my darling. We both know it's no use, don't we? I was such a fool to let you go all those years ago. We were always meant for each other and now we have to be together, no matter what.'

They ate Krista's supper without tasting it, barely taking their eyes from each other. Afterwards they talked. Patrick told her that his marriage was over. It had been a mistake — a failure from the beginning. They both knew it.

They made love in the big white bed with the curtains drawn back from the balcony windows and the shutters open. Only the moonlit mountains standing sentinel. For Elaine it was like the first time all over again. Afterwards, as she lay in his arms, he said perceptively: 'It's been a long time, my love, hasn't it? Not just since *we* made love, but a long time for you — with anyone.'

'Paul and I haven't shared a bed or anything else for years,' she confided. 'He doesn't want me any more. As a wife, yes; as a status symbol, but not as a woman. It was never that kind of marriage.'

He raised his head to stare incredulously down at her. 'Why have you stayed with him all this time? You're a warm, loving woman. How could you bear to live with anyone on those terms, Elaine?'

She smiled gently. 'It's simple. There's only ever been one man for me, Patrick. And as I couldn't have you, it didn't really matter. As a headmaster Paul needed a wife. Tricia deserved security. It seemed like a fair bargain. So I stayed.'

An expression of pain crossed his face and he pulled her close. 'God, if I'd only know. But we'll be together from now on, darling. I'll make it all up to you, I promise.' He looked down into her eyes. 'You won't change your mind? You won't go back to him again through some misguided sense of duty?'

'No.' She nestled close, burying her face in his neck. 'No, I won't change my mind. How can you think it?'

There were two days left of the holiday and they spent them idyllically, as close to each other as it was possible to get. They went to the top of the Schatzalp in the cable car and stood hand in hand in the brilliant sunshine at what seemed like the very top of the world, gulping in the heady, iced-wine air till they felt drunk with it. They travelled down again, stopping for lunch in the restaurant halfway, and as they ate they planned their future.

Patrick went back to the lace factory with her when she ordered fabric for wedding dresses, and in the back of her mind was a dream

289

of the one she'd design and make for herself, to wear on the day she married him.

On the last day they went again to Lichtenstein. But this time Elaine saw so much more than she'd seen the first time. With her hand clasped tightly in his, everything looked so much better; the colours brighter, the mountains more awesome − even the people seemed to smile more.

They drank coffee at a pavement cafe in the shadow of the *schloss*, then strolled through the quaint, colourful streets.

They bought ice cream and sat in a little park to eat it, but Elaine's expression was sad as she looked around her. Suddenly none of it seemed real. She couldn't lose the feeling that it was all a dream - one that would fade when they returned to England.

'I can't believe it will really happen,' she said. 'That things will really work out as we want and we'll be together.'

'It will. Of course it will,' he promised, tipping her face up to his.

'Paul will be difficult,' she warned. 'It won't be easy, getting a divorce. He might contest it.'

'Let him,' he said, drawing her head on to his shoulder. 'We'll face whatever comes together. And I'll make you a promise: We'll come here again when it's all over and we're free to marry. We'll come for our honeymoon. This will always be our special place, the place where we found each other at last.' He laughed down at her. 'This time next year we'll be laughing at all our fears. You wait and see.'

She closed her eyes, praying with all her heart that he was right; wishing that the coming weeks were behind them.

Mary struggled up the path with the two heavy bags of shopping bumping uncomfortably against her legs. Pausing for a moment at the foot of the steps, she rummaged in her handbag for her front door key. At the top of the steps she inserted the key, but to her surprise found the door unlatched. Dumping the bags in the hall she sank gratefully on to the telephone seat. Those new supermarkets were supposed to be labour-saving but in her opinion they were sheer hard work − for the customer anyway. A far cry from the days when one could simply ring for an order to be delivered at the tradesman's entrance by a respectful little man in a brown overall. She'd had the greatest difficulty finding all the things she'd wanted in the maze of shelves and alleyways and she'd had to queue interminably at the check-out. The sour-faced girl sitting at the adding machine thing had been ill-mannered too, positively rude. If she hadn't been so exhausted she'd have complained to the manager. She was too old for this kind of marathon, she told herself resentfully. This was one of her bridge afternoons too. She'd had to cancel when she discovered that there was nothing in the house for dinner. Thank goodness Elaine would be home tomorrow. She'd be more than glad to hand the household duties over to her again.

She hung her outdoor things on the hallstand and carried the bags through to the kitchen, putting the kettle on for a cup of tea. Paul would be home soon. She would have to make a start on the dinner. But first she would go upstairs and change into her comfortable slippers.

In the hall she paused, thinking she heard a sound. Of course the front door had been on the latch, so Paul must be home. He would be in his study, working as usual. At the top of the stairs she paused, puzzled to hear a murmur of voices coming from his bedroom. Crossing the landing she stood at the half open door, her hand raised to tap. She had opened her mouth to speak his name when a sudden movement caught her eye. On the opposite side of the room she could see the bed reflected in the dressing table mirror. Paul was on it. For a moment she thought he must be ill. She made to walk into the room − then he moved and she saw that he was naked, also that he was not alone. She froze. Paul's companion was a young man. The sudden realisation of what was happening brought an involuntary cry of horror from her lips.

The next moment chaos broke loose. Paul suddenly caught sight of his mother's reflection in the mirror and his eyes widened in stunned surprise as they met hers. Momentarily confused, Mary backed away, making for the stairs, anxious to escape. From the bedroom behind her came the sounds of breathless voices raised in confusion.

She was at the bottom of the stairs when a figure rushed past, almost overbalancing her. She turned, clinging to the bannisters for support, and for a moment looked into the startled face of a youth she remembered being head boy at St Jasper's two years ago. He ran through the hall in a panic, his shoes skidding perilously on the tiled floor. The front door banged shut behind him, while Mary clung desperately to the newel post, feeling sick and dizzy.

Looking up, she saw that Paul stood at the top of the stairs, staring down at her. He wore a crumpled sweater and was fastening the belt of his trousers. His thin hair stood up around his head and his eyes were blank and colourless.

'You *fool*,' she hissed at him breathlessly. 'How could you? In your own home and with one of your own boys − after all these years? You promised me all that was over when you married Elaine. I thought you were cured.'

'Shut up, Mother. Just shut up, do you hear? You saw nothing. You understand nothing. You never did.' His voice shook. 'What I do is none of your bloody business. I thought this was your bridge day anyway. What the hell do you mean by coming back to spy on me?' He came down the stairs towards her, a threatening look in his eyes. But Mary was not to be intimidated. Snatching an umbrella from the hallstand she advanced towards him up the stairs again and brandished it under his nose.

'You *pervert*,' she screamed. 'You filthy, disgusting creature. I've tried with you, God only knows how I've tried, but you've never been anything but a failure and a disappointment. I lost the best of my two sons. *You* should have died, not Richard. I just thank God that your father never lived to find out.' She prodded him in the chest with the umbrella. 'What's Elaine going to say when I ...?'

She crumpled instantly under the blow he dealt her and fell backwards. The umbrella dropped over the bannisters and skittered across the tiles. There was a series of dull thuds as her back bumped over the stair treads, then a sickening crack as her head struck the newel post.

She lay spread-eagled upside down across the bottom two stairs, limp as a rag doll; her raised skirt displayed skinny nylon-clad knees and her arms outstretched like a scarecrow's.

Paul stood, poised halfway up the staircase, numb with shock as he stared down at his mother's prone body. A feeling of overwhelming revulsion filled his chest and he clasped a hand over his mouth as he tasted bile. Christ, what had he done? More times than he cared to remember he had wished he had the courage to tell his mother to go to hell, and now he had killed her. Hatred filled his whole being as he stared down at the crumpled body. It seemed to him that his whole life had been dominated by women. How he hated them. All they ever did was deceive and despise him. He wished with all his heart that he *had* died instead of his brother. Now his life wouldn't be worth living anyway. He thought of what was to come: the police; the trial; then prison. He had heard about what happened to his kind in prison.

Stepping over his mother's body into the hall, he lifted the telephone, carefully dialling 999. When he had requested an ambulance and given the address he went out to the garage and got into the car. It would be an accident. No one need ever know now. The A1. He knew just the spot. With luck it would be over quickly.

He was deadly calm, his mind as clear and calculating as a

292

computer. Automatically, he checked the fuel gauge to make sure he had enough petrol, then backed out of the garage and headed for the motorway.

He'd been driving for about half an hour when he recognised that he was nearing the place. He'd seen it many times before. A high bank with trees at the bottom. There was a crash barrier but he knew that the car was powerful enough to break through it. He pressed his foot down to the floor and felt the car leap forward − the speedometer needle spun to ninety. He came to the bend in the road, saw the dull gleam of the metal barrier and felt the surge of adrenalin quicken his heartbeat and tighten his stomach. *This was it.*

Metal screamed against metal as the car struck the barrier, then, with a terrible rending noise, it gave way and the car somersaulted crazily, down the bank. Gouging a path through the soft turf, uprooting young trees and saplings in its path, it finally came to rest on its battered roof, engine roaring and wheels spinning.

The cable reached Davos half an hour after they had left for the airport. On the flight back to London they made their plans. Elaine would tell Paul she wanted a divorce. She didn't look forward to confronting him. One never knew with Paul. He could be so fiendishly devious when he chose. Patrick had promised to travel up to Edinburgh to see Cathy next weekend. He was sure the news would be welcome to her too, pretty certain that she already had a lover.

As they sat side by side on the plane, Elaine looked down at the billowing clouds below and wondered if this was the right moment to tell Patrick that Tricia was his child. She decided against it. She would wait until everything had been settled. The most difficult hurdle was yet to come as far as she was concerned. Telling Paul she was leaving him and his mother − then breaking the news to Grace. All that was going to take courage, and she must do it alone. When it was all behind her, then she would tell Patrick. It would be a special moment; something to look forward to. Then the three of them could look forward to being a complete family at last.

At Heathrow they decided to part company, saying goodbye at the carousel when they collected their luggage. Promising to keep in close touch, they clung to each other in a secluded corner for one final kiss.

Patrick whispered, 'It won't be for long, darling. Soon we'll be together for always.'

When she came through customs Elaine was surprised to see

Morgan waiting. She had assured him that she would make her own way home. One look at his face was enough to tell her that something was wrong. As he took her case she searched his eyes.

'Morgan, what is it?'

'You didn't get the cable?'

'Cable?' Her heart leapt. 'No. What is it? Is it Mum?'

'No.' He drew her to one side. Putting the case down he took both her hands. 'Your mother is with me. She's waiting in the car.'

'Here? But why?' Her heart almost stopped and she grasped his arm for support. 'My God, *Tricia!* It's Tricia, isn't it?'

'No, no, Elaine. Tricia's fine. Listen, it's Paul. He had an accident late yesterday afternoon.'

She stared at him. 'Accident? What kind of accident?'

'In the car. He was very badly injured. I'm afraid. He's in hospital – intensive care. They didn't expect him to live through the night, but he's still alive. I'll drive you straight there now.'

Grace was waiting in the back of the car. She put an arm around Elaine's shoulders. 'I had to come. I thought you might need me, darling. Morgan will drive us straight to the hospital.'

'What happened?' Elaine's numbed mind was only just beginning to assimilate the facts.

'He was driving – on the A1. He went over a bank. The police said the car must have gone out of control. He was lucky that someone saw it happen and managed to pull him clear before the car burst into flames. But I'm afraid he's in a bad way, dear.'

'What about his mother? Has someone told her?'

'Not yet. As it happens she had a bad fall herself yesterday. She seems to have fallen on the stairs and knocked herself unconscious. They took her to hospital, but apart from slight concussion and shock she's all right.' Grace looked into her daughter's face. 'Elaine darling, I think you should prepare yourself. I talked to the doctors this morning. They didn't expect Paul to survive, but he did. If he continues to live the chances are that he'll be a helpless invalid for the rest of his life. You're going to have to be very strong.

Mary lay in the end bed of the geriatric ward. She'd been furious when she found out they'd put her in with a lot of senile old people. When Elaine arrived she was fractious.

'They say Paul's been in an accident. I could have told him, rushing out of the house like that.' She poked at Elaine with a sharp forefinger. 'I knew something would happen if you went away.'

Elaine gently patted her arm. 'Where was he going at that time of day, Mother? What happened?'

Mary frowned. 'Can't remember. I'd been shopping. I was going to make the dinner. He just — rushed out.'

'How did you fall?'

Mary shook her head. 'I was going to get my slippers. I started to go upstairs. After that it's all a blank.' She grasped Elaine's arm with a grip like steel. 'You won't go away again, will you? They say I can go home tomorrow, but I can't manage the house any more. And Paul will need nursing by the sound of it.'

'No, Mother. I won't go away.'

The blue eyes peered into hers. They looked as sharp and keen as ever. 'How is he? Any improvement?'

'He's — progressing.'

The grip on her arm relaxed and after a moment or two Mary appeared to fall into a doze. Elaine sighed. The whole thing was like some terrible nightmare. She had learned from the doctor at the hospital this morning that Paul was paralysed. Paraplegic, he called it. It meant there was no feeling in his body from the waist down. There was a fear he might have suffered some brain damage too, but they wouldn't know for sure until the swelling went down and they could see the X-rays more clearly. There had been talk of a rehabilitation centre — having the house adapted to accommodate a wheelchair; of sending someone to teach her the special nursing care he would need. Slowly, little by little, she had realised that what they were talking about was the shattering of her dream — a life sentence.

She had telephone Patrick immediately afterwards. Trying hard to keep the tears out of her voice she had told him what had happened, and explained what it meant. He had been appalled, disbelieving — and unaccepting.

'Elaine, what are you saying? You can't stay after all that's happened. What about me? What about us?'

'I can't walk out now, Patrick. You must see that. And I can't lose the feeling that it would never have happened if I'd been here.'

'How can you say that? You can't possibly know.'

But she could. Deep inside was the memory of the things he'd said on the night he told her that he knew Tricia was not his child. She felt guilty and ashamed — feelings she could not share with Patrick now. Whatever Paul was — whatever he had said — she had still cheated him. How could she desert him now?

'How can you put him first?' Patrick was saying. 'Surely to God he'd be better off in hospital? For heaven's sake think what you're doing to us both. You can't mean it, Elaine.'

He had pleaded with her, on and on, urging her not to waste her life — not to throw away their chance of happiness like this. She had listened to his voice tearing at her heart until finally, unable to bear any more, she had very quietly hung up on him to weep her own silent, aching tears.

Mary watched Elaine through the slits of her half closed eyes. They had all swallowed her story about not being able to remember. No one need ever know. Paul was a fool; a weak, stupid fool. He never could do anything right. She'd always had to push him in the right direction, plan and scheme and cover up for him. God only knew where he'd be if it wasn't for her — mixed up in some unsavoury scandal, most likely; a social outcast without a job. But if Elaine ever found out the truth about what had happened that afternoon, she wouldn't stay. Who could expect her to? And what would they do then?

In her mind she went over the sequence of events again. She'd regained consciousness by the time the ambulance man came and found her. He said someone had telephoned to say there'd been a 'fatal accident'. In his own panic-stricken way, Paul must have thought he'd killed her and rushed off typically to take the coward's way out — to do away with himself. And he hadn't even managed to make a good job of that. Still, it wasn't her problem any more. Elaine would take care of them both now. After all, it was her fault in a way, wasn't it? If she hadn't gone selfishly swanning off to Switzerland none of it would have happened.

Chapter Twenty

1987

As usual Harry had arrived early at the rehearsal theatre in Camden Town. Climbing the steps at the side of the stage he took the dust sheet off the piano and opened the lid. Then he sat down and ran his fingers experimentally over the keys. He pursed his lips. It could do with tuning. He'd mentioned it the last time he was here but they never seemed to take any notice. He flexed his fingers, wincing slightly and trying to ignore the twinges of pain in the joints. Arthritis — the dread of every musician. If he refused to acknowledge it, kept on playing and exercising his fingers, perhaps it would go away.

As he let his hands drift up and down the keyboard he thought of the dreams he had once had. Concert pianist, solo entertainer ... He smiled. Deep inside he'd always known he'd never reach those heights. It wasn't that he wasn't good, more that he'd never had the necessary drive. A good jobbing musician, that's what he'd always been. When he was with Stella, in her heyday, there had been a little reflected limelight. That had been the nearest he had ever come to fame. It had touched him like she had, with the transitory warmth and colour of a flame. And with her it had died. Without realising it he had begun to play one of her songs, 'Where Has Our Love Gone?' Poor Stella. He still missed her.

The pain in his fingers gradually eased and he began to warm up. He took off his jacket and hitched up his shirt sleeves, securing them with the expanding arm bands he always wore. The caretaker greeted him cheerily as he walked down the centre aisle, his cockney voice echoing slightly in the empty theatre:

'Mornin', Mr Wendover. Fancy a nice cuppa coffee?'

'Thanks very much, Jack. I'd love one.'

The little man climbed on to the stage and poured the coffee from a flask, grinning at Harry as he put the plastic mug on top of the piano. ''ow many 'opefuls this mornin' then?'

'About a dozen, I think. Mr Crichton will be here soon. Got any more of that coffee for him?'

Jack winked. 'I'll nip round the caff in a bit and get a refill. Can't 'ave 'is lordship goin' without, can we?'

'Certainly can't.'

Max Crichton, the conductor of the New World Youth Orchestra, arrived ten minutes later, filling the dingy little auditorium immediately with his luminous presence. Max was a young conductor who Harry admired very much. At twenty-nine he was already a well-known and respected name in the music world; a professional to his fingertips. But Harry knew all too well that professionalism wasn't enough in the entertainment world. You needed dynamism — something he now recognised that he had never had. You needed a powerful personality and charisma, that elusive, magic quality that Max Crichton had in abundance.

He stood at the orchestra rail, looking up at Harry with a smile on his handsome dark-bearded face. He wore his favourite clothes, cord trousers and a leather blouson over a rollneck sweater.

'Good morning, Harry. I'm glad to see they've allocated you. Looks as though we've got a heavy morning ahead of us. I hope you're feeling strong.'

Harry grinned back. 'When there's a vacancy to work with you, there's always a rush. And the standard's usually high. I like playing for your auditions. It's nice to see youngsters getting on.'

It seemed no time at all to Harry since he was a young hopeful himself, burning with brash confidence and youthful enthusiasm. Sometimes he wondered where the years had gone — what had happened to his life since the days when he had played in the pit orchestras of variety theatres and travelled up and down the country with dance bands.

A sudden flurry of activity at the back of the auditorium told him that the candidates were beginning to arrive. He stood up and took the list of names from Max, preparing to meet them.

Two hours later they were coming to the end of the auditions. One after the other, the young violinists had climbed on to the stage to stand beside him and play a piece of their own choice, followed by the set piece, chosen by Max Crichton. The standard had been average, ranging from the merely competent to the technically accomplished, but Harry knew from the look on Max's face as he sat there in the front row that none of them quite came up to his

298

high standards. 'People expect so little of youth, especially today,' he'd said to Harry once. 'I want to show them that we have the best young musicians in the world. Nothing but the best will do for us.'

They were just about to conclude the morning session when there was a commotion at the back of the hall. Max had come up on to the stage and had begun to speak. He paused, frowning as the sound of raised voices cut through his speech. Shading his eyes he peered into the gloom at the back of the theatre, trying to see who was causing the fracas.

'Is there anything wrong back there?'

The caretaker appeared, his chirpy face bristling with indignation. 'Young woman 'ere, sir — says she wants to audition. I've told 'er she's too late and you're done for the mornin' but she won't 'ave none of it.'

Max's dark eyes twinkled with amusement. 'It's all right, Jack. Let her come in.'

Everyone turned to see a slender girl with straight blonde hair step through the doors at the back of the auditorium. She looked cool, except for the light of defiance in her bright blue eyes which was directed straight at Jack.

'I'm sorry I'm late, Mr Crichton,' she called out to Max in a cool, clear voice. 'There was some sort of dispute on the Underground and I got held up.'

'That's quite all right, Miss ...' Max consulted his list.

'Kingston. Patricia Kingston.' The girl had reached the front row and stood staring straight up into his eyes with her direct blue gaze. She seemed to exude confidence and her presence was such that it was all he could do to stop himself from moving instinctively towards her.

'Well, now that you *are* here, I take it you'd like to play for us?'

'Certainly.' She removed her scuffed denim jacket. Underneath, she wore faded jeans and a plain white tee shirt. Her figure was slender, almost as straight as a boy's, but her arms were sinuous; the hands strong with long sensitive fingers. She took the violin and bow from its case, walked purposefully up the steps on to the stage and passed Harry her music. Then she tucked the instrument under her chin and tightened her bow.

'I'll take it from there to there,' she said to Harry, pointing with her bow to the numbers on the page. He was impressed by her cool manner — and her choice; part of the second movement of the Brahms concerto. That took nerve. He smiled and gave her an

299

A on the piano, wishing it could have been truer. She tuned her instrument briefly, then, bow poised, nodded her readiness.

Harry had heard more than a dozen violinists that morning. He had heard those whose technique was more accomplished, those who had more polish and control. But this girl had something that all the others lacked. She had style and inspiration. Her playing had a life and a spirit he had heard only rarely. She loved her music and her instrument and it showed. Her compellingly blue eyes shining and her strong young face rapt, she brought something of her own character to the music. She drew light and shade from the piece; brought out all the fire, the colour, the very *soul* of the music. She made all the other violinists he had heard that morning sound mechanical and dull.

The audition piece that Max had set was designed to show up all the candidates' weaknesses, but it gave her no problems. Her sight reading was faultless and she tackled the tricky harmonics and double stopping with a panache that had Harry hiding a smile of triumph. As they came to the end of the piece he felt a little thrill of pleasure. If Max Crichton had any sense at all he would snap this girl up. She was a find, the best they had heard today – the best in months. He glanced across at the conductor's face. It wore the enigmatic expression Harry knew so well; the one he adopted when he didn't want to give away his true feelings.

'Thank you, Miss Kingston,' he said brusquely, getting to his feet. She watched expectantly as he turned to the other candidates. 'And thank you everyone. You'll all be hearing from me quite soon. Thank you all very much for attending.'

They began to drift away in ones and twos, but Harry noticed that the girl remained on stage, in no hurry to put away her violin. He caught her eye and they smiled at each other.

'Have you come far, Miss – er ...'

'Tricia,' she said with a sudden disarming grin. 'No. I share a flat in Chelsea – well, Fulham really – with a friend who's a drama student. My real home is in East Anglia.'

'A nice part of the world. You're lucky.'

'I don't go there very often. Do you know it?'

'Not well. But I have been there – once.'

She glanced round and noted with satisfaction that all the other candidates had gone. Tossing back the straight blonde hair that hung to her shoulders, she looked straight at Max. 'Well, Mr Crichton, how did I do?'

He was clearly taken aback and Harry watched his reaction with amusement. Max Crichton was used to being treated with awe and reverence by young musicians, especially the female ones. This girl's naive, slightly brash approach clearly threw him.

'Surely you heard what I said – I'll be in touch.'

'Oh. But can't you give me some idea?'

Max turned on her with the blistering stare he reserved for those who overstepped the mark. 'I didn't comment on the other performances I heard this morning. What makes you think that I should make an exception in your case?' He raised an arrogant eyebrow at her in a way that usually reduced young musicians to a pile of ashes. 'You couldn't even manage to get yourself here on time.'

'That wasn't my fault,' she said indignantly. 'I told you, there was a strike on the Underground.'

'Then you should have caught a bus.' Max picked up his blouson and threw it carelessly over his shoulder. 'I'll be in touch.' Already he was walking away.

'Don't call us, we'll call you' she muttered under her breath, putting a defiant face behind his back, but Harry thought he detected a slight quiver in her voice. She wasn't quite as tough as she would like people to think. He watched, noting the droop of her shoulders as she carefully put away her instrument and pulled on the denim jacket. Pulling her silky, child-like hair free of its collar, she suddenly looked very young and vulnerable.

'I'm going for a coffee. Would you like one?' he asked her impulsively.

She looked up at him with the sunny smile of a twelve-year-old. 'Oh, yes please.'

'Good.' Harry closed the piano and began to replace the dust cover. She put down her violin case and moved to give him a hand. 'There's a McDonald's just across the road,' he told her. 'And I don't know about you but I could murder a Big Mac too.'

It was too early for the lunchtime rush and Tricia found them a table in a quiet corner while Harry collected coffee and burgers and brought them across. He found her looking pensive.

'What's up?' he asked as he unloaded the tray.

Her shoulders drooped. 'I blew it, didn't I? It isn't professional to ask. I knew that, but I've wanted to play with the New World ever since I first started at the Guildhall. It means a lot to me.'

'You don't look old enough to have completed a course at the Guildhall,' he told her.

'I'm not. I'm nineteen. I dropped out in the middle of my second year. I didn't like all the rules, and frankly I didn't feel I was learning

301

much. Besides, they didn't approve of my playing with a jazz group in my spare time.'

He laughed. 'No. I don't suppose they would.'

She stirred her coffee reflectively. 'It was so bigotted and stupid. Other people did jobs to augment their grants. It was no different really.' She grinned her sudden, impish grin. 'And a damned sight more fun than waitressing in some grotty restaurant and getting my bum pinched black and blue by foreign tourists.'

Harry laughed. 'You play jazz violin then?'

'No. Tenor sax,' she said, taking a bite of her burger. 'With a group that plays in a little club in Greek Street. I love it. They say girls don't have enough wind to be really good, but I reckon I'm as good as most. It pays the rent okay, but the violin's my real love.'

'I could certainly tell that.'

'Could you?' She leaned forward eagerly. 'What do you think my chances are, Mr ...'

'Harry — just call me Harry. I thought you were good — very good.'

'Did you really?'

'Yes. But that's only my opinion, mind. It's Crichton's that matters.'

Her smile vanished and she nodded. 'No doubt he thought I was pushy and rude.'

'Well, you need plenty of push to get on nowadays. No good hiding your light — waiting around to be discovered. You've got to get out there and sock it to 'em.' He smiled. 'But I'm sure I don't have to tell you that. How long have you been playing?'

'About as long as I can remember,' she told him. 'My mother always regretted not taking up music herself, so she got me at it at an early age.'

'Good for her. What about your father — is he musical?'

She shook her head. 'Not at all. He was a headmaster till he was badly injured in an accident. He's paraplegic now. In a wheelchair.'

'I see. I'm sorry. That must make life tough for your mother.'

She shrugged. 'It did at first. She and a friend run a complete wedding service called "Happy Ever After". They'd only just started it at the time and at first she thought she'd have to give it up. But luckily my grandmother stepped in and helped out till she was able to get organised. My mother designs these glamorous wedding gowns and her friend does the catering. They've done really well — opened several branches in other towns now.'

302

Harry smiled. 'You must be very proud of her.'

'Oh, I am.' Tricia stirred her coffee thoughtfully. 'The only thing is, she doesn't seem to have much time for . . .'

'For you?'

She looked up at him. 'That's about it.'

'Is that why you live in London?'

'Partly, but not just that. Somehow I've never really felt I fitted in at home. Maybe it's because I went away to boarding school when I was seven. Then on to the Guildhall.' She pushed the silky hair behind her ears. 'It isn't their fault. What with Dad's accident and Mum's work, they haven't had much time to spare for me. I go home at Christmas and every now and again for a weekend, but . . .' She shrugged. 'You know how it is.'

He nodded. 'I know.'

'What about you?' she asked, looking up at him with her level blue gaze. 'Do you have a family?'

'No. There's just me.'

'Oh. Don't you mind that?'

'Sometimes,' He smiled at her. 'But I'm lucky. I enjoy my work.'

She regarded him. He was really quite old − sixty or more. People of his age had usually retired. 'Do you do this all the time,' she asked. 'Play for auditions?'

'I do a bit of everything; accompanying, deputising − you know. I'm freelance − my own boss.' He laughed. 'Have fingers − will travel, weddings and barmitzvah's a speciality.'

She laughed with him. 'Sounds like fun. So where do you find all these interesting jobs?'

'My agent. I'm with Joan Sefton in Old Bond Street. I've been with her a long time now and she knows the kind of jobs I like.'

'I see. So what do you think my chances are, Harry?'

'Pretty good, I'd say. But you'll just have to wait patiently. It's a pity you ducked out of college.'

'Yeah. I suppose that'll be a black mark against me,' she said, pulling a face. 'What's he really like, Max C? He looks as though he could be a bit of a pain to work for.'

'He's tough, but he's a good conductor; he knows what he wants and how to get it − with or without making friends along the way. I can promise you one thing − working for Max wouldn't be dull. But underneath it all he's a nice guy.'

She smiled wistfully. 'He sounds fantastic. Bet I never have the luck to land a job with him though. How old is he? It's hard to guess under all that hair.'

Harry laughed. 'Well, all members of the NW have to be under thirty,' he told her. 'And that includes the conductor.'

He had already decided that he'd have a word with Max himself on her behalf if he got the chance. He'd taken a real shine to Patricia Kingston and he reckoned she deserved a chance to show what she could do.

His chance to speak up for Tricia presented itself sooner than he'd imagined. He was working at the BBC two days later when he ran into Max in the canteen. They were both alone and automatically shared a table for lunch. Max had been recording a concert. He wore jeans and a plaid shirt, the sleeves rolled up above the elbow. His hair was rumpled where he had carelessly pulled off his headphones and he looked more like a lumberjack than an orchestral conductor.

Harry asked him: 'What did you think of the batch of young violinists we auditioned the day before yesterday?'

'Nothing special,' Max said. 'I suppose I might fill the two vacancies in the second violin section. But what I really want is a good leader. Donald Latimer is leaving at the end of the year.'

'How about the blonde girl — the one who came late?' Harry asked. 'I thought she had talent.'

Max's eyes flickered with interest for a moment, but he shook his head. 'Talent, yes, but too much fire. No discipline.'

Harry grinned. 'I'm sure you wouldn't find that a problem. Surely you could soon lick her into shape?'

'I'm not looking for the kind of leader I have to lick into shape. I want one who'll take all that kind of thing off my shoulders for me.'

'Yes, I see your point,' Harry said thoughtfully. 'So why not promote someone and give Miss Kingston a try out in the seconds.'

Max frowned. 'It's just this feeling I have about her. She seems like trouble to me. Too damned confident.'

'That's just bravado,' Harry said. 'Look, I took her for a coffee after the auditions. She's just an insecure kid like we all were once. But she's got guts and determination, and she's got her heart set on working with the NWYO. If you don't give her a job, someone else will. And I have this gut feeling about her. Something tells me she's going to make a name for herself.' He said no more. What Tricia Kingston had told him about her background and her penchant for jazz playing was confidential. If she wanted anyone else to know it was up to her to tell them.

Max was looking at him curiously. 'I don't think I've ever heard you so enthusiastic, Harry.'

He shrugged. 'It's just a hunch. As I said: a gut feeling. I may not have made much of a career for myself, but I've been in the business a hell of a long time and I think I can spot a natural.'

But Max still looked doubtful. 'I can't see her taking kindly to the discipline of playing with an orchestra,' he said. 'I may be wrong but she seemed to have too much individuality.'

'She's soloist material, you mean?'

Max pulled a face. 'That's what *she* thinks, no doubt. Miss Kingston has a lot to learn first though. And I'm not sure I want the hassle of teaching her.'

Harry was thoughtful. There was a lot in what Max said. The girl had walked out on her course. She was certainly a rebel. And for all her innocent openness, she promised to be as stubborn and uncompromising as Max when it came to getting her own way.

The conductor was looking at him with a hint of amusement in his dark eyes 'But you think I should give the girl a chance, don't you?'

Harry decided to put his money where his mouth was. 'Yes, I do.'

Max chuckled. 'Okay. If I find I can't handle her, I'll send for you, shall I?'

'Handle her — *you*?' Harry looked at the large young man sitting opposite. With his powerful personality and dark good looks he exuded authority despite his lack of years. Harry had seen strong men quail before the force of his biting sarcasm. Yet here he was, unsure of whether he could handle a slip of a teenage girl. Patricia Kingston must have even more charisma than he had given her credit for.

When Paul first came home from the rehabilitation centre he had been paralysed from the waist down and had no use of his right arm. As result of the slight brain damage he had sustained, his speech was also impaired.

At first Elaine had been able to do little more than look after his basic needs. As the months went by the ground floor of Langmere Lodge had been adapted for his use and she had learned all the necessary nursing skills from the resident nurse who came for the first few weeks of his homecoming. If she had not been so desperately busy she would have been deeply unhappy. But at the end of each day she had been so exhausted that sleep had overtaken her almost before she'd had time to fall into bed. Thoughts of

Patrick were never out of her mind. Letting him go had been the hardest and most painful thing she had ever had to do. Thinking of him, and of their brief, ecstatic time together in Switzerland, hurt unbearably and the hurt grew no less as the months passed. The only way to get through the pain was work. Fortunately there was no shortage of that.

As time passed things gradually improved. With physio and speech therapy Paul regained the partial use of his arm and his speech improved, so that at least the frustration of not being able to communicate his needs was eased and his temper improved.

At 'Happy Ever After' Grace stepped in to fill the breach, falling naturally into the job as though it had been made for her. Elaine was obliged to watch with a mixture of feelings as the business she and Alison had started with such enthusiasm, gathered momentum and went from strength to strength without her.

Gradually, little by little, they were able to expand and employ more staff. Alison's catering became popular and with the help of her mother and a young helper she catered for other functions besides weddings, to help swell the business's finances.

A year passed, then another, and things grew a little easier for Elaine at home. She found she was able to design exclusive dresses for HEA again. Now they could afford outworkers for the making up. Generally she worked late at night, when Paul had gone to bed. It was wonderful therapy for her; an oasis in her endless round of caring for a man whose every word and look accused and reproached her; who deeply resented his helplessness and reliance on her. He blamed himself relentlessly every day of his life for not succeeding in his attempt to end his life that day in the car. The only good thing about it was that his mother remembered nothing of what had happened on that terrible afternoon.

Mary had volunteered to move into a private home for the elderly soon after Paul's accident, though the reason had never been altogether clear to Elaine. She came to visit her son once a week, but the two would sit together over tea and biscuits, hardly saying a word to each other. Sometimes Elaine wondered why she came at all. She often asked herself just what had happened that day. But Mary doggedly insisted that she remembered nothing.

An added difficulty for Elaine was that Paul was always extra fractious and agitated when Tricia was in the house. And although Elaine longed to see more of her daughter, she had to admit that the girl's presence only made life harder for everyone. It was clearly no fun for her either. In trying to explain to her, Elaine blamed Paul's attitude on his illness, but she guessed that he saw in the girl the root cause of all his misfortune.

Four years after its initiation, 'Happy Ever After' had become a registered company with a board of directors that included Grace and Morgan, who had put up the money for their expansion. 'You filled a gap in the market at the right time,' he told them. 'You deserve to succeed. I'll back you all the way.' With his help three provincial branches had been successfully launched and were flourishing. Elaine allowed her mother to persuade her to employ a full-time nurse for Paul so that she could go back into the business.

'I'm not getting any younger,' she'd argued. 'For some years now Morgan has been pressing me to join him in London, retire and enjoy myself. I might just take him up on it while I'm still able to enjoy that kind of life. And besides . . .' She looked at the tiny lines of strain and weariness round Elaine's eyes, the streaks of premature grey in her hair. 'It's high time you did something you really want to do again. I know Paul isn't the easiest of patients and you deserve more out of life than you're getting.'

Soon after that Josh Grey had moved in to take up residence in the specially converted flat on the second floor at Langmere Lodge. Josh was a young West Indian State Registered nurse who specialised in paraplegic cases. He'd had special training in the field and had worked at Stoke Manderville until he had decided to take up private nursing. Fortunately Paul took to him on sight and right from the first day Josh seemed to be able to get him to cooperate in a way that Elaine never had. It was like having a great weight removed from her shoulders. At last she was able to go back to work full time in the smart new office block close to the town centre that now housed the HEA complex. As well as an office and board room on the first floor of the building, they had their own showroom and shop window at street level, where Elaine's gowns and other bridal wear could be displayed. There was also a comfortably furnished room where prospective brides and their mothers could view on video some of the weddings HEA had coordinated in the past. They prided themselves on organising down to the smallest detail, any kind of wedding, from the quietest family affair to the most lavish society occasion.

Every week without fail, however busy she was, Elaine managed somehow to visit Zoe. She was Elaine's only link with Patrick — the one and only person who fully understood what Elaine had given up to nurse Paul. From Zoe she learned that Patrick was divorced and lived alone. That he had given up the hated job in advertising to take a teaching post at a London school of art where he was now the Principal. His promotion had come only recently and as Zoe gave her the news over coffee in her studio, she remarked wryly that if her son had been completely happy he would probably not be the successful man he was today.

'It's strange, the way our emotional state can alter the whole course of our life,' she said reflectively as they sat over their tea . . .

'Sometimes I wonder if it's good for us to be completely happy. It makes us lazy and complacent.' She laughed. 'Look at Tom, for instance, still stuck in the same school he was in twelve years ago, just because he's so besotted with his wife and kids.' She shook her head. 'You should see him with those girls of his. Who would ever have imagined Tom living happily in a Midland suburb with a houseful of kids and a mortgage round his neck? She laughed.

Six years ago Tom had fallen in love with and married a pretty young gym mistress who taught at the same school, and together they had plunged headlong into domesticity by producing twin daughters within a year of their wedding.

Red still had his antique shop. Luckily for him the building had just escaped the redevelopment. Zoe insisted that they would both continue to work till — as she put it — they dropped in their tracks. The carefree parties they loved to give had settled into more sedate affairs and puppet plays in the little barn theatre were now a rarity, neither Patrick nor Tom being on hand to help.

'Everything's changing,' Zoe said with a sigh. 'We're all getting older. Even Cambridge itself has changed, what with all the redevelopment and the new Grafton shopping centre. I hate to see the character of the place fading. I have this nightmare vision of an England where every town looks alike; all concrete and glass and those horrid bricks, the colour of dried blood.'

'That will never happen,' Elaine said. 'Not here at least. The colleges will always be here; the river and the backs and the little streets with their cosmopolitan mix of people. And Parker's Piece and Midsummer Common will never be allowed to turn into housing estates.'

'I sincerely hope you're right.' Zoe looked at Elaine with her sudden disconcertingly direct look. 'What would have happened, I wonder, if Paul hadn't had his accident?'

'Patrick and I would have been married,' Elaine said quietly. 'Perhaps we would have had a family of our own by now.'

Zoe laid a hand on her arm. 'He'll never stop loving you, make no mistake about that. Patrick had never confided his private feelings to me until the day you sent him away. It completely shattered him, you know. Don't you think that even now you could . . .?'

'No.' Elaine drew her arm away. 'It's too late. We had our chance. I would have died for Patrick once, but he wasn't ready. He didn't want me then and I married Paul. Now my duty lies with him. I can't walk out on him and leave him helpless.' She looked appealingly at Zoe. 'Well can I?'

'Are you asking me or telling me?' Zoe shook her head. 'Sometimes I think that you're punishing yourself for something — punishing Patrick too. Don't you think you've both paid enough penance? I'm sure that Paul wouldn't blame you for keeping in touch with Patrick. Even if you can't marry you could see each other; at least give each other a little comfort. What's to stop you?'

Elaine stood up, her cheeks pink. 'It's time I was going,' she said, pulling on her coat.

'Time you were ducking out, you mean.'

Elaine looked thoughtfully at Zoe for a moment, then she sat down again. 'Oh, Zoe. Look, I'll try to explain how I feel,' she said. 'I should never have married Paul. I didn't make him happy. We never really got along. Now is my chance to make it up to him. Caring for him is the least I can do to pay for the way I deceived him.'

'Deceived him?' Zoe's sharp eyes pierced hers.

'Into thinking I loved him,' Elaine said quietly. 'Because I never have.' She got to her feet. Once again she'd almost said too much. Zoe was so perceptive. 'I must go,' she said abruptly.

Zoe reached out to grasp Elaine's arm. 'Listen, don't you feel you owe Patrick something too? After all, he loves you. Paul just despises you. You've told me that often enough.'

Slowly Elaine sank down in her chair again. 'If you only knew what it cost me to say goodbye to him. When we were together in Switzerland I somehow knew it was all too good to be true. And I was right. I couldn't offer him anything, Zoe. It wouldn't be fair. It's better that he forgets all about me.'

'You know he'll never forget. A few days together now and again would be better than nothing. Look, you could afford to get a housekeeper for Paul now. He had his resident nurse — everything he needs. Which is more than can be said for Patrick, or for you. Are you going to make him pay for the rest of his life for not knowing what he wanted when you were both scarcely more than kids?' She paused to peer into Elaine's eyes. 'And what about Tricia?'

Elaine shook her head. 'What do you mean?'

'What kind of home life does she have? If you're not careful you'll lose her, Elaine. Don't leave it any longer. The world is changing so fast. One day, quite suddenly, it could be too late. You'd never forgive yourself.' She laid a hand on Elaine's arm and smiled softly. 'I want so much to see you both happy before I die.'

Elaine stood up. She'd never seen Zoe in this mood before and she didn't know quite how to react. 'I — I'll think about it. I promise. Look, I'm sorry, Zoe, but it's getting late. I really must be going now,' she said.

'Please remember what I've said.'

'I will.' On a sudden impulse she bent and dropped a kiss on the older woman's cheek. 'And thanks.'

'What on earth for?' Suddenly the anxiety left Zoe's face and she laughed. 'I should have been your mother-in-law if I hadn't been done out of it. I might as well boss you about a bit.'

Tricia was beginning to worry. So far the kindly audition pianist who had bought her a burger and let her talk about herself, was the only person she had told about leaving the Guildhall School of Music. She'd hoped to get a job first and then break the news to her mother. But she'd been applying and auditioning for almost a month now and so far, nothing. Her bank balance was rapidly diminishing. Soon she would have to go home and face the music. She didn't look forward to that at all. She was poring over the Sits Vac column in the paper the evening that her grandmother rang.

'Hello, darling. How are you?'

'Granny Grace, lovely to hear you. I'm fine. What can I do for you?'

'I'm coming up to Town for a few days and I wondered if you could put me up?'

Tricia frowned. 'Here at the flat?'

'Is it inconvenient?'

'No, I'd love to have you, and as it happens Tracey will be away. But it's not much like Uncle Morgan's posh penthouse in Mayfair,' Tricia said doubtfully. Had it not been for the fact that the tiny mews flat she shared belonged to Tracey's parents, the girls could never have afforded the rent. As it was they were happy to have the place occupied when they weren't using it, and only charged a minimal rent.

'It'll be fine,' Grace said. 'I wouldn't ask only I particularly want to come tomorrow. Anything will do, darling,' Grace said into the ensuing pause. 'A sleeping bag on the floor — anything.'

Tricia laughed. 'I think I can manage better than that. With Tracey away we'll have the place to ourselves.'

'That sounds lovely. I'm coming up on the two o'clock train, so I'll see you about half-past.'

'I'm playing at the club tomorrow evening, but you can come with me if you like,' Tricia said mischievously.

'We-ell . . .'

'Don't worry. I'm only kidding. See you tomorrow.' Tricia laughed as she replaced the receiver. The thought of Granny Grace in one of her immaculate designer outfits, sitting there in the smoke-filled atmosphere of the Lizard Club, among the wild hairdo's and way-out clothes, drinking and listening to jazz, was an image to savour. Not that Gran wouldn't go there if she took it into her head that it might be useful to her. She might be in her fifties but she was still game for any new experience, especially where business was concerned.

On the following afternoon Tricia was at King's Cross to meet the two o'clock train. She stood at the barrier waiting as her grandmother walked up the platform. Grace wore a black coat with a wide fur collar high-heeled shoes and sheer black stockings, and Tricia reflected that her Gran still had the sexiest pair of legs she'd ever seen.

When she saw Tricia waiting, Grace's eyes lit up. 'Darling, how sweet of you to meet me. But shouldn't you be at college?'

'It's a long story. I'll tell you later.' Tricia linked her arm through her grandmother's. 'We're going to have such fun this weekend, catching up with all the gossip, but first shall we go and have tea and lashings of squishy cream cakes?'

They took the Underground to Oxford Circus and had tea at John Lewis's. Over it Grace reminded her: 'You were going to tell me something about college.'

Tricia met her grandmother's eyes across the table. 'As a matter of fact, Gran, I've left the Guildhall.'

Grace's face fell. 'Oh, *Tricia*. Have you told your mother?'

'No. I was sort of hoping you might help me out with that.'

'I thought you were so happy there.'

'Not really. Look, Gran, I've been at a school of some sort or other since before I was eight. That's eleven years. I've had rules and regulations up to here. I want to be my own woman now – live my own life.'

'Yes, but without qualifying . . .' Grace looked at her grand-daughter. It seemed no time at all since she was starting her first music lessons. Since the child first went away to school, and especially since Paul's accident, she had tried to do what she could for her. The poor child had had hardly any real home life at all. It was hardly surprising that she wanted to strike out on her own.

'I wish you'd have stopped to talk it over before taking a step like that. You know you can always talk to me if there's anything worrying you, don't you darling?'

'Of course I do, Gran. But this was something I felt I had to do for myself. To tell the truth, I thought I'd get a job fairly easily. Then I could have stayed on up here with Tracey in the flat and told Mum when I was settled.'

'But the jobs aren't as easy to come by as you thought?'

'No. And what I earn at the club doesn't pay my way. I did manage to get an audition for the New World Youth Orchestra last week, but everything went wrong that morning. I overslept — then there was a strike on the Underground and I arrived late.'

'*Too* late?'

'I did get to play. But Max Crichton, the conductor, didn't seem very impressed. I haven't heard from him anyway.'

'Well, all I can say is, he must be stone deaf if he didn't snap you up on the spot.'

'You wouldn't be prejudiced by any chance?' Tricia laughed. 'Oh, Gran, it *is* good to see you.' Her smile faded. 'I've decided to give it one more week. After that my money will have run out. I can't afford to stay in London on what I get from the DHSS.'

'Well, if I can help ...'

'No,' Tricia said firmly. 'I'll make it on my own some way or other, even if I have to get a job in a shop or something. I don't want to have to come home and admit defeat.'

'No one would blame you.'

'Dad would. He's always disapproved of me.'

'I'm sure that's not true.'

'Oh, yes, it is. Look, Gran ...' Tricia looked up. 'If the worst comes to the worst, I suppose I couldn't come and stay with you?'

Grace bit her lip. 'Oh, darling. Normally of course you'd have been welcome. But the truth is, I've decided to retire and move up here. Uncle Morgan has always wanted me to come and share his flat and now I've made up my mind to accept his offer.' She smiled. 'I haven't said so to your mother, but I want to get out from under her feet — hand over the reins. I don't think she'll ever feel free to make her own decisions while I'm around. That's why I'm here this weekend. I'm going to surprise Morgan.'

Tricia frowned. 'You're opting out of HEA?'

Grace shook her head. 'Oh, no. I shall keep my seat on the board.

312

But I can always travel up for meetings. I shall be putting the house up for sale next week.'

'Oh, I see.' Tricia tried hard to keep her smile from slipping. 'Well, not to worry. I might get the next job I apply for. You never know what's round the corner, do you?'

The long black Alison Moyet-style dress that Tricia wore to play with the jazz group at the Lizard caused Grace's jaw to drop in dismay.

'Why do all the young people one meets nowadays have to make themselves look so dreary?' she wailed. 'I see it wherever I look. If it isn't scruffy denim with holes in the knees, it's bedraggled weeds one would hesitate to wear to a funeral.'

Tricia laughed as she pulled on her coat. 'I thought I looked rather good,' she said. 'What do you think I should wear, Gran?' She held up her hand, her eyes dancing. 'Don't tell me − pale pink net with sequins. And if I gave you half a chance you'd have my hair in ringlets too.'

Grace bridled. 'Rubbish! I hope I have better taste than that. A black skirt − yes, fine. But with a pretty Laura Ashley blouse or something. You're only young once, Tricia. Do try to make the most of it.'

Tricia kissed her grandmother indulgently. 'Okay, I'll bear it in mind. But now I'll have to go or I'll be late.'

'There's no hurry, I'll drop you off,' Grace said decisively, picking up her own coat. 'I've just rung for a minicab to take me to Morgan's. I hate the idea of you travelling on the Underground at night, and Soho isn't too far out of the way.' She opened her bag. 'Now, if I give you the fare, will you promise to take a cab home later?'

'Oh, all right, Gran, but I don't know what you think I do when you're not here.'

'Well, tonight I *am* here.'

'And I bet you'll be waiting up for me with cocoa when I get home.'

Grace laughed. 'Naturally I will. Isn't that what grandmothers are for?'

Chapter Twenty-One

Tricia had seen the party arrive at about half-past eleven. There were six of them, three couples. They looked a little out of place in the shabby gloom of the Lizard in their dinner jackets and elegant evening dress, but they seemed to be enjoying themselves for all that. When she had a few bars rest she peered through the smoke-laden atmosphere at them as they sat there at their corner table. Max Crichton looked slightly out of character in a dinner jacket. Apart from when he was conducting at formal concerts, his usual mode of dress was casual to the point of scruffiness. His companion was very attractive, slightly gipsyish-looking woman. Her glossy black hair was caught back with a diamante clip and she wore a garnet-red dress that left her shoulders bare and showed off her flawless olive complexion. Was she his wife, Tricia speculated, or just the latest girlfriend? They certainly looked very close.

She edged her chair in a bit, hoping Max hadn't seen her. Then she asked herself if it was really necessary. he probably wouldn't recognise or even remember her. By the look of relaxed enjoyment on his face, she doubted whether he'd bother to acknowledge her even if he did.

Ever since she first saw a photograph of Max Crichton in a magazine three years ago, she had wanted to meet him. Since then she had eagerly devoured every article ever written about him; never missed one of his concerts, either live or on TV and avidly watched his every appearance on chat shows and art magazine programmes. Tracey teased her and called her a 'classical groupie'. But Tricia refused to let her friend's teasing put her off. To her, Max epitomised music as she herself had always perceived it: exciting and open to a million different interpretations. He had original and innovative ideas that struck a deep chord within her, and he put the individual stamp of his own personality on everything he touched. Max Crichton brought a breath of fresh air to music many young people had previously seen as stuffy and boring. He had even had two of his albums in the charts — something no other classical conductor had achieved.

She longed to work for him, hoping that some of his charisma would rub off on her. In her dreams she saw herself embarking on long earnest discussions with him. But that was just a fantasy — an indulgence she only allowed herself late at night when she was alone with the lights out.

So preoccupied was she with thoughts of Max that she almost missed her solo. But as she looked up from the music after her five bars, she saw that he was watching. He had stopped talking to his companion and was staring intently at her. Her heart sank, and she was grateful for the gloom, feeling the hot colour flood her cheeks. If she'd had any chance at all of impressing him at the audition, she'd have lost it after this.

It was as the group were preparing to leave the stand to take their break that she turned and found herself looking straight into the penetrating brown eyes.

'I know you, don't I? Didn't you audition for me a couple of weeks ago?'

'That's right. Patricia Kingston.'

He nodded, smiling to himself. 'I thought so. Do you work here permanently?'

She shook her head. 'It's just a part-time job to help out my grant — two nights a week.'

'I see.' He smiled suddenly, completely disarming her. 'Come and have a drink.'

'Oh, thank you.'

He didn't take her back to his table but led her across to the bar. 'What will you have — er — Pat, is it?'

'Tricia. A Perrier, please.'

'You don't drink?'

'Not alcohol. I don't like the taste — or the way it blunts the senses.'

He laughed aloud. 'Good for you. Not many people would share your opinion.' He sat on one of the stools and indicated that she should do the same. 'I've been meaning to get in touch with you.'

Her heart leapt, but she managed to keep her expression cool. 'Really? Why?'

He looked surprised. 'Well, you did audition for me.'

She sipped at her Perrier, resisting the urge to roll the cold glass against her burning cheek. He probably felt guilty about not telling

315

her he'd filled the vacancies. 'That's all right. I might be leaving London soon — going home to Cambridge.' Instantly she was appalled. What on earth had made her say that?

'I see. That's a pity. Any particular reason?'

She looked at him. She'd better come clean. He'd have to know anyway. 'I opted out of my course at the Guildhall,' she said. 'Left in the middle of term.'

He looked at her enquiringly. 'A row?'

She shook her head. 'Call it impatience if you like. I didn't feel I was getting anywhere. Well, I can't afford to stay in London any longer on what I earn here, so I'll have to go home.'

'Supposing you got a job though?'

She caught her breath. 'Oh, well, yes of course — that would make all the difference.'

'I'd like you to audition for me again,' he said.

Her eyes snapped up to meet his. 'Why? I've already auditioned. If I wasn't any good the first time ...'

'Woaah ...' He held up his hand. 'Who said you were no good? I've filled the second violin section vacancies I was auditioning for the other day.'

'And you don't see me as a first violin?'

'No.' His eyes twinkled. 'But then, I didn't see you as a tenor sax player either.' He smiled. 'My leader is leaving soon and there'll be a re-shuffle. It would help not to have to advertise again, but I'd still like to re-appraise your work.'

She relaxed a little. 'Well, all right then. Fair enough. When and where?'

He regarded her for a moment. 'Give me your phone number. I'll have to let you know.'

He took a pen from and inside pocket and offered her the back of a menu card from the bar. She scribbled the number and he slipped it carefully into his wallet. Tossing back the last of his drink, he stood up.

'I'd better join my party again. I promised faithfully not to talk shop this evening. I'll be in touch, Tricia, Goodnight.'

In the staff cloakroom she looked at herself in the chipped mirror. If she'd known he was going to be here tonight she would have put on some make-up. Tracey was always going on at her for not making the most of her looks. And tonight there was Gran chiding her for her poor taste in dress. She pressed cool palms against her hot cheeks. 'I'll be in touch,' he'd said. Would he really ring her? Or would he forget all about it tomorrow morning? A good thing she'd thought to write her name above the telephone number, otherwise

316

he'd probably have puzzled over whose number it was. Just wait till she told Gran.

Back on the stand she noticed that Max and his party had left, but in a way she was glad. She would have felt so terribly self-conscious with him watching and listening. As it was she played with a renewed zest that brought a smile to the faces of her older, male colleagues.

It was half-past one when she arrived back at the flat. She'd taken a taxi home — partly in celebration and partly to satisfy her grandmother. As she climbed the stairs her heart quickened in anticipation. She couldn't wait to tell Grace her news.

Grace had been waiting for hours, though she had hardly noticed the time passing. She felt stunned. If only she had telephoned first to let Morgan know she was coming. How could she have been so naive as to expect him to welcome her decision after she had kept him waiting so long?

She'd arrived at his flat in Park Lane soon after eight. Taking the lift up to the second floor she had rung the bell and waited, looking forward to seeing the look of surprise light up his face. The surprise had been there all right, but from the moment he set eyes on her it was clear that he had been expecting someone else.

'You're early ...' he began as he threw open the door. Then he stopped in mid-sentence, his eyes startled. 'Grace! I'd no idea you were even in Town. Why didn't you let me know?'

'I'm sorry. Were you going out?'

'No — no, of course not. Come in.' Collecting himself, he held the door open for her. Through the open dining-room door she could see that the table was carefully laid for two, with tall red candles in a silver candelabra. Grace looked at it, then at Morgan.

'You're expecting someone?'

'Well, yes. But I can easily lay another place.'

'No, I wouldn't dream of intruding. Look, perhaps we can meet tomorrow?'

Morgan looked acutely uncomfortable. 'Grace, don't go. Look, is there anything you particularly wanted to see me about?'

She shook her head. Something was badly wrong. They were behaving like strangers. It was so unlike the easy, relaxed manner in which Morgan always greeted her.'

'My visit was meant to be a surprise,' she said. 'What I really came to tell you was that I've decided to accept your offer to share the flat. I know it's long overdue but ...' She trailed off. Morgan was staring at her.

317

'Oh, I see.'

'Look, I can see that this isn't the right moment.' She backed towards the door. 'I'll ring you tomorrow, Morgan.'

He glanced briefly at his watch, then reached out to take her hand. 'Grace, please listen. Oh, God, I feel terrible about this. I'd given up all hope of your taking me up on it.' He drew her down on to the settee with him. 'Perhaps I should have told you this before. I've met someone – someone who means a great deal to me. I never thought I would. Not again. I didn't tell you because I wanted to be quite sure.'

'And now you are?'

'Yes, Grace. I'm sure.' His eyes met hers and suddenly her heart contracted. She stepped towards him and framed his face with her hands.

'Oh, Morgan. My dear, I'm so glad for you. Don't be uncomfortable about it. You've been alone for so long.'

'No, Grace, I was never alone while I had you. I thought you'd never join me here. You have family, Elaine and Tricia. That's where you belong. I had no right even to ask.'

'You had every right.' Standing on tiptoe she kissed his cheek. 'You've meant so much to me over the years. You've been my best friend, son, confidant, all rolled into one. A mirror of myself, almost.'

'I'd have been nothing but for you,' he said quietly. 'All my success is yours really. You were the first person to believe in me, even before I did myself. If I ever thought I'd hurt you – that I'd failed to be there for you when you needed me ...'

She shook her head. 'No. It's nothing like that. You could never hurt me by being happy.' For a moment they looked at each other, then she said: 'I'll go now. Before you friend comes.'

'There's no need. He knows all about you. I'd like you to meet.'

She shook her head. 'Maybe some other time. You must bring him to Cambridge. But not now, Morgan. Not tonight.'

She took a taxi back to Fulham and climbed the stairs to the empty flat. Changing into a dressing gown and slippers, she settled down in front of the TV but found herself unable to concentrate on the programme. Deep inside she recognised this evening as a watershed in her life. All these years Morgan had been the only man in her life and now she examined her true feelings towards him. She was fond of him in the way she would have been fond of a son or a younger brother. Perhaps she had been unfair to him in a way. Perhaps they had both been hiding from reality

318

all these years; each of them afraid of facing up to their own sexuality. But nowadays these things were brought out into the open much more freely; discussed and resolved in ways that had been unheard of in Grace's younger days. Now Morgan had found happiness again in the only way he could find it. For her it was too late.

Her thoughts went inevitably to Harry. Since her talk with Rachel it was as though a mist had cleared in her mind. She no longer felt the deep revulsion she had once felt towards anything of a sexual nature. And now she realised with surprise that in some inexplicable way Morgan had unwittingly helped to cure her of that.

Where was Harry now? She thought of him more and more lately. In the eyes of the law they were still married. He had never asked her for a divorce again. She knew that Stella Rainbow had died. She'd seen it quite by chance five years ago — a few lines of print in an old newspaper wrapped around something she had bought in the market. 'Fifties singing star dies of cancer in Australia'. Smoothing out the paper she'd seen that it was already two months old. Had Harry stayed out there or had he returned to England? Either way he hadn't been in touch with her — or with Elaine as far as she knew. Harry. She smiled wistfully to herself. With a pang of surprise she realised he would be sixty now. How quickly the time went as one grew older. It was hard to imagine him getting old. How was he coping with life on his own? Had he found someone else? Was he still working? She sighed. She had loved Harry so very much. If only he could have understood why she couldn't respond to him. If only she could have told him. Everything might have been so different for them all.

She'd fallen into a doze by the time Tricia returned. Hearing the door slam and the light footsteps on the stairs she roused herself and went into the kitchen to heat the milk for the promised cocoa.

Tricia was full of her meeting with Max Crichton. 'He didn't seem to disapprove of my playing with the group,' she said excitedly. 'And he's going to audition me again. Oh, Gran, I *know* I shan't be able to sleep a wink tonight. I can't *wait* till Tracey gets back so that I can tell her.'

Grace looked at her granddaughter's shining eyes, remembering herself at that age — married with a baby; her life already beginning to disintegrate.

Elaine's youth had been short-lived too. She often agonised over the life her daughter had had — suspecting that she herself might be to blame for that disastrous marriage. She'd guessed that Elaine had been pregnant before she and Paul had married, of course, but been unable to talk to her about it. She'd been cowardly about everyone knowing – afraid of the shame and disgrace had Paul refused to marry her after all. And she was ashamed at the relief she had felt when the knot was safely tied. Marriage to Paul had seemed ideal to her at the time. He'd been so stable and steady, unlike the Carne boy. But she'd been wrong – so very wrong. Now, she hoped fervently that life would be better for Tricia. She was their stake in the future. Maybe through her they could recoup the happiness they had missed. To this end she must have all the help they could give her.

'But what about you, Gran?' Tricia was saying. She too had changed into a dressing gown and sat, feet tucked under her in a corner of the settee, her hands wrapped round her mug of cocoa. 'Was Uncle Morgan surprised to see you? Was he pleased about your decision?'

Grace sighed. 'I should have let him know I was coming. I should have given him some warning.'

Tricia laughed. 'Warning? You make your visit sound more like an invasion.'

'It almost was.' Grace smiled wryly. 'He was expecting a friend for dinner – the friend who is about to move in and share the flat with him.'

'Oh, I see.' Tricia nodded. 'As a matter of fact I've seen him around with someone once or twice. I did wonder.' She glanced apprehensively at her grandmother. 'Granny, you did realise that Uncle Morgan was gay, didn't you?'

Grace's eyebrows rose. At nineteen she had been a wife and mother, yet she hadn't known half of what young girls knew nowadays. And maybe it was a good thing they did. At least they were prepared for life – something she had never been. In spite of herself, she laughed.

'Yes, darling. I've always known that.' A thought occurred to her and her eyes widened. 'Oh, you didn't think that I had any romantic ideas?'

'Of course not.' Tricia looked shocked. 'I thought you just wanted to mother him.' She peered anxiously at Grace. 'Are you terribly disappointed?'

Grace shook her head resolutely. 'No, I'm glad. Things are working out very well. Morgan seems to have found a partner he'll be happy with. Your mother is able to take and active part in her business again. Your future looks promising ...'

'Yes, but what about *you*, Gran?' Tricia asked. 'What are you going to do with your retirement?'

Grace stifled a sigh. 'Retirement' sounded so very elderly. 'Never you mind about me,' she said. 'I've had my life.'

'But you're not old. You have lots of energy and you still look wonderful. You have so much to offer. You can't just merge into the wallpaper.'

Grace laughed. 'I've no intention of doing any such thing. I'll think of something to do with my spare time. Now I'll have time for all the things I've always meant to do. I might travel. Follow Morgan's example and buy myself a little place somewhere in the sun.'

'Do you ever wish ...' Tricia glanced at her grandmother hesitantly. 'Do you ever wish that you and – and grandfather were still together?'

Grace smiled. 'It was all so long ago, Tricia. I daresay we're both different people now. In marriage you grow together down the years. You change together – mould to each other's ways. If I met your grandfather in the street now, I probably wouldn't even recognise him.'

'Oh, that's so sad,' Tricia whispered, her eyes bright. 'Because I know you loved him. I've always known that by the way you speak about him. Do you think he'd have liked me? Do you think ...?'

'I'm certain he'd have been very proud of you.' Grace stood up. 'Have you seen the time, young lady? Off to bed with you this minute. Plenty of time for talking tomorrow.' In the doorway of her room Grace took Tricia's face between her hands and kissed her.

'Don't worry yourself about me or what's past,' she said softly. 'Your future is what matters now. You have talent and plenty of common sense. Make good use of both those things and you won't go far wrong. Goodnight, my darling. Sleep well.'

But they both lay awake through the last dark hours before dawn; thinking about themselves and each other. About the regretted past and the hoped for future.

It was five days before Max Crichton rang. Tricia had given up hope of hearing from him. She imagined him finding the card on which she'd written her name and number in his pocked and tossing it away without remembering who she was. But she was wrong. She arrived home from shopping the following Friday afternoon to hear the telephone ringing inside the flat. She hastily found her key, fell in through the door and snatched up the receiver.

'He-hello?'

'Hello. It's Max Crichton. You sound breathless.' He sounded amused.

'I've been out. I heard the phone as I came up the stairs.'

'No rush. I'd have rung again. Any chance of you coming round to play for me tomorrow morning?'

'Tomorrow?'

'If it's inconvenient . . .'

'*No*. No, it's fine. Er − where?'

He gave her an address in Knightsbridge. 'Make it about eleven. Okay?'

'Yes. Fine. I'll be there.'

'I'll see you tomorrow then. Goodbye.' And before she could say another word he had rung off.

Tracey, coming in a few minutes later had been sceptical. 'Knightsbridge? I take it that's *his* place eh? You want to watch it. He sounds like a dirty old man if you ask me.'

'Nobody is asking you. And he's *not* old,' Tricia said indignantly. 'Anyway, he's a dedicated musician. It's in *your* profession they have casting couches, not mine.'

Tracey laughed and tossed her beautiful auburn head. 'Want to bet?'

'Anyway, he's got an absolutely *gorgeous* girlfriend. I've seen her,' Tricia said. 'She might even be his wife, for all I know.'

'When did a little thing like a wife ever stop any of them?' asked Tracey cynically. 'Just you watch yourself, young Trish. You're far too innocent and trusting for your own good.' Then she grinned. 'Mind you − you'll be boringly safe if you turn up dressed like that.'

'What's wrong with the way I look?'

'What's right with it?' Tracey, who bought clothes like other people buy food, and never wore anything that didn't bear a designer label, looked her up and down critically. 'You never do anything with your hair and you absolutely live in a tee-shirt and jeans. It's not much of a turn-on, is it.'

'Look, Tracey, I'm a musician, not a model,' Tricia retorted. 'This is *me* − this is the way I am. Take me or leave me.'

Tracey sighed and shook her head. 'Okay, but it wouldn't hurt to make the most of yourself just for once, would it?'

'And just what does that mean?'

'That you're a very pretty girl. You have great, naturally blonde hair and a lovely complexion. Your figure's not bad either. So what's wrong with playing up your assets?' She looked at Tricia's doubtful expression and added: 'Look, put it this way − would you buy a Stradivarius and play Chopsticks on it?'

Tricia collapsed into giggles. 'Chopsticks is a piano piece.'

322

'Exactly. I rest my case.'

The address Max Crichton had given her did indeed turn out to be his flat, but it wasn't nearly as opulent as Tricia had imagined. It was on the second floor of a large converted Edwardian house in a small square. As she rang the doorbell she could hear the piano playing inside. At her second ring, it stopped abruptly and a few minutes later Max himself opened the door. When he saw her his eyebrows rose a fraction and Tricia was instantly self-conscious about her appearance.

'Ah – come in.' He wore cord jeans and a black cashmere sweater. His dark hair was rumpled where he had constantly raked his fingers through it. 'Perhaps you'd like a coffee before we begin? I was just going to make some.'

'Thank you.' She felt suddenly uncomfortable, wishing fervently that she hadn't let Tracey loose on her this morning, allowing her to do her hair in a riot of spiral curls. The flowered pedal pushers and red cotton bomber jacket she had insisted on lending her felt all wrong too. At least she'd drawn the line at the awful Barbie doll make up Tracey had applied, surreptitiously scrubbing it off in the bathroom before she set out.

Max showed her into the studio. It had a spartan look. The walls were painted plain white and the polished oak floor was strewn with white Indian rugs. A Picasso that looked suspiciously like an original hung over the fireplace, but the room was dominated by a full-sized grand piano. Under the long window was a black leather Chesterfield and a coffee table. Apart from these, the room was bare. As she took off her jacket Tricia began to wish she hadn't come. She didn't feel right in these awful clothes. She wouldn't be able to play dressed up like a dog's dinner, she knew it.

Max came back carrying a tray with two mugs of coffee which he put down on the coffee table. He looked at her.

'Relax. You're all tense,' he said perceptively. 'There's nothing to be scared of.'

'I know.' She took the mug he handed her and trust out her chin defensively. 'I'm not scared.'

'Good.' He sat down on the piano stool and smiled at her. 'So what are you going to play for me this morning?'

'A bit of Vivaldi's Four Seasons.'

'Good. That's a favourite of mine. Right, shall we begin?'

Once she had begun to play her nerves calmed. She had practised the piece for hours the day before and knew it thoroughly. She even added some little innovative re-phrasing of her own that she had dreamed up last night. When she had finished, she looked up at him.

His face completely impassive, he stood up, removed the music from her stand and placed another sheet on it.

'Right – play this for me. Unaccompanied this time.'

She did as he said. It was a fiendishly tricky piece, but she enjoyed the challenge and was fairly satisfied with her execution of it.

When she came to the end he got up without a word and walked out of the room. Returning after a few moments with the coffee pot, he refilled the two empty mugs, handed one to her, then sat astride the piano stool and regarded her thoughtfully.

'Tell me about Patricia Kingston,' he said.

She was taken aback. 'About me? There isn't much. I'm nineteen. I was born in Cambridge. I have no brothers or sisters. I've been playing the violin since I was five years old. I told you about opting out of college.' She shrugged. 'That's all.'

'Why are you here today?'

She frowned. 'Because – because you asked me to come.'

'That's all, is it? No other reason?'

'Yes. I came because I want to play with the New World Orchestra. I've wanted to ever since I can remember.'

'And what is your ultimate ambition?'

'Just – just to earn my living doing what I love most – with my music. If I'm good enough,' she added, hoping that a touch of humility was what he was looking for.

'Right, now tell me the truth,' he said looking her straight in the eye. 'And don't try to be what you think I *expect* you to be.'

She paused, slightly thrown by his directness. 'All right. I want to be a concert violinist,' she said defiantly.

'Great. That's what I thought. Now we're getting somewhere.' He took a deep draught of his coffee, studying her over the rim of the mug. 'I take it you've heard about my reputation as a brute and a bully?'

'No.' She glanced up at him and grinned. 'Well, all right, yes.'

'Would it bother you to know that you might be shouted at in rehearsal – made to look foolish – humiliated?'

'Yes, it would.'

'Why?'

'Because I feel that kind of thing is unnecessary and unprofessional. I wouldn't respond to it, because I'm a good player. I don't need bullying.'

He gave a shout of laughter. 'I like you, Tricia Kingston. You've got guts. But let me tell you that if you came to work for me, you'd have to break some of the rather individual habits you've formed. You'd have to learn to do as you're told — without arguing. And that might be traumatic for you. Because in spite of what you say, I've a feeling you don't take kindly to discipline or criticism.'

She wanted to tell him that for him she'd climb up Everest or swim the Atlantic. Instead she bit the inside of her lip hard and said: 'I'm willing to learn. And I don't mind taking orders — as long as it's from a person who knows better than I do. A person I can respect.'

'Really? That's encouraging. But do you feel that *I* fit that description?'

She glanced at him out of the corner of her eye. Was he laughing at her? Never mind. She was determined to stick it out no matter what. 'Yes, Mr Crichton, I do,' she said firmly. 'I've wanted to work with — *for* you — for years. If you give me the chance I'll prove that I can take discipline and criticism as well as anybody.'

He stood up and held out his hand. 'Right. In that case, welcome to the New World Orchestra, Miss Kingston. You'll be getting your contract in the post. I'll get my secretary to send you a rehearsal schedule and a list of forthcoming concerts.' He studied her hard as her hand lay in his. 'By the way, I've been dying to ask ever since you arrived — what have you done to yourself today?' He frowned. 'You look different.'

She flushed. 'My flatmate thought I should smarten myself up for the audition.'

'And is *this* your idea of smartening up?' he asked scathingly.

Her hand went to her stiffly lacquered hair. 'No. It was hers, to be honest.'

'Do you like it?'

'I hate it.'

'The feeling's mutual. Come with me.' He walked out through the door, still holding on to her hand so that she was obliged to go with him. At the end of the corridor he opened a door and drew her into a green and white bathroom. Without a word he turned on the tap at the wash basin and, ignoring her indignant protests, put one hand behind her head and thrust it under the tap, holding it there until her hair was thoroughly wet. Pulling her upright again, he grabbed a towel and rubbed it dry.

'Comb it,' he ordered, handing her a comb. When she had done so, he took her by the shoulders and turned her to face the mirror.

'There. Look,' he said. 'That was your first lesson. Don't try to be something you're not. It doesn't work. *That's* the real Patricia

325

Kingston. Stay just like that and don't let anyone talk you into changing, right?'

Her eyes blazed furiously back at his reflection in the mirror. 'There was no need to go to those lengths,' she told him breathlessly. 'I would have done it myself when I got home anyway.'

He laughed. 'I can see that we're going to get along like a house on fire.' He gave her a little push. 'Off you go now. And don't forget to practise.'

Looking back afterwards, Tricia remembered nothing about the journey home that afternoon. She didn't remember much about the audition either. What she did remember with crystal clarity was the moment that her eyes had met Max Crichton's in the bathroom mirror. At that moment she hated him with an intensity she could almost taste. Hated and adored him.

Elaine had been surprised when Mrs Freer, the matron of St Hilda's Retirement Home, telephoned her at the office.

'Your mother-in-law would like to see you, Mrs Kingston,' she said in her clipped impersonal voice.

'Is she ill?'

'She's had a mild attack of influenza, but apart from a little chestiness she's well. She just seems anxious to see you, that's all.'

'I see. Well, I'll come as soon as I can.'

'She'd like it to be this afternoon, if that's possible.'

'Does she need anything?' Elaine was growing more puzzled by the minute. Mary had made her routine visit only a week last Sunday.

'Not as far as I know,' Mrs Freer said coolly. She cleared her throat. 'May I tell her to expect you then?'

Elaine flipped open her appointment book. There was nothing that couldn't wait till tomorrow. 'All right,' she said. 'I'll come round at about half-past two.'

She went through to Alison's office to tell her she'd be taking an hour off. 'I can't think why she wants to see me,' she said. 'If I know Mary there'll be a snag of some kind. All I hope is that she hasn't had a row with Mrs Freer and plans to move back to Langmere Lodge.'

Alison smiled. 'As long as there's nothing much doing, why don't you take the rest of the afternoon off?' she suggested. 'Heaven knows you've worked enough overtime lately.'

Their most recent bride had embarked on a crash slimming course just a month before her wedding and as a result the wedding dress had had to undergo some drastic last minute alterations.

'Actually, I was going to ask *you* a favour,' Alison was saying.

326

Elaine looked up, surprised to find Alison looking slightly embarrassed. 'Fine. What is it?'

'I was going to ask you if you'd stay on through the lunch hour. I've been asked out to lunch.'

'Of course I'll stay,' Elaine assured her. She smiled. 'Who's your date?'

'Robert Hannan.' Alison made a great show of tidying her desk, avoiding Elaine's curious eyes.

'Our account? There's nothing wrong with the books, is there?'

'No, nothing like that. It's − well, purely social.'

'Ah, I see.' Elaine smiled her encouragement. 'In that case, why lunch? I'd have thought dinner ...' Suddenly she *did* see. All these years Alison had steered clear of all but the most casual relationships; afraid to become involved again; terrified of being hurt. Lunch was safe. It could not develop into a situation that might be embarrassing to get out of.

'Tell you what, why don't you take an extra hour?' she suggested 'That'll still leave me time to get round to St Hilda's.' She smiled to herself as she made her way back to her office. It was time Alison found a new man. And she'd already noticed the rapport between her partner and Robert Hannan, their handsome accountant. In fact, it had been there right from the moment the two had first met.

At St Hilda's Mary was sitting alone in her room, wrapped in a crochet shawl. Normally she looked younger than her eighty years, but today she looked white and drawn; her hair, usually neatly dressed, was unkempt and straggly and as she slumped in her chair she suddenly looked like a very old woman.

'I'd almost given you up,' she grumbled as Elaine bent to kiss her cheek.

She looked at her watch. 'I'm only ten minutes late.'

Mary sighed noisily. 'When you're sitting here all day with nothing to think about but the passing time, it becomes an obsession,' she said.

Elaine put the box of chocolates she had brought on the table, took off her coat and sat down. 'What did you want to see me about, Mother?' she asked.

'I've been ill.'

'Matron said you'd had a slight attack of flu.'

Mary grunted. 'What does *she* know? She isn't even a real nurse. I thought my last hour had come the night before last − couldn't get my breath.' She peered at Elaine with beady eyes. 'They thought they'd have to send for the doctor, you know.'

'She didn't tell me that.'

Mary pulled the shawl more closely around her shoulders. 'Well, they got the nurse to have a look at me in the end. But I really did have a bad chest. I still have.' She coughed wheezily as though to prove her point.

'I'm sorry, Mother. I'd have come before if I'd known.'

Mary's expression softened. 'Oh, it's all right. I know how busy you are.' She sighed. 'It's just that I got to thinking – lying there gasping for breath. There are things I should have told you, Elaine, serious things. I feel you'd better know them before anything happens to me.'

'Nothing is going to happen to you, Mother.'

'It might. It easily could.' Mary looked agitated. 'And if it did . . .'

'All right, what is it you want to say? Are you sure you want to . . .'

'Oh, be quiet. I'm trying to *tell* you,' Mary snapped with sudden impatience. 'I've made up my mind. That's why I sent for you, so just listen.' She reached for a glass of water on the table at her side and took a sip, then dabbed at her mouth with a handkerchief.

'It's about Paul. His accident. I don't believe what happened that day *was* an accident.'

Elaine frowned. 'What do you mean?'

'I believe he tried to commit suicide.'

Elaine stared at her mother-in-law. 'Really, Mother, why should he do that?'

'That day – that afternoon . . . You were away. I came home and went upstairs – found him in bed with – with someone.'

Elaine stared disbelievingly at her mother-in-law. The idea that Paul of all people . . . Mary must be getting confused.

'No, not an affair.' Mary snapped. 'It was a young man. Not much more than a boy.'

Elaine was stunned. Surely Mary must be rambling. She'd always insisted that she didn't remember anything of what happened that day. Could her flu have made her light-headed?'

'Don't look at me like that,' Mary said. 'I'm not ga-ga, if that's what you're thinking. It's true. Paul is homosexual. I always knew he had latent tendencies that way, but I hoped he'd grow out of them.'

Elaine took a deep breath to steady the rapid beating of her heart. She felt as though the world had suddenly tipped sideways. What Mary was saying would account for so much if it were true. Bitter

328

resentment sharpened her voice as she said: 'You *knew* that? You knew and yet you let me marry him. How could you?'

Mary's lip curled. 'You were pregnant — frightened to tell your mother. You were glad enough to get a husband at the time, so you needn't be so self-righteous.'

'You knew that too?' Elaine got to her feet as the blank corners of the past years were suddenly filled in. 'It was *you* who told him, wasn't it? You kept it to yourself all those years — and then you told him. To spite me. Why, Mother? *Why?*'

The old woman in the chair suddenly seemed to crumple before her eyes. Her voice cracked as she said: 'I didn't do it just to spite you, Elaine. I told him because I was afraid you were going to leave him. You'd started this new business with your friend. Tricia was going away to school. I knew you weren't happy, and then there was that day I came home and found you with that man — Patrick Crown or whatever his name was.' She looked up, her eyes watery with remorse. 'I thought you might leave Paul — leave me too. I was afraid.' She glanced up hesitantly. 'I — I tried to urge him to make you pregnant. I thought if you had another baby ...'

'*Another baby* ...?' Elaine fought hard to control the urge to laugh hysterically. She took a deep breath and swallowed the lump in her throat. 'So you tried to manipulate us as you'd done so many times in the past. And it misfired.'

'I only meant to make him face it,' Mary said. 'I quite thought he would have guessed — that he'd simply turned a blind eye. I had no idea he really didn't know, or that he'd take it so badly — use it against you. I didn't foresee that you'd go away — or that he'd take up his predilection for young men again.' Mary took another anxious gulp from the glass of water. 'It was as though I'd opened a Pandora's box. We quarrelled violently that afternoon when I found them. I fell down the stairs and I think he thought he'd killed me — or that if I was alive I'd tell you about him. I don't know which. Either way, you can imagine how desperate he must have been. He meant to take his own life, Elaine, I'm convinced of it. Instead he sentenced himself to life imprisonment.'

Elaine sat down again, her legs suddenly too weak to support her. 'Yes,' she said quietly. 'And he sentenced me too.'

'I know.' Mary reached out to touch her daughter-in-law's hand. It was the first gesture of communication she'd ever offered her. 'It was my fault — all of it. I had to tell you. If I'd died with it on my conscience ...'

'And now you've told me. Thank you for that at least,' Elaine said bitterly. She stood up. 'I'll have to go now, Mother.'

Mary seemed not to have heard her. She stared into space, the tears dripping on to her shawl as she said: 'All my life, every man I've ever loved has disappointed me. I lost my Richard, my brilliant, lovely boy. Paul — well, I don't have to tell you about *him*. But I always thought my memories of Henry were safe. I looked up to him so, thought him a perfect husband. I always considered myself so lucky. Then when Edna was dying she told me that she and Henry had been lovers. They'd been seeing each other, sleeping together behind my back, for years before he died.' She thumped the arm of the chair in sudden impotent rage. 'Bloody cringing, mousey little *Edna* of all people! All those years sucking up to me, when all the time ... The lying bitch said she wanted to die with a clear conscience. Never mind about the agony she left me with.'

Elaine looked at the shrunken figure in the chair. She couldn't see — Mary really couldn't see — that she was doing precisely what she was blaming poor Edna for. But somehow she couldn't find it in herself to reproach the frail old woman. In her own way she had suffered too. Anyway, it was too late now to alter anything. Much too late.'

She said: 'I'm sorry, Mother.'

'Never mind. It's all over now — all over a long time ago.' The old woman looked up, her pale eyes pleading. 'You won't hold it against me, will you, Elaine?'

'No, Mother. I won't hold it against you. There's little point now, is there?'

Mary sighed. 'Thank you. I feel so much better now that I've told you. So much better.'

Elaine stood with the door half open, her hand on the handle. She felt numb. Her heart was so heavy, and yet there was nothing left to say to the woman who had done so much to help wreck her life. Mary looked at peace now, her eyelids already heavy with drowsiness. She was happy in the knowledge that she had repaid her debt.

Little did she know that the coin she had used was counterfeit.

330

Chapter Twenty-Two

Tricia was happy. She was playing with an orchestra — the one she'd dreamed of playing with. So far she'd enjoyed every minute of it: rehearsals, concerts, even the travelling. The New World Youth Orchestra had just completed a summer tour of cathedrals up and down the country. It had been hard work, but Tricia thrived on it. The musicians travelled in their own bus. A large blue van carried their instruments whilst another carried all the sound equipment, plus technicians. She loved being part of it all. She felt she truly belonged as she had never belonged anywhere before. In the whole ten months that she'd been with the orchestra she'd only been home once. And that was only on a flying visit to attend Granny Mary's funeral last February.

At Peterborough the BBC came along and televised the concert. Their programme included the Bach double violin concerto, and the soloists were husband and wife violinists, Marc and Juliette Kass. From her place right at the back of the first violin section, Tricia watched and listened raptly. One day she would be standing up there instead of providing a small part of the background. But she was impatient. She wanted to begin preparing right away. But how did one start?

Since she had been playing with the orchestra she and Max Crichton had hardly exchanged a word. Apart from the occasional nod of acknowledgement as they passed in the corridor or on the stairs, she might not have existed. She was disappointed. After her audition at his flat when he'd washed all the curl out of her hair, she'd imagined there would be some kind of rapport between them. Naturally he couldn't single her out for attention, but all the same she hadn't expected him to resume the remote, godlike aura he had had before.

Max's rehearsals were an education. She learned so much in those

331

first months — about Max himself as well as music. He seemed two different people. The shaggy giant in jeans and sweatshirt who threw so much emotional and physical energy into the preparation of a concert, seemed to put on the cool, suave, sex symbol image that the media had given him along with the formal evening dress he wore for concerts. Tricia found the enigma a little bewildering. Which one was the real Max Crichton? Or maybe underneath it all there was yet another man hiding.

She found most of her fellow musicians friendly but she had made two special friends among her colleagues in the first violin section. Eunice Holtby, who sat next to her, was a year older, whilst Terry, her brother, who occupied a slightly more elevated position two desks in front, was twenty-one. They were from Bolton in Lancashire and their warm Northern personalities had embraced Tricia from the first day. However, apart from Max, she had confided to no one her ambition to be a concert soloist. It was something she hugged to herself, believing that somehow, someday, a miraculous opportunity would arrive and it would all happen for her. It was her fate, written in her stars, she was certain of it.

At the end of the tour there was talk of an overseas tour, to take place sometime in the New Year. The excited buzz of rumour went round. Some said it was America — the East Coast: Boston; New York; Philadelphia. Others said it was Australia. But Tricia didn't much care where it was. She had always wanted to travel and to travel with music — and to do it with Max seemed to her the best of all worlds.

But before their next round of engagements they were to have a two-week break. There was just one concert to record, to go out on BBC television later in the autumn. After that she could go home for the much delayed visit to see her mother and Granny Grace.

It was after the recording session, when she and Eunice and Terry were having lunch in the canteen, that she spotted a familiar figure at a corner table. Telling the others that she would catch them up later, she went across to him.

'Harry, how are you?'

He looked up and smiled in surprise. 'Hello there. It's Tricia, isn't it?'

'That's right.' She looked at the empty chair opposite him. 'Are you waiting for someone or can I join you?'

'No, please do.'

'I'm not holding you up — I mean, do you have to rush off?'

'No. I've just finished accompanying Ben Seton, the tenor, on the midday magazine programme "Today Live".'

'Oh, that's all right then.' She slipped into the seat opposite. 'I just wanted to tell you that I got a job with the NW.'

He could have told her that he already knew. Some weeks ago he'd seen Max who'd made a special point of telling him that he'd taken his advice and engaged the young girl violinist with the blonde hair and the cocky air of self-confidence.

'That's wonderful,' he said with a smile.

'First violins − not second,' she added with a smile. 'And we've just finished a tour of cathedral concerts. It's been fantastic. And now there's talk of an overseas tour next year. But I've got a break to look forward to right now.'

'Good.' Harry looked at the shining blue eyes and swinging fair hair and felt a pang of nostalgia. All that enthusiasm. All that vibrant energy. What it was to be young. 'So are you going home? East Anglia, isn't it?'

'That's right.'

'And ambition-wise, what's the next step on the way to stardom?'

She looked wistful. 'What I really want is to be a soloist,' she told him earnestly. 'People younger than me have achieved it. I'm getting older all the time.'

'You poor old lady.' He laughed. 'You've got all the time in the world.'

'Not really,' she told him earnestly. 'You know about these things. What could I do, Harry? I mean, how are the people who matter ever going to hear me at the back of the first fiddles in the New World Orchestra?'

'You'd be surprised − never know who's listening.'

She shook her head impatiently. 'That's no good. I want them to hear *me*. What can I do?'

'Make a demo tape like the pop people do,' he suggested, half jokingly.

Her eyes brightened and she latched on to the idea eagerly. 'Hey − that's a great idea. But I couldn't do it on my own. I'd need an accompanist ...' She broke off to look appealingly into his eyes. 'Harry − I suppose you wouldn't ...?'

He laughed. 'I walked right into that, didn't I? Okay, why not? I've got a reasonably good tape machine at home, and the piano of course. When would you like to come?'

'I'm free from this afternoon onwards,' she told him eagerly.

He took an envelope out of his wallet and removed the letter inside. 'Here, that's my address. It's not far from the Underground station. Think you can find it?'

'You bet. Would tomorrow morning be okay − around ten?'

333

His eyebrows shot up. 'Fine, if you think you'll be ready by then.'

'I've been ready for months,' she told him confidently. 'I've been practising hard and I've got at least four pieces I could do. If I go home now and work on them this afternoon and tonight ...'

He laughed. 'Okay then. I hope you have tolerant neighbours. Tomorrow it is. I'll look forward to seeing you.'

She was still practising that evening when her mother rang.

'Tricia, you haven't been in touch, darling. I wondered when you were coming home.'

'Would Friday be all right? I'm making a demo tape tomorrow.'

'That sounds exciting.'

'It'll only be an amateur one. A friend is helping me with it.'

'So you'll be home at the end of this week?'

'Yes. And I can stay for a week, if that's all right.'

'That's lovely. Tricia – I'm staying at Granny Grace's at the moment, so you'll be coming there too.'

'That's okay.' Tricia frowned. 'Are you all right, Mum?'

'I'm fine.'

'Gran isn't ill or anything?'

'Good heavens, no. You know Granny. She's as fit as a flea. I'll explain everything when I see you. Listen, darling, Alison had an idea this morning. I don't know how you feel about working during your holiday, but we need some live music for a wedding on Saturday.'

Tricia paused. Why had her mother changed the subject so abruptly? Was she really all right? 'I thought most people booked a disco nowadays,' she remarked.

Elaine laughed. 'Oh, they do, and they have – for later on. But this is rather a classy affair and they want some live musicians to play during the formal reception in the afternoon. You'd get paid proper union rates and everything.'

'Oh, well, in that case I'll do it,' Tricia said, laughing. 'Any idea what kind of programme they'll want?'

'Oh, light popular classics, you know the kind of thing. I'll leave it to you.'

'Andrew Lloyd Webber – "Evita", "Phantom", that kind of thing?'

'Lovely. Maybe some oldies too.'

'Mum ...' An idea suddenly came into her head. 'You'll be wanting a pianist too. Do you have one?'

'Not yet. I was going to make some enquiries today.'

334

'Well, I think I can save you the trouble. Would you like me to fix one for you?'

'Certainly, if you know of someone good.'

'I do. The person who's helping me make this demo tape. I owe him a favour. I know he'd be grateful for the work.'

'Ah, do I detect romance in the air?' Elaine asked.

Tricia's laugh trilled down the line. 'Good lord, no. He's really old – must be well over sixty. But he's a real sweetie. I'm sure you'll like him.'

'Well, fine, if you can fix it all up, it'll save me another job. See you on Friday then, darling. Bye.'

Elaine put down the telephone with a sigh. Tricia seemed so happy and fulfilled in her new job. She had been worried last year at the news that she had opted out of college. As her daughter grew older, Elaine saw Patrick in her again and again. She had the same restlessness; the same impulse to snatch at everything life had to offer. Elaine had been so relieved when things had worked out well for her. They might easily have been otherwise.

It would be so lovely to have Tricia home for a few days and hear all her news. But she wasn't looking forward quite so much to the talk they would have to have. She told herself that surely anything would be better than the atmosphere at Langmere Lodge over the past years, but nevertheless, it was the only home the girl had ever known.

Elaine had thought for a long time about what Mary had told her on the afternoon she had visited her. A week of sleepless nights had been spent agonising about the wasted years. Should she face Paul with it or leave it alone? Finally she decided that she must at least find out if what Mary said was really true. After that she would make a decision about the future.

As it happened, Paul made it for her. Apart from his paraplegia he had made a good recovery from his devastating accident. But for a slight slurring when he grew agitated, his speech was fluent again and he had regained the use of both hands and arms. Josh, his young West Indian nurse, and he got along well. They had a lot in common and seemed to enjoy being together as friends as well as patient and nurse. Because of this Elaine had to wait some time for an opportunity to speak to Paul alone. She had no wish to face him with his mother's accusations in front of Josh.

At first he waved them away, dismissing them as the ramblings of a senile old woman.

'She doesn't know what she's saying nowadays. Surely you can

335

see that? She probably dreamed the whole thing. You know as well as I do that she was amnesic after the accident.'

'She only said she was because she was afraid I might leave if I'd known the truth,' Elaine told him. 'Is it true, Paul? I think I have a right to know. Did she find you with someone that afternoon? Was the accident really an unsuccessful suicide attempt?'

His eyes suddenly flashed with anger. 'What the hell does it matter now anyway? Don't you feel I've been punished enough? You and Mother between you – you never stopped twisting me this way and that, trying to turn me into the person you wanted me to be. Well, now I'm nothing. Just a thing in a wheelchair. Can't you be satisfied with that?'

'It isn't my fault, Paul,' she said patiently. 'And if I did something wrong in marrying you, I think you'll agree that I've paid too.'

'Do you think I don't know that?' he shouted at her. 'Do you think I don't see it in your eyes every day of the week? How do you think it feels to realise that you stayed with me only out of some misplaced sense of duty? I don't *want* your long suffering martyrdom any longer, Elaine. If you really want to know, all I want is for you to get the hell out of here and leave me to make some kind of life for myself again.'

She stared at him. 'You know I can't do that.'

'Why not?' He laughed harshly. 'Because of what people might say – is that it? Because of the way it would make you look? Tell them all to get stuffed. To hell with what they think. I'm sick of having to pretend just to satisfy convention.' He wheeled his chair closer to her and stared at her intently. 'I don't want you here any longer, Elaine. I'm sick of the sight of you. Can't you get that through your thick head?'

Shocked, she backed away. 'But – how would you manage? What would you do?'

His lip curled scathingly. 'You really think you're indispensable, don't you? Well, you're not. Listen, Mother left me the house and the rest of her estate. Josh and I have been making plans. We want to turn the place into a home for the disabled; convert it into self-contained flats – install a lift. I believe there's even some kind of grant we could get, but we haven't looked into that yet. He and I would live here on the ground floor and run the place. I'd manage the administrative side. Josh would be on hand for medical help. It could really work, if only ...'

'If only I got out and left you to it – is that what you're saying?'

'That's it in a nutshell. But for you I'd have a fighting chance to be a person again. So why don't you sod off?' he said brutally.

She was stunned. 'All right, Paul, if that's what you want, I'll leave immediately.'

Later that night, when Paul was asleep, she'd tapped on Josh's door and asked to speak to him. She asked him if the plan was real of just something Paul had thought up on the spur of the moment in order to get back at her. The nurse looked uncomfortable.

'The plan is real enough, Mrs Kingston,' he said. 'But I only went along with it because I thought it was just a pipe dream. I hope you don't think I was plotting to turn you out of your home.'

'Of course not, Josh.' She smiled, trying to put him at his ease. 'Perhaps you already know that our marriage was over long before Paul's accident?' The young West Indian looked acutely distressed and Elaine went on: 'I'd like an honest opinion, Josh. And I *mean* honest. Does Paul really want me to leave?'

'Mrs Kingston – what you ask is very difficult ...'

'It needn't be. Just tell me. Is he sincere? I'm not going to be upset. It's important that you tell me the truth.'

'He – it's true that he would like to be independent,' he said after a pause. 'I think he feels that – tied together you might both drown, but cut free there's a chance for you both to swim and be free again.'

Elaine smiled wryly. 'I like your turn of phrase, Josh. Thank you for telling me.'

She moved in with Grace three days later. On the first night they sat up talking till dawn. It had been a shock to Elaine to realise that Paul actually wanted her out of the house – wanted to be free as much as she did. Suddenly it seemed to her that her whole life had been a sham. She had been so misguided, wasted so much time; not only her own but other people's too.

'Oh, Mum, what have I done with my life?' she asked despairingly. 'I was so convinced that what I was doing was right, and all the time ... I'm such a failure.'

Grace was silent. She felt that she was the real failure. She had allowed the trauma of her early years to cloud her whole life; to go on leaving its mark – multiplying and spreading like ripples on a pond, wreaking havoc on the lives of those she loved. And the tragedy of it was that some of that damage could never be undone.

'You're still young,' she said gently. 'There's still plenty of time for you to make a new life. Look for a new place to live. Make a real home, for yourself and for Tricia. Then there's the business. You and Alison have done so well. How can you call yourself a failure?'

Elaine tried to smile. 'Thank God I've still got you,' she said. 'You've always been so strong.' She hugged her mother.

But the face that looked over her shoulder was full of sadness. Strong, yes — if only it had been the right kind of strength. Her eyes filled with the stinging tears of regret.

It wasn't until Tricia got out of the train at Notting Hill that she pulled out the envelope Harry had given her to look at the address. It was only then that she noticed the name: 'Mr H. Wendover'. She stood in the station booking hall, staring down at the tattered envelope in her hand, oblivious to the crowds milling round her. Wendover. That was Granny Grace's name. Could this Harry also be *her* Harry? Excitement quickened her heartbeat as the implications began to pile one upon the other in her mind. Everything seemed to point to the fact that she was right. It wasn't a terribly common name, and the chances of there being two Harry Wendovers who were also pianists were surely slim. It wasn't really such a coincidence that they should have met either. The world of music was comparatively small. Even in her own limited experience she had discovered that.

But what should she do about it? She had promised to ask Harry to play at the wedding on Saturday. Should she warn him first? Warn her mother and Granny Grace? Or should she keep it as a wonderful, gigantic surprise? She'd always known that deep down Gran longed to find him again. And Harry seemed so lonely.

As she made her way along the busy street her mind raced, making one plan — discarding it to make another, then going back over it again. First and foremost she must make absolutely sure — and do it discreetly. It would be too embarrassing if she were to speak out only to find that she was wrong after all.

Harry was impressed with Tricia's playing. He had been so afraid that playing with an orchestra would rob her of her individuality; take away some of the spirit and zest he had admired so much at the audition. As they came to the end of the last piece, he rose and turned off the tape recorder.

'Want to hear it through?' he asked as he pressed the rewind button.

Tricia shook her head. 'Not for a minute. Could we have a cup of coffee first, please?'

He looked at his watch and was surprised to see that it was three o'clock. 'Good heavens. I'd no idea it was as late as that. I'd planned to give you lunch.'

'Oh, Harry, there's no need for that. I've already taken up too much of your day.'

He grinned. 'Rubbish. I've enjoyed myself. I wasn't doing anything today anyway. As a matter of fact the jobs are a bit thin on the ground at the moment.'

'Ah, that reminds me.' Tricia put her violin in its case, turning her back so as to hide the excitement in her eyes. 'I told you I was going home, didn't I? Well, I've been asked to play for a wedding reception on Saturday. I've also been asked to find a pianist. Would you like the job?'

Harry looked pleased. 'Good of you to think of me. Where is it?'

'Cambridge. It's quite a classy wedding, and they'll pay proper rates.' She grinned. 'I daresay there'll be some posh nosh and the odd glass of champers too if we play our cards right.'

He laughed. 'Right, you're on. Never could resist champagne. Had you thought about a programme?'

'Yes. I've brought some music along with me. Maybe we could have a run through if you agree.' She passed him a sheaf of music, which he glanced through.

'Looks fine. All stuff I'm familiar with so it shouldn't be a problem. Just give me the details, will you? Time and venue. Write it down while I go and get us something to eat. You must be starving.'

Tricia scribbled down the details on Harry's telephone pad, then wandered through to the small kitchen and asked if she could help. It was strange and exciting to think she was about to sit down to lunch with her grandfather.

'Nothing to do,' Harry said, expertly slicing French bread. 'It's all ready. Just some cold meat and a salad.'

She watched him thoughtfully for a moment, then said, 'You look very much at home in the kitchen. How long have you been on your own, Harry?'

'Quite a while.'

'So you're a widower?' She saw him hesitate and bit her lip. 'Oh, look, sorry. Take no notice of me. I'm famous for putting my foot in it. You don't have to answer my silly questions.'

He smiled. 'It's just that I had to think. I was married once — well, still am as far as I know. But the marriage broke up years ago. The woman I used to share my life with died. She was ill for a long time which is how I got so domesticated.' He began to spread butter on the bread. 'I think of myself as a widower, though as far as I know, I'm not.'

339

Tricia tried hard to keep her voice from rising. It all added up. 'I see. I'm sorry,' she said.

He smiled. 'Don't be. I'm fine. Now — shall we listen to the tape while we eat?' He carried the plates through to the living room.

Tricia was fairly satisfied with the tape, though she had some reservations, which she aired when it came to an end. Harry waved them away.

'You can't expect to be completely satisfied. One never is. What are you going to do with your demo tape now you've got it?' She looked blank and he laughed. 'Would you like me to pass it on to my agent?'

'Oh, Harry, *would* you?'

He shrugged. 'I can try. I can't promise anything, of course, but even if she can't represent you herself, she might have some ideas.' He got up and began to clear away the used dishes. 'Now you can help me with the washing up if you like. Then we'll have a look at this programme you've got planned for Saturday.'

Elaine received the telephone call from Red at the office on the day Tricia was due home. When her secretary put the call through to her she was surprised.

'Red, how nice to hear from you. How are you?'

'I'm fine, Elaine. Look, if you're not too busy could you meet me for lunch?'

'Of course. Is there something wrong?'

'I'm afraid there is, but I'll tell you about it when we meet. Shall we say The Anchor at twelve-thirty?'

'Right. I'll see you later then.'

He had rung off abruptly, leaving Elaine wondering for the rest of the morning what it was he wanted to talk to her about.

When she arrived at the pub by the river Red was already there. He looked worried, his lean face pinched and drawn. He bought drinks for them both and they found a quiet corner table.

'What's wrong, Red?' Elaine asked, seriously worried by now.

He looked up at her. 'It's Zoe. She's ill.'

'Zoe? But I saw her last week. She was all right then.'

'I thought so too. We all did. It was only two days ago that I found out the truth.'

'Found out? Please, Red, what is it?'

He took a long pull of his beer. 'She has to have major surgery quite soon. It's cancer, Elaine.'

She gasped. 'Oh, *no*. Oh, Red, what can I say?'

'She's known about it for months and kept it to herself.'

Elaine shook her head. 'That sounds like Zoe.' She reached across the table to touch his hand. 'Have you talked to the doctor yourself, Red? Do you know just how serious it is?'

He nodded. 'I saw her consultant yesterday. He won't know how much he can do until he operates. He may be able to get it all. On the other hand . . .'

She pressed his hand. 'Red, if sheer will power can help, Zoe will be all right. She's the strongest person I know.'

'I hope you're right.' When he looked up at her she was dismayed to see that there were tears in his eyes. 'I can't imagine life without her, Elaine,' he said brokenly. 'She's got to get well again. She's just *got* to.'

A lump filled her throat. 'She will, Red. I know that if it's possible to will herself better, she'll do it.' She moistened her dry lips. 'Do Tom and Patrick know?'

'I telephoned them both last night. They were as shocked as me.'

'Naturally. When is the operation?'

'The week after next. They're taking her in a week on Monday — operating next day.' He looked at he. 'Will you go and see her? She's very fond of you, Elaine. She's often said that you're the nearest she's ever had to a daughter of her own.'

'Of course I'll go and see her.'

All afternoon thoughts of Zoe filled her mind. How could she have kept her illness form them all? Why hadn't she mentioned it to anyone? Her eyes kept straying to the head of Tricia that Zoe had done almost twelve years ago. Since she'd left Langmere Lodge it had stood on her desk where she could see it all the time. Zoe loved Tricia. If only she could have known that she was her own granddaughter. Suddenly she recalled a conversation they had had not so long ago. 'The world is changing so fast,' Zoe had said. 'One day, quite suddenly, it could be too late. I want so much to see you both happy before I die.' She must have known she was ill then. Poor Zoe. If only she could have shared it with them. Surely it would have made it easier to bear?

Elaine heard their excited voices as soon as she opened the front door. Tricia was telling her grandmother all about Max Crichton and the cathedral tour. When she heard the front door slam, she ran into the hall.

'Mummy.' She threw her arms round Elaine and hugged her. 'Oh, it's lovely to be home and see you both. Gran's got the most sumptuous meal waiting. Wait till you see.'

341

The meal was a happy affair. But later, when Grace left them to make coffee, Tricia asked: 'Why aren't you at home, Mum? What's going on? Is it Dad?'

'Hasn't Granny told you?'

'She said it would be better coming from you.'

Elaine looked at her daughter. 'There isn't much to tell, darling. I'm sure it won't come as too much of a shock to you to hear that Dad and I have finally parted. He wants to turn Langmere Lodge into a home for the disabled — with Josh Grey's help. He feels we'd be happier apart.'

Tricia's eyes widened. 'Just like *that*? After you've sacrificed so much for him?'

Elaine shook her head. 'It's not quite that simple, darling. Believe me, it's better for everyone this way.' She smiled. 'All these years he's resented his dependence on me. And if I'm truthful, I've resented it too. It doesn't make for a happy relationship.'

'Yes, but what will you do now?'

'Well, to begin with I'm looking for a nice house where we can make a home, you and I,' Elaine hurried on. 'Maybe we can look together while you're home?'

'Just tell me one thing,' Tricia said. 'Was it anything to do with me — your parting with Dad?'

'Darling, of course not.'

'Why has he always hated me?' Tricia looked up at her mother. 'Don't say he didn't, because he did. I always felt it. Langmere Lodge never felt like home to me. He didn't really want me there, did he?'

Elaine knew that this was the moment. Tricia had given her the perfect cue. 'It's not your fault. It's mine,' she said slowly. 'Our marriage hadn't been happy for a long time — from the very beginning, in fact.' She looked up apprehensively at her daughter. Would she see her in a different light after what she was about to say? 'You see, Paul Kingston isn't your true father, Tricia.'

For a long moment mother and daughter looked at each other. Then Tricia said dazedly: 'I think I always knew, deep inside me somewhere. There was never any real closeness between us. So who was he? My real father, I mean?'

'Someone I loved very much,' Elaine told her. 'Someone I expected to share the rest of my life with — at the time.'

Tricia's eyes were misty. 'And he let you down?'

'No. He never knew about you. And he never will — which is why I can't tell you either. It was all over a long time ago and there

342

isn't any point. No one else knows, Tricia, not even Gran, so I'd be grateful if we could keep it between ourselves.'

Tricia was disappointed and a little let down. After learning something so dramatic, it seemed something of an anti-climax.

'We must look to the future now, not the past,' Elaine went on. 'It's so long since Granny, you and I spent any time together. Let's make the most of it, shall we? She's helping the florist with the flowers tomorrow, so all three of us will all be taking part.'

Tricia smiled to herself. 'All *four* of us,' she corrected excitedly under her breath. Finding Harry would make up a little for what felt like the loss of her father.

Harry had told Tricia he'd arrive at the bride's home early on Saturday afternoon. The wedding party wasn't expected until four-thirty, so they'd have plenty of time to run through their programme of music before the reception. In actual fact he was a little early, having caught an earlier train. A housekeeper took him through the house to the marquee where the reception was to be held. He took off his coat and sat down at the piano, running his hands experimentally over the keys. It was in tune and well maintained. That was a bonus.

'Harry, you're early.'

He looked up to see Tricia coming towards him. 'Yes. I was so anxious not to be late that I caught the train before the one I intended. The piano's good, listen.' He played a snatch of Cole Porter.

'Sounds great. Shall we have a little run-through? Or maybe you'd like coffee first. I've brought a flask.'

'We'll have that later. Let's get started.'

They worked their way through the programme of music they had chosen: a selection of old favourites, Cole Porter, Rogers and Hart, and some of the more modern work of Andrew Lloyd Webber. They rehearsed for about half and hour, pausing now and then to re-phrase a passage and mark their music accordingly. Tricia liked the way she and Harry played together. They seemed to have an almost telepathic rapport, each knowing instinctively what the other was thinking and following effortlessly. It was just as one would expect, she told herself, between close relatives. If there were butterflies in her stomach it wasn't because of the coming performance.

Grace had been hard at work all morning, helping to decorate the marquee for the reception, and had promised to go back to the bride's house to collect surplus flowers and florists' paraphernalia. As she loaded the last of it into the boot of the car she heard strains of music coming from the marquee and realised that Tricia and her accompanist must be running through their programme. She paused to listen, feeling the glow of pride she always felt, listening to Tricia playing.

'They're rehearsing for the wedding. Lovely, isn't it?' Grace turned to see the housekeeper watching her.

'It's my granddaughter playing the violin,' she said proudly. 'She's with the New World Youth Orchestra but she's at home for a few days.'

The woman smiled. 'Well, she's certainly very talented. You must be very proud.'

'We are,' Grace told her. 'Today is a real family occasion for us at HEA. Three generations of us, all working together.' She nodded towards the floral equipment. 'I've collected up all the debris. I'll get if out of your way now.'

'There's no hurry. Why not go in and listen to your granddaughter for a few minutes, if you'd like to?'

Grace hesitated. 'It would be nice,' she said. 'I'll slip in quietly without letting them see me.'

Going round by the garden, she slipped into the marquee by one of the side entrances and stood behind a bank of plants she'd arranged earlier. The two musicians were playing on a small dais in the far corner. Tricia looked very pretty in her black velvet skirt and white frilled blouse. She was wearing her hair as Grace liked to see it, swinging loose; straight and silky. At the piano sat a rather distinguished-looking man with grey hair, his back half turned to her.

Grace watched and listened for a few moments. They paused briefly to discuss something and the pianist turned his face in her direction. Grace caught her breath sharply. Harry! Dear God, it was Harry, she was sure of it. Slowly, her heart thudding against her ribs, she went out into the garden. Her heart raced sickeningly and her legs felt like jelly as she made her way back to the car and when she reached it she stood for a moment, leaning against the door as she tried to steady the sickening thudding of her heartbeat.

The housekeeper noticed her from the window and came out onto the drive, concerned at the sight of the woman's ashen face.

'Are you feeling ill? Can I get you something?'

Grace shook her head. 'N-No, thank you. I'm quite all right. It's just − just rather warm.'

'Let me get you a glass of water.'

Grace straightened her shoulders and took a firm hold of herself. 'No, thank you,' she said. 'It's very kind but I'm fine now. And I have some other jobs to do.'

She got into the car and drove away, her mind still spinning. What would Tricia say if she knew that the man accompanying her was actually her own grandfather?

Once safely home her thoughts seemed to slow down and she found she was able to think logically. What about Elaine? She hadn't seen her father since she was eleven years old. She wasn't likely to recognise him now. If she simply said nothing, Harry would go back to London without ever knowing, and no one would be any the wiser. On the other hand ...

She made herself a strong cup of coffee and sat for several minutes thinking of the opportunity she held in the palm of her hand. It was almost as though fate was offering her an option. Should she let it pass? It would be so nice to see Harry again — talk to him. Lately he had been in her thoughts so much. What had happened was all so long ago now. And Stella was dead after all.

Making up her mind quite suddenly, she got up and went to the telephone. When the housekeeper's pleasant voice answered she said: 'It's Mrs Wendover speaking. I'm so sorry to trouble you when you're so busy, but would you give my granddaughter a message for me? Will you ask her to bring her accompanist home with her for a meal when they've finished playing?'

For the rest of the afternoon Harry remained in her mind. He'd looked fit; older of course, like her, but really quite distinguished and handsome. And he played as well as ever. When she had slipped into the marquee to listen he and Tricia had been playing a selection from the old musical Bless the Bride. That show had been all the rage when they'd first married. The hit song 'This Is My Lovely Day' had been a special favourite of theirs. As she worked, in spite of herself, she found herself humming it.

The wedding reception went without a hitch. Everyone enjoyed the music and some of the guests even asked Elaine if the musicians would be available for other functions. It gave her quite a buzz to be able to tell them that the violinist was her daughter and only playing as a special favour.

When the marquee was being cleared in preparation for the evening dance she went in search of Tricia, hoping to catch her before she left for home. She found her alone and freshening up

345

in a bedroom on the first floor that had been set aside for staff.

'Darling, I'm glad I caught you before you left. The music was lovely. Everyone enjoyed it so much.'

'Thanks, Mum. We enjoyed playing. It was fun.'

'What are you doing now?'

'Gran's invited us back for dinner,' Tricia told her as she applied a little lip gloss. Suddenly she could contain herself no longer. 'Mum,' she said, looking at her mother through the mirror, 'did the pianist look familiar to you?'

Elaine frowned. 'No, Should he?'

Tricia took a deep breath. 'I was hoping you might have recognised him. Mum, his name is Harry — Harry Wendover.'

Elaine stared at her daughter. 'Wendover? But that's ...' She shook her head. 'You *can't* possibly mean what I think you mean?'

Tricia laughed delightedly. 'Yes! Isn't it the most exciting thing? And to think I'd known him for *ages* and never guessed. I only knew him as Harry, you see. It wasn't until I ...' She broke off, her smile fading as she caught the look on her mother's white face. 'What is it, Mum? I know it's a surprise but ...'

'What are you thinking of, Tricia? You can't walk into Gran's house with him just like that. It could be an awful shock for her after all these years.'

But Tricia was shaking her head. 'Gran is stronger than that. I've always had the impression that she'd love to see him again.' She looked hard at her mother. 'Are you sure you didn't recognise him?'

'Of course I didn't.' Elaine's voice was sharp with annoyance. 'I was only eleven years old the last time I saw him. That's a lifetime ago.'

'But don't you *want* to see him again?' Tricia's heart was sinking. It wasn't going at all as she'd visualised.

'No, I don't' Elaine stood up. 'Have you said anything to him?'

'No. It was going to be a — a surprise.'

Elaine snorted. 'That's the under-statement of the year. If you take my advice you'll get him on the first train for London as quickly as you can and say nothing to Gran about it. You can take my car. Alison will give me a lift home.'

'All right, if you say so. But I thought you'd be pleased too. I've been looking forward to it all day.'

'I'm sorry, Tricia, but you really should have spoken to me about it first. You don't understand how Gran and I feel. It isn't easy to forgive or forget the way he walked out and left us.'

346

Elaine felt shocked and upset. Not only by the sudden reappearance of her father and the prospect of meeting him again, but by the depth of her own resentment. She had a sudden and vivid recollection of herself as a desperately unhappy teenager — of the letter she had written to her father, to which he had never even bothered to reply.

'Get him out of here, Tricia,' she said shakily. 'I don't want to see him. I won't!'

There was a lump in Tricia's throat as she dropped Harry off at the station. Her mother didn't seem to have worried that *she* might be upset by the sudden announcement last night that Paul Kingston wasn't her father. Perhaps she hadn't stopped to imagine the impact that news like that would have. The notion that there was a man out there somewhere who wasn't even aware that he had a daughter made her ache in a strange, restless way. They could pass each other in the street without even knowing. For almost twenty years she had been Patricia Kingston. Now suddenly she didn't know who she was — didn't even know her real name.

Fortunately she hadn't had time to tell Harry about her grandmother's invitation, so she was saved the embarrassment of thinking up an excuse. As she stopped the car on the station forecourt, he looked anxiously at her.

'Tricia, are you all right? You're very quiet.'

She shook her head, forcing a smile. 'No, I'm fine, thank you, Harry. Thanks for coming today. I'll give you a ring when I get back to London.' As she drove back to her grandmother's house her heart was full and heavy. She'd looked forward so much to introducing Harry and then standing back to watch the reaction. She might have known it would blow up in her face. Maybe she just hadn't thought it through properly.

She drove her mother's car into the drive and got out, but she hadn't reached the front door when it opened and her grandmother stepped out into the porch.

'I saw you arrive.' She looked agitated. 'Where is he?'

Tricia stared at her. 'Who?'

'Harry. I invited you both back here for a meal.'

'I know — but I — Mum didn't want — I took him straight to the station.'

'Oh, *no*.' Grace's face drained of colour. 'Has he gone then?'

Tricia shook her head. 'I left him waiting. The train wasn't due for another ten minutes. He might not have ...'

Grace was already getting into the car. 'Come on. If we hurry

347

we might catch him,' she urged. 'Well, don't just stand there, Tricia. What you don't realise is that the man you call Harry is your grandfather.'

Tricia looked at her grandmother as she hurriedly fastened her seat belt. 'You *knew*?'

'Yes. I saw the two of you rehearsing when I came to collect the florist's stuff. That's when I telephoned with the invitation to bring him home.'

A grin spread over Tricia's face as she began to back out of the drive. Gran knew all the time. Knew and, unlike her mother, actually wanted to see him again. She glanced at her watch. The train was already a minute overdue. Unless it was running late they wouldn't catch him. As she pressed her foot down on the accelerator she was saying a silent prayer under her breath.

As they drove on to the station forecourt the hands of the clock stood at six fifty-five. Tricia looked apologetically at her grandmother.

'I'm horribly afraid we must be too late, Gran,' she said. 'But you go and see. I'll wait here for you.'

Grace got out of the car and hurried into the booking hall. She could see that the platform was still full of people. Maybe the train hadn't gone yet after all. She bought a platform ticket and asked the ticket collector.

'Running ten minutes late, madam,' he told her. 'Due any minute now.'

On the platform she searched the crowds for him without success. Maybe he was in the buffet. She made her way towards it. Then she saw him turning away from the newsagent's stand, and evening paper in his hand as he paused to put away his change.

She stopped in her tracks, suddenly at a loss. Till now she hadn't thought what she would do or say, but now that the moment was here she found she hadn't any idea how to approach him. Suppose she had aged beyond recognition? Suppose he didn't know her?

The public address system bleeped and a voice announced that the train arriving on platform two was the six forty-eight for London. Apologies were made for delay and inconvenience. The crowds around her surged forward, jostling and pushing; bumping her legs with bags and suitcases. She lost sight of Harry and panicked. Then she saw him again and let the crowds carry her forward towards him as he waited. It was as the train drew to a stop that she found herself close enough to touch his sleeve.

'Harry?'

He turned and looked at her, frowning a little. Then his face cleared. 'Grace?'

'Yes, it's me.' As she looked up at him there was only one thing to say; 'Please, Harry, don't go.'

They stood there while the other passengers pushed impatiently past them to climb on to the crowded train; stood looking at each other as the doors banged and the guard blew his whistle. Then as the train began to pull out of the station, Harry held out his hand and Grace put her own into it.

In the station forecourt the car was empty. Tricia had gone, leaving a note under the windscreen wiper. It read: 'Two's company. See you later, Gran. Good luck. Tricia.' Grace passed it to Harry.

'Maybe this will explain.'

He read it and looked at her, a smile spreading over his face. 'I might have known. God, I might have known,' was all he said. But his eyes said more — much more.

Chapter Twenty-Three

'Thank you, ladies and gentlemen. I'm glad to see that your holiday has refreshed you. 'Max Crichton laid down his baton. 'We'll take a lunch break now and assemble again at two-thirty. Then we'll tackle the Brahms.'

Terry Holtby turned in he chair and raised and eyebrow at his sister. 'Coming across the road for a burger?'

Eunice nodded eagerly. 'You bet. I'll just get my coat. See you in ten minutes.' She looked at Tricia. 'Coming?'

Tricia smiled. 'Yes, please. I'm starving — didn't have time for breakfast this morning.'

The girls put away their instruments and started to leave, but as they passed the rostrum Max glanced up and said: 'Miss Kingston, I'd like a word with you. Would you mind staying behind?'

Tricia looked at Eunice. 'You go on. I'll catch up with you later.'

Eunice pulled a face and lowered her voice. 'Hello, what have you been up to then? He doesn't look best pleased.'

Max clearly had no intention of speaking until they were alone and Tricia felt conspicuous, standing waiting for him while the other members of the orchestra filed past. Finally, when they were alone, she looked up enquiringly.

'What did you want to see me about?'

He'd been studying a score. He closed it with a snap and stepped down from the rostrum. 'Come with me,' he said shortly.

Puzzled, she followed him to the small bare dressing room he used backstage. Beckoning her inside he closed the door. 'Sit down.' he indicated a chair in the corner. Apprehensively she did as he said. Reaching into his briefcase he brought out a pocket tape recorder and switched it on. Immediately the room was filled with the sound of Vivaldi. She was listening to her own demo tape. Flushing scarlet, she looked at him.

'Oh.'

'Exactly.' He switched it off. 'Perhaps you'd care to explain.'

She shrugged and lifted her chin defiantly. 'It's a demo tape. We thought it might be a way of getting heard.'

'And who is "we"?'

'A friend and I.' She cleared her throat. 'How − how did you come to have it?'

'An agent sent it to me. Obviously she was unaware that it had been made by a member of my own orchestra.' He glowered at her. 'You are aware that you are under contract − and that your contract precludes this kind of thing?'

'I wasn't aware of it, no.'

'Then I suggest that you go home and read it − *all* of it. And don't let me catch you doing anything like this again. At least, not while you are with the NWYO.'

'No.' It was a long time since she'd been spoken to so arbitrarily. She stood up, her face red. 'Is that all?'

'No, it is *not* all,' he thundered. 'I'm still waiting for an apology.'

'Oh − yes, of course. I'm sorry.' She moistened her lips and glanced up at him. Might as well be hanged for a sheep as a lamb. 'Er − did you listen to the tape right through?'

He paused. 'And if I had ...?'

She cleared her throat. 'Nothing really − I just wondered what you thought of it.'

His dark eyes narrowed and for a moment he looked as though he might explode with anger, then he drew up another chair and sat astride it facing her, his face on a level with hers.

'I'd intended to spare you that,' he told her. 'But seeing that you have the barefaced effrontery to ask, I'll tell you. I thought it was quite the most audacious, presumptuous, *arrogant* piece of playing that I've ever had the misfortune to listen to.' He registered her discomfort with obvious satisfaction. 'And if I were continuing as conductor of this orchestra, I would certainly be tempted to dismiss you.' He waited for this to sink in, then went on: 'However, as I shall be leaving shortly, I have decided to let you off with a warning.'

Dismayed, she stared at him. 'You're *leaving*?'

'I leave at the end of the year.'

'But why?' She looked at him with enormous blue eyes. 'Why are you leaving? Have you had a better offer?'

He blinked, slightly taken aback by her directness. 'If it's any of your business − which it isn't − I do happen to have had several very good offers, but I've made no decision as yet,' he said. 'The

351

reason I'm leaving the orchestra is very simple. By then end of this year, I shall have reached the age limit.'

'I see. I'll miss you,' she said simply.

His eyebrows rose a fraction, then he picked up the tape recorder. 'Quite clearly you weren't thinking of that when you made this.'

'I didn't intend to leave the orchestra.'

'What did you intend then?'

'I just wanted to be heard,' she said. 'No one can hear me playing with all the rest of the orchestra and I want to be a soloist. But if you think my playing is as bad as that, maybe it's just as well that no one else heard it.' She rose to go, her shoulders drooping a little. Her confidence had taken a battering, and the news that Max would be leaving had shaken her too, even more than she would have anticipated.

'Wait,' he commanded. 'Did I say you could go?'

She turned to look at him. His eyes were dark and intense as he glared at her.

'I'm sorry. I did apologise. Is there something else you wanted to say to me?'

'Are you going to give up just like that?'

'Isn't that what you're trying to tell me I should do?'

'I don't *try* to tell people things. If I thought you should give up, I'd leave you in no doubt.'

'Oh.' She frowned. 'Then what ...?'

'If you're really hell bent on becoming a concert artist, you'll need to work hard at it. You'll have to find yourself a professor – a good one.'

'Yes. But who?'

He stood up. 'Me.' He folded his arms and looked at her. 'Can you think of anyone better?'

'N-no, but ...'

'It won't be easy – for either of us, so don't think that.'

They stood facing each other for what seemed to Tricia like a very long moment. Her heart quickened and she felt the hot colour warm her face.

'Are you serious?' she whispered.

'Is the idea so repellent to you?'

'Oh, n-no,' she stammered. 'But I thought ...'

'I warn you, I'll make life hell for you.'

'I know.'

'And you'll loathe me by the time we've finished.'

Her lips twitched. 'Would that worry you?'

'Not in the least.'

352

'Then it doesn't matter, does it?'

'But if you can stand the pace — which I very much doubt — I'll make a virtuoso of you. If that's what you really want.'

'You really think I have the talent?'

He shook his head. 'It's *I* who have the talent. The talent to get the best out of you. Whether you have the stamina and the resilience to learn, remains to be seen.'

'When can we start?' Her eyes were shining.

'Don't look so eager,' he warned. 'You don't know what you're letting yourself in for.'

'I think I do.'

'By the end of one month you'll wish you'd taken up law, architecture, clog dancing ...'

'No, I won't.' She laughed. 'Please, Max. When can I start?'

His stern expression softened. 'Ten o'clock tomorrow morning — at my place. And don't be late.'

'I'll be there.'

'And, Tricia ...' She turned at the door to look at him. 'Just for the moment, it's between ourselves. Right?'

She gave him her most brilliant smile. 'You got it.'

Elaine found the ward without too much difficulty. Zoe had been admitted to Addenbrookes's Hospital the previous day and now awaited her operation. A young nurse at the desk answered her enquiry, pointing to a bed at the far end of the ward.

As she walked towards it, she racked her brain for what to say. How could she make normal, light conversation with a woman who knew she had cancer and faced an operation with a fifty-fifty chance of recovery, especially a woman as vital and life-loving as Zoe? When Red had telephoned to tell her that Zoe had been admitted he had sounded devastated.

'The surgeon has promised to do what he can,' he told her. 'I'm praying it'll be curable, but there's nothing any of us can do now but wait and hope.'

The words echoed in her head as she walked the length of the ward. But when she reached the end bed she found Zoe sitting up and looking quite cheerful. Her long hair was neatly coiled and she wore an incongruous frilly pink bed jacket. Elaine found it oddly touching to see her wrists bare of the silver bangles she always wore.

'Hello, stranger,' she said, looking up from the book she was reading. 'It's good to see a friendly face.'

Elaine put down the flowers she had brought and kissed Zoe's cheek. 'How are you feeling?'

'Bloody bored.' Zoe threw aside her book. 'Got that thing from the woman with the library trolley. The most fatuous rubbish I've ever read. I'll be glad to get this damned op' over with and get back to my work.'

'Of course you will. Any idea how long you're likely to be in?'

'I daresay they'll be glad to get rid of me as soon as they can.' Zoe looked up with a wry smile. 'I'm already making a sodding nuisance of myself. I expect you know that I might not get over it completely?'

Elaine caught her breath. 'Zoe, don't say that.'

'Why not? It has to be faced.' She laid a hand on Elaine's arm. 'Don't look like that, my dear. I've had a damned good innings – and we all have to go sometime. If they can put me right – fine. If not, well, fair enough.'

'Please, Zoe ...' Elaine swallowed hard. 'I wish you wouldn't ...'

'Sorry, love.' Zoe squeezed her hand. 'I know I'm a bit too blunt at times. I've had longer than everyone else to come to terms with it.' She smiled wryly. 'It was almost a relief in a way, having it confirmed.'

'You knew? But why didn't you tell anyone before?'

'I suppose I tried to ignore it for a while. Kidded myself that it might just go away.' She shrugged. 'What was the point of worrying everyone? That's not my style. You know how I hate fuss.'

'But if they'd got it sooner ...' Elaine bit her lip, but Zoe just smiled.

'They'll do what they can. The consultant seemed quite optimistic. Now let's talk about something else. What about you? Are you definitely divorcing Paul?'

Elaine nodded. 'It's all in the hands of a solicitor. Paul won't contest, so everything is in progress.'

Zoe settled herself more comfortably. 'That's good news.' She looked intently at Elaine. 'Tricia wrote to me, such a happy letter. She told me about how she found your father playing the piano for auditions or something, and brought him home to play at one of your weddings. Got him and your mother on to speaking terms again.'

Elaine nodded. 'That's right.'

'You don't seem too thrilled about it.'

'I'm not.'

'Dare one ask why?'

'He's bad news, Zoe. He let us down all those years ago. I'm afraid he might hurt Mother all over again.'

354

'Surely that's not very likely after all this time?'

Elaine looked down at her hands. 'I've never told anyone this before, but I wrote to him once — it was when I was in my teens and very unhappy. I asked to see him again. He never even replied.'

'I see.'

'No, you don't.' Elaine looked up with accusing eyes. 'You think I'm just nursing a childish grudge, but I'm not.'

'Maybe there was a good reason for his not replying,' Zoe said. 'Maybe he never even got your letter.'

'And maybe he just didn't want to know.'

'So you won't see your father? And you're avoiding Patrick too, aren't you? I quite thought you'd try to get in touch with him after your separation.'

Elaine shook her head. 'I'm not deliberately avoiding him, Zoe. It's just that I can't handle anything else at the moment. I just want to get the divorce over with and have some peace.'

'And the future?' Zoe asked. 'You're still young — and very attractive.'

'There's the business. From now on I intend to put all my energy into that.'

Zoe took in Elaine's tight-lipped expression. 'Ah, yes, of course. The business.'

Her whimsical tone brought Elaine's eyes up to meet hers. 'I've decided that in the end the business is my best bet, Zoe,' she said. 'At least I'm in control of that.' She shook her head. 'I've come to the conclusion that I'm just no good at relationships. I seem to have wasted my own life and everyone else's, trying to make them work. Maybe I should steer clear of people.'

'You and I both know that isn't true.' Zoe squeezed her hand tightly. 'None of us can do without people. Each one we meet as we go through life brings out a small facet of our personality. Some bring out the worst — show us the darker side that none of us likes to admit we have. Others, the ones we love, bring out the best. But the more people, the more facets to make us sparkle. Like a finely cut diamond.'

Elaine smiled wryly. 'How philosophical. You make life sound so simple.'

Zoe chuckled. 'I can tell by the way you're looking at me that you think I'm a bit batty, waxing lyrical like that. Maybe I'm a little high on the dope they're shoving into me. I suppose what I'm trying to say is that nothing is actually wasted unless you let it be. Even the most arid relationship tells us something about ourselves — shows us our faults and

355

weaknesses. We can learn from that, build on it. If we choose to.'

Elaine was silent for a moment. 'It's too late in my case,' she said at last.

Zoe laughed softly. 'Of course it isn't. It's never too late. Ask your mother.'

Elaine looked thoughtful. 'I sometimes wonder what our lives would have been like if my parents had stayed together.'

Zoe shrugged. 'Who can tell?'

'I wouldn't have come to live in Cambridge — wouldn't have known Alison and started HEA. Wouldn't have known you and Red and ...'

'And Patrick?'

'And Patrick wouldn't have known me. Maybe I messed up his life too.'

'Patrick's marriage would never have worked, if that's what you mean,' Zoe put in. 'Cathryn was never right for him. At heart it was always you, Elaine, whether he knew it or not.' She leaned back against her pillows, looking suddenly tired and drawn.

'Elaine stood up. 'I've tired you. I'll go now. You must get your rest.'

Zoe reached out her hand. 'You'll come again afterwards — if there is an afterwards, won't you?'

'Of course I will.' Elaine bent to kiss her. 'And I'll be thinking about you all day tomorrow. You'll be fine, I know you will.'

Tricia flung herself through the door of the flat, pulled off her coat and threw it into a chair. Tracey looked at her, one eyebrow raised.

'Oh dear, I know that look,' she said. 'Do I take it that the music lesson didn't go too well?' she asked mildly.

Tricia growled. 'Aaagh! That man. He's an arrogant, self-opinionated, *rude* ...'

'Brilliant musician — as you're always telling me,' Tracey finished for her.

'I must have been stark, staring mad to agree to let him tutor me.'

Tracey laughed. 'As bad as that, eh?'

'*Worse.* Do you know, he had that woman in the flat? She must have heard every insulting word he said to me. She even made coffee for us — came calmly waltzing in with the tray. A big smile on her ravishing bloody face.'

'What woman is this?' Tracey asked.

356

'The one he brought to the Lizard that night — the one with the dramatic black hair and the flashing eyes. Oh, Tracey, it was awful. I can't go there again. I just *can't*.'

'So that's the end of the concert career, is it?'

Tricia was silent, chewing at a thumb nail as she remembered the morning's humiliation. 'The rotten thing is, if I give up now he'll say I've no guts,' she said. 'He said it would be hell. Now I know he wasn't kidding.'

'So what are you going to do?'

Tricia stood for a moment, her shoulders slumped as she stared out of the window, then suddenly she straightened up and took a deep breath. Pulling her case towards her she opened it and drew out a sheet of music. 'I'm going to practise,' she said firmly. 'Tomorrow I'm going to be so damned *good* he won't be able to find a single fault. That's what I'm going to do.'

Elaine was about to break for lunch at the office the following morning when Red telephoned.

'Elaine, it's all over. Zoe's through her operation. I've just spoken to Blake-Thomas, her consultant.'

'Yes? What did he say?'

'He was cautiously optimistic,' he told her. 'We'll have to keep our fingers crossed — wait and see. She'll have to be carefully monitored over the next twelve months, but he's fairly sure he's cracked it.'

'Oh, Red, I'm so glad. Have you seen her? When can I go?'

'I'm ringing from the hospital now. I've already seen her. She came round from the anaesthetic but now she's asleep. She'll be in intensive care for a couple of days. I'll let you know when you can go.'

'I'll tell Alison. She'll be so pleased. Is there anyone else you'd like me to contact for you?'

There was a pause, then he said: 'Could you ring the boys for me? If you've got a pencil, I'll give you their numbers. I want to be there beside her when she wakes up, you see.'

'Of course, Red. Leave it to me. And let me know if there's anything else.' Elaine scribbled down the numbers he gave her and found suddenly that her eyes were full of tears. Coming into the room a moment later Alison saw them and stopped short.

'Elaine?'

'That was Red.'

'Oh, God — Aunt Zoe. It's not bad news if it?'

'No. Zoe's going to be all right,' Elaine assured her, swallowing the lump in her throat. 'At least, things are looking hopeful so far.'

'Oh, thank God for that.' Alison drew up a chair. 'Elaine – maybe this isn't the right time to bring this up, but I have something to tell you and I want to do it before my nerve fails.' She paused, eyeing Elaine apprehensively. 'Robert and I are engaged. We plan to get married at Christmas.'

'Oh, Alison, that's great.' Elaine got up and went to hug her, but Alison held her at arms' length. 'Wait – you might not feel quite so pleased when I tell you the rest. Robert has been offered a very good job in Canada. Toronto. They want him to start in the New Year, but of course I won't leave till you've found a suitable replacement for me ...' She stopped, dismayed at the look on Elaine's face. 'Oh dear, you're shocked.'

'No. I'm pleased for you, of course. It's lovely news. And you must go with Robert when he starts his new job. Don't worry about the business. Everything runs smoothly nowadays. And Mum will always help out in an emergency.'

Alison looked relieved. 'Are you really sure? I feel I'm leaving you in the lurch. After all, the business was always a joint venture and it's meant so much to us both.'

'Life comes first though.' Elaine said, remembering Zoe's words. 'And people. You and Robert are perfect for each other. You really deserve to be happy, Alison, and I couldn't be happier for you both.' She paused for a moment. 'There is a favour you could do for me though.'

'Please – just say the word.'

'You couldn't find a corner for me at your place this weekend, could you?'

Alison looked puzzled. 'Isn't it this weekend that your father is coming to stay?'

'That's right. But I'd rather not be around. Could you possibly put me up for a couple of nights?'

'Robert has to go up to London this weekend, to finalise arrangements. I had planned to go with him, but of course you're welcome to stay at the flat.' She paused. 'Tell me to mind my own business if you like, but don't you think you should be around – for your mother's sake?'

'Why?'

Alison shrugged. 'Well, as support, chaperone, whatever. She's bound to be nervous.'

Elaine shook her head. 'Don't you believe it. She can hardly wait.. She's like a teenager going on her first date. No, I'd prefer to stay at the flat, if that's all right?'

'Well, if you're sure that's what you really want ...'

358

'Well, if you're sure that's what you really want ...'

'It *is*.' Elaine's face was tight and closed and she busied herself with tidying her desk, refusing to meet Alison's eyes.

'Look, Elaine, if your mother if prepared to let bygones be bygones ...'

'That's her affair,' Elaine said abruptly. 'She may be prepared to forget the way he behaved, I'm not. I want nothing to do with him.'

'Isn't that a little hard on your mother?'

Elaine looked up at her friend. 'It's up to her. She must do as she chooses. I have my own life to live and I've made up my mind that it won't include my father again − *ever*.'

When Alison had left for lunch Elaine rang Grace. After she had passed on the news about Zoe she said: 'Oh, and by the way, I'll be away this weekend. Alison is going away and I said I'd keep an eye on the flat. Anyway, I have some work to catch up with.'

There was a small silence at the other end, then Grace said: 'All right, dear, just as you like. You must do whatever you think. I understand.'

Ringing off, Elaine sat thinking for some minutes. Everything around her seemed to be changing. Her divorce; Zoe's illness; her father's reappearance; and now Alison's bombshell. It felt as though life was caving in on her. People were moving on, leaving her behind. Maybe it was time she moved on too. But where to − and to what?'

She remembered the two calls she had promised to make and pulled the pad towards her. She dialled Tom's number first. It was his home number and his wife answered. Elaine gave her the message, asked after the children and made polite small-talk, then rang off. For some minutes she sat staring at the other number − Patrick's. Although she heard news of him from Zoe, it was years since they had actually been in touch. It would be strange, hearing his voice again. She lifted the receiver and dialled the London code.

Patrick's secretary answered.

'I'm sorry but Mr Carne is lecturing at the moment.'

Elaine felt weak with a mixture of disappointment and relief as she passed Red's message on.

'That's good news,' the girl said pleasantly. 'I'll see that he gets it as soon as possible, of course. But I happen to know he's planning to drive up to Cambridge this evening anyway.'

When she put the receiver down Elaine found that her hands were shaking. Patrick would be here this evening. It was quite likely that she'd see him tomorrow. Now that they were both free again, now

359

that there was nothing to stop them being together, were her feelings for him still the same? There was no need to ask. The clamour in her heart at the thought of seeing him again answered the question for her.

'It's no use, I'll never get the hang of calling you Grandad,' Tricia laughed. 'It's got to be Harry or nothing.'

'Make it Harry then. I don't think I could bear to be called "Nothing".'

They were having lunch together in a wine bar in The Strand. On the weekend of the wedding they had made a standing arrangement to meet there every Wednesday to have lunch and share their news. Today Tricia had poured out all her woes, but Harry had refused to take them seriously.

'I get the distinct impression that you're a bit of a masochist when it comes to music,' he said. 'Come on now, admit it. You'd much rather have someone who pulls no punches than a wimp who'd be soft with you.'

She pulled a face. 'We-ell − I suppose so,' she said grudgingly. 'It's just that he's so rude. I can't seem to do anything right at the moment. I practised the Schubert really hard all week and then when I played it for him he laughed − *laughed*, Harry. Said if he hadn't laughed he'd have had to cry. Can you imagine how that made me feel?'

Harry hid a smile. He'd already guessed that Tricia was more used to praise than criticism. Her doting mother and grandmother − perhaps even the teachers at St Cecilia's − had made her feel she had a special talent, which she did. But Harry knew Max Crichton wasn't in the business of dishing out compliments. Nothing but perfection would do for him, and he'd get it − even if he had to batter it out of her. At the moment he was treating her like a high-spirited young colt − breaking her in.

'He must have great faith in your ability,' he said quietly.

'How can you *say* that?' Tricia wailed. 'Sometimes I think he feels I'm absolutely hopeless.'

'Would he bother with you at all if he really thought that? Would he even have given you a job in the orchestra?'

'Perhaps not.'

'Well then. Come on, cheer up and have another of those fizzy drinks you're so fond of. What's it called, a spritzer?'

'Thanks, Harry. You always cheer me up. What would I do without you?'

He grinned at her, inordinately proud of his beautiful and talented granddaughter. 'You know, I still can't get over finding you. It's a miracle. One I don't deserve.'

She touched his hand. 'When are you and Gran seeing each other again?'

His face suddenly grew serious. 'I'm going to Cambridge at the weekend.'

'You're nervous, aren't you?' She peered into his eyes. 'Don't be. Gran's the loveliest person I know.'

'She hasn't much reason to think kindly of me.'

'Do you know, when I was a little girl she was always talking to me about you,' she told him. 'To hear her talk, you were all the most brilliant musicians the world has ever known, all rolled up into one.'

He stared at her. 'She said that — about me?'

She pursed her lips, her head on one side. 'Mmm, implied rather than said. She always said I got my musical talent from you.'

'What else did she tell you?' he asked warily.

'I know about the break-up — and Stella Rainbow. But it was all a very long time ago now, wasn't it?'

He smiled wryly. 'To you it's history, something that happened to two other people long before you were born. To us — to your grandmother and me — it's still comparatively recent. I left her, Tricia. And I left your mother. Just at the time when they both needed me.' He shook his head. 'I'm not sure if your mother will ever truly understand or forgive me for that.'

'She'll come round.' Tricia looked thoughtful for a moment, then she said: 'Mummy hasn't had an easy time. You know of course that she's divorcing Dad?' He nodded. 'They've never been happy together, so it's probably just as well.' Tricia looked at him for a moment, wishing she could tell him the rest. But she had promised to keep it to herself. It seemed all wrong. Families shouldn't have secrets from each other.

'I should have been there for her all those years,' he said thickly. 'Maybe if I had ...' The remorse in his eyes tugged at Tricia's heart and she looked away.

'You must have had a reason for leaving as you did — a good one.'

'Of course it *seemed* a good reason, at the time. Values are so different when you're young. In retrospect I don't come out of it so well. It's your grandmother who was the strong one in the end. Look what she made of her life — and then look at me.'

'You mustn't say that, mustn't put yourself down. You've had a good career.'

He shook his head. 'I've rubbed along. Nothing more than

that. Stella was the one with the talent. All I did was bask in
her reflected glory. Even that didn't last long. There were a lot
of bad times too.'

Tricia looked at her watch. 'I'm sorry, Harry. I've got to go now
Rehearsal at three.' She grinned. 'Must try to keep on the right side
of Max, mustn't I?'

He watched her go, swinging across the restaurant with long
confident strides, her violin case under one arm and her blonde
hair swinging. Elaine's girl. In spite of the fact that she wore no
make-up, made no attempt to glamorise herself, there wasn't a
male head that didn't turn in her direction as she passed. It was
her freshness, her youthful charm and exuberance that was her main
attraction. Harry sighed. He hoped Max wouldn't be too tough with
her. It would be criminal to break a spirit like that.

Grace had cleaned the house from top to bottom. In the spare room
she had put carefully chosen books and magazines by the bed, fresh
flowers on the dressing table. In the oven a beef casserole and an
apple pie stood ready to be served. Were they still Harry's favourites?
Her hair was freshly shampooed and set and she was wearing the new
dress she had taken so much trouble in choosing. It was coral – a
soft shade that flattered her colouring and enhanced the rich velvet
brown of her eyes. She stood looking round the neat, comfortable
room. Yes, everything was ready.

For the tenth time that day she rearranged the vase of
flowers on the little table in the window, glancing up the
road as she did so. Around four o'clock, he had said. It
was almost a quarter past now. Maybe she should have
gone to meet the train. But she hadn't wanted to seem
too eager.

She turned from the window to sit on the edge of the settee,
her ear alert for the softest step on the path outside. If only
Elaine wasn't so disapproving. It wasn't that she'd actually
said anything, more what she *hadn't* said. All those years
ago it was Elaine who had always upheld her father. They
had been so close, often made Grace feel left out in those
old, far-off days. And he had never forgotten her birthdays
and Christmas, so why was she so reluctant to meet him
again now?

She was still puzzling over the problem when a sudden ring at the
front doorbell brought her to her feet. He was here. Passing the
hall mirror she took a last glance at herself, then went to answer
the door.

362

Do you know what struck me about this house the moment I saw
it?' Harry leaned back in his chair, replete after his second helping
of Grace's apple pie.

'No. What was that?' She cleared away the used plates and began
to pour coffee.

'That it was like the little house in Stanmore. There are even
cherry trees in the road outside.'

Grace smiled. 'I know. That's what made me buy it after I gave
up the shop. It reminded me too. I loved that house.' She passed
him the sugar. 'I always promised myself I'd buy another just like
it when I retired.' She looked at him. 'I daresay you've lived in all
sorts of places on your travels.'

He nodded. 'All sorts. Posh hotels, grotty hotels, apartments,
rented houses . . . but oddly enough, never anything permanent. The
little flat where I live now, in Notting Hill, is the most permanent
place I've had. But it isn't a patch on this.' He looked round
approvingly at the light oak furniture and pastel green carpet, the
dainty china ornaments and tastefully arranged flowers. 'This feels
like a real home.' He smiled at her. 'But you always had the knack
of making a place homely, Grace.'

She stirred her coffee thoughtfully. 'You and Stella – you never
wanted to marry, make a home and have a family? You never asked
me again for a divorce.'

He was silent for a moment, then he looked up at her. 'There was
a time once – she had a miscarriage. She was very ill afterwards.
After that her career started to fall apart and she got very nervy and
insecure. She badly wanted us to be married then.' He paused. 'I even
came here to Cambridge once, to ask you again for a divorce.' He
smiled reminiscently. 'I stood on the other side of the road and I saw
you come out of your shop with this good-looking young fellow.'
He looked at her. 'I couldn't do it, Grace. Suddenly, I just knew
I couldn't do it.'

She frowned. 'Why not? If you'd asked me then I might have
agreed.'

'In a way I think that was what I was afraid of,' he confessed.
'You looked so happy.' He avoided her eyes. 'I was – well,
jealous, I suppose, though God knows I'd no right to be.'
He shrugged, smiling sheepishly. 'Anyway, when I got home
that night Stella seemed much better. She seemed to have
forgotten all about it – never mentioned marriage again. A
few months later we went to Australia. Somehow it didn't seem
to matter to her whether we were married or not over there.

363

For a few more years we were reasonably happy, till she got ill again.'

'I'm sorry . . .' She touched his hand. 'About Stella, I mean. It must have been awful for you.'

He nodded. 'It was. Her illness is something I don't like to remember.' He patted her hand. 'Still, all over now.'

'It must have been Morgan you saw that day,' Grace said thoughtfully. 'He's a young knitwear designer I helped when he was starting out. We worked together and were close friends, though he was much younger than me. But there was never anything more between us. Morgan was – has other preferences.'

'Ah, I see.' Harry nodded. Morgan Owen wasn't interested in Grace as anything but a business partner. That was why they were such good friends. He glanced at her. She was still beautiful. Her skin glowed with health and her eyes shone. She'd kept her figure too. He'd always known she would. Grace had the kind of feminine pride not often seen nowadays.

'Did you ever patch things up with your family?' he asked suddenly.

Grace felt the colour rise to her face. 'I ran into my sister Rachel a few years ago,' she told him quickly. 'She's a headmistress now – somewhere in Yorkshire. She gave me news of my other sisters. They're all fine.'

'And your father?'

Grace drew a deep breath. 'He died. He took his own life.'

Harry winced. 'I'm sorry, Grace. I shouldn't have asked.'

'No, I'm glad you did. It was a relief to me, Harry, seeing Rachel and hearing about the rest of them. Father didn't – he didn't mistreat the other girls. I was relieved about that. It had always worried me.'

He looked at her and found himself speculating about her father. It had always seemed to him that the man was twisted. He was surely more than simply a strict father. Could his mistreatment have extended to more than physical abuse? he wondered. He sighed, wishing the thought had occurred to him all those years ago. That could have been the cause of her inhibitions. If he could have got her to talk about it . . . Had she ever managed to overcome her revulsion for physical contact? Slightly ashamed, he thrust the thought aside and said: 'I daresay it would be a simple matter to get the marriage dissolved now, if that's what you'd like? It's been so long. It'd be no more than a formality by now, I daresay.'

Grace rose and began to clear the table, avoiding his eyes. 'Yes, I daresay you're right.'

They tidied up companionably together in the kitchen, Grace washing whilst Harry dried.

'Will Elaine be joining us?' Harry asked at last. 'Tricia tells me she's living with you while she looks for a place of her own.'

Grace avoided his eye. 'She's staying at her partner's flat this weekend. I believe they have some work they want to catch up with.'

'I see.' Harry put down the plate he was drying. 'Look, Grace, if my coming here is causing you any trouble . . .'

She turned to look at him. 'Elaine has had a hard time for some years — her husband's illness and the divorce have taken their toll of her. She hasn't said anything, but I think she might find the situation a little difficult to come to terms with. But she'll come round eventually.'

He searched her eyes. 'Does that mean what I hope it means — that we're going to continue to see each other?'

For a long moment they looked at each other, then Harry took both her hands and drew her to him.

'I know it's no use saying we can take up where we left off,' he said. 'It was so long ago, and too much went wrong between us for that. It wouldn't be realistic. But I daresay the years have changed us both. We're two different people now. We could have a try at getting to know each other again. Take it a step at a time.' He looked down at her. 'What do you say, Grace.'

She nodded, her throat tight. 'Yes, Harry. I'd like that very much.'

'I'd hate to lose you again now that I've found you.'

They talked until long after the hands of the clock had passed midnight, filling in the gaps in each of their pasts. Sitting side by side on the settee, it seemed to Grace like turning the clock back to the time when they had first met. In spite of the fact that they had both grown older and matured, she felt now just as she had then. Harry was a little heavier and his hair greyer, but for all that he was the same Harry she had met and fallen in love with when she was sixteen.

'Do you like living in London?' she asked him. 'I thought of moving up there recently, but then I changed my mind.'

'You made a wise decision.' He sighed. 'Sometimes I get so tired of the noise and bustle — of never knowing where I'll be working next week. It was exciting once, but now I tire more easily and I'm getting the odd twinge of arthritis in my fingers.' He smiled wistfully. 'There are times when I'd give anything to live in a place like this. You have everything here; beautiful architecture; a pleasant town. There's the river and the countryside not far away.'

Grace had a sudden idea — one that made her heart quicken with excitement. 'Harry . . .' She turned to look at him, her eyes shining. 'You could always come here and help with HEA. You could be our resident pianist. Elaine would be so . . .'

He was shaking his head ruefully. 'It sounds wonderful, but somehow I feel Elaine might not share your enthusiasm. Do us all a favour and sound her out first, eh?' He smiled as he saw her stifle a yawn. 'You're tired,' he said. 'I think it's time to call it a day.'

On the landing Grace paused. Her cheeks were pink and she couldn't quite meet his eyes as she said: 'I've put you in the spare room, Harry.'

He smiled gently. 'I'm sure I'll sleep like a log after that wonderful dinner.' He saw the uncertainty in her eyes and put his hands on her shoulders. 'Grace, my dear. We said we'd take it a step at a time, didn't we: I've enough sense to know that I have to win your trust all over again.' He kissed her very gently on the lips and smiled down into her eyes. 'You know it's funny, but the older you get, the less hurry there seems to be. Goodnight, love.'

'Goodnight, Harry.'

As she sat at her dressing table, taking off her make-up and preparing for bed, she thought how comforting it was, hearing him moving about in the room next door. Perhaps, someday soon . . . She found to her surprise that the thought of sharing a room — a bed — the intimacy of close contact with him, held no fears for her.

'It's a second chance,' she whispered to her reflection. 'I've been given a second chance.'

Chapter Twenty-Four

'That's *it*!' Tricia strode across the studio and began to put her violin into its case. 'This isn't working, Max. I can't go on any longer.'

She had been at his flat since late morning and had worked now for five hours without a break, playing the same piece over and over. Max, it seemed, was never satisfied. There was nothing about her playing that was right. Now, after hours of explosive, sometimes heavily sarcastic, criticism, he sat at the piano, smiling calmly at her as she began to struggle into her jacket.

'Just calm down,' he instructed. 'We'll have a break if you like, then you can try again. The trouble is that at the moment you're letting your temper play the damned violin.'

She rounded on him. 'Well, what do you expect? You make me go over and over it just for the sake of finding fault. I've practised that damned thing for hours at home. I work and *work*, yet you call me lazy and careless.'

'All right, all right. I admit that was uncalled for . . .;'

'And you yell at me loud enough for that woman to hear.'

'Woman?' He frowned. 'What woman?'

'Your – your *mistress* or whatever she is. She's always here, popping in and out to make sheep's eyes at you and gloat over my humiliation.'

Max got to his feet. His face was angry now. 'Don't be bloody impertinent. Consuela is *not* my mistress. Neither is she here to humiliate you.'

'Then who is she? And if she doesn't live here, why does she always have to be hanging around when I'm here?'

'That is none of your business,' he thundered. 'I will not have you questioning me about my guests. Perhaps it would be better if you left now, and came back when your manners have improved.'

'I shan't be coming back again,' she told him, gratified that she'd managed at last to arouse his anger. 'I've had you and your arrogant, high-handed attitude right up to here. And as for *manners* – you've got a lot of room to talk, I must say.' She snapped her case shut and began to cross the room, but he moved quickly to stand in her path.

'You're not leaving here in this mood.'

'But you've just told me to go.'

'Not like this.'

'Please get out of my way.'

'No. You're far too angry.'

She pushed at him, but he was like a solid wall. 'Get away. I want to go – ho-ome.' The last three words came out like a child's defenceless wail and to her horror she found herself crying with impotent fury. Hating him for forcing this final humiliation upon her, she kicked viciously at his ankle. 'Oh, I hate you,' she sobbed. 'Why can't you just let me go and forget all about me? I'll never make a concert artist. I'm no good. I'm useless. I'm not even even *me* any more.' Scalding, helpless tears were pouring down her cheeks now. It no longer mattered that he was seeing her at her weakest – her most vulnerable. She just didn't care any more.

Very gently he took her violin case out of her arms and put it aside, then he put an arm around her shoulders and led her firmly across the room to the settee.

'Sit down,' he commanded. 'First, you're going to tell me what all this is about, then I'm going to make you something to eat. Maybe hunger is your problem.' He took out a clean handkerchief and dabbed at her face, soaking up the tears that trembled on the ends of her fair-tipped lashes. 'Now what's wrong, Tricia?' he asked. 'What's *really* wrong?'

At the new, softer tone in his voice, the tears gathered afresh in her throat. 'You wouldn't understand,' she said thickly.

'Try me. We've got plenty of time.'

'I've had some news.'

'What kind of news?'

'I've been told something rather disturbing. It's made me feel – odd ever since.'

'Do you want to talk about it?'

She paused, biting her lip, wondering where on earth to begin. 'Have you ever heard the expression, "lost a shilling and found a sixpence"?' she said at last.

'Yes.'

She took the handkerchief from him and blew her nose. 'My

grandmother used to say that to me when I was little. Well, I've lost a father and found a grandfather.'

He looked nonplussed. 'Sorry, but I'm afraid you've lost me. I think you're going to have to elucidate on that one, Tricia.'

'My parents are divorcing at the moment. But my mother has just told me that my father — *isn't* — if you see what I mean. And she won't tell me who is.'

'And that gives you an identity problem?'

'Yes.' She looked at him. 'Well, wouldn't it you?'

'I'm not sure.' He frowned. 'But you mentioned your grandfather. Where does he come into it?'

'He and my gran split up years ago, when my mother was a child. He was a musician. I always knew that. Then, a few weeks ago and quite by accident, I discovered that he was none other than Harry Wendover.'

'*Our* Harry Wendover, you mean?' Max's eyes widened. 'But that's great.' He peered at her enquiringly. 'Isn't it?'

'It is to me. And to my Gran too. But my mother won't have anything to do with him. She can't forgive him for leaving all those years ago.' She looked up at him. 'The whole bloody thing is getting me down. I'm torn in two directions and I can't stop wondering who I am and where we're all going.'

'Then don't.' He took her firmly by the shoulders. 'Look, *I* know who you are. You're Patricia Kingston and you're going to be a concert violinist. I've taken you on as my protégée and no one I've taught has *ever* failed. Do you understand that?'

She stared at him. 'Yes, but . . .'

He put a finger over her lips. 'No buts. That was a positive statement. There'll be no doubts, no thought of failure — no excuses, or negative thoughts. *You are going to succeed.*' She opened her mouth to speak, but he went on: 'Names don't mean a thing, Tricia. Parents give us our physical bodies and, if we're lucky, some useful genes. The rest is up to us. You're *you*. That's all you need to know. You have talent and guts and stamina. I have the ability to mould all that into a professional career for you. If you'll let me, and if it's what you want.' He looked at her. '*Is* that what you want, Tricia? Because that's all you really have to ask yourself.'

She gave a shuddering sigh. 'Yes, Max. Oh, yes — please.'

He looked at her for a long moment, his dark eyes softening, then he drew her slowly into his arms and kissed her. He knew he was probably giving both of them a whole new set of problems — ruining all he'd just said; even shattering the chance of a truly professional

369

relationship between them, but he couldn't help himself. She looked so lost and so young with her wide blue eyes looking up at him and her mouth soft and tremulous. But he found her response astonishingly adult. Under all that child-like naivety she was all woman and as her body arched towards him and her lips parted beneath his he found her surprising fire arousing him to unexpected passion. What had started as a light kiss developed into a passionate embrace that left them both breathless and shaken.

'Tricia,' he murmured her name wonderingly. 'We shouldn't . . .'

'Yes — yes, we should,' she breathed against the corner of his mouth. 'It had to happen, Max. Can't you understand that? Now everything will be all right. Now you won't have to be angry with me any more.' She drew her head back to look into his eyes. 'Because it wasn't my music that was getting under your skin, was it?'

The deep blue eyes teased him wickedly and he felt laughter rise in his throat. 'You're not as green as you look, are you? I've half a mind to put you to the test.'

Her lips teased his playfully. 'Only half a mind? What happened to all that positive thinking?'

Getting to his feet, he held out his hand to her. 'All right, challenge accepted. Let's find out whether your theory is right, shall we?'

'Not when there's a chance that Consuela might walk in.'

'She won't.'

'But she might. And if she did . . .?'

He stood for a moment, looking down at her. Then he said: 'Tricia — do you trust me?'

She put her head on one side. 'I trust you as a musician — and as my teacher. As a man, I'm not so sure.'

He sat down and pulled her down again beside him, pulling her hand through his arm as though to hold her captive. 'Tell me, who do you *really* imagine Consuela is?' When she paused he urged her: 'Come on, cards on the table. Tell the truth. What have you been thinking?'

'We-ell, what I said: that she's your girlfriend.'

'Do you want to know the truth? Are you grown up enough to bear it? Will it make a difference to the way you feel? The truth now. If I'm going to be completely honest, I shall expect the same from you.'

She caught her lower lip between her teeth. 'I want to hear the truth. And it won't make any difference to the way I feel, but it might make a difference to what I allow to happen.'

'I see.' His face was grave. 'A woman of integrity.'

She frowned. 'You're making fun of me. Are you going to tell me or aren't you?'

370

'Of course I am.' He looked into her eyes. 'Consuela is my ...'

'Yes, she's your *what*?'

'She's my step-mother.'

She stared at him for a moment, then pulled her hand away and began to get up. 'If you're going to be facetious ...'

He took her hand and jerked her down again. 'It's the truth, Tricia. My mother died when I was ten. Five years later, my father went to Argentina to stay with a friend. He met and fell in love with his twenty-two-year-old daughter.' Tricia was silent, lost for words, and Max went on: 'I hated them both for a long time. I deeply resented having a stepmother who was only a few years older than me. But Consuela won me over in the end and we became good friends. She was like the older sister I'd never had. And she really did – *does* – love my father.'

'Where is he now?' Tricia asked in a whisper.

'In Argentina. They live there. My father went into partnership with Consuela's father. They breed horses. She comes over for the occasional week in London, to buy clothes and to see her friends. She stays at the Savoy, but she usually spends some time with me because we enjoy one another's company.'

'Did you ask her to chaperone me?' Her eyes were beginning to twinkle again now.

He laughed. 'No, that was her idea. Consuela was brought up very strictly. Our English freedom and sex equality shocks her profoundly. She thinks you're very talented and very attractive.' His eyes danced. 'She also thinks you fancy me.'

'Really? And what do *you* think? She reached up to stroke his beard and found it smoother and softer than she imagined.'

He stood up and scooped her up into his arms. 'Actions speak louder than words,' he informed her, his face close to hers. 'Maybe it's time I showed you.'

Elaine wakened to the sound of church bells. Alison's flat was in the heart of the city within hearing of several churches. Just for a drowsy, half-awake moment she fancied she was in Switzerland. She lay for a moment, thinking of the magic, idyllic days she had spent there with Patrick twelve years ago, wondering if he remembered and sometimes thought of it too.

Maybe I'll see him today, she told herself. And felt her heart lift and quicken. Yesterday it had seemed as though her life was grinding inexorably to a halt. Her own divorce; Alison's imminent departure for Canada; Tricia's independence ... they all seemed to point to the fact that she was becoming redundant, that her life was hurtling the fact that she was becoming redundant, that her life was hurtling downhill out of control. Her mother's reunion with her father had been the final straw. She would never come to terms with that. She deeply resented her father's selfishness. He hadn't replied to her letter, hadn't cared when she needed him. But now that he was alone and getting old he had come back to insinuate himself into their lives again — at the instigation of her own daughter too. But her mother's obvious pleasure at the prospect hurt most of all. It was as though all the people she had devoted her life to, wanted and needed her no more. They were all casting her aside.

In three more years she would be forty. A landmark. It was too young to retire and yesterday she had told herself despairingly that it was too late to begin again. But this morning, with the sun shining through the window and the leaves turning golden on the trees outside, things looked brighter. Zoe believed that Patrick still wanted her; that he had always loved her. If it were true, perhaps it would be possible to start again — to share their lives at last. After all, there was nothing standing in their way any more.

'What shall we do today?'

Grace and Harry sat at breakfast in the kitchen. Outside the window with its frilled blue gingham curtains the sky was blue and the autumn sun bathed the small neat garden in a rich golden glow.

'You choose,' Harry said. 'You live here. You know all the best places to visit.'

Grace considered. 'Well, I could take you to Grantchester where Rupert Brook used to live. It's such a pretty village with real picturebook thatched cottages and everything. We could have a pub lunch. Or we could take a picnic to Gog Magog Hills and look at the iron-age fort at Wandlebury Ring. Then again, if you don't mind travelling a bit further, we could visit Sandringham House.'

He was smiling at her across the table. She'd changed so much — grown in confidence and assurance. Yet she was still the Grace he had known all those years ago, delighted by small things; a sunny morning, the prospect of a day out. 'Anywhere will do as long as we can do it together,' he said softly. As she passed on her way to refill the teapot, he caught her hand and squeezed it. 'This weekend — I was so nervous and apprehensive ...'

She looked down at him. 'Oh, Harry, so was I.'

'But it's been marvellous. I can't tell you what it's meant.'

'You make it sound as though it's over,' she laughed. We've got all today yet.' She freshened the pot and refilled his cup, unaware that he hadn't asked for more — her sub-conscious memory reminding

372

her that he always drank two cups at breakfast. 'So come on. It's make-your-mind-up time. Where shall we go?'

'I won't have you packing lunch,' he said decisively. 'Let's make it Grantchester, and I'll take you out to a slap-up lunch. We can see all those other places some other time.'

Tricia opened her eyes and stretched like a cat. She turned to look at Max. He lat on his back, one arm flung out, the other above his head. In sleep he looked much younger and she noticed for the first time how long and thick his eyelashes were. Now, perhaps for the first time ever, I'm looking at the real Max Crichton, she told herself. Just for this moment he's an open book – and he's all mine.

Raising herself on one elbow she studied him long and hard, savouring his oblivious defencelessness. His shoulders were wide and powerful, his arms strong and muscular. And the thick, curling hair on his chest was as dark as his hair and beard.

She sighed reminiscently. Last night had been wonderful. When she first wakened she thought she had dreamed it all. She had often secretly fantasised about what it would be like to make love with Max. She had guessed that he would be positive, even slightly ruthless, but never in her wildest dreams had she imagined that he could be so gentle and tender. Clearly he was experienced. Her own sexual experience was sketchy. There had never been anyone she had cared for enough to spend a whole night with, or even to make love 'all the way', and Max had somehow known this without having to be told.

Someone – she couldn't remember who – had once said that when one fell in love, everything came naturally. Last night she had discovered this to be true. Making love with Max had been gloriously instinctive. There was obviously a lot to learn, but that was something to look forward to, a wonderful adventure. And she was happily convinced that he would be as good a teacher in matters of that kind as he was in music.

Would their new relationship improve her playing? she wondered excitedly. Suddenly she couldn't wait to find out. Rising to her knees she threw one leg across him and shook him hard.

'Wake up, lazy slob,' she shouted. 'Don't you know what the time is?'

Max drowsily half opened his eyes and peered at the naked girl perched unselfconsciously astride him. She had skin like ivory and small bouncing, rose-tipped breasts. Her face was aglow with life and her eyes were shining. She was totally irresistible.

373

'Come *on*.' She leaned forward to shake him again and her blonde hair brushed his chest tantalisingly.

He grasped her slender waist and turned her swiftly so that their positions were reversed. 'Are you always this disgustingly energetic first thing in the morning?' he growled.

She giggled. 'Absolutely. Without fail.'

'Mmmm.' He lowered himself on to her and covered her lips with his. And as his hand stroked along the length of her body to cup one breast her breath caught in her throat and he had the satisfaction of feeling her eager, quivering arousal.

'The idea was to – get up and – and begin work,' she said breathlessly as their lips parted.

'And so we will,' he murmured as he gently parted her thighs. 'All in good time. First things first, my love. First things first.'

Elaine made herself a snack lunch, then got ready to visit the hospital. As she showered she wondered whether she should telephone Red first. Tom and his wife might come for the weekend as well as Patrick. Zoe had had major surgery. They probably wouldn't allow too many visitors at this stage.

She dialled the number and waited, listening to the ringing at the other end. But there was no reply. Perhaps they had all gone out to lunch and would go straight on to the hospital afterwards. Well, she would go anyway.

She locked up the flat carefully and went down in the lift. It came to a halt on the ground floor and the doors opened to reveal a man waiting, his back turned towards herr. He wore a trenchcoat with the collar turned up. The sound of the doors made him turn and Elaine caught her breath. It was Patrick. For a moment they stared at each other in surprise, then he said: 'Hello, Elaine. I was on my way to see Alison. I've been ringing you at your mother's house but there was no reply.'

'No. I've been here all weekend. Alison's away.'

'I didn't know.'

There was something wrong. His face was white and drawn and his mouth moved wordlessly. She reached out a hand to him instinctively.

'Come back up to the flat. There's no one there.'

It seemed to take an age to get out her key again and unlock the door. At last, in the small hallway, she looked at him.

'Tell me.'

He looked at her with eyes that seemed to fill his face. 'She's dead, Elaine. Zoe's dead.'

Her hand flew to her mouth and she stared at him disbelievingly. 'But — she *can't* be. She was doing so well. What went wrong? The operation ...'

'It was nothing to do with the operation,' he told her. 'A heart attack at ten o'clock this morning. It was sudden and unexpected — all over in half an hour. There wasn't even time for us to get there.'

'Oh, *Patrick*.' She held out her arms to him and he walked into them. They held each other silently for a long moment. It seemed hopelessly unreal to her, ludicrous even, that someone as alive and vital as Zoe could suddenly just not *be* any more. She couldn't feel anything. No grief, no regret, no sense of loss — not even shock. Just numbness. Inside her heart there was nothing but a hollow, empty space. In the silence she could hear the muffled sounds of traffic in the street below and Alison's antique wall clock busily ticking. Suddenly, over Patrick's shoulder, she noticed a mark on the door handle and found herself making a mental note to clean it off. Patrick felt cold and heavy; a dead weight in her arms as he leaned against her. The stiff unyielding stuff of his trenchcoat rubbed coldly against her cheek.

At last she pushed him gently and said: 'Let me make you some coffee.'

He nodded. 'Thanks.'

It was good to have something with which to busy her hands. She put the kettle on and arranged cups on a tray, took biscuits out of the tin and found a plate for them. She was struck by the ludicrous normality of everything around her. It was all exactly the same as it had been an hour ago. How could that be when something so outrageously unacceptable had happened? While she worked she watched Patrick out of the corner of her eye. He sat slumped on a stool at the breakfast bar, his eyes unfocussed.

'What about the — the arrangements?'

'Next Wednesday,' he said dully. 'At least, that's what we think. Being Sunday, all the business will have to be done tomorrow. I'm staying to help Red.'

'Of course. How is he?'

'I don't think he's taken it in yet. Tom is with him. It fell to me to do the rounds.'

'Patrick — look, I don't want to keep you.'

He looked up, startled. 'What? Oh, no. This is my last call.' he took the cup from her and swallowed his coffee gratefully. 'I'm sorry. I haven't asked you how you are,' he said. 'It's been a long time, Elaine.'

375

'Yes, it has. I'm fine. And you?'

'Fine too — apart from . . .'

'Of course.' He was the same Patrick, yet suddenly he seemed like a stranger. 'You may have heard that Paul and I are divorcing,' she said.

'Yes. Zoe told me. She seemed pleased about it. She always said you deserved better.'

'She was my closest friend. Closer in some ways than Alison or even my own mother. She understood things without having to be told. I shall miss her terribly.'

He nodded unhappily. 'We all shall. I just wish I'd seen more of her these past few years.' He looked up. 'But at least I was able to give her some good news.'

'You were?'

'Yes. She was always worrying about my single state. I'm getting married again, Elaine. I thought — after us, you and me, that there'd never be anyone else. Then I met Jessica. She's my secretary. Fifteen years my junior, which raised a few eyebrows, but I've never been one for following convention, as you know. She's very mature for her years. A cultured, intelligent girl, and very beautiful. I'm a very lucky man.'

Her mouth was dry and she had difficulty in forcing her voice past the sudden constriction in her throat. 'I'm — sure you are,' she managed to say. 'Congratulations. When — when is the wedding to be?'

'Next month. It's to be a very quiet affair. No fuss, so we shan't postpone it. Zoe wouldn't have wanted that.'

'No. No, of course she wouldn't.'

He glanced at his watch. 'Well, I'd better get back.' At the door he turned. 'We'll see you at the funeral?'

'Naturally.'

'I'll let you know the details. Thanks for the coffee.' He walked out into the hall, Elaine following. 'Goodbye.' He bent to kiss her cheek briefly. 'I'll ring you as soon as the arrangements are made.'

She closed the door and leant against it, listening, still numb, to his footsteps going along the corridor to the lift.

'I'm sorry, Zoe,' she whispered. 'I was too late after all.'

She heard the clatter of the lift gates and then the hum of the lift descending. He had gone — this time for ever. Then the blackness descended on her. It came down like a heavy, stifling cloak; dense and suffocating, making her heart thud and the breath catch in her throat. Gasping, she rushed to open a window, and as she leaned out to gulp in the air she felt as through she were drowning; as

376

through black waters were closing over her head, pressing down on her relentlessly.

Suddenly she knew that there was only one person in the world who could stop the blackness for devouring her. One name rose in terrified desperation to her lips, like the cry of a wounded animal.

'That was better — *much* better.' Max beamed at her from the piano.

They'd been practising for three hours and Tricia had never enjoyed playing more in her life. She put her violin down and threw herself full-length on the Chesterfield.

'Yes, I thought so too,' she said, clasping her hands behind her head. 'But are you sure you're not saying that just because you've had your wicked way with me?'

He raised his eyebrows at her. 'Really! What kind of way is that for a nice young lady to talk? Anyway, I rather got the impression that it was the other way round.'

She frowned. 'Damn. You've guessed.'

'Guessed what?'

'That I seduced you simply to stop you yelling at me. Still ...' She grinned impishly. 'It worked, didn't it?'

He took her hand and drew her to her feet. 'Come on, get your coat. We're going out.'

'Why? Where to?'

'To lunch. I can't remember when I last ate properly, but I do vaguely recollect that we somehow missed dinner last night. Besides, if we don't go out, we'll probably finish up back in bed.'

'Max — about us.' Her face was suddenly serious, all teasing gone from her eyes. She laid a hand on his arm. 'What happened last night ... it isn't — wasn't casual, was it?'

He looked down at he in surprise. 'Casual? Of course it wasn't.'

'I don't go in for casual sex, you know, one night stands — that sort of thing. I know most people do, but I don't.'

He took her shoulders and drew her to him, smiling indulgently. 'Do you think I didn't know that?'

'You did — but how?'

The corners of his mouth twitched. 'How can you be such a steamy little sexpot one minute and as innocent as a babe in arms the next?'

He kissed her forehead and held her close. Already he felt a tenderness for her that he had felt for no other woman. He had felt the germ of it right from that day when she turned up late for

377

the audition. He admired her talent, which he truly believed he could channel into greatness. She maddened and infuriated him with her headstrong manner and her stubborness. Yet all the time, deep within him, something else had been steadily growing, developing. He had tried his hardest to ignore it, telling himself it would get in the way, cloud his judgement and ruin their professional relationship. But last night he'd been able to suppress it no longer. She had finally captivated him. He looked down at her upturned face. 'Do I really have to tell you?'

'I just wanted you to know that I wouldn't have slept with you unless I'd felt something — something very special,' she said, her voice muffled as she pressed her face against his chest.

'Nor would I — in spite of what you seem to think.' He shook her gently. 'But just for the moment we'll have no declarations or soul baring. Just music and love. That'll do nicely to be going on with, don't you think?'

She smiled up at him. 'Sounds lovely. What could be better? Music and love.'

'And food,' he said. 'Because I don't know about you, but I'm starving.'

The sun was setting when Grace and Harry got home. She put the car away and unlocked the front door.

'We'll have time for tea before I take you to the station?' she said as she took off her coat.

Harry sighed. The moment he had been dreading was almost here. He thought of the flat in Notting Hill, comparing its impersonal austerity with the warmth and attractiveness of Grace's house. 'It's been such a perfect day, a perfect weekend,' he said. 'I wish I didn't have to go.'

Grace turned and looked at him. 'Well, do you really have to?'

He smiled ruefully. 'I'm afraid I do. I have several gigs booked next week.' He hesitated. 'I suppose you wouldn't like to come and visit *me* next week maybe?'

She smiled delightedly. 'That would be lovely. Thank you, Harry.'

His face brightened. 'I'd meet you at the station and we could go to a show or something.'

'And I could take you to see Morgan, if you'd like that. I'm sure he'd like to meet you.'

'So that's a date?'

'It's a date.' She looked at her watch. 'Now I'd better get the kettle on.'

The sound of a car on the drive outside made her pause and frown. 'Who can that be at this time?'

Harry looked out of the hall window. 'A blue Metro. Mean anything to you?'

'Elaine?'

She used her own key to open the door and when she stepped inside she showed no surprise at finding them standing expectantly in the hall. Grace caught her breath in alarm at her pale face and blank, staring eyes.

'Darling, what is it? Are you ill?'

'Zoe.' Elaine swallowed painfully as though her throat hurt. 'Zoe – died this morning. Patrick came to tell me.'

'Oh, darling, how dreadful.' Shocked, Grace held out her arms, but Elaine seemed oblivious to the gesture, standing where she was, motionless as a statue.

'Did I tell you that Alison is going to Canada?' she said. Her voice was unnaturally high, as though on the edge of hysteria. 'And now Zoe's abandoned me too. And guess what? Patrick – Patrick tells me he's getting married again next month. Isn't *that* good news?' Tears welled up in her eyes and began to slip unchecked down her chalk-white cheeks. 'I thought – I really believed that now I'm free again we'd ...' She shook her head disbelievingly. 'But he's marrying his secretary. She's called Jessica, and she's young and cultured and beautiful.' With a sudden harsh sob she turned to Harry.

'Please help me, Daddy. It hurts so much. I don't know how to bear it any more. Oh God, *God* – what am I going to do?'

Without a word he stepped forward and folded her tightly in his arms. 'There, don't cry, baby.' He rocked her gently in the way he had done when she was a little girl. 'It's all right, love. Daddy's here – Daddy's got you.'

Chapter Twenty-Five

The September evening air was warm and fragrant with the scent of pines. Grace and Harry had left their hotel half an hour before the start of the concert to take a walk along the cliffs and through the pleasure gardens before taking their seats.

They had been together again now for almost four years and sometimes it seemed to Grace as though they had never been apart. They had settled into the easy relationship of all happily married, middle-aged couples, enjoying one another's company in a way that had never before been possible; drawn ever more closely together by the traumatic events of the year following Zoe Carne's death.

Bournemouth held so many memories for them both. Happy ones for Grace, and for Harry a mixture of both bitter and sweet. As they crossed the road and began to climb the winding path to the Winter Gardens Concert Hall, memories flooded back: of the new start Elaine's birth had seemed to give their marriage; idyllic days in the sun and the joy of motherhood, for Grace. For Harry, later ones of the sad end of Stella's career and the loss of their unborn child. It was here that he had tried so hard to regain earlier joy and peace, and failed sadly.

Grace squeezed his arm. 'A penny for your thoughts.'

He smiled down at her. 'I was just thinking, when we were in Bournemouth last, all this was brand new.'

'I know. And now it all looks so mature,' she said. 'And who would have guessed that we'd be coming here all these years later? After all that's happened ...'

'To hear our own granddaughter play solo violin in a symphony concert,' Harry completed the sentence proudly. He smiled reminiscently, looking at the bill outside the concert hall which gave the

380

programme for tonight's concert. Max and Tricia had top billing: Guest Conductor Max Crichton. Soloist Patricia Crichton (violin).

Harry smiled with satisfaction. 'The Mendelssohn violin concerto was always a favourite of mine – and Elaine's. I remember buying her Menuhin's recording of it when we lived in Stanmore. LPs had just come out at the time.'

'I remember.' Grace looked up at him. 'Harry – she is happy now isn't she?'

He pressed her fingers. 'No doubt about that, love. I think she's found her true vocation in life at last.'

'I hope so.' Grace sighed. 'I do hope so.'

After Zoe's sudden death, Elaine had suffered a serious collapse and become very ill. The doctor told Grace that the strain she had suffered over a long period of years had taken its toll of her. Zoe's death and the news of Patrick's engagement had finally tipped the balance. She had sunk into a deep clinical depression that had lasted for almost a year. Harry had been marvellous. He had given up his flat in London and moved to Cambridge to be near her, visiting her in hospital every day. After a conference with Alison and the other directors it had been decided to franchise the three branches of HEA. This would provide Elaine with an income – something that worried Grace who, at the time, could see no prospect of her ever working again.

One bonus was that during Elaine's illness the three of them had become close again – a family. It had helped her on to the road to recovery in the way that nothing else could.

Morgan had proved to be a tower of strength too, both as a friend and a business colleague. He visited Elaine every weekend while she was ill, and when she was on her feet again he had taken her on holiday. Not to Switzerland, which he knew would bring back too many memories, but to his villa in Spain. Whilst there he had offered her a job with his London firm. There was a vacancy on his team at the luxury end, for a designer who could create wedding and ball gowns. He told her that he had the utmost faith in her. The job was hers if she wanted it, if – and the challenge was intentional – she thought she was up to the hard work involved.

His confidence in her was just the boost she needed. As for the hard work, she revelled in it. Morgan sent her to New York, to Paris and to Rome to study current trends and glean ideas. She had always longed to travel and enjoyed every minute, coming back bursting with a new health and energy, her note book and drawing pad bulging with ideas, impatient to begin work. At last Grace and Harry were able to breathe a sigh of relief and take up the threads of their own life again.

381

In her hotel room Elaine put the finishing touches to her make-up. She was nervous. Becoming a mother-in-law at thirty-nine and a grandmother at forty-one had been traumatic enough, but her daughter's English concert debut promised to be the most dramatic development yet. Her own contribution was the dress that Tricia would wear, designed especially for the occasion.

It was a very special evening for Tricia, her English concert platform debut. It had been delayed by the birth of her baby son, Greg, born six months ago. Elaine had been too ill to attend the wedding, which had taken place in the early spring of '88, just in time for Max's overseas tour, and she had missed Tricia's concert debut in Canada six months later. Since then she and Max had earned themselves a stunning reputation as a soloist-conductor team, touring Canada and Australia and the Continental capitals. They had worked non-stop until earlier this year when Tricia's pregnancy had forced her to take a break. This would be the first time Elaine had heard her perform as a soloist and she felt as nervous as she imagined her daughter did at the prospect.

She leaned forward to take a long hard look at herself in the dressing table mirror. In spite of her illness and the strain of the past years she looked much younger than forty-one. Her hair was thick and springy as ever, and the silver highlights merely added to her new sleek sophistication. Her figure was still slim and supple and, thanks to Morgan's unshakable faith in her, she had never felt fitter or happier. She loved her new job and was making a name for herself as a luxury designer. There was even a whisper that she might be chosen to design something for minor royalty in the coming months.

The news that Patrick hadn't married after all reached her through Tom, whom she ran into one weekend in Cambridge a little over a year ago.

'Couldn't bring himself to go through with it in the end,' he told her with characteristic bluntness. 'Well, silly devil. I always said it was sheer flattery on his part anyway. You know – middle-aged man and young girl. A touch of mid-life crisis, if you ask me.'

The news had left Elaine feeling strangely detached. It was then that she had realised that she was over the heartache once and for all. The girlhood heartbreak that had haunted her through the whole of her life now belonged to the past. At last her heart was her own. She no longer needed anyone in whom to invest her dreams. She was whole, a complete person at last.

She stood up smoothed the skirt of the slim black sheath dress she had designed especially for tonight. The dresses she created for clients were lavish and sumptuous, but the ones she designed for herself were plain to the point of starkness; glamorously understated, like the single diamond that hung around her neck on a cobweb-fine chain.

Picking up her evening bag she took a last look at herself then, smiling with anticipation, went to find Morgan.

'Zip me up, please.' Tricia flicked nervously at her fringe with a comb as Max stepped forward to fasten her dress.

She peered at him anxiously through the mirror. 'Oh, God, do I look all right?'

Max stood back to look at his wife. Privately he thought she had never looked more lovely. 'Love and music' had suited her, but the more recent addition of motherhood had added a new, almost luminous radiance.

He had never in his life been as happy as he had during the three and a half years of their marriage. Although their tempers sometimes still flared, it was an undisputable fact that they brought out the best in each other. Musically they were like instrument and player. Although each was talented independent musician, the real magic only occurred when they performed together. Then they fitted like the two halves of an intricate puzzle.

The dress Elaine had created was slim and, like her own, perfectly plain. 'It must be glamorous without taking the attention away from the music,' Tricia had instructed. It was made in a taffeta with a soft sheen that caught the light; its colour a shade of blue shot with green that complemented her colouring dramatically. The strapless bodice lay against her skin in petal-like points and clung to her slender waist and hips, to froth out below the knee into a tulle 'fishtail'. This was delicately starred with tiny brilliants that caught pinpoints of light as she moved.

'You're sure it's not too distracting?' she asked, turning to face anxiously up to Max.

'No, but you are. You look like some magical kind of mermaid.' He took her face between his hands and kissed her gently so as not to spoil her make-up. 'Darling, you're trembling. There's no need to be nervous. You've played the Mendelssohn before, I don't know how many times.'

'But not *here*, Max — not in England.' She glanced at the huge basket of flowers on the dressing table, sent by her grandparents, and the other flowers and cards crowding the room, all wishing her luck. 'So many of my friends and family will be out there. Uncle Red and

383

Tom. Alison and Robert. Morgan, Granny Grace and Harry. Then there's Mum.' She threw up her hands. 'Even Tracey has taken time off to be here. They're all expecting so much of me. Suppose I let them down?'

'You *won't*.' He held her chin firmly and looked into her eyes. 'Remember what I told you once, a long time ago? My students never fail.' He kissed the tip of her nose. 'And my wife certainly won't.'

For Max half the concert was already over. They had played a Beethoven overture and a Sibelius tone poem. Now the interval was almost finished and the audience had begun to filter back to their seats. It was time for the violin concerto, the highlight of the evening. On the dressing room intercom they heard the orchestra tuning up and a round of applause as the leader of the first violins took his place. Max smiled and took her hand. 'Darling, it's time,' he said.

As he led her on to the platform there was a burst of welcoming applause. In the front row she caught sight of her mother and Morgan; her grandparents; Conseula, looking radiant in a white dress and holding tightly to the arm of Max's father. But the time for nerves was over. Max had mounted the rostrum. Stunningly handsome in white tie and tails, he towered above her. He was looking at her – tapping and raising his baton. A hush fell. The orchestra poised, ready to begin.

As always, once into her music she lost all sense of time and place. The rows of faces below her melted and merged into a mist as she became one with her instrument and her interpretation of the great music she loved so much.

In the front row Grace surreptitiously held Harry's hand under cover of her programme. She could hardly believe that she was here and that it was all really happening. Tricia looked so beautiful, so happy and fulfilled. She had everything – success in her chosen career; the man she loved; and a beautiful baby son to seal their happiness. And tonight, the admiration and love of all those watching and listening would be hers. It was as though all the bitterness and regrets – all the broken dreams and dashed hopes of the past years – were being redeemed at last in Tricia.

The first movement evolved into the second, the hauntingly beautiful slow movement. Elaine sat next to her father. Tricia's playing was faultless. Surely tomorrow the critics would rave. She would be made.

Reaching out her hand she touched her father's fingers and they exchanged a brief smile, each knowing what the other was thinking.

The slow movement came to an end and the rousing third began. In the back row of the concert hall sat a solitary figure. Although his father and brother were in the audience, neither knew that Patrick was coming this evening. In fact he had tried hard to stay away. He had arrived in Bournemouth at the last minute, to find the car park packed and the concert sold out. He'd had to hang around the box office till the very last minute, waiting hopefully for a cancellation.

Listening to the music he watched the lovely young woman on the platform with curious nostalgia, his heart full of regrets and misgivings. The sealed letter his mother had written for him had been left with the solicitor, attached to the Will she had made without the knowledge of her family. He had received it two days after the funeral.

Elaine has never told me so herself and I can't prove it, but I know with all a mother's instincts that Tricia is your daughter, Patrick. I know it just as surely as I know you are my son. As far as I know, no one else does. What you do about it is up to you, but you must promise not to show this letter to anyone. My only wish is for your happiness.

At first he had dismissed it as the fevered imaginings of a sick woman, then he had begun to remember so many little things, clues, that when put together and added up, told him that what Zoe suspected must be true. But why had Elaine never told him? he asked himself repeatedly. When they were in Switzerland and so close − about to be together for always − even then she'd said nothing.

By the time he received the letter, Elaine was ill; too ill to see anyone. He knew then that all the things that had gone wrong with her life were his fault. Her unhappy marriage, her wasted, desolate life − they were all down to him.

He had broken off his engagement, knowing then that he had been deluding himself just as he had before, with Cathy. No one had ever been or ever could be what Elaine was to him.

Later, when he heard about her recovery, he asked himself if he had the right to walk back into her life. He'd done nothing but bring her misery so far. He'd made other people unhappy too. Perhaps it would be better all round to stay away, to put everything he had into his work and let Elaine rebuild her life safely and happily − without him.

385

Now, sitting at the back of the hall, he ached to take his rightful place at her side. He could see them all sitting there in the front row, friends and relatives in all their party finery, sharing this special occasion. No doubt there would be some kind of celebration later; one from which he must be excluded. He tried to imagine how it would be to stand proudly at the side of his daughter, sharing her triumph, basking in her happy smile — being the person her eyes searched the crowd for, her hands reached out to. There was a child now, he understood, a baby boy. He was a grandfather. He tried, momentarily, to feel like one, but it was totally beyond his comprehension. Anyway, it was too late for all that, he told himself. Much, much too late.

The music reached its climax and suddenly the concerto was over. The audience broke into a frenzy of applause, calling the soloist back again and again. The orchestra was applauding too, the violinists tapping their bows on music stands in the time honoured way. Max stepped down from the rostrum and took Tricia's hand to lead her forward yet again. He looked at her with unconcealed pride and love in his eyes, and bent to kiss her hand, bringing forth a fresh burst of clapping.

At the back of the hall the doors swung open and Patrick walked out into the vestibule. Eager to get away before the rush, he was already halfway through the outer doors when he heard a familiar voice call his name.

'Patrick?'

Turning, he saw Tom staring disbelievingly at him.

'Patrick, what are you doing here? I thought you were too tied up.'

'I made up my mind at the last minute — found I could make it. Managed to get a cancellation ...' Patrick trailed off. 'Look, I can't stop — have to be in London first thing tomorrow.'

'Rubbish.' Tom grasped his arm. 'There's a party at the hotel. We're all staying the night. I'm just going to get the car — bring it round for the others. Everyone you know is here — even Red. You can't go without saying hello.'

'Well ...' Patrick searched his mind for a valid excuse. 'Look, I can't gatecrash.'

'Stuff that. It's a special occasion. You can't disappear without seeing Tricia and wishing her all the best — not after a stunning performance like that.' Tom punched his shoulder. 'Tell you what, Elaine's here. She looks fantastic. Come on, don't tell me you wouldn't like to see her. It must be ages ...' Tom frowned, puzzled at the agony of indecision he saw in his brother's eyes.

386

'Look,' he said at last as the crowds began to mill around them, 'I'm going to be in the dog-house if the car isn't here when they come out. The party is at the Millroy Heights Hotel. It's overlooking Poole Harbour. Do come, even if it's only for half an hour. Surprise everyone. See you there, eh?'

Tom backed away and a moment later was gone, swallowed up in the throng of concert-goers that jostled Patrick as they streamed down the steps.

It was dark as he nosed the car into the queue snaking its way out of the car park, but the sky was pale with the reflection of a thousand multi-coloured neon lights. Traffic was heavy as he reached the main road. As he hesitated the driver behind him hooted impatiently. It was time to make a decision. Perhaps the most important he had ever made. Should he go to the party – see Elaine – try to win her love again? Was there really still a chance for them? And if not, could he bear to risk the pain of her rejection? Or should he take the coward's way – go back to London now and try to forget?

The driver behind him hooted again, persistently this time. Patrick pressed his foot down and took advantage of a gap in the traffic to turn left. Joining the stream of cars he followed the curve in the road, then turned left again to climb Poole Hill. He felt his heart lift as the traffic thinned and he gathered speed. Now that he was on his way, he couldn't wait to get there; couldn't wait to see Elaine and the lovely young woman who was their daughter.

He had a powerful feeling that the foundations of his whole future life were about to be laid tonight.

You have been reading a novel published by Piatkus Books. We hope you have enjoyed it and that you would like to read more of our titles. Please ask for them in your local library or bookshop.

If you would like to be put on our mailing list to receive details of new publications, please send a large stamped addressed envelope (UK only) to:

Piatkus Books, 5 Windmill Street
London W1P 1HF

PIATKUS

The sign of a good book